FORBIDDEN JOURNEYS

FORBIDDEN JOURNEYS

Fairy Tales and Fantasies by Victorian Women Writers

Edited by Nina Auerbach and
U. C. Knoepflmacher

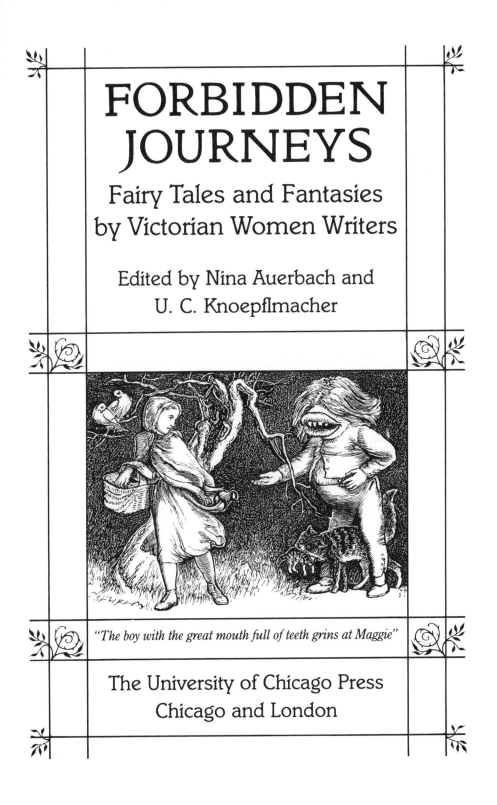

"The boy with the great mouth full of teeth grins at Maggie"

The University of Chicago Press
Chicago and London

NINA AUERBACH, professor of English at the University of Pennsylvania, is the author of *Romantic Imprisonment* and *Private Theatricals.*
U. C. KNOEPFLMACHER, professor of English at Princeton University, is the author of *Laughter and Despair: George Eliot's Early Novels* and *Brontë: Wuthering Heights.*

The University of Chicago Press, Chicago 60637
The University of Chicago Press, Ltd., London
© 1992 by the University of Chicago
All rights reserved. Published 1992
Printed in the United States of America

01 00 99 98 97 96 95 94 93 92   5 4 3 2 1

ISBN (cloth): 0-226-03203-5

Library of Congress Cataloging-in-Publication Data
Forbidden journeys : fairy tales and fantasies by Victorian women
writers / edited by Nina Auerbach and U. C. Knoepflmacher.
    p.   cm.
Includes bibliographical references.
ISBN 0-226-03203-5 (cloth)
1. Fantastic fiction, English.   2. English fiction—Women authors.
3. English fiction—19th century.   4. Children's stories, English.
5. Fairy tales—Great Britain.   I. Auerbach, Nina, 1943-   .
II. Knoepflmacher, U. C.
PR1309.F3F6   1992
823'.08766089287—dc20   91-31824
                                                   CIP

Contents

Introduction

Victorian readers found the association of women with children's books natural, even inevitable, but it wasn't. Cultural and economic pressures made it more acceptable for women to write for children than for other adults, but the most acclaimed writers of Victorian children's fantasies were three eccentric men—Lewis Carroll, George MacDonald, and James Barrie—whose obsessive nostalgia for their own idealized childhoods inspired them to imagine dream countries in which no one had to grow up. The most moving Victorian children's books are steeped in longing for unreachable lives. Carroll, MacDonald, and Barrie envied the children they could not be; out of this envious longing came their painful children's classics.

Most Victorian women, including those whose stories we reprint here, envied adults rather than children. Whether they were wives and mothers or teachers and governesses, respectable women's lives had as their primary object child care. British law made the link between women and children indelible by denying women independent legal representation. As Frances Power Cobbe pointed out in a witty essay, "Criminals, Idiots, Women, and Minors" were identical in the eyes of the law. In theory, at any rate, women lived the condition Carroll, MacDonald, and Barrie longed for. If they were good, they never grew up.

Written under subtle cultural compulsion, the stories reprinted here are more abrasive than the better-known, more lovable children's books by Victorian men; our authors often seem to chafe against childhood rather than to envy or idealize it. Yet constraint gives their stories a wonderful edge. Few readers will find them heartwarming; some, in fact, might be repelled or even shocked by their anger and violence. For though their choices were severely limited, women who wrote for children had surprising freedom of expression compared to writers of juvenile fiction today. The literary marketplace, like Victorian society in general, rewarded women for adhering to stereotyped roles. Once women conformed outwardly, an age still free of psychoanalytic suspicion exempted their emotions from close inspection.

In *New Grub Street* (1891), a grimly realistic novel about the pressures the literary marketplace imposed on late-Victorian authors, George Gissing portrays the ease with which an untalented woman carves out a career writing for children. All the authors in *New Grub Street* who have some authentic

1

connection to literature starve, die, or fail humiliatingly, but Dora Milvain simply obeys her careerist brother and adapts her wares to the market he describes: "But it's obvious what an immense field there is for anyone who can just hit the taste of the new generation of Board school children. Mustn't be too goody-goody; that kind of thing is falling out of date. But you'd have to cultivate a particular kind of vulgarity."

And Dora does. At the end, as literary lives fall into wreck around her, she is contentedly writing "a very pretty tale which would probably appear in *The English Girl.*" She marries Whelpdale, one of her successful brother's sycophants, who woos her in literary gush: "You seem to me to have discovered a new *genre;* such writing as this has surely never been offered to girls, and all the readers of [*The English Girl*] must be immensely grateful to you."

In Gissing's context, Dora's success as a children's hack is bitterly ironic. We never learn what she writes, and the narrative implies that it doesn't matter; any formulaic hackwork will fill the pages of *The English Girl,* a magazine founded by a "Mrs. Boston Wright," whose mixed background, respectable and yet also sufficiently unconventional, has apparently helped in setting the right tone. It is possible, though, that Whelpdale is right: for all we know Dora may have discovered a new genre. Juvenile literature was produced in such volume that it could flourish uncensored. Since Victorian children were perceived as secure in their innocence, there was no felt need to expurgate anger, subversion, or literary experimentation from their reading. Moreover, in the 1870s and 1880s, changes in the juvenile marketplace empowered some astonishingly bold and innovative writing by women.

In the 1840s and '50s, rigid didacticism had held children's fiction in thrall. Had George Eliot, the three Brontë sisters, or Elizabeth Gaskell—all of whom turned to fiction writing in the late 1840s and 1850s—wanted to write for children, they would have had no choice but to join the ranks of female forbidders. In Charlotte Brontë's angry account of a suppressed childhood, Jane Eyre's passion for truth, her insistence on an "exact tale," as well as her powerful romantic imagination, are exacerbated by her enforced reading, the drab "book entitled the *Child's Guide.*" Jane scornfully suggests to Mrs. Reed that she give this sententious narrative "to your girl, Georgiana, for it is she who tells lies, and not I." To Jane Eyre, moralism is simply "telling lies," but when the next generation of children's literature expanded into wilder romance and fairy tale plots, even Jane Eyre would have been attracted to the forbidden emotional and psychic truths whose expression had now become possible.

Fairy tales and romances were grounded in an oral narrative tradition that may well have been initiated by women. The antiquity of fairy tales, their anonymous origins, had the feel (and perhaps the fact) of a lost, distinctively female tradition. Moreover, the wild magic of fairy tales, so guardedly approached even by the finest of the didacticists who dominated earlier juvenile literature, now seemed to license a new generation of writers as well as readers to be deviant, angry, even violent or satirical. For the most part, the trespassers in our anthology are untamed if not unpunished. Thus, while Gissing's *New Grub Street* allows us to assume that Dora Milvain is a happy hack, her stories may replace the "goody-goody" with the startling subversion of the actual writers whose work this collection introduces: Jean Ingelow (1820–1897), Christina Rossetti (1830–1894), Anne Thackeray Ritchie (1837–1919), Maria Louisa Molesworth (1839–1921), Juliana Horatia Gatty Ewing (1841–1885), Frances Hodgson Burnett (1849–1924), and E. Nesbit (1858–1924).

Most of the works presented here appeared within a span of twelve years, from 1867 to 1879; Nesbit's two "unlikely tales" are slightly later. A shift in outlook had led to an erosion of the "goody-goody" standards to which Gissing refers. Female romance was now considered appropriate reading matter for the young of both sexes; even *Jane Eyre* and *Silas Marner* (though not *The Mill on the Floss*) had become acceptable as juvenile texts. What is more, children's journals that encouraged the publication of imaginative fiction began to replace the earlier magazines devoted to "useful" moral and intellectual instruction. In England, *Aunt Judy's Magazine* (founded in 1866), *Good Words for the Young* (1868), *The Boy's Own Paper* (1879), *The Girl's Own Paper* (1880—perhaps the model for Gissing's *The English Girl*), and in America, *St. Nicholas* (1873), soon attracted some of the finest writers of both sexes. Still decorously Victorian in their observance of the proprieties, still affiliated with religion, still stressing morality and useful subjects such as history, biography, and geography, these and other magazines nonetheless printed unconventional works, and hence did much to stimulate the production of something like "a new genre."

Without the existence of this fresh field, several of the women writers we present in this volume would have been denied a literary career; few would have attained the high reputation they enjoyed among their contemporaries. Admittedly, Anne Thackeray Ritchie, whose fairy tales were intended for adults rather than children, did not require the opportunities offered by the newly defined market. Neither did Christina Rossetti and Jean Ingelow, both of whom were respected as major poets. Nevertheless, Ingelow's *Mopsa the Fairy* (1869), which we reprint in its entirety, proved far more of a financial success than her earlier, still moralistic *Stories Told to a Child* (1865), while Rossetti's splendid *Speaking Likenesses* (1874), which we also reproduce in full as our last selection, was meant to capitalize on the popularity of her *Sing-Song, A Nursery Rhyme Book* (1872). The success of the other four writers rests entirely on their acclaim as innovators in the field of children's fiction.

Juliana Ewing was the literary mainstay of the fine monthly magazine for girls edited by her mother Margaret Gatty, *Aunt Judy's Magazine,* which ran the two stories we offer here, "Christmas Crackers" and "Amelia and the Dwarfs," from December 1869 to March 1870. Far more prolific, Maria Louisa Molesworth and Frances Hodgson Burnett, who lived well into the twentieth century, are remembered for their major children's books rather than for their many adult novels. Whereas Molesworth's career as the pseudonymous novelist "Ennis Graham" only proved that she was neither a George Eliot nor a "Currer Bell," her fortunes rose dramatically when she began to publish the tales she had written down to amuse her own children. Illustrated by Walter Crane, her first such venture, *Tell Me a Story* (1875), was followed in quick succession by the sentimental but highly popular *Carrots* (1876), *The Cuckoo-Clock* (1877) and *The Tapestry Room* (1879), the haunting fantasy from which we have extracted "The Brown Bull of Norrowa," the interpolated tale heard by two dreaming children who wander behind an arras.

Burnett, who emigrated from England to Tennessee as a teenager, was able to count on an adult readership appreciative of her adaptations of British romances to American tastes. Thus, unlike Molesworth, she enjoyed considerable popularity before she became convinced that children's stories would prove an even more profitable undertaking. Her dream story, "Behind the White Brick," appeared in *St. Nicholas Magazine* (1879) before her *Little Lord Fauntleroy* (1885) took the nation by storm. Although Burnett never gave up the writing of adult fiction, her best-selling work thereafter was always aimed at children. She repeated the success of *Fauntleroy* with the much-reprinted *A Little Princess* (1905) and *The Secret Garden* (1910), and also adapted these and other works to the London and New York stage.

Like Molesworth (who chose to live apart from her husband) and Burnett (who eventually divorced the husband whose medical career she had financed through her writings), E. Nesbit published her fiction and poetry to provide for her children. (Two of these five children were not her own, but the illegitimate offspring of her philandering mate.) Starting out as an anonymous hack writer in order to supplement her husband's meager income, she too followed the familiar path of marketing stories originally composed for her own children. No longer bound by Victorian conventions even a "new woman" like Burnett adhered to, moving in the socialist circle of Shaw and Wells, Nesbit eventually chose to give prominence to the subversive subtexts that the earlier writers had handled far more circumspectly. Her sense of the anachronism not just of the late-Victorian respectability she was still expected to uphold as a children's writer, but also of the literary conventions she was expected to deploy, finds a wonderful expression in both "Melisande, or, Long and Short Division" and "Fortunatus Rex & Co.," the intensely funny stories she wrote in 1901, the year of Queen Victoria's death.

The alliance between comedy and "metaphoric magic" in Nesbit's work is justly celebrated in Alison Lurie's recent *Don't Tell the Children: Subversive Children's Literature* (1990). Yet Lurie, who offers valuable insights into the work of other late-Victorian and Edwardian women who produced books for children—Kate Greenaway, Lucy Clifford, and Beatrix Potter, in addition to Nesbit and Burnett—tends to regard the authors she likes as "modern" or protomodern. Ewing and Molesworth are bunched together with a much earlier writer such as Frances Browne and quickly dismissed in a single sentence for exhibiting the "conservative moral and political bias" of standard Victorian literary fairy tales. Rossetti is noted merely as the "aunt by marriage" of Ford Madox Ford, to whose modern fairy tales Lurie devotes an entire chapter; she entirely ignores Jean Ingelow and Ritchie, although as the sister of the first wife of Virginia Woolf's father, Leslie Stephen, Ritchie was also a modernist's aunt by marriage.

But Nesbit's and Burnett's immediate predecessors, male as well as female, initiated and refined the subversiveness Lurie prizes in children's books. In *Alice to the Lighthouse: Children's Books and the Radical Experiments in Art* (1987), Juliet Dusinberre shows the relevance of Victorian literary fairy tales to the dissident art of Virginia Woolf. Dusinberre grants Nesbit and Burnett, along with such earlier figures as Molesworth and Ewing, almost as much prominence as Lewis Carroll or Robert Louis Stevenson. Yet she slights the gender distinctions Victorian constraints on the female imagination make necessary. There is a considerable difference between the open subversiveness (and artistic experimentation) of Lewis Carroll's two *Alice* books (1865, 1871), or even of George MacDonald's fantasies of the late 1860s and 1870s, and the ironic indirections that mark some of the texts by women writers of the same period. Whereas male writers encroaching on "feminine" material could be as wicked as they liked, their female contemporaries had to speak gently (like Lewis Carroll's Duchess) even when they were most enraged.

As we note in our introductions, the anger in such major texts as *Amelia and the Dwarfs* (in part 1), "Fortunatus Rex" (in part 2), *Mopsa the Fairy* (part 3), and *Speaking Likenesses* (part 4), is directed not only at the targets male fantasists had themselves attacked; it also undermines the ideological assumptions and literary conventions of those privileged men. As our frequent references to works such as "A Christmas Carol" or *Alice in Wonderland* indicates, writers like Ewing, Ingelow, and Rossetti deliberately evoke Dickens and Carroll in a mode of subtle but firm repudiation.

Thus, paradoxically, the special indebtedness of these women to Lewis Carroll, who institutionalized amorality in juvenile literature, was also a burden. If, on the one hand, the success of the *Alice* books had licensed female dreaming and liberated aggressive subtexts for women writers, Carroll's nostalgia, his resistance to female growth and female sexuality, could hardly inspire Ewing, Ingelow, and Rossetti as they transported their own child heroines into realms of the forbidden. As they recognized, the frustration of Carroll's intense desire to keep his beloved dream child forever young, forever enshrined in "happy summer days" unaffected by change, led him to indulge in fantasies of containment and domination that were totally inimical to their own yearning for autonomy and authority. Although the author of the Alice books may impersonate ineffectual male creatures such as the White Rabbit and the White Knight, he is also angry at the girl who refuses to "leave off at seven" and prefers, instead, to grow into an adult woman. His need to detain, refrain, and contain the growing girl by insisting that this dreamer is a part of his own dream makes Carroll a distant but distinct cousin of those aestheticizing male dominators Robert Browning had exposed in poems such as "My Last Duchess," or "Porphyria's Lover." And, more to the point, he is a cousin, too, of the two male foils E. Nesbit creates for the elderly heroine of "King Fortunatus Rex." In that story Miss Robinson successfully opposes both the weepy king who mourns for lost Princess Daisy as well as the aggressive magician who specializes in making girls disappear at the very edge of puberty.

From a woman writer's point of view, Lewis Carroll's great *Alice* books appropriated the central plot of this anthology: a little girl's journey into forbidden countries. In the same spirit, male redactors like Perrault and the brothers Grimm had appropriated and moralized the genre that was once associated with authoritative women, the *sages femmes* or *Märchenfrauen*, whom male experts demoted to the status of mere informants. The male writer's sentimental return to a myth of matriarchal origins was for the woman writer a colonization of one of the few literary spheres she was allowed to consider her own.

Even a post-Victorian, astringent adult writer like Virginia Woolf looks longingly toward the lost authority of fairy tales. When, in *To the Lighthouse*, her key modernist text, Mrs. Ramsay tells her son that misogynist fable popularized by the Brothers Grimm, "The Fisherman's Wife," Woolf, like the writers we anthologize, makes us aware of moralistic male revisions of female journeys. Like the fictional Shahrazad (who may have been the Persian Princess Homai, or an "Anon" living in fifteenth-century Cairo), and like the imaginative woman punished in the Grimm tale, Mrs. Ramsay struggles against male narrative power. She invests herself with magic by promising her son a "passage" to a distant tower in a "fabled land," but her magic and the promised voyage are illusory. Mrs. Ramsay is not one of those weavers or spinners traditionally associated with the fairies or fays and their pagan ancestors, the Fates. Her knitting and her journey will be left undone until her husband claims them for his reality. The dissipation of Mrs. Ramsay's magic into a cautionary tale punishing an overweening wife is a symptom of the violated female tradition whose restoration Woolf urges in her great address to the next generation of woman writers, "A Room of One's Own."

As a herald of that restoration, Woolf inserts in *To the Lighthouse* a glimpse of one of those wise old women like the fictional Mother Goose or Dame Bunch, who symbolize the narrative power secreted in fay tales. As Mrs. Ramsay tells her child the tale of the Fisherman's Wife—the Woman Who Would Be God—an unnamed stranger enters the house: "there was an old woman in the kitchen with very red cheeks, drinking soup out of a basin." The figure, probably Mrs. McNab, is left unidentified, but her presence is portentous: she is one of those old wise women so prominent in the folktales. Though not an instructress, as she would be in the hands of George MacDonald, Molesworth, Ewing, or Ingelow, this female ancient is not a powerless wife. Her red cheeks mock the fragility Mrs. Ramsay shares with the overweening wisher in "The Fisherman's Wife." Mrs. McNab, if the red-cheeked stranger is she, will restore the Ramsays' house. Unnamed, primitive, resilient, this quasimythological figure will also restore the broken female vision whose resurrection was the central aim of Woolf's literary enterprise.

We find the same fragmentation, accompanied by quasimystical longings for magic integration, in such hitherto obscure or misconstrued works as *Mopsa the Fairy* or *Speaking Likenesses.* These tales do not yield the fusions or idealizations sentimentalists might expect. Instead, they defy convention in their deliberate fragmentation, their refusal to provide integrated happy endings. No female child with pure unclouded brow walks through these dreamworlds; in fact, most of the children in this collection are defiantly impure, even unappealing. Though female energies are released, they remain elliptical, subversive, open-ended. They convey not so much triumph as rage against the constraints that distort them.

But if the female *Kunstmärchen* often insists on the frustration of the energies it unleashes, it taps those energies with rare vigor and inventiveness. As Woolf's Mrs. McNab repairs the Ramsay house, which has come to resemble the dilapidated and overgrown palace of "Sleeping Beauty"— the tale Woolf's "aunt" Ritchie reappropriated so wittily—so female art of a special sort resuscitates sleeping ambitions. Like *The Arabian Nights,* these stories transmit broken visions of a forbidden completion. In the spirit of this vision, Woolf's art endows Mrs. Ramsay with the power that eludes her in life. Like the ageless old women in the Victorian tales of magic Woolf knew so well, she still sits, by her window, to this very day. In the same way, the tales anthologized here affirm their imaginative power by implicitly protesting against the conditions that forbid it.

✳

There is more to read than the stories we have chosen. A more wide-ranging collection would have started with earlier nineteenth-century texts by writers such as Margaret Gatty and Frances Browne, whose collected fairy tales had appeared in 1851 and 1857, respectively. It might have concluded with Woolf's own story for children, "The Widow and the Parrot." Such a continuum would have allowed the reader to detect both continuities and generational contrasts by emphasizing, say, the differences between Gatty's didactic mode and the far more sophisticated mixture of moralism and fantasy found in the work of her daughter, Juliana Horatia Ewing. This broader anthology might also juxtapose one of the stories by Julia Duckworth, Woolf's mother, to that of her daughter.

We might have presented more thematic, less chronological contrasts by printing both Frances Browne's "The Story of Fairy-foot" and Frances Burnett's revision, a quarter of a century later, of her predecessor's story. In the same spirit, we might have devoted an entire section to Victorian retellings of a single story—for example, the Cinderella story, that archetypal tale of femininity rewarded, a staple of adult British fiction at least since Richardson's *Pamela.* Among the writers such a section might have included were several lesser known figures such as Jane Leeson, author of *The Lady Ella; or, The Story of 'Cinderella' in Verse* (1847), and Louisa (Mrs. George) MacDonald, who converted the story of the Glass Slipper into a "chamber drama" intended "for very young children only" (1870).

Like the Fisherman's Wife, however, we contracted our scope, selecting only stories both of us loved. The artistic power of the texts we chose to include took precedence over representativeness and historical range. Moreover, the availability of some of the best stories in the recent, excellent anthologies edited by Jack Zipes and Michael Patrick Hearn led us to eliminate such first-rate authors as Lucy Lane Clifford and Mary DeMorgan. Seeing no point in duplicating other editors' selections, we are happy to refer our readers to these and other such reprints. We hope the materials we have included will stimulate the reader to further forbidden journeys into the rich, weird world of Victorian fantasies by women.

*

Each of the four sections of this anthology is headed by an introductory essay that explicates and contextualizes the stories that follow, but of course those stories speak for themselves. Like those stories, this book is intended for a varied audience. All but Ritchie's two stories were originally designed for juvenile readers, but the tales that are ostensibly for children have an imaginative power rarely released in more respectable, adult fiction by Victorian women. Like the original Grimm fairy tales which Bruno Bettelheim read too exclusively as stories for children, these fantasies carry adult subtexts. Burlesque fairy tales such as Nesbit's "Melisande," or fantasy novels such as *Mopsa the Fairy,* thus hold a multiple appeal for child and adult readers, for students of Victorian literature and children's literature, for feminists and historians of culture. Above all, though, the collection should interest those readers of all ages and genders who care about the seditious truths secreted in literary fantasy.

In addition to our introductory essays, we have provided explanatory notes and a concluding bibliography designed to allow the reader further access to these and other writers. We have also retained, wherever feasible, the illustrations by the male artists who collaborated with our female authors. These drawings, many of which are superb, provided Victorian readers with an immediate (if not always reliable) interpretation of the text.

Arthur Hughes' illustrations for Christina Rossetti's *Speaking Likenesses* are particular unnerving gems. Savage, violent, at times almost surreal, Hughes' illustrations provide a startling tribute not only to Christina Rossetti's bizarre imagination, but to the Victorian child imagined by adults: a creature always presumed innocent, but in these illustrations at least, far more resilient, even monstrous, than sentimentalists, in the nineteenth century and now, dare imagine.

NINA AUERBACH
U. C. KNOEPFLMACHER

Part One

REFASHIONING FAIRY TALES

�֍

Women writers of the Victorian era regarded the fairy tale as a dormant literature of their own. When Charlotte Brontë's Jane Eyre hears hoofbeats approaching her in the dark, ice-covered Hay Lane, "memories of nursery stories" immediately flood her mind, especially the recollection of "a North-of-England" monster capable of assuming several bestial forms. But the beastly apparition Jane expects turns out to be Rochester, the "master" whom she promptly causes to fall off his horse and who will eventually become her thrall. Rochester himself soon shows his own conversance with, and respect for, powers he associates with the magical women of traditional fairy tales. "When you came on me in Hay Lane last night," he tells Jane, "I thought unaccountably of fairy tales, and had half a mind to demand whether you had bewitched my horse. I am not sure yet. Who are your parents?" When Jane replies that she is parentless, Rochester endows her with a supernatural ancestry. Surely, he insists, she must have been "waiting for [her] people," the fairies who hold their revels in the moonlight: "Did I break one of your rings, that you spread the damned ice on the causeway?" (chapter 13).

Here and elsewhere in *Jane Eyre,* Charlotte Brontë takes even more seriously than her two characters do the potency of the female fairy-tale tradition to which she has them refer. Karen E. Rowe, who has so ably written on that tradition, was the first to show how fully saturated *Jane Eyre* is with patterns drawn from major folktales such as "Cinderella," "Sleeping Beauty," "Blue Beard," and, as a prime analogue for Jane's developing relationship with the homely Rochester, from "Beauty and the Beast," the 1756 *Kunstmärchen* (or literary fairy tale) adapted and popularized by Madame Le Prince de Beaumont.

Proscribed for its paganism by successive religious authorities, the orally transmitted fairy tale lingered in the popular imagination just as fays and gnomes had themselves presumably survived in the less populated regions of the British Isles. In literature written for children, however, such fantastic narratives had been forced to vie, for an entire century, with the moral fables preferred by even such eminent women educators as Maria Edgeworth, whose fine stories for children display her wariness of a demonic imagination. Even though French *precieuses* such as d'Aulnoy, L'Heritier, de Villeneuve and, eventually, a writer like Beaumont (whose 1756 *Magasin des Enfans* was actually printed in London) had penned fairy tales of their own, the earlier oral tradition of the *contes de vieilles,* or old wives' tales, continued to be regarded as crude and subliterary. Not until the Romantic fascination with primitivism, childhood, and peasant folklore redirected collectors like the Grimms to female informants such as Dorothea Viehmann, did the genre's rich mythical veins again become accessible, and its female origins become fully apparent to a dominant literary culture.

Victorian male writers promptly appropriated these materials. As much attracted to the imaginative wealth of this storehouse as to its female sources, they soon assimilated for their own creative purposes the folktales—English, Scottish, Irish, and Scandinavian—which antiquarians, mythographers, and folklorists now were assiduously collecting in emulation of the Brothers Grimm. Victorian women writers, however, still expected by their culture to adhere to and propagate the realism of everyday, were at a decided disadvantage. Unwilling to be stereotyped as fantasists, eager to be valued for their social realism, they found themselves prevented from overtly acknowledging the importance for their own creative efforts of the fantasy lore bequeathed to them by their anonymous foremothers. Whereas male writers such as Tennyson, Dickens, or Ruskin could openly enlist fairy tale materials they found in the collections by Thomas Keightley or the Grimms or even in the treasure trove of *The Arabian Nights,* that product of another female story-spinner's craft, their female counterparts had to proceed far more covertly. Jane Eyre disparages her belief in the North-of-England "Gytrash" as childish "rubbish," even though she adds that her credulity actually was strengthened during the period of her "maturing youth." To mine the mythic richness of the fairy tales so important to Brontë's own imaginative development thus required the adoption of authorial strategies of indirection and disguise. Such tactics prevail even in the texts we present in the second, third, and fourth parts of this anthology, where the fantastic is far more directly embraced than in *Jane Eyre.*

By recasting known folktales, as the three authors introduced in this first part so skillfully do, Victorian women writers could tap more openly the mythic female sources Brontë must half deny. Like Brontë, the three novelists we have chosen—Ritchie, Molesworth, and Ewing—possess a powerful imagination of their own. Yet by posing as mere translators or adapters, they can activate the traditional materials they appropriate without having to risk being accused of indulging in child-like fantasies. Indeed, in the first two selections, "The Sleeping Beauty in the Wood" and "Beauty and the Beast," which open Anne Thackeray Ritchie's *Fairy Tales for Grown Folks,* childishness is kept at bay by the invitation to reinspect from an ironic adult perspective the archetypal relevance of tales removed from the confines of the nursery. A similar sophistication deepens Maria Louisa Molesworth's "The Brown Bull of Norrowa" and Juliana Horatia Ewing's "Amelia and the Dwarfs." These enlargements of a Scottish fairy tale and an Irish fairy tale are addressed to the child reader as much as to the adult. Although both readers can equally appreciate the resourcefulness of each tale's young female protagonist, only the grown-up can also grasp the cultural poignancy of parables as concerned with female empowerment as *Jane Eyre.*

Significantly enough, old women—some of them superannuated—play a major role in each of these selections. Ritchie's narrator is gradually revealed to be an aged spinster called Miss Williamson, a name that befits the real-life daughter whom *William* (Thackeray) had brought up as his literary *son.* (For her *Blackstick Papers,* a collection of essays, Ritchie even chose to impersonate the wise centenarian Fairy Blackstick, who dominates in the fairy tale Thackeray had originally written for her sister and herself, *The Rose and the Ring.*) Miss Williamson lives with the widow known as "H.," and with her friend's grandchildren, in a placid community of women that seems to be patterned after Gaskell's *Cranford.* The quiescent, ordinary, drab lives she observes in the minutely detailed fashion expected of Victorian realists introduce us to other old ladies: the appropriately named Mrs. Dormer, for instance, "long past eighty now," who seems to have been nodding for years before she notices that her great-niece and godchild is no longer eighteen but twenty-five. This dozing benefactress must be roused in order to enact the traditional role of fairy godmother in "The Sleeping Beauty of the Woods." Her "arts" have become rusty after such long disuse. Nonetheless, as the artlessly artful narrator herself makes us see, fairy-tale patterns still obtain in everyday life. Whereas the goody-goody children of didactic children's fiction have long since expired, fairy-tale creatures like Mrs. Dormer and Miss Williamson still thrive, "everywhere and every day."

Their immortality is explained by H.: "All these histories are the histories of human nature, which does not seem to change very much in a thousand years or so, and we don't get tired of the fairies because they are so true to it."

Although Ritchie's stories end with marriage, it is significant that her narrator should be an old single woman. Originally used to denote the occupation of those women capable of spinning wool as well as stories, the term "spinster" did not become attached to unmarried women until the seventeenth century. The title page to Perrault's 1695 *Contes de Ma Mere Loye* offered an etching of the wool-spinning crone, seated with children and adults before an open hearth, that became an icon for all future verbal and pictorial representations of the figure variously known as Mother Goose or Dame Bunch. Ritchie's Miss Williamson, though a genteel Victorian lady, is this figure's latter-day incarnation. Her aged youthfulness makes her perfectly suited as a purveyor of the old but ever-fresh tales she merely needs to replant.

Comfortably situated with her female friend H. on "either side of the warm hearth," Miss Williamson does not have to rake up coals for any frozen Rochester. The two women spend the winter evenings of their lives "without fear of fiery dwarfs skipping out of the ashes." In *Villette,* the novel that revises *Jane Eyre,* Charlotte Brontë made sure that her new heroine would not be compelled to wed the ugly male Beast who desires a mate. Though Miss Williamson is most sympathetic to the young men to whom she assigns the roles of Prince and Beast in her two narratives, her own sexual segregation (like that of unmarried writers such as Rossetti and Ingelow) allows her to treat marriage plots with wry detachment.

Old women also figure prominently in the selections from Molesworth and Ewing. The white-haired woman, "spinning busily," encountered in a dream by the children in Molesworth's *The Tapestry Room,* is of an undetermined age, as the narrator makes sure to stress: "No doubt she was old, as we count old, but, except, for her hair, she did not look so." This strange white lady, who proceeds to tell the story of the Princess and the Brown Bull, acts as an intermediary between the children's old nurse Marcelline and the two old women within the tale (one of whom seems to be the same fairy who gave the princess her magical balls). Molesworth relishes these refractions and blendings of a figure who also stands for her own authorial self. Marcelline, the dream-narrator, the "kind old woman" who shelters the princess, are all purveyors of an oft-told tale honed and embellished by a succession of female spinners.

Ewing's "Amelia and the Dwarfs" calls attention even more prominently to its venerable ancestry in female folklore. The opening sentence invites us to go back five generations to the grandmother of "my godmother's grandmother." Ewing's acknowledged dependence on a distant old wife's tale makes her narrator assume the role of transmitter. And it is true that this deliciously comic masterpiece faithfully follows the contours of the tale of "Wee Meg Barnilegs," the folktale still told to Ruth Sawyer in the 1890s by her Irish nurse and reprinted in Sawyer's *The Way of the Storyteller.* But Ewing does much more than reset a peasant tale in the genteel Victorian society she so relentlessly satirizes. Among her many improvisations is the addition of the "old woman" Amelia encounters in the underground into which she has been thrust by the sadistic dwarfs. Like the Apple Woman in Ingelow's *Mopsa the Fairy* (reprinted in part 3), this fellow captive is "a real woman, not a fairy." She has lost all sense of time in her long period of servitude. Though she prefers the timelessness of surroundings unmarked by days and nights, and hence has decided to remain in the penumbra (and anonymity) of her underground existence, she nonetheless instructs Amelia how to escape through the sexual wiles her clever pupil promptly exploits. Whereas, in the Irish folktale, the male dwarfs bring about Wee Meg's reform, in Ewing's version it is the dwarfs' slave who remains Amelia's prime tutor.

In all of these tales, then, older women come to the aid of the young. Ritchie's Miss Williamson and Mrs. Dormer act as marriage brokers for the clumsy and the naive; Molesworth's enchantresses provide shelter and magical tools; Ewing's slave woman discharges the role that neither Amelia's fumbling mother nor her impotent nurse were able to perform in a stratified and genteel Victorian order. But if these figures are invested with powers traditionally assigned to fairy godmothers, young women themselves are credited with an ingenuity and resilience that restores some of the power they possessed in a matriarchal culture.

Dull Cecilia Lulworth, to be sure, in Ritchie's "The Sleeping Beauty in the Wood," is the exception that proves the rule. Lacking all wit, she insists on discoursing about slugs at the dinner table; lacking any taste or even an awareness of her own attractiveness, she chooses "a sickly green dress," hideously trimmed, as her "dinner-costume." In her portrait of sluggish Cecilia, Ritchie mocks the female passivity that so attracted Victorian males to the sleeping beauties they tried to awaken with a kiss. Cecilia's tears exasperate her outspoken godmother, who declares that the "girl is a greater idiot than I took her for." But they utterly disarm young Frank Lulworth, the "young prince" touched by her "simplicity and beauty." As Ritchie implies, simplicity and beauty appear to be largely in the eyes of prospective princes. Frank is as charmed by Cecilia's "silly" crying as George Eliot's Lydgate is moved by the teardrops shed by his imaginary water nixie in *Middlemarch,* the novel which Virginia Woolf described as written for truly "grown-up people" in an essay in which she also cites her mentor and step-aunt, Lady Ritchie. Ritchie's tale for "grown folks," however, permits "fairy transformations" that would be impossible in *Middlemarch.*

Ritchie's revision of "Beauty and the Beast" features a far more energetic heroine than stolid Cecilia. It is true that the bestial male whom Belle Barley is compelled to serve is neither as frightening as the monster who tries to detain Beauty in his mansion in the original tale nor as wonderfully duplicitous as the bigamist who conceals the existence of his vampiric, attic wife in order to keep Jane Eyre at Thornfield. Brontë's Rochester must be demasculinized as much as the senseless and broken Beast whom Beauty finds near death in the original fairy tale. But in Ritchie's revision, masculinity is never a threat. Guy Griffiths, the Beast to Belle's Beauty, may be "rough-looking" and clumsy, especially when he smashes crockery or wields a "huge seal, all over bears and griffins." But his empathy and susceptibility to female guidance are apparent from the story's outset.

Indeed, Guy's resemblance to his presumed foil, Belle's impotent father, is much more marked than in the original. Both men are excessively prone to self-pity and self-derogation. Both are decidedly subservient to stronger females. Guy transfers this submissiveness from his unloving mother to Miss Williamson and the widow H., who become the story's good fairies. Belinda's father, on the other hand, allows himself to be so utterly dominated by her mean-spirited older sisters that he cannot even value the sacrifices he exacts from his sanest and most loving child. By dwelling so extensively on this patriarch's pathology, and by removing from her cast of characters the three loving brothers Beauty possessed in the original tale—soldiers willing to fight for her against the all-powerful Beast—Ritchie further accentuates the passivity of the male figures. It is the women who decide the story's outcome.

Ritchie invites us to regard Belle's preference for her shaggy jailer to her feckless father as a sign of her maturation. Guy does not undergo anything resembling the miraculous transformation which, in the original tale, changes an agonized monster "into one of the loveliest princes that ever eye beheld." But Guy's agonies were never as profound as either Beast's or Rochester's. Though found "lying on the grass" by Belle, he is hardly near death. He has merely fallen asleep and, in a reversal of "Sleeping Beauty," this ugly male can now be awakened by a female kiss. Like Belle's merchant father, he is still prone to protest that he does not deserve such abundant recompense. But under her tutelage, he will soon be cured of both his propensity for self-belittlement and his tendency to treat romance as some sort of barter.

If Ritchie's story ends on a note more prosaic than passionate, Maria Louisa Molesworth's "The Brown Bull of Norrowa" revises "Beauty and the Beast" to more effervescent effect. Molesworth's princess moves deftly through a fantastic landscape because of endowments most fairy tale princesses would shun: cocky intelligence and acrobatic skill. Fairy tales conventionally exhort us to admire beauty and passive virtue in their heroines; this one champions "good sense and ready wit." This princess is vain, not about her looks, but about her dexterity at juggling. In fact, Molesworth slyly gives her heroine all the virtues generally reserved for boys: "She was not a silly Princess at all. She was clever at learning, and liked it, and she was sensible and quick-witted and very brave."

Above all, the narrator reiterates, she is brave. Most princesses wait and pine and endure until the prince comes to save them; this one, however, makes daring choices and takes repeated risks for a debilitated prince who manages to stay passive even when he is a rampaging bull. She may live in a fairy tale, but she breathes feminist air. Like Louisa May Alcott's ambitious tomboys, or the rugged little girls *Ms. Magazine* used to feature in its revisionist children's stories, this brave young woman goes beyond Ritchie's Belle in challenging the conservative ideologies of gender that often seem embedded in the very form of fairy tales.

The princess's unremitting competence—not only does she throw a mean ball, but she makes a fire, and binds the prince's wound with the same deft dispatch—is Molesworth's witty addition to the Scottish tale that was her source. In earlier versions (such as those reprinted by Chambers, Lang, Jacobs, and Grierson), the heroine does not willingly offer herself as a sacrifice to a Minotaur-like bull in order to redeem her father's kingdom. Instead, the protagonist (a commoner rather than a princess) is told by an "auld witch-wife" that she is as fated to be carried away by a bull as her luckier older sisters were when carted off by a coach-and-six. She remains as submissive throughout all her subsequent adventures. Although she, too, must climb a glass hill after becoming separated from the bull, she cannot obtain her iron shoes until after she has spent seven entire years serving still another master, a blacksmith. Betrayed by her next employer, this uncomplaining drudge manages to gain her prince's attention only after he accidentally overhears her singing about her "lang years" of service and devotion.

The initiative of Molesworth's princess thus contrasts with the inactivity of her folktale progenitor, who seems closer to the more familiar figures of Beauty and Cinderella. Beauty need only love her benevolent abductor to dispel the enchantment that transformed him; she crosses no sea, climbs no mountains, explores no wastelands, to find him. Cinderella, at least in her most popular incarnation, proves herself to a fastidious prince because she is delicate enough to wear that token of virginity and fine breeding, a tiny glass slipper. By contrast, the fairy godmother of Molesworth's princess provides magic walking shoes tough enough for a strenuous journey. Feminine tenderness and patience, aristocratic delicacy, are eclipsed by the sturdy feet of Molesworth's vigorous traveler.

The activism of this princess challenges the fortitude even of Jane Eyre. Jane too embarks on difficult journeys, but these never humanize her surly master; only his demonic bride can finally transform Rochester. Moreover, Brontë's earnest protagonist, like so many heroines of traditional fairy tales, lacks the most winning attribute of Molesworth's princess: she does not love to play. The ordeals the princess undergoes are as intense as those experienced by her forerunner in the original folktale of "The Brown Bull of Norrowa." This princess is unique, however, in her zest for proving herself: Molesworth has created a character whose energy matches her ordeals. She loves adversity because, like the golden balls with which she is so skilled, it is a congenial mode of performance.

"Catch," she says after a romantic supper with her prince, and throws a golden ball at him. This princess likes to be good at things. Her infectious spirit of play teases the adult reader with hints of a sophisticated sexuality that fuels her adroitness at work and her virtuoso suffering. She likes to act in every sense of the word. Her final ordeal is a literal performance, in which she wins a husband by out-juggling princesses who are too arrogant to excel. Victorian heroines were exhorted to radiate virtue only in seclusion. "The Brown Bull of Norrowa" is unique in the impropriety of its princess, who wins her prize by showing off.

Little Amelia in Ewing's story about a bratty child's socialization is also a show-off—and as consummate a tease. Her ability to manipulate the mindless and impotent adults whose permissiveness she exploits may be faulted by the narrator for its "rudeness, wilfulness, and powers of destruction." Nonetheless, as the opening account of her activities clearly suggests, this clever and "very observing child" also acts as the satirical narrator's agent and ally. Amelia's ineffectual mother, with her "rolling Rs," is no match for the shrewd little demon who purports to spill finger glasses by accident or not to understand the workings of the bracelets she infallibly breaks. Even blackmail is not beyond the pale of Amelia's provocative activities. Though stewing in anger, the "well-bred and amiable" Victorian adults who are Amelia's victims are too polite to remonstrate. The retaliation she courts can therefore come only from aggressive creatures unbound by such hypocrisy.

In her everyday world, a snow-white bulldog plays Beast to Amelia's Beauty; in the fantasy world below, the sadistic dwarfs exact the revenge the bland adults forbore to carry out. Rolling "as many warning Rs as Amelia's mother," the bulldog—unlike that indulgent mamma—makes good on his warning. Refusing to be teased, he bites Amelia. The adults are as befuddled as ever: Amelia's mother must quickly correct herself when she ponders aloud whether to "shoot Amelia and burn the bull-dog—at least I mean shoot the bull-dog and burn Amelia with a red-hot poker" to cauterize the wound. (By assigning this Freudian slip to the mother, Ewing subtly improves on the original Irish folktale, where one annoyed neighbor quite seriously proposed shooting the pesky Meg and rewarding the dog who bit her.) But the wound is hardly as deep as that suffered by another wild child in need of canine discipline, Catherine Earnshaw in *Wuthering Heights*. Unsurprisingly, the bulldog, described as a "great deal more sensible than anybody in the house," now becomes Amelia's closest friend and confidant.

At the end, the dog will be the only one to know how Amelia's underground descent taught her to use her "clever head" more productively. But he can no more act as Amelia's mentor than her well-meaning nurse can go against the parental permissiveness that prevented Amelia from understanding that her destructive energies might be better employed. Thus it is that a new set of enforcers now needs to take over. The bulldog's gentle nip was hardly hurtful. But the nasty little men who pinch Amelia's funny bone and tread on her heels clearly enjoy their sadism. Like the grotesque goblins in Rossetti's poem "Goblin Market," the wizened dwarfs undergo such "horrible contortions as they laughed, that it was hideous to behold."

In "Wee Meg Barnilegs," the gnomes merely bring about the chastening of a rebellious little girl. Ewing's story goes further by stressing Amelia's resourcefulness. This rebel outwits her captors as decisively as she had earlier eluded the authority of the adults in her own world. Amelia accepts from the old slave woman the instructions she refused to receive from the nurse in the world above. The girl who bled a little when bitten by the dog is close to puberty. The old woman advises her to exploit her sexual appeal by dancing "all your dances, and as well as you can," while seeming "content" to remain with the dwarfs. The ruse works. Amelia "cunningly" concentrates her deceptions on one specially "grotesque and grimy old dwarf" who is so enamoured of her coquettish mazurkas that he wants to detain her forever. This "very smutty" old man puts his arms around Amelia's waist in proprietary fashion but finds himself stumbling over his protruding shoes. Unlike Ritchie's clumsy Guy, or Molesworth's Bull of Norrowa, he will hardly turn into a handsome young prince. Amelia has no intention of staying with this diminutive representative of male beastliness.

Back in her own world, however, Amelia must compromise. She has learned how to feign compliance in the underworld of the dwarfs; she must now accept the limits of the social world she had repudiated. Her mother's "amiable" friends prove to be no wiser than before when they decide to rename the unexpectedly compliant young woman by calling her "Amy, that is to say, 'Beloved.'" In the Irish folktale, Meg produces offspring proverbial for their acquiescence and sociability. But the unmarried Amelia's popularity, Ewing seems to suggest, stems less from conformism than from a willingness to mask her superiority. Beneath the "good and gentle" grown-up lurks her earlier self. Thus, after extolling the adult Amelia's unselfishness, Ewing's narrator is quick to add: "She was unusually clever, as those who have been with the 'Little People' are said always to be." The anarchic child is mother of the woman.

Juliana Ewing's conclusion symbolically applies to the ways in which she and Ritchie and Molesworth were able to harness and discipline the powerful energies of more primitive narratives. As translators of this older material, they relocated it and made it conform as much as Charlotte Brontë did in *Jane Eyre* to the literary conventions and social decorum of their own time. Yet even if their happy-ever-after heroines accept marriage or, in Amelia's case, domestication, they have been vitalized by their contacts with a primal world—a world the writers whose work we introduce in subsequent sections of this anthology recast even more radically.

ANNE THACKERAY RITCHIE

The Sleeping Beauty in the Wood

A kind enchantress one day put into my hand a mystic volume prettily lettered and bound in green, saying, "I am so fond of this book. It has all the dear old fairy tales in it; one never tires of them. Do take it."

I carried the little book away with me, and spent a very pleasant, quiet evening at home by the fire, with H. at the opposite corner, and other old friends, whom I felt I had somewhat neglected of late. Jack and the Beanstalk, Puss in Boots, the gallant and quixotic Giant-killer, and dearest Cinderella, whom we every one of us must have loved, I should think, ever since we first knew her in her little brown pinafore: I wondered, as I shut them all up for the night between their green boards, what it was that made these stories so fresh and so vivid. Why did not they fall to pieces, vanish, explode, disappear, like so many of their contemporaries and descendants? And yet, far from being forgotten and passing away, it would seem as if each generation in turn, as it came into the world, looks to be delighted still by the brilliant pageant, and never tires or wearies of it. And on their side princes and princesses never seem to grow any older; the castles and the lovely gardens flourish without need of repair or whitewash, or plumbers or glaziers. The princesses' gowns, too, —sun, moon, and star color, —do not wear out or pass out of fashion or require altering. Even the seven-leagued boots do not appear to be the worse for wear. Numbers of realistic stories for children have passed away. Little Henry and his Bearer, Poor Harry and Lucy,[1] have very nearly given up their little artless ghosts and prattle, and

---

1. **Little Henry . . . and Lucy** Mary Martha Sherwood's *Little Henry and His Bearer* (1814), the story of an Anglo-Indian boy who converts his Hindoo bearer to Christianity before dying, was a best-seller especially popular in Evangelical circles. As didactic but less sentimental was Maria Edgeworth's *Harry and Lucy* (1801).

21

ceased making their own beds for the instruction of less excellently brought up little boys and girls; and, notwithstanding a very interesting article in the *Saturday Review,* it must be owned that Harry Sandford and Tommy Merton[2] are not familiar playfellows in our nurseries and school-rooms, and have passed somewhat out of date. But not so all these centenarians,—Prince Riquet,[3] Carabas,[4] Little Red Riding-hood, Bluebeard, and others. They seem as if they would never grow old. They play with the children, they amuse the elders, there seems no end to their fund of spirits and perennial youth.

H., to whom I made this remark, said, from the opposite chimney-corner, "No wonder; the stories are only histories of real, living persons turned into fairy princes and princesses. Fairy stories are everywhere and every day. We are all princes and princesses in disguise, or ogres or wicked dwarfs. All these histories are the histories of human nature, which does not seem to change very much in a thousand years or so, and we don't get tired of the fairies because they are so true to it."

After this little speech of H.'s, we spent an unprofitable half-hour reviewing our acquaintance, and classing them under their real characters and qualities. We had dined with Lord Carabas only the day before, and met Puss in Boots; Beauty and the Beast were also there. We uncharitably counted up, I am ashamed to say, no less than six Bluebeards. Jack and the Beanstalk we had met just starting on his climb. A Red Riding-hood; a girl with toads dropping from her mouth: we knew three or four of each. Cinderellas—alas! who does not know more than one dear, poor, pretty Cinderella; and as for sleeping princesses in the woods, how many one can reckon up! Young, old, ugly, pretty, awakening, sleeping still.

"Do you remember Cecilia Lulworth," said H., "and Dorlicote? Poor Cecilia!"

Some lives are *couleur de rose,* people say; others seem to be, if not *couleur de rose* all through, yet full of bright, beautiful tints, blues, pinks, little bits of harmonious cheerfulness. Other lives, if not so brilliant, and

2. **Harry . . . Merton** Another former staple of middle-class households, *The History of Sandford and Merton* (1783–1789) counterpointed the education of a virtuous farmer's son and spoilt merchant's son through linked tales and parables. Once hailed for its progressive ideas, the book had lost some of its appeal after the proliferation of more artistic and complicated texts for Victorian children.

3. **Prince Riquet** Perrault's "Riquet of the Tuft" had been recently retold by Dinah Maria Mulock Craik in her *Fairy Book* (1863) and was later adapted by Ritchie herself in *Bluebeard's Keys and Other Stories* (1874).

4. **Carabas** Puss in Boots gives his master the spurious title of marquis of Carabas.

seeming more or less gray at times, are very sweet and gentle in tone, with faint gleams of gold or lilac to brighten them. And then again others, alas! are black and hopeless from the beginning. Besides these, there are some which have always appeared to me as if they were of a dark, dull hue; a dingy, heavy brown, which no happiness, or interest, or bright color could ever enliven. Blues turn sickly, roses seem faded, and yellow lilacs look red and ugly upon these heavy backgrounds. Poor Cecilia, —as H. called her, —hers had always seemed to me one of these latter existences, unutterably dull, commonplace, respectable, stinted, ugly, and useless.

Lulworth Hall, with the great, dark park bounded by limestone walls, with iron gates here and there, looked like a blot upon the bright and lovely landscape. The place from a distance, compared with the surrounding country, was a blur and a blemish as it were, —sad, silent, solitary.

Travellers passing by sometimes asked if the place was uninhabited, and were told, "No, shure, —fam'ly lives thear all the yeaurr round." Some charitable souls might wonder what life could be like behind those dull gates. One day a young fellow riding by saw rather a sweet woman's face gazing for an instant through the bars, and he went on his way with a momentary thrill of pity. Need I say that it was poor Cecilia who looked out vacantly to see who was passing along the high-road. She was surrounded by hideous moreen, oil-cloth, punctuality, narrow-mindedness, horsehair, and mahogany. Loud bells rang at intervals, regular, monotonous. Surly but devoted attendants waited upon her. She was rarely alone; her mother did not think it right that a girl in Cecilia's position should "race" about the grounds unattended; as for going outside the walls it was not to be thought of. When Cecilia went out with her gloves on, and her goloshes, her mother's companion, Miss Bowley, walked beside her up and down the dark laurel walk at the back of the house, —up and down, down and up, up and down. "I think I am getting tired, Maria," Miss Lulworth would say at last. "If so we had better return to the hall," Maria would reply, "although it is before our time." And then they would walk home in silence, between the iron railings and laurel-bushes.

As Cecilia walked erectly by Miss Bowley's side, the rooks went whirling over their heads, the slugs crept sleepily along the path under the shadow of the grass and the weeds; they heard no sounds except the cawing of the birds, and the distant monotonous, hacking noise of the gardener and his boy digging in the kitchen-garden.

Cecilia, peeping into the long drab drawing-room on her return, might, perhaps, see her mother, erect and dignified, at her open desk, composing, writing, crossing, re-reading, an endless letter to an indifferent cousin in Ireland, with a single candle and a small piece of blotting-paper, and a pen-wiper made of ravellings, all spread out before her.

"You have come home early, Cecil," says the lady, without looking up. "You had better make the most of your time, and practise till the dressing-bell rings. Maria will kindly take up your things."

And then in the chill twilight Cecilia sits down to the jangling instrument, with the worn silk flutings. A faded rack it is upon which her fingers had been distended ever since she can remember. A great many people think there is nothing in the world so good for children as scoldings, whippings, dark cupboards, and dry bread and water, upon which they expect them to grow up into tall, fat, cheerful, amiable men and women; and a great many people think that for grown-up young people the silence, the chillness, the monotony and sadness of their own fading twilight days is all that is required. Mrs. Lulworth and Maria Bowley, her companion, Cecilia's late governess, were quite of this opinion. They themselves, when they were little girls, had been slapped, snubbed, locked up in closets, thrust into bed at all sorts of hours, flattened out on backboards, set on high stools to play the piano for days together, made to hem frills five or six weeks long, and to learn immense pieces of poetry, so that they had to stop at home all the afternoon. And though Mrs. Lulworth had grown up stupid, suspicious, narrow-minded, soured, and overbearing, and had married for an establishment, and Miss Bowley, her governess's daughter, had turned out nervous, undecided, melancholy, and anxious, and had never married at all, yet they determined to bring up Cecilia as they themselves had been brought up, and sincerely thought they could not do better.

When Mrs. Lulworth married, she said to Maria, "You must come and live with me, and help to educate my children some day, Maria. For the present I shall not have a home of my own; we are going to reside with my husband's aunt, Mrs. Dormer. She is a very wealthy person, far advanced in years. She is greatly annoyed with Mr. and Mrs. John Lulworth's vagaries, and she has asked me and my husband to take their places at Dorlicote Hall." At the end of ten years Mrs. Lulworth wrote again: "We are now permanently established in our aunt's house. I hear you are in want of a situation; pray come and superintend the education of my only child, Cecilia (she is named after her godmother, Mrs. Dormer). She is now nearly three years old, and I feel that she begins to require some discipline."

This letter was written at that same desk twenty-two years before Cecilia began her practising that autumn evening. She was twenty-five years old now, but like a child in inexperience, in ignorance, in placidity; a fortunate stolidity and slowness of temperament had saved her from being crushed and nipped in the bud, as it were. She was not bored because she had never known any other life. It seemed to her only natural that all days should be alike, rung in and out by the jangling breakfast, lunch, dinner, and prayer-bells. Mr. Dormer—a little chip of a man—read prayers suitable for every day in the week; the servants filed in, maids first, then the men. Once Cecilia saw one of the maids blush and look down smiling as she marched out after the others. Miss Dormer wondered a little, and thought she would ask Susan why she looked so strangely; but Susan married the groom soon after, and went away, and Cecilia never had an opportunity of speakng to her.

Night after night Mr. Dormer replaced his spectacles with a click, and pulled up his shirt-collar when the service was ended. Night after night old Mrs. Dormer coughed a little moaning cough. If she spoke, it was generally to make some little, bitter remark. Every night she shook hands with her nephew and niece, kissed Cecilia's blooming cheek, and patted out of the room. She was a little woman with starling eyes. She had never got over her husband's death. She did not always know when she moaned. She dressed in black, and lived alone in her turret, where she had various old-fashioned occupations, —tatting, camphor-boxes to sort, a real old spinning-wheel and distaff among other things, at which Cecilia, when she was a child, had pricked her fingers trying to make it whirr as her aunt did. Spinning-wheels have quite gone out, but I know of one or two old ladies who still use them. Mrs. Dormer would go nowhere, and would see no one. So at least her niece, the master-spirit, declared, and the old lady got to believe it at last. I don't know how much the fear of the obnoxious John and his wife and children may have had to do with this arrangement.

When her great aunt was gone it was Cecilia's turn to gather her work together at a warning sign from her mother, and walk away through the long, chilly passages to her slumbers in the great green four-post bed. And so time passed. Cecilia grew up. She had neither friends nor lovers. She was not happy nor unhappy. She could read, but she never cared to open a book. She was quite contented; for she thought Lulworth Hall the finest place, and its inmates the most important people in the world. She worked a great deal, embroidering interminable quilts and braided toilet-covers and fish-napkins. She never thought of anything but the utterest commonplaces and platitudes. She considered that being respectable and decorous, and a little pompous and overbearing, was the duty of every well-brought-up lady and gentleman. To-night she banged away very placidly at Rhodes' air,[5] for the twentieth time breaking down in the same passage and making the same mistake, until the dressing-bell rang, and Cecilia, feeling she had done her duty, then extinguished her candle, and went upstairs across the great, chill hall, up the bare oil-cloth gallery, to her room.

Most young women have some pleasure, whatever their troubles may be, in dressing, and pretty trinkets and beads and ribbons and necklaces. An unconscious love of art and intuition leads some of them, even plain ones, to adorn themselves. The colors and ribbon ends brighten bright faces, enliven dull ones, deck what is already lovable, or, at all events, make the most of what materials there are. Even a Maypole, crowned and flowered and tastily ribboned, is a pleasing object. And, indeed, the art of decoration seems to me a charming natural instinct, and one which is not nearly enough encouraged, and a gift which every woman should try to acquire. Some girls, like birds, know how to weave, out of ends of rags, of threads and morsels and straws, a beautiful whole, a work of real genius for their habitation. Frivolities, say some; waste of time, say others,—expense, vanity. The strong-minded dowagers shake their heads at it all,—Mrs. Lulworth among them; only why had Nature painted Cecilia's cheeks of brightest pink, instead of bilious orange, like poor Maria Bowley's? why was her hair all crisp and curly? and were her white, even teeth, and her clear, gray eyes, vanity and frivolity too? Cecilia was rather too stout for her age; she had not much expression in her face. And no wonder. There was not much to be expressive about in her poor little stinted life. She could not go into raptures over the mahogany sideboard, the camphene lamp in the drawing-room, the four-post beds indoors, the laurel-bushes without, the Moorish temple with yellow glass windows, or the wigwam summer-house, which were the alternate boundaries of her daily walks.

Cecilia was not allowed a fire to dress herself by; a grim maid, however, attended, and I suppose she was surrounded, as people say, by every comfort. There was a horsehair sofa, everything was large, solid, brown as I have said, grim, and in its place. The rooms at Lulworth Hall did not take the impression of their inmate; the inmate was moulded by the room. There were in Cecilia's no young lady-like trifles lying here and there; upon the chest of drawers there stood a mahogany workbox, square, with a key,—

5. **Rhodes' air** Hugh Rhodes wrote religious verses and choral songs in the sixteenth century.

that was the only attempt at feminine elegance,—a little faded chenille, I believe, was to be seen round the clock on the chimney-piece, and a black and white check dressing-gown and an ugly little pair of slippers were set out before the toilet-table. On the bed, Cecilia's dinner-costume was lying,—a sickly green dress, trimmed with black,—and a white flower for her hair. On the toilet-table an old-fashioned jasper serpent-necklace and a set of amethysts were displayed for her to choose from, also mittens and a couple of hair-bracelets. The girl was quite content, and she would go down gravely to dinner, smoothing out her hideous toggery.

Mrs. Dormer never came down before dinner. All day long she stayed up in her room, dozing and trying remedies, and occasionally looking over old journals and letters until it was time to come downstairs. She liked to see Cecilia's pretty face at one side of the table, while her nephew carved, and Mrs. Lulworth recounted any of the stirring events of the day. She was used to the life,—she was sixty when they came to her, she was long past eighty now,—the last twenty years had been like a long sleep, with the dream of what happened when she was alive and in the world continually passing before her.

When the Lulworths first came to her she had been in a low and nervous state, only stipulated for quiet and peace, and that no one was to come to her house of mourning. The John Lulworths, a cheery couple, broke down at the end of a month or two, and preferred giving up all chance of their aunt's great inheritance to living in such utter silence and seclusion. Upon Charles, the younger brother and his wife, the habit had grown, until now anything else would have been toil and misery to them. Except the old rector from the village, the doctor now and then, no other human creature ever crossed the threshold. For Cecilia's sake Miss Bowley once ventured to hint,—

"Cecilia with her expectations has the whole world before her."

"Maria!" said Mrs. Lulworth, severely; and, indeed, to this foolish woman it seemed as if money would add more to her daughter's happiness than the delights, the wonders, the interests, the glamours of youth. Charles Lulworth, shrivelled, selfish, dull, worn-out, did not trouble his head about Cecilia's happiness, and let his wife do as she liked with the girl.

This especial night when Cecilia came down in her ugly green dress, it seemed to her as if something unusual had been going on. The old lady's eyes looked bright and glittering, her father seemed more animated than usual, her mother looked mysterious and put out. It might have been fancy, but Cecilia thought they all stopped talking as she came into the room; but then dinner was announced, and her father offered Mrs. Dormer his arm immediately, and they went into the dining-room.

It must have been fancy. Everything was as usual. "They have put up a few hurdles in Dalron's field, I see," said Mrs. Lulworth. "Charles, you ought to give orders for repairing the lock of the harness-room."

"Have they seen to the pump-handle?" said Mr. Lulworth.

"I think not." And then there was a dead silence.

"Potatoes," said Cecilia, to the footman. "Mamma, we saw ever so many slugs in the laurel walk, Maria and I, —didn't we, Maria? I think there are a great many slugs in our place."

Old Mrs. Dormer looked up while Cecilia was speaking, and suddenly interrupted her in the middle of her sentence. "How old are you, child?" she said; "are you seventeen or eighteen?"

"Eighteen! Aunt Cecilia. I am five-and-twenty," said Cecilia, staring.

"Good gracious! is it possible?" said her father, surprised.

"Cecil is a woman now," said her mother.

"Five-and-twenty!" said the old lady, quite crossly. "I had no idea time went so fast. She ought to have been married long ago; that is, if she means to marry at all."

"Pray, my dear aunt, do not put such ideas—" Mrs. Lulworth began.

"I don't intend to marry," said Cecilia, peeling an orange, and quite un-moved, and she slowly curled the rind of her orange in the air. "I think people are very stupid to marry. Look at poor Jane Simmonds; her husband beats her; Jones saw her."

"So you don't intend to marry?" said the old lady, with an odd inflection in her voice. "Young ladies were not so wisely brought up in my early days," and she gave a great sigh. "I was reading an old letter this morning from your poor father, Charles, —all about happiness, and love in a cot, and two little curly-headed boys, —Jack, you know, and yourself. I should rather like to see John again."

"What, my dear aunt, after his unparalleled audacity? I declare the thought of his impudent letter makes my blood boil," exclaimed Mrs. Lul-worth.

"Does it?" said the old lady. "Cecilia, my dear, you must know that your uncle has discovered that the entail was not cut off from a certain property which my father left me, and which I brought to my husband. He has there-fore written me a very business-like letter, in which he says he wishes for no alteration at present, but begs that, in the event of my making my will, I should remember this, and not complicate matters by leaving it to yourself, as had been my intention. I see nothing to offend in the request. Your mother thinks differently."

Cecilia was so amazed at being told anything that she only stared again, and, opening a wide mouth, popped into it such a great piece of orange that she could not speak for some minutes.

"Cecilia has certainly attained years of discretion," said her great-aunt; "she does not compromise herself by giving any opinion on matters she does not understand."

Notwithstanding her outward imperturbability, Cecilia was a little stirred and interested by this history, and by the little conversation which had preceded it. Her mother was sitting upright in her chair as usual, netting with vigorous action; her large foot outstretched, her stiff, bony hands working and jerking monotonously. Her father was dozing in his arm-chair. Old Mrs. Dormer, too, was nodding in her corner. The monotonous Maria was stitching in the lamplight. Gray and black shadows loomed all round her. The far end of the room was quite dark; the great curtains swept from their ancient cornices. Cecilia, for the first time in all her life, wondered whether she should ever live all her life in this spot,—ever go away? It seemed impossible, unnatural, that she should ever do so. Silent, dull as it was, she was used to it, and did not know what was amiss . . .

Young Frank Lulworth, the lawyer of the family—John Lulworth's eldest son—it was who had found it all out. His father wrote that with Mrs. Dormer's permission he proposed coming down in a day or two to show her the papers, and to explain to her personally how the matter stood. "My son and I," said John Lulworth, "both feel that this would be far more agreeable to our feelings, and perhaps to yours, than having recourse to the usual professional intervention; for we have no desire to press our claims for the present; and we only wish that in the ultimate disposal of your property you should be aware how the matter really stands. We have always been led to suppose that the estate actually in question has been long destined by you for your grand-niece, Cecilia Lulworth. I hear from our old friend, Dr. Hicks, that she is remarkably pretty and very amiable. Perhaps such vague possibilities are best unmentioned; but it has occurred to me that in the event of a mutual understanding springing up between the young folks,—my son and your grand-niece,—the connection might be agreeable to us all, and lead to a renewal of that family intercourse which has been, to my great regret, suspended for some time past."

Old Mrs. Dormer, in her shaky Italian handwriting, answered her nephew's letter by return of post:—

"MY DEAR NEPHEW,—I must acknowledge the receipt of your epistle of the 13th instant. By all means invite your son to pay us his proposed visit. We can then talk over business matters at our leisure, and young Francis can be introduced to his relatives. Although a long time has elapsed since we last met, believe me, my dear nephew, not unmindful of by-gone associations, and yours, very truly, always,

"C. DORMER."

The letter was in the postman's bag when old Mrs. Dormer informed Mrs. Charles of what she had done.

Frank Lulworth thought that in all his life he had never seen anything so dismal, so silent, so neglected, as Dorlicote Park, when he drove up, a few days after, through the iron gates and along the black laurel wilderness which led to the house. The laurel branches, all unpruned, untrained, were twisting savagely in and out, wreathing and interlacing one another, clutching tender shootings, wrestling with the young oak-trees and the limes. He passed by black and sombre avenues leading to mouldy temples, to crumbling summer-houses; he saw what had once been a flower-garden, now all run to seed,—wild, straggling, forlorn; a broken-down bench, a heap of hurdles lying on the ground, a field-mouse darting across the road, a desolate autumn sun shining upon all this mouldering ornament and confusion. It seemed more forlorn and melancholy by contrast, somehow, coming as he did out of the loveliest country and natural sweetness into the dark and tangled wilderness within these limestone walls of Dorlicote.

The parish of Dorlicote-cum-Rockington looks prettier in the autumn than at any other time. A hundred crisp tints, jewelled rays,—grays, browns, purples, glinting golds, and silvers,—rustle and sparkle upon the branches of the nut-trees, of the bushes and thickets. Soft blue mists and purple tints rest upon the distant hills; scarlet berries glow among the brown leaves of the hedges; lovely mists fall and vanish suddenly, revealing bright and sweet autumnal sights; blackberries, stacks of corn, brown leaves crisping upon the turf, great pears hanging sweetening in the sun over the cottage lintels, cows grazing and whisking their tails, blue smoke curling from the tall farm chimneys; all is peaceful, prosperous, golden. You can see the sea on clear days from certain knolls and hillocks . . .

Out of all these pleasant sights young Lulworth came into this dreary splendor. He heard no sounds of life,—he saw no one. His coachman had opened the iron gate. "They doan't keep no one to moind the gate," said the driver; "only tradesmen cooms to th'ouse." Even the gardener and his boy were out of the way; and when they got sight of the house at last, many of the blinds were down and shutters shut, and only two chimneys were smoking. There was some one living in the place, however, for a watch-dog who was lying asleep in his kennel woke up and gave a heart-rending howl when Frank got out and rang at the bell.

He had to wait an immense time before anybody answered, although a little page in buttons came and stared at him in blank amazement from one of the basement windows, and never moved. Through the same window Frank could see into the kitchen, and he was amused when a sleepy, fat cook came up behind the little page and languidly boxed his ears, and seemed to order him off the premises.

The butler, who at last answered the door, seemed utterly taken aback,—nobody had called for months past, and here was a perfect stranger taking out his card, and asking for Mrs. Dormer, as if it was the most natural thing in the world. The under-butler was half-asleep in his pantry, and had not heard the door-bell. The page—the very same whose ears had been boxed—came wondering to the door, and went to ascertain whether Mrs. Dormer would see the gentleman or not.

"What a vault, what a catacomb, what an ugly old place!" thought Frank, as he waited. He heard steps far, far away; then came a long silence, and then a heavy tread slowly approaching, and the old butler beckoned to him to follow,—through a cob-web-color room, through a brown room, through a gray room, into a great, dim, drab drawing-room, where the old lady was sitting alone. She had come down her back stairs to receive him; it was years since she had left her room before dinner.

Even old ladies look kindly upon a tall, well-built, good-looking, good-humored young man. Frank's nose was a little too long, his mouth a little too straight; but he was a handsome young fellow, with a charming manner. Only, as he came up, he was somewhat shy and undecided,—he did not know exactly how to address the old lady. This was his great-aunt. He knew nothing whatever about her, but she was very rich; she had invited him to come, and she had a kind face, he thought; should he,—ought he to embrace her? Perhaps he ought, and he made the slightest possible movement in this direction. Mrs. Dormer, divining his object, pushed him weakly away. "How do you do? No embraces, thank you. I don't care for kissing at my age. Sit down,—there, in that chair opposite,—and now tell me about your father, and all the family, and about this ridiculous discovery of yours. I don't believe a word of it."

The interview between them was long and satisfactory on the whole. The unconscious Cecilia and Miss Bowley returned that afternoon from their usual airing, and, as it happened, Cecilia said, "O Maria! I left my mittens in the drawing-room last night. I will go and fetch them." And, little thinking of what was awaiting her, she flung open the door and marched in through the ante-room, —mushroom hat and brown veil, goloshes and dowdy gown, as usual. "What is this?" thought young Lulworth; "why, who would have supposed it was such a pretty girl?" for suddenly the figure stopped short, and a lovely, fresh face looked up in utter amazement out of the hideous disguise.

"There, don't stare, child," said the old lady. "This is Francis Lulworth, a very intelligent young man, who has got hold of your fortune and ruined all your chances, my dear. He wanted to embrace me just now. Francis, you may as well salute your cousin instead: she is much more of an age for such compliments," said Mrs. Dormer, waving her hand.

The impassive Cecilia, perfectly bewildered, and not in the least understanding, only turned her great, sleepy, astonished eyes upon her cousin, and stood perfectly still as if she was one of those beautiful wax-dolls one sees stuck up to be stared at. If she had been surprised before, utter consternation can scarcely convey her state of mind when young Lulworth stepped up and obeyed her aunt's behest. And, indeed, a stronger-minded person than Cecilia might have been taken aback, who had come into the drawing-room to fetch her mittens, and was met in such an astounding fashion. Frank, half laughing, half kindly, seeing that Cecilia stood quite still and stared at him, supposed it was expected, and did as he was told.

The poor girl gave one gasp of horror, and blushed for the first time, I believe, in the course of her whole existence. Bowley, fixed and open-mouthed from the inner room, suddenly fled with a scream, which recalled Cecilia to a sense of outraged propriety; for, blushing and blinking more deeply, she at last gave three little sobs, and then, O horror! burst into tears!

"Highty-tighty! what a much ado about nothing!" said the old lady, losing her temper and feeling not a little guilty, and much alarmed as to what her niece Mrs. Lulworth might say were she to come on the scene.

"I beg your pardon. I am so very, very sorry," said the young man, quite confused and puzzled. "I ought to have known better. I frightened you. I am your cousin, you know, and really, —pray, pray excuse my stupidity," he said, looking anxiously into the fair, placid face along which the tears were coursing in two streams, like a child's.

"Such a thing never happened in all my life before," said Cecilia. "I know it is wrong to cry, but really—really—"

"Leave off crying directly, miss," said her aunt, testily, "and let us have no more of this nonsense." The old lady dreaded the mother's arrival every instant. Frank, half laughing, but quite unhappy at the poor girl's distress, had taken up his hat to go that minute, not knowing what else to do.

"Ah! you're going," says old Mrs. Dormer; "no wonder. Cecilia, you have driven your cousin away by your rudeness."

"I'm not rude," sobbed Cecilia. "I can't help crying."

"The girl is a greater idiot than I took her for," cried the old lady. "She has been kept here locked up until she has not a single idea left in her silly noddle. No man of sense could endure her for five minutes. You wish to leave the place, I see, and no wonder!"

"I really think," said Frank, "that under the circumstances it is the best thing I can do. Miss Lulworth, I am sure, would wish me to go."

"Certainly," said Cecilia. "Go away, pray go away. Oh, how silly I am!"

Here was a catastrophe!

The poor old fairy was all puzzled and bewildered: her arts were powerless in this emergency. The princess had awakened, but in tears. The prince still stood by, distressed and concerned, feeling horribly guilty, and yet scarcely able to help laughing. Poor Cecilia! her aunt's reproaches had only bewildered her more and more; and for the first time in her life she was bewildered, discomposed, forgetful of hours. It was the hour of calisthenics; but Miss Lulworth forgot everything that might have been expected from a young lady of her admirable bringing-up.

Fairy tales are never very long, and this one ought to come to an end. The princess was awake now; her simplicity and beauty touched the young prince, who did not, I think, really intend to go, though he took up his hat.

Certainly the story would not be worth the telling if they had not been married soon after, and lived happily all the rest of their lives.

※

It is not in fairy tales only that things fall out as one could wish, and indeed, H. and T. agreed the other night that fairies, although invisible, had not entirely vanished out of the land.

It is certainly like a fairy transformation to see Cecilia nowadays in her own home with her children and husband about her. Bright, merry, full of sympathy and interest, she seems to grow prettier every minute.

When Frank fell in love with her and proposed, old Mrs. Dormer insisted upon instantly giving up the Dorlicote Farm for the young people to live in. Mr. and Mrs. Frank Lulworth are obliged to live in London, but they go there every summer with their children; and for some years after her marriage, Cecilia's godmother, who took the opportunity of the wedding to break through many of her recluse habits, used to come and see her every day in a magnificent yellow chariot.

Some day I may perhaps tell you more about the fairies and enchanting princesses of my acquaintance.

ANNE THACKERAY RITCHIE

Beauty and the Beast

I

Fairy times, gifts, music, and dances are said to be over; or, as it has been said, they come to us disguised and made familiar by habit that they do not seem to us strange. H. and I, on either side of the hearth, these long past winter evenings could sit without fear of fiery dwarfs skipping out of the ashes, of black puddings coming down the chimney to molest us. The clock ticked, the window-pane rattled. It was only the wind. The hearth-brush remained motionless on its hook. Pussy, dozing on the hearth, with her claws quietly opening to the warmth of the blaze, purred on and never once startled us out of our usual placidity by addressing us in human tones. The children sleeping peacefully upstairs were not suddenly whisked away and changelings deposited in their cribs. If H. or I opened our mouths pearls and diamonds did not drop out of them; but neither did frogs and tadpoles fall from between our lips. The looking-glass, tranquilly reflecting the comfortable little sitting-room, and the stiff ends of H.'s cap-ribbons, spared us visions of wreathing clouds parting to reveal distant scenes of horror and treachery. Poor H.! I am not sure but that she would have gladly looked in a mirror in which she could have sometimes seen the images of those she loved; but our chimney-glass, with its gilt moulding and bright polished surface, reflects only such homely scenes as two old women at work by the fire, some little Indian children[1] at play upon the rug, the door opening and Susan bringing in the tea-things. As for wishing-cloths and little boiling pots, and such like, we have discovered that instead of rubbing lamps, or spread-

---

1. **Indian children** H.'s grandchildren, though raised in England, were presumably born in India, like Ritchie's father, W. M. Thackeray.

ing magic table-cloths upon the floor, we have but to ring an invisible bell
(which is even less trouble), and a smiling genius in a white cap and apron
brings in anything we happen to fancy. When the clock strikes twelve, H.
puts up her work and lights her candle; she has not yet been transformed
into a beautiful princess all twinkling with jewels, neither does a scullion ever
stand before me in rags; she does not murmur farewell forever and melt
through the key-hole, but "Good-night," as she closes the door. One night
at twelve o'clock, just after she had left me, there was indeed a loud ortho-
dox ring at the bell, which startled us both a little. H. came running down
again without her cap; Susan appeared in great alarm from the kitchen. "It
is the back-door bell, ma'am," said the girl, who had been sitting up over
her new Sunday gown, but who was too frightened to see who was ringing.

I may as well explain that our little house is in a street, but that our back
windows have the advantage of overlooking the grounds of the villa belonging to our good neighbor and friend Mr. Griffiths, in Castle Gardens, and
that a door opens out of our little back garden into his big one, of which we
are allowed to keep the key. This door had been a postern gate once upon a
time, for a bit of the old wall of the park is still standing, against which our
succeeding bricks have been piled. It was a fortunate chance for us when
our old ivy-tree died and we found the quaint little doorway behind it. Old
Mr. Griffiths was alive then, and when I told him of my discovery he good-
naturedly cleared the way on his side, and so the oak turned once more upon
its rusty hinges to let the children pass through, and the nurse-maid, instead
of pages and secret emissaries and men-at-arms; and about three times a
year young Mr. Griffiths stoops under the arch on his way to call upon us. I
say young Mr. Griffiths, but I suppose he is over thirty now, for it is more
than ten years since his father died.

When I opened the door, in a burst of wind and wet, I found that it was
Guy Griffiths who stood outside bareheaded in the rain, ringing the bell that
winter night. "Are you up?" he said. "For heaven's sake come to my mother;
she's fainted; her maid is away; the doctor doesn't come. I thought you might
know what to do." And then he led the way through the dark garden, hurrying along before me.

Poor lady! when I saw her I knew that it was no fainting-fit, but a paralytic
stroke, from which she might perhaps recover in time; I could not tell. For
the present there was little to be done. The maids were young and frightened; poor Guy wanted some word of sympathy and encouragement. So far
I was able to be of use. We got her to bed and took off her finery, —she had
been out at a dinner-party, and had been stricken on her return home, —

Guy had discovered her speechless in the library. The poor fellow, frightened and overcome, waited about, trying to be of help, but he was so nervous that he tumbled over us all, and knocked over the chairs and bottles in his anxiety, and was of worse than no use. His kind old shaggy face looked pale, and his brown eyes *ringed* with anxiousness. I was touched by the young fellow's concern, for Mrs. Griffiths had not been a tender mother to him. How she had snapped and laughed at him, and frightened him with her quick, sarcastic tongue and hard, unmotherlike ways! I wondered if she thought of this as she lay there cold, rigid, watching us with glassy, senseless eyes.

The payments and debts and returns of affection are at all times hard to reckon. Some people pay a whole treasury of love in return for a stone; others deal out their affection at interest; others again take everything, to the uttermost farthing, and cast into the ditch and go their way and leave their benefactor penniless and a beggar. Guy himself, hard-headed as he was, and keen over his ledgers in Moorgate Street, could not have calculated such sums as these. All that she had to give, all the best part of her shallow store, poor Julia Griffiths had paid to her husband, who did not love her; to her second son, whose whole life was a sorrow to his parents. When he died she could never forgive poor Guy for living still, for being his father's friend and right hand, and sole successor. She had been a real mother to Hugh, who was gone; to Guy, who was alive still and patiently waiting to do her bidding, she had shown herself only a step dame; and yet I am sure no life-devoted mother could have been more anxiously watched and tended by her son. Perhaps, —how shall I say what I mean?—if he had loved her more and been more entirely one with her now, his dismay would have been less, his power greater to bear her pain, to look on at her struggling agony of impotence. Even pain does not come between the love of people who really love.

The doctor came and went, leaving some comfort behind him. Guy sat up all that night burning logs on the fire in the dressing-room, out of the bedroom in which Mrs. Griffiths was lying. Every now and then I went in to him and found him sitting over the hearth shaking his great shaggy head, as he had a way of doing, and biting his fingers, and muttering, "Poor soul! poor mother!" Sometimes he would come in creaking on tiptoe; but his presence seemed to agitate the poor woman, and I was obliged to motion him back again. Once, when I went in and sat down for a few minutes in an armchair beside him, he suddenly began to tell me that there had been trouble between them that morning. "It made it very hard to bear," he said.

I asked him what the trouble had been.

"I told her I thought I should like to marry," Guy confessed, with a rueful face.

Even then I could hardly help smiling.

"Selfish beast that I am! I upset her, poor soul! I behaved like a brute."

His distress was so great that it was almost impossible to console him, and it was in vain to assure him that the attack had been produced by physical causes.

"Do you want to marry any one in particular?" I asked, at last, to divert his thoughts, if I could, from the present.

"No," said he; "at least,—of course she is out of the question,—only I thought perhaps some day I should have liked to have a wife and children and a home of my own. Why, the counting-house is not so dreary as this place sometimes seems to me."

And then, though it was indeed no time for love-confidences, I could not help asking him who it was that was out of the question.

Guy Griffiths shrugged his great round shoulders impatiently, and gave something between a groan and sigh, and a smile, dark and sulky as he looked at times, a smile brightened up his grim face very pleasantly.

"She don't even know my name," he said. "I saw her one night at the play, and then in a lane in the country a little time after. I found out who she was. She's a daughter of old Barly the stockbroker. Belinda, they call her,—Miss Belinda. It's rather a silly name, isn't it?" (This, of course, I politely denied.) "I'm sure I don't know what there is about her," he went on, in a gentle voice. "All the fellows down there were head over ears in love with her. I asked,—in fact I went down to Farmborough in hopes of meeting her again. I never saw such a sweet young creature, never. I never spoke to her in my life."

"But you know her father?" I asked.

"Old Barly? Yes," said Guy. "His wife was my father's cousin, and we are each other's trustees for some money which was divided between me and Mrs. Barly. My parents never kept up with them much, but I was named trustee in my father's place when he died. I didn't like to refuse. I had never seen Belinda then. Do you like sweet, sleepy eyes that wake up now and then? Was that my mother calling?" For a minute he had forgotten the dreary present. It all came rushing back again. The bed creaked, the patient had moved a little on her pillow, and there was a gleam of some intelligence in her pinched face. The clock struck four in quick, tinkling tones; the rain seemed to have ceased, and the clouds to be parting; the rooms turned suddenly chill, though the fires were burning.

When I went home, about five o'clock, all the stars had come out and were shooting brilliantly overhead. The garden seemed full of a sudden freshness and of secret life stirring in the darkness; the sick woman's light was burning faintly, and in my own window the little bright lamp was flickering which H.'s kind fingers had trimmed and put there ready for me when I should return. When we reached the little gate Guy opened it and let me pass under some dripping green creeper which had been blown loose from the wall. He took my cold hand in both his big ones, and began to say something that ended in a sort of inarticulate sound, as he turned away and trudged back to his post again. I thought of the many meetings and partings at this little postern gate, and last words and protestations. Some may have been more sentimental, perhaps, than this one, but Guy's grunt of gratitude was more affecting to me than many a long string of words. I felt very sorry for him, poor old fellow, as I barred the door and climbed upstairs to my room. He sat up watching till the morning. But I was tired and soon went to sleep.

II

Some people do very well for a time. Chances are propitious; the way lies straight before them up a gentle inclined plane, with a pleasant prospect on either side. They go rolling straight on, they don't exactly know how, and take it for granted that it is their own prudence and good driving and deserts which have brought them prosperously so far upon their journey. And then one day they come to a turnpike and destiny pops out of its little box and demands a toll, or prudence trips, or good sense shies at a scarecrow put up by the wayside,—or nobody knows why, but the whole machine breaks down on the road and can't be set going again. And then other vehicles go past it, hand-trucks, perambulators, cabs, omnibuses, and great, prosperous barouches, and the people who were sitting in the broken-down equipage get out and walk away on foot.

On that celebrated and melancholy Black Monday of which we have all heard, poor John Barly and his three daughters came down the carpeted steps of their comfortable sociable for the last time, and disappeared at the wicket of a little suburban cottage,—disappeared out of the prosperous, pompous, highly respectable circle in which they had gyrated, dragged about by two fat bay horses, in the greatest decorum and respectability; dining out, receiving their friends, returning their civilities. Miss Barlys had left large cards with their names engraved upon them in return for other large cards upon which were inscribed equally respectable names, and the addresses of other equally commodious family mansions. A mansion—so the house-agents tell us—is a house like another with the addition of a back staircase. The Barlys and all their friends had back staircases to their houses and to their daily life as well. They only wished to contemplate the broad, swept, carpeted drawing-room flights. Indeed, to Anna and Fanny Barly, this making the best of things, card-leaving and visiting, seemed a business of vital importance. The youngest of the girls, who had been christened by the pretty silly name of Belinda, had only lately come home from school, and did not value these splendors and proprieties so highly as her sisters did. She had no great love for the life they led. Sometimes looking over the balusters of their great house in Capulet Square, she had yawned out loud from very weariness, and then she would hear the sound echoing all the way up to the skylight and reverberating down from baluster to baluster. If she went into the drawing-room, instead of the yawning echoes the shrill voices of Anna and of Fanny were vibrating monotonously as they complimented Lady Ogden upon her new barouche, until Belinda could bear it no longer, and would jump up and run away to her bedroom to escape it all. She had a handsome bedroom, draped in green damask, becarpeted, four-posted, with an enormous mahogany wardrobe, of which poor Belle was dreadfully afraid, for the doors would fly open of their own accord in the dead of night, revealing dark abysses and depths unknown, with black ghosts hovering suspended or motionless and biding their time. There were other horrors: shrouds waving in the blackness, feet stirring, and low creaking of garroters, which she did not dare to dwell upon, as she hastily locked the doors and pushed the writing-table against them.

It must, therefore, be confessed, that to Belinda the days had been long and oppressive sometimes in this handsomely appointed Tyburnean palace. Anna, the eldest sister, was queen-regnant; she had both ability and inclination to take the lead. She was short, broad, and dignified, and some years older than either of her sisters. Her father respected her business-like mind, admired her ambition, regretted sometimes secretly that she had never been able to make up her mind to accept any of the eligible young junior partners, the doctor, the curate, who had severally proposed to her. But then, of course, as Anna often said, they could not possibly have got on without her at home. She had been in no hurry to leave the comfortable kingdom where she reigned in undisputed authority, ratifying the decisions of the ministry downstairs, appealed to by the butler, respectfully dreaded by both the housemaids. Who was there to go against her? Mr. Barly was in town all day and left everything to her; Fanny, the second sister, was her faithful ally. Fanny was sprightly, twenty-one, with black eyes, and a curl that was much admired. She was fond of fashion, flirting, and finery; inquisitive, talkative, feeble-minded, and entirely devoted to Anna. As for Belle, she had only come back from school the other day. Anna could not quite understand her at times. Fanny was of age and content to do as she was bid; here was Belle, at eighteen, asserting herself very strangely. Anna and Fanny seemed to pair off somehow, and Belle always had to hold her own without assistance, unless, indeed, her father was present. He had a great tenderness and affection for his youngest child, and the happiest hour of the day to Belinda was when she heard him come home and call for her in his cheerful, quavering voice. By degrees it seemed to her, as she listened, that the cheerfulness seemed to be dying out of his voice, and only the quaver remained; but that may have been fancy and because she had taken a childish dislike to the echoes in the house.

At dinner-time Anna used to ask her father how things were going in the City, and whether shirtings had risen any higher, and at what premium the Tre Rosas shares were held in the market. These were some shares in a Cornish mine company of which Mr. Barly was a director. Anna thought so highly of the whole concern that she had been anxious to invest a portion of her own and her sister Fanny's money in it. They had some small inheritance from their mother, of part of which they had the control when they came of age; the rest was invested in the Funds in Mr. Griffiths' name, and could not be touched. Poor Belle, being a minor, had to be content with sixty pounds a year for her pin-money, which was all she could get for her two thousand pounds.

When Anna talked business Mr. Barly used to be quite dazzled by her practical clear-headedness, her calm foresight, and powers of rapid calculation. Fanny used to prick up her ears and ask, shaking her curls playfully, how much girls must have to be heiresses, and did Anna think they should ever be heiresses? Anna would smile and nod her head, in a calm and chastened sort of way, at this childish impatience. "You should be very thankful, Frances, for all you have to look to, and for your excellent prospects. Emily Ogden, with all her fine airs, would not be sorry to be in your place."

At which Fanny blushed up bright red, and Belinda jumped impatiently upon her chair, blinking her white eyelids impatiently over her clear gray eyes, as she had a way of doing. "I can't bear talking about money," said she; "anything is better. . . ." Then she too stopped short and blushed.

"Papa," interrupted Fanny, playfully, "when will you escort us to the pantomime again? The Ogdens are all going next Tuesday, and you have been most naughty, and not taken us anywhere for such a long time."

Mr. Barly, who rarely refused anything anybody asked him, pushed his chair away from the table and answered, with strange impatience for him, — "My dear, I have had no time lately for plays and amusements of any sort. After working from morning to night for you all, I am tired, and want a little peace of an evening. I have neither spirits nor—"

"Dear papa," said Belinda, eagerly, "come up into the drawing-room and sit in the easy-chair, and let me play you to sleep."

As she spoke, Belinda smiled a delightful fresh, sweet, tender smile, like sunshine falling on a fair landscape. No wonder the little stockbroker was fond of his youngest daughter. Frances was pouting. Anna frowned slightly as she locked up the wine and turned over in her mind whether she might not write to the Ogdens and ask them to let Frances join their party. As for Belinda, playing Mozart to her father in the dim drawing-room upstairs, she was struck by the worn and harassed look in his face as he slept, snoring gently in accompaniment to her music. It was the last time Belle ever played upon the old piano. Three or four days after, the crash came. The great Tre Rosas Mining Company (Limited) had failed, and the old-established house of Barly & Co. unexpectedly stopped payment.

If poor Mr. Barly had done it on purpose, his ruin could not have been more complete and ingenious. When his affairs came to be looked into, and his liabilities had been met, it was found that an immense fortune had been muddled away, and that scarcely anything would be left but a small furnished cottage, which had been given for her life to an old aunt just deceased, and which reverted to Fanny, her godchild, and the small sum which still remained in the three per cents., of which mention has been made, and which could not be touched until Belle, the youngest of three daughters, should come of age.

After two or three miserable days of confusion,—during which the machine which had been set going with so much trouble still revolved once or twice with the force of its own impetus, the butler answering the bell, the footman bringing up the coals, the cook sending up the dinner as usual,— suddenly everything collapsed, and the great mass of furniture, servants, human creatures, animals, carriages, business and pleasure engagements, seemed overthrown together in a great struggling mass, panting and bewildered and trying to get free from the confusion of particles that no longer belonged to one another.

First the cook packed up her things and some nice damask table-cloths and napkins, a pair of sheets, and Miss Barly's umbrella, which happened to be hanging in the hall; then the three ladies drove off with their father to the cottage, where it was decided they should go to be out of the way of any unpleasantness. He had no heart to begin again, and was determined to give up the battle. Belle sat with her father on the back seat of the carriage, looking up into his haggard face a little wistfully, and trying to be as miserable as the others. She could not help it,—a cottage in the country, ruin, roses, novelty, clean chintzes instead of damask, a little room with mignonette, cocks crowing, had a wicked, morbid attraction for her which she could not overcome. She had longed for such a life when she had gone down to stay with the Ogdens at Farmborough last month, and had seen several haystacks and lovely little thatched cottages, where she had felt she would have liked to spend the rest of her days; one in particular had taken her fancy, with dear little latticed windows and a pigeon-cote, and two rosy little babies with a kitten toddling out from the ivy porch; but a great rough-looking man had come up in a slouched wide-awake and frightened Emily Ogden so much that she had pulled Belinda away in a hurry . . . but here a sob from Fanny brought Belle back to her place in the barouche.

Anna felt that she must bear up, and nerved herself to the effort. Upon her the blow fell more heavily than upon any of the others. Indignant, injured, angry with her father, furious with the managers, the directors, the shareholders, the secretary, the unfortunate company, with the Bankruptcy Court, the Ogdens, the laws of fate, the world in general, with Fanny for sobbing, and with Belle for looking placid, she sat blankly staring out of the window as they drove past the houses where they had visited, and where she had been entertained an honored guest; and now—she put the hateful thought away—bankrupt, disgraced! Her bonnet was crushed in; she did not say a word; but her face looked quite fierce and old, and frightened Fanny into fresh lamentations. These hysterics had been first brought on by the sight of Emily Ogden driving by in the new barouche. This was quite too much for her poor friend's fortitude. "Emily will drop us, I know she will," sobbed Fanny. "O Anna! will they ever come and ask us to their Thursday luncheon-parties any more?"

"My children," said Mr. Barly, with a placid groan, pulling up the window, "we are disgraced; we can only hide our heads away from the world. Do not expect that any one will ever come near us again." At which announcement Fanny went off into new tears and bewailings. As for the kind, bewildered, weak-headed, soft-hearted little man, he had been so utterly worn out, harassed, worried, and wearied of late, that it was almost a relief to him to think that this was indeed the case. He sat holding Belle's hand in his, stroking and patting it, and wondering that people so near London did not keep the roads in better repair. "We must be getting near our new abode," said he at last almost cheerfully.

"You speak as if you were glad of our shame, papa," said Anna, suddenly, turning round upon him.

"Oh, hush!" cried Belle, indignantly. Fortunately the coachman stopped at this moment on a spot a very long way off from Capulet Square; and, leaning from his box, asked if it was that there little box across the common.

"Oh, what a sweet little place!" cried Belinda. But her heart rather sank as she told this dreadful story.

Myrtle Cottage was a melancholy little tumbledown place, looking over Dumbleton Common, which they had been crossing all this time. It was covered with stucco, cracked and stained and mouldy. There was a stained-glass window, which was broken. The veranda wanted painting. From outside it was evident that the white muslin curtains were not so fresh as they might have been. There was a little garden in front, planted with durable materials. Even out of doors, in the gardens in the suburbs, the box-edges, the laurel-bushes, and the fusty old jessamines are apt to look shabby in time, if they are never renewed. A certain amount of time and money might, perhaps, have made Myrtle Cottage into a pleasant little habitation; but (judging from appearances) its last inhabitants seemed to have been in some want of both these commodities. Its helpless new occupants were not likely to have much of either to spare. A little dining-room, with glass drop candlesticks and a rickety table, and a print of a church and a dissenting minister on the wall. A little drawing-room, with a great horse-hair sofa, a huge round table in the middle of the room, and more glass drop candlesticks, also a small work-table of glass over faded worsted embroidery. Four little bedrooms, mousey, musty, snuffy, with four-posts as terrific as any they had left behind, and a small, black dungeon for a maid-servant. This was the little paradise which Belle had been picturing to herself all along the road, and at which she looked round half-sighing, half-dismayed. Their bundles, baskets, blankets were handed in, and a cart full of boxes had arrived. Fanny's parrot was shrieking at the top of its voice on the narrow landing.

"What fun!" cried Belinda, sturdily, instantly setting to work to get things into some order, while Fanny lay exhausted upon the horse-hair sofa; and Anna, in her haughtiest tones, desired the coachman to drive home, and stood watching the receding carriage until it had dwindled away into the distance,—coachman, hammer-cloth, bay horses, respectability, and all. When she re-entered the house, the parrot was screeching still, and Martha, the under-housemaid—now transformed into a sort of extract of butler, footman, ladies'-maid, and cook,—was frying some sausages, of which the vulgar smell pervaded the place.

III

Belle exclaimed, but it required all her courage and natural brightness of spirit to go on looking at the bright side of things, praising the cottage, working in the garden, giving secret assistance to the two bewildered maids who waited on the reduced little family, cheering her father, smiling, and putting the best face on things, as her sisters used to do at home. If it had been all front stairs in Capulet Square, it was all back staircase at the cottage. Rural roses, calm sunsets, long shadows across the common are all very well; but when puffs of smoke come out of the chimney and fill the little place; when, if the window is opened, a rush of wind and dust—worse than smoke—comes eddying into the room, and careers round the four narrow walls; when poor little Fanny coughs and shudders, and wraps her shawl more closely round her with a groan; when the smell of the kitchen frying-pan perfumes the house, and a mouse scampers out of the cupboard, and black beetles lie struggling in the milk-jugs, and the pump runs dry, and spiders crawl out of the tea-caddy, and so forth; then, indeed, Belle deserves some credit for being cheerful under difficulties. She could not pretend to very high spirits, but she was brisk and willing, and ready to smile at her father's little occasional puns and feeble attempts at jocularity. Anna, who had been so admirable as a general, broke down under the fatigue of the actual labor in the trenches which belonged to their new life. A great many people can order others about very brilliantly and satisfactorily, who fail when they have to do the work themselves.

Some of the neighbors called upon them, but the Ogdens never appeared. Poor little Fanny used to take her lace-work, and sit stitching and looping her thread at the window which overlooked the common and its broad roads, crossing and recrossing the plain; carriages came rolling along, people came walking, children ran past the windows of the little cottage; but the Ogdens never. Once Fanny thought she recognized the barouche,—Lady Ogden and Emily sitting in front, Matthew Ogden on the back seat;

surely, yes, surely it was him. But the carriage rolled off in a cloud of dust, and disappeared behind the wall of the neighboring park; and Frances finished the loop, and passed her needle in and out of the muslin, feeling as if it was through her poor little heart that she was piercing and sticking; she pulled out a long thread, and it seemed to her as if the sunset stained it red like blood.

In the meanwhile, Belle's voice had been singing away overhead, and Fanny, going upstairs presently, found her, with one of the maids, clearing out one of the upper rooms. The window was open, the furniture was piled up in the middle. Belle, with her sleeves tucked up, and her dress carefully pinned out of the dust, was standing on a chair, hammer in hand, and fixing up some dimity curtains against the window. Table-cloths, brooms, pails and brushes were lying about, and everything looked in perfect confusion. As Fanny stood looking and exclaiming, Anna also came to the door from her own room, where she had been taking a melancholy nap.

"What a mess you are making here!" cried the elder sister, very angrily. "How can you take up Martha's time, Belinda? And oh! how can you forget yourself to this degree? You seem to *exult* in your father's disgrace." Belinda flushed up.

"Really, Anna, I do not know what you mean," said she, turning round, vexed for a minute, and clasping a long curtain in both arms. "I could not bear to see my father's room looking so shabby and neglected; there is no disgrace in attending to his comfort. See, we have taken down those dusty curtains, and we are going to put up some others," said the girl, springing down from the chair and exhibiting her treasures.

"And pray where is the money to come from," said Anna, "to pay for these wonderful changes?"

"They cost no money," said Belinda, laughing. "I made them myself with my own two hands. Don't you remember my old white dress that you never liked, Anna? Look how I have pricked my finger. Now, go down," said the girl, in her pretty, imperative way, "and don't come up again till I call you."

Go down at Belle's bidding . . .

Anna went off fuming, and immediately set to work also, but in a different fashion. She unfortunately found that her father had returned, and was sitting in the little sitting-room down below by himself, with a limp paper of the day before him open upon his knees. He was not reading. He seemed out of spirits, and was gazing in a melancholy way at the smouldering fire, and rubbing his bald head in a perplexed and troubled manner. Seeing this, the silly woman, by way of cheering and comforting the poor old man, began to exclaim at Belinda's behavior, to irritate him, and overwhelm him with allusions and reproaches.

"Scrubbing and slaving with her own hands," said Anna. "Forgetting herself; bringing us down lower indeed than we are already sunk. Papa, she will not listen to me. You should tell her that you forbid her to put us all to shame by her behavior."

When Belle, panting, weary, triumphant, and with a blackened nose and rosy cheek, opened the door of the room presently, and called her father exultingly, she did not notice, as she ran upstairs before him, how wearily he followed her. A flood of light came from the dreary little room overhead. It had been transformed into a bower of white dimity, bright windows, clean muslin blinds. The fusty old carpet was gone, and a clean crumb-cloth had been put down, with a comfortable rug before the fireplace. A nosegay of jessamine stood on the chimney, and at each corner of the four-post bed, the absurd young decorator had stuck a smart bow, made out of some of her own blue ribbons, in place of the terrible plumes and tassels which had waved there in dust and darkness before. One of the two armchairs which blocked up the wall of the dining-room had been also covered out of some of Belinda's stores, and stood comfortably near the open window. The sun was setting over the great common outside, behind the mill and the distant fringe of elm-trees. Martha, standing all illuminated by the sunshine, with her mop in her hand, was grinning from ear to ear, and Belle turned and rushed into her father's arms. But Mr. Barly was quite overcome.

"My child," he said, "why do you trouble yourself so much for me? Your sister has told me all. I don't deserve it. I cannot bear that you should be brought to this. My Belle working and slaving with your own hands through my fault,—through my fault."

The old man sat down on the side of the bed by which he had been standing, and laid his face in his hands, in a perfect agony of remorse and regret. Belinda was dismayed by the result of her labors. In vain she tried to cheer him and comfort him. The sweeter she seemed in his eyes, the more miserable the poor father grew at the condition to which he had brought her.

For many days after he went about in a sort of despair, thinking what he could do to retrieve his ruined fortunes, and if Belinda still rose betimes to see to his comfort and the better ordering of the confused little household, she took care not to let it be known. Anna came down at nine, Fanny at ten. Anna would then spend several hours regretting her former dignities, reading the newspaper and the fashionable intelligence, while the dismal strains of Fanny's piano (there was a jangling piano in the little drawing-room) streamed across the common. To a stormy spring, with wind flying, and dust dashing against the window-panes, and gray clouds swiftly bearing across the wide, open country, had succeeded a warm and brilliant summer, with sunshine flooding and spreading over the country. Anna and Fanny were able to get out a little now, but they were soon tired, and would sit down under a tree and remark to one another how greatly they missed their accustomed drives. Belinda, who had sometimes at first disappeared now and then to cry mysteriously a little bit by herself over her troubles, now discovered that at eighteen, with good health and plenty to do, happiness is possible, even without a carriage.

One day Mr. Barly, who still went into the city from habit, came home with some news which had greatly excited him. Wheal[2] Tre Rosas, of which he still held a great many shares, which he had never been able to dispose of, had been giving some signs of life. A fresh call was to be made: some capitalist, with more money than he evidently knew what to do with, had been buying up a great deal of the stock. The works were to be resumed. Mr. Barly had always been satisfied that the concern was a good one. He would give everything he had, he told Anna that evening, to be able to raise enough money now to buy up more of the shares. His fortune was made if he could do so; his children replaced in their proper position, and his name restored. Anna was in a state of greater flutter, if possible, than her father himself. Belle sighed; she could not help feeling doubtful, but she did not like to say much on the subject.

"Papa, this Wheal has proved a very treacherous wheel of fortune to us," she hazarded, blushing, and bending over her sewing; "we are very, very happy as we are."

"Happy?" said Anna, with a sneer.

"Really, Belinda, you are too romantic," said Fanny, with a titter; while Mr. Barly cried out, in an excited way, "that she should be happier yet, and all her goodness and dutifulness should be rewarded in time." A sort of presentiment of evil came over Belinda, and her eyes filled up with tears; but she stitched them away and said no more.

Unfortunately the only money Mr. Barly could think of to lay his hands upon was that sum in the three per cents upon which they were now living; and even if he chose he could not touch any of it, until Belinda came of age; unless, indeed, young Mr. Griffiths would give him permission to do so.

2. **Wheal** a mine

"Go to him, papa," cried Anna, enthusiastically. "Go to him; entreat, insist upon it, if necessary."

All that evening Anna and Frances talked over their brilliant prospects.

"I should like to see the Ogdens again," said poor little Fanny.

"Perhaps we can if we go back to Capulet Square."

"Certainly, certainly," said Anna.

"I have heard that this Mr. Griffiths is a most uncouth and uncivilized person to deal with," continued Miss Barly, with her finger on her chin. "Papa, wouldn't it be better for me to go to Mr. Griffiths instead of you?" This, however, Mr. Barly would not consent to.

Anna could hardly contain her vexation and spite when he came back next day dispirited, crestfallen, and utterly wretched and disappointed. Mr. Griffiths would have nothing to say to it.

"What's the good of a trustee," said he to Mr. Barly, "if he were to let you invest your money in such a speculative chance as that? Take my advice, and sell out your shares now, if you can, for anything you can get."

"A surly, disagreeable fellow," said poor old Mr. Barly. "I heartily wish he had nothing to do with our affairs."

Anna fairly stamped with rage. "What insolence, when it is our own! Papa, you have no spirit to allow such interference."

Mr. Barly looked at her gravely, and said he should not allow it. Anna did not know what he meant.

Belinda was not easy about her father all this time. He came and went in an odd, excited sort of way, stopping short sometimes as he was walking across the room, and standing absorbed in thought. One day he went into the city unexpectedly about the middle of the day, and came back looking quite odd, pale, with curious eyes; something was wrong, she could not tell what. In the mean time Wheal Tre Rosas seemed, spite of Mr. Griffiths' prophecies, to be steadily rising in the world. More business had been done; the shares were a trifle higher. A meeting of directors was convened, and actually a small dividend was declared at midsummer. It really seemed as if there was some chance after all that Anna should be reinstated in the barouche, in Capulet Square, and her place in society. She and Fanny were half wild with delight. "When we leave,"—was the beginning of every sentence they uttered. Fanny wrote the good news to her friend Miss Ogden, and, under these circumstances, to Fanny's unfeigned delight, Emily Ogden thought herself justified in driving over to the village one fine afternoon and affably partaking of a cracked cupful of five o'clock tea. It was slightly smoked, and the milk was turned. Belinda had gone out for a walk and was not there to see to it all; I am afraid she did not quite forgive Emily the part she had played, and could not make up her mind to meet her.

One morning Anna was much excited by the arrival of a letter directed to Mr. Barly in great round handwriting, and with a huge seal, all over bears and griffins. Her father was forever expecting news of his beloved Tre Rosas, and he broke the seal with some curiosity. But this was only an invitation to dine and sleep at Castle Gardens from Mr. Griffiths, who said he had an offer to make Mr. Barly, and concluded by saying that he hoped Mr. Barly forgave him for the ungracious part he had been obliged to play the other day, and that, in like circumstances, he would do the same by him.

"I shan't go," said Mr. Barly, a little doggedly, putting the letter down.

"Not go, papa! Why you may be able to talk him over if you get him quietly to yourself. Certainly you must go, papa," said Anna. "Oh! I'm sure he means to relent. How nice!" said Fanny. Even Belinda thought it was a pity he should not accept the invitation, and Mr. Barly gave way as usual. He asked them if they had any commands for him in town.

"Oh, thank you, papa," said Frances. "If you are going shopping, I wish you would bring me back a blue alpaca, and a white grenadine, and a pink sou-poult, and a—"

"My dear Fanny, that will be quite sufficient for the short time you remain here," interrupted Anna, who went on to give her father several commissions of her own, —some writing-paper stamped with Barly Lodge and their crest in one corner; a jacket with buttons for the knife-boy they had lately engaged upon the strength of their coming good fortune; a new umbrella, house-agent's list of mansions in the neighborhood of Capulet Square, the *Journal des Modes,* and the *New Court Guide.* "Let me see, there was something else," said Anna.

"Belle," said Mr. Barly, "how comes it you ask for nothing? What can I bring you, my child?"

Belle looked up with one of her bright, melancholy smiles, and replied, "If you should see any roses, papa, I think I should like a bunch of roses. We have none in the garden."

"Roses!" cried Fanny, laughing. "I didn't know you cared for anything but what was useful, Belle."

"I quite expected you would ask for a saucepan, or a mustard-pot," said Anna, with a sneer.

Belle sighed again, and then the three went and stood at the garden-gate to see their father off. It made a pretty little group for the geese on the common to contemplate,—the two young sisters at the wicket, the elder under the shade of the veranda, Belle upright, smiling, waving her slim hand; she was above the middle height, she had fair hair and dark eyebrows and gray eyes, over which she had a peculiar way of blinking her smooth white eyelids;—and all about, the birds, the soft winds, the great green common with its gorgeous furze-blossom blazing against the low bank of clouds in the horizon. Close at hand a white pony was tranquilly cropping the grass, and two little village children were standing outside the railings, gazing up open-mouthed at the pretty ladies who lived at the cottage.

IV

The clouds which had been gathering all the afternoon broke shortly before Mr. Barly reached his entertainer's house. He had tried to get there through Kensington Gardens, but could not make out the way, and went wandering round and round in some perplexity under the great trees with their creaking branches. The storm did not last long, and the clouds dispersed at sunset. When Mr. Barly rang at the gate of the villa in Castle Gardens at last that evening he was weary, wet through, and far less triumphant than he had been when he left home in the morning. The butler who let him in gave the bag which he had been carrying to the footman and showed him the way upstairs immediately, to the comfortable room which had been made ready for him. Upholsterers had done the work on the whole better than Belle with all her loving labor. The chairs were softer than her print-covered horse-hair cushions. The waxlights were burning although it was broad daylight. Mr. Barly went to the bay-window. The garden outside was a sight to see: smooth lawns, arches, roses in profusion and abundance, hanging and climbing and clustering everywhere, a distant gleam of a fountain, of a golden sky, a chirruping and rustling in the bushes and trellises after the storm. The sunset which was lighting up the fern on the rain-sprinkled common was twinkling through the rose-petals here, bringing out odors and aromas and whiffs of delicious scent. Mr. Barly thought of Belle, and how he should like to see her flitting about in the garden and picking roses to her heart's content. As he stood there he thought too with a pang of his wife whom he had lost, and sighed in a sort of despair at the troubles which had fallen upon him of late. What would he not give to undo the work of the last few months, he thought—nay, of the last few days? He had once come to this very house with his wife in their early days of marriage. He remembered it now, although he had not thought of it before.

Sometimes it happens to us all that things which happened ever so long ago seem to make a start out of their proper places in the course of time, and come after us, until they catch us up, as it were, and surround us, so that one can hear the voices, and see the faces and colors, and feel the old sensations and thrills as keenly as at the time they occurred,—all so curiously and strangely vivid that one can scarcely conceive it possible that years and years perhaps have passed since it all happened, and that their present shock proceeds from ancient and almost forgotten impulse. And so, as Mr. Barly looked and remembered and thought of the past, a sudden remorse and shame came over him. He seemed to see his wife standing in the garden, holding the roses up over her head, looking like Belle,—like, yet unlike. Why it should have been so, at the thought of his wife among the flowers, I cannot tell; but as he remembered her he began to think of what he had done,—that he was there in the house of the man he had defrauded,—he began to ask himself how could he face him? how could he sit down beside him at table, and break his bread? The poor old fellow fell back with a groan in one of the comfortable armchairs. Could he confess? Oh, no—no, that would be the most terrible of all!

What he had done is simply told. When Guy Griffiths refused to let Mr. Barly lay hands on any of the money which he had in trust for his daughters, the foolish and angry old man had sold out a portion of the sum belonging to Mr. Griffiths which still remained in his own name. It had not seemed like dishonesty at the time, but now he would have gladly—oh, how gladly!— awakened to find it all a dream. He dressed mechanically, turning over every possible chance in his own mind. Let Wheal Tre Rosas go on and prosper, the first money should go to repay his loan, and no one should be the wiser. He went down into the library again when he was ready. It was empty still, and, to his relief, the master of the house had not yet come back. He waited a very long time, looking at the clock, at the reviews on the table, at the picture of Mrs. Griffiths, whom he could remember in her youth, upon the wall. The butler came in again to say that his master had not yet returned. Some message had come by a boy, which was not very intelligible,—he had been detained in the city. Mrs. Griffiths was not well enough to leave her room, but she hoped Mr. Barly would order dinner,—anything he required,—and that her son would shortly return.

It was very late. There was nothing else to be done. Mr. Barly found a fire lighted in the great dining-room, dinner laid, one plate and one knife and fork, at the end of the long table. The dinner was excellent,—so was the wine. The butler uncorked a bottle of champagne, the cook sent up chickens and all sorts of good things. Mr. Barly almost felt as if he, by some strange metempsychosis, had been converted into the owner of this handsome dwelling, and all that belonged to it. At twelve o'clock Mr. Griffiths had not yet returned, and his guest, after a somewhat perplexed and solitary meal, retired to rest.

Mr. Barly breakfasted by himself again next morning. Mr. Griffiths had not returned all night. In his secret heart Mr. Griffiths' guest was almost relieved by the absence of his entertainer; it seemed like a respite. Perhaps, after all, everything would go well, and the confession, which he had contemplated with such terror the night before, need never be made. For the present, it was clearly no use to wait any longer at the house. Mr. Barly asked for a cab to take him to the station, left his compliments and regrets and a small sum of money behind him, and then, as the cab delayed, strolled out into the front garden to wait for it.

Even in the front court the roses were all abloom; a great snow-cluster was growing over the doorway, a pretty tea-rose was hanging its head over the scraper; against the outer railing which separated the house from the road rose-trees had been planted. The beautiful pink fragrant heads were pushing through the iron railings, and a delicious little rose-wind came blowing in the poor old fellow's face. He began to think—no wonder—of Belle and her fancy for roses, and mechanically, without much reflecting upon what he was about, he stopped and inhaled the ravishing sweet smell of the great dewy flowers, and then put out his hand and gathered one; and as he gathered it a sharp thorn ran into his finger, and a heavy grasp was laid upon his shoulder . . .

"So it is you, is it, who sneak in and steal my roses?" said an angry voice. "Now that I know who it is, I shall give you in charge."

Mr. Barly looked round greatly startled. He met the fierce glare of two dark-brown eyes under shaggy brows that were frowning very fiercely. A broad, thick-set, round-shouldered young man of forbidding aspect had laid hold of him. The young man let go his grasp when he saw the mistake he had made, but did not cease frowning.

"Oh! it is you, Mr. Barly," he said.

"I was just going," said the stockbroker, meekly. "I am glad you have returned in time for me to see you, Mr. Griffiths. I am sorry I took your rose. My youngest daughter is fond of them, and I thought I might, out of all this gardenful, —you would not—she had asked—"

There was something so stern and unforgiving in Mr. Griffiths' face that the merchant stumbled in his words, and stopped short, surprised, in the midst of his explanations.

"The roses were not yours, not if there were ten gardens full. I won't have my roses broken off," said Griffiths; "they should be cut with a knife. Come back with me; I want to have a little talk with you, Mr. Barly."

Somehow the old fellow's heart began to beat, and he felt himself turn rather sick.

"I was detained last night by some trouble in my office. One of my clerks in whom I thought I could have trusted, absconded yesterday afternoon. I have been all the way to Liverpool in pursuit of him. What do you think should be done with him?" And Mr. Griffiths, from under his thick eyebrows, gave a quick glance at his present victim, and seemed to expect some sort of answer.

"You prosperous men cannot realize what it is to be greatly tempted," said Mr. Barly, with a faint smile.

"Do you know that Wheal Tre Rosas has come to grief a second time?" said young Mr. Griffiths, abruptly, holding out the morning's *Times,* as they walked along. "I am *not* a prosperous man; I had a great many shares in that unlucky concern."

Poor Barly stopped short and turned quite pale, and began to shake so that he had to put his hand out and lean against the wall. Failed! Was he doomed to misfortune? Then there was never any chance for him,—never. No hope! No hope of paying back the debt which weighed upon his conscience. He could not realize it. Failed! The rose had fallen to the ground; the poor unlucky man stood still, staring blankly in the other's grim, unrelenting face. "I am ruined," he said.

"You are ruined! Is that the worst you have to tell me?" said Mr. Griffiths, still looking piercingly at him. Then the other felt that he knew all.

"I have been very unfortunate—and very much to blame," said Mr. Barly, still trembling;—"terribly to blame, Mr. Griffiths. I can only throw myself upon your clemency."

"My clemency! my mercy! I am no philanthropist," said Guy, savagely. "I am a man of business, and you have defrauded me!"

"Sir," said the stockbroker, finding some odd comfort in braving the worst, "you refused to let me take what was my own; I have sold out some of your money to invest in this fatal concern. Heaven knows it was not for myself, but for the sake of—of—others; and I thought to repay you ere long. You can repay yourself now. You need not reproach me any more. You can send me to prison if you like. I—I—don't much care what happens. My Belle, my poor Belle,—my poor girls!"

All this time Guy said never a word. He motioned Mr. Barly to follow him into the library. Mr. Barly obeyed, and stood meekly waiting for the coming onslaught. He stood in the full glare of the morning sun, which was pouring through the unblinded window. His poor old scanty head was bent, and his hair stood on end in the sunshine.

His eyes, avoiding the glare, went vacantly travelling along the scroll-work on the fender, and so to the coal-scuttle and to the skirting on the wall, and back again. Dishonored,—yes. Bankrupt,—yes. Three-score years had brought him to this,—to shame, to trouble. It was a hard world for unlucky people; but Mr. Barly was too much broken, too weary and indifferent, to feel very bitterly even against the world. Meanwhile, Guy was going on with his reflections, and like those amongst us who are still young and strong, he could put more life and energy into his condemnation and judgment of actions done, than the unlucky perpetrators had to give to the very deeds themselves. Some folks do wrong as well as right, with scarcely more than half a mind to it.

"How could you do such a thing?" cried the young man, indignantly, beginning to rush up and down the room in his hasty, clumsy way, knocking against tables and chairs as he went along. "How could you do it?" he repeated. "I learned it yesterday, by chance. What can I say to you that your own conscience should not have told you already? How could you do it?"

Guy had reached the great end window, and stamped with vexation and a mixture of anger and sorrow. For all his fierceness and gruffness, he was sorry for the poor feeble old man, whose fate he held in his hand. There was the garden outside, and its treasure and glory of roses; there was the rose, lying on the ground, that old Barly had taken. It was lying broken and shining upon the gravel,—one rose out of the hundreds that were bursting, and blooming, and fainting and falling on their spreading stems. It was like the wrong old Barly had done his kinsman,—one little wrong Guy thought, one little handful out of all his abundance. He looked back, and by chance caught sight of their two figures reflected in the glass at the other end of the room,—his own image, the strong, round-backed, broad-shouldered young man, with gleaming white teeth and black bristling hair; the feeble and uncertain culprit, with his broken, wandering looks, waiting his sentence. It was not Guy who delivered it. It came,—no very terrible one after all,— prompted by some unaccountable secret voice and impulse. Have we not all of us sometimes suddenly felt ashamed in our lives in the face of misfortune and sorrow? Are we Pharisees, standing in the marketplace, with our phylacteries displayed to the world? We ask ourselves, in dismay, does this man go home justified rather than we? Guy was not the less worthy of his Be-

linda, poor fellow, because a thought of her crossed his mind, and because
he blushed up, and a gentle look came into his eyes, and a shame into
his heart,—a shame of his strength and prosperousness, of his probity and
high honor. When had he been tempted? What was it but a chance that
he had been born what he was? And yet old Barly, in all his troubles, had a
treasure in his possession for which Guy felt he would give all his good fortune and good repute, his roses,—red, white, and golden,—his best
heart's devotion, which he secretly felt to be worth all the rest. Now was
the time, the young man thought, to make that proposition which he had in
his mind.

"Look here," said Guy, hanging his great shaggy head, and speaking
quickly and thickly, as if he was the culprit instead of the accuser. "You imply
it was for your daughter's sake that you cheated me. I cannot consent to act
as you would have me do, and take your daughter's money to pay myself
back. But if one of them,—Miss Belinda, since she likes roses,—chooses
to come here and work the debt off, she can do so. My mother is in bad
health, and wants a companion; she will engage her at—let me see—a
hundred guineas a year, and in this way, by degrees, the debt will be
cleared off."

"In twenty years!" said Mr. Barly, bewildered, relieved, astonished.

"Yes, in twenty years," said Guy, as if that was the most natural thing in
the world. "Go home and consult her, and come back and give me the answer."

And as he spoke, the butler came in to say that the hansom was at the
door.

Poor old Barly bent his worn, meek head and went out. He was shaken
and utterly puzzled. If Guy had told him to climb up the chimney he would
have obeyed. He could only do as he was bid. As it was, he clambered with
difficulty into the hansom, told the man to go to the station for Dumbleton,
and he was driving off gladly when some one called after the cab. The old
man peered out anxiously. Had Griffiths changed his mind? Was his heart
hardened like Pharaoh's[3] at the eleventh hour?

It was certainly Guy who came hastily after the cab, looking more awkward and sulky than ever. "Hoy! Stop! You have forgotten the roses for your
daughter," said he, thrusting in a great bunch of sweet foam and freshness.
As the cab drove along, people passing by looked up and envied the man

3. **like Pharaoh's** See Exodus 10:27.

who was carrying such loveliness through the black and dreary London streets. Could they have seen the face looking out behind the roses they might have ceased to envy.

Belle was on the watch for her father at the garden-gate and exclaimed with delight, as she saw him toiling up the hill from the station with his huge bunch of flowers. She came running to meet him with fluttering skirts and outstretched hands, and sweet smiles gladdening her face. "O papa, how lovely! Have you had a pleasant time?" Her father hardly responded. "Take the roses, Belle," he said. "I have paid for them dearly enough." He went into the house wearily, and sat down in the shabby arm-chair. And then he turned and called Belinda to him wistfully and put his trembling arm round about her. Poor old Barly was no mighty Jephthah;[4] but his feeble old head bent with some such pathetic longing and remorse over his Belle as he drew her to him, and told her, in a few simple, broken words, all the story of what had befallen him in those few hours since he went away. He could not part from her. "I can't, I can't," he said, as the girl put her tender arms round his neck . . .

Guy came to see me a few days after his interview with old Mr. Barly, and told me that his mother had surprised him by her willing acquiescence in the scheme. I could have explained matters to him a little, but I thought it best to say nothing. Mrs. Griffiths had overheard and understood a word or two of what he had said to me that night, when she was taken ill. Was it some sudden remorse for the past? Was it a new-born mother's tenderness stirring in her cold heart, which made her question and cross-question me the next time that I was alone with her? There had often been a talk of some companion or better sort of attendant. When the news came of poor old Barly's failure, it was Mrs. Griffiths herself who first vaguely alluded again to this scheme.

"I might engage one of those girls—the—the—Belinda, I think you called her?"

I was touched, and took her cold hand and kissed it.

"I am sure she would be an immense comfort to you," I said. "You would never regret your kindness."

The sick woman sighed and turned away impatiently, and the result was the invitation to dinner, which turned out so disastrously.

---

4. **mighty Jephthah** the warrior who rashly sacrificed his only daughter in Judges, 11:1–40

V

When Mr. Barly came down to breakfast, the morning after his return, he found another of those great, square, official-looking letters upon the table. There was a check in it for 100*l*. "You will have to meet heavy expenses," the young man wrote. "I am not sorry to have an opportunity of proving to you that it was not the money which you have taken from me I grudged, but the manner in which you took it. The only reparation you can make me is by keeping the enclosed for your present necessity."

In truth the family prospects were not very brilliant. Myrtle Cottage was resplendent with clean windows and well-scrubbed door-steps, but the furniture wanted repairing, the larder refilling. Belle could not darn up the broken flap of the dining-room table, nor conjure legs of mutton out of bare bones, though she got up ever so early; sweeping would not mend the hole in the carpet, nor could she dust the mildew-stains off the walls, the cracks out of the looking-glass.

Anna was morose, helpless, and jealous of the younger girl's influence over her father. Fanny was delicate; one gleam of happiness, however, streaked her horizon; Emily Ogden had written to invite her to spend a few days there. When Mr. Barly and his daughter had talked over Mr. Griffiths' proposition, Belle's own good sense told her that it would be folly to throw away this good chance. Let Mrs. Griffiths be ever so trying and difficult to deal with, and her son a thousand times sterner and ruder than he had already shown himself, she was determined to bear it all. Belinda knew her own powers, and felt as if she could endure anything, and that she should never forget the generosity and forbearance he had shown her poor father. Anna was delighted that her sister should go; she threw off the shawl in which she had muffled herself up ever since their reverses, brightened up wonderfully, talked mysteriously of Fanny's prospects as she helped both the girls to pack, made believe to shed a few tears as Belinda set off, and bustled back into the house with renewed importance. Belinda looked back and waved her hand, but Anna's back was already turned upon her.

Poor Belinda! For all her courage and cheerfulness her heart sank a little as they reached the great bronze gates in Castle Gardens. She would have been more unhappy still if she had not had to keep up her father's spirits. It was almost dinner-time, and Mrs. Griffiths' maid came down with a message. Her mistress was tired, and just going to bed, and would see her in the morning; Mr. Griffiths was dining in town; Miss Williamson would call upon Miss Barly that evening.

Dinner had been laid as usual in the great dining-room, with its marble columns and draperies, and Dutch pictures of game and of birds and flowers. Three servants were in waiting, a great silver chandelier lighted the dismal meal, huge dish-covers were upheaved, decanters of wine were handed round, all the *entrées* and delicacies came over again. Belle tried to eat to keep her father in company. She even made little jokes, and whispered to him that they evidently meant to fatten her up. The poor old fellow cheered up by degrees; the good claret warmed his feeble pulse; the good fare comforted and strengthened him. "I wish Martha would make us ice puddings," said Belle, helping him to a glittering mass of pale-colored cream, with nutmeg and vanilla, and all sorts of delicious spices. He had just finished the last mouthful when the butler started and rushed out of the room, a door banged, a bell rang violently, a loud scraping was heard in the hall, and an echoing voice said, "Are they come? Are they in the dining-room?" And the crimson curtain was lifted up, and the master of the house entered the room carrying a bag and a great-coat over his arm. As he passed the sideboard the button of the coat caught in the fringe of a cloth which was spread upon it, and in a minute the cloth and all the glasses and plates which had been left there came to the ground with a wild crash, which would have made Belle laugh, if she had not been too nervous even to smile.

Guy merely told the servants to pick it all up, and put down the things he was carrying and walked straight across the room to the two frightened people at the end of the table. Poor fellow! After shaking hands with old Barly and giving his daughter an abrupt little nod, all he could find to say was, —

"I hope you came of your own free will, Miss Barly?" and as he spoke he gave a shy scowl and eyed her all over.

"Yes," Belle answered, blinking her soft eyes to see him more clearly.

"Then I'm very much obliged to you," said Guy.

This was such an astonishingly civil answer that Belinda's courage rose.

Poor Belinda's heart failed her again when Griffiths, still in an agony of shyness, then turned to her father, and in his roughest voice said, —

"You leave early in the morning, but I hope we shall keep your daughter for a very long time."

Poor fellow! he meant no harm and only intended this by way of conversation. Belle in her secret heart said to herself that he was a cruel brute; and poor Guy, having made this impression, broken a dozen wine-glasses, and gone through untold struggles of shyness, now wished them both goodnight.

"Good-night, Mr. Barly; good-night, Miss Belle," said he. Something in his voice caused Belle to relent a little.

"Good-night, Mr. Griffiths," said the girl, standing up, a slight, graceful figure, simple and nymph-like, amidst all this pomp of circumstance. As Griffiths shuffled out of the room he saw her still; all night he saw her in his dreams. That bright, winsome young creature dressed in white, soft folds, with all the gorgeous gildings and draperies, and the lights burning, and the pictures and gold cups glimmering round about her. They were his, and as many more of them as he chose; the inanimate, costly, sickening pomps and possessions; but a pure spirit like that, to be a bright, living companion for him? Ah, no! that was not to be, —not for him, not for such as him. Guy, for the first time in his life, as he went downstairs next morning, stopped and looked at himself attentively in the great glass on the staircase. He saw a great loutish, round-backed fellow, with a shaggy head and brown glittering eyes, and little strong, white teeth like a dog's; he gave an uncouth sudden caper of rage and regret at his own appearance. "To think that happiness and life itself and love eternal depend upon tailors and hair-oil," groaned poor Guy, as he went down to his room to write letters.

Mrs. Griffiths had not seen Belle the night before; she was always nervously averse to seeing strangers, but she had sent for me that evening, and as I was leaving she asked me to go down and speak to Miss Barly before I went. Belinda was already in her room, but I ventured to knock at the door. She came to meet me with a bright, puzzled face and all her pretty hair falling loose about her face. She had not a notion who I was, but begged me to come in. When I had explained things a little she pulled out a chair for me to sit down.

"This house seems to me so mysterious and unlike anything else I have ever known," said she, "that I'm very grateful to any one who will tell me what I'm to do here. Please sit down a little while."

I told her that she would have to write notes, to add up bills, to read to Mrs. Griffiths, and to come to me whenever she wanted any help or comfort. "You were quite right to come," said I. "They are excellent people. Guy is the kindest, best fellow in the whole world, and I have long heard of you, Miss Barly, and I'm sure such a good daughter as you have been will be rewarded some day."

Belle looked puzzled, grateful, a little proud, and very charming. She told me afterwards that it had been a great comfort to her father to hear of my little visit to her, and that she had succeeded in getting him away without any very painful scene.

Poor Belle! I wonder how many tears she shed that day after her father was gone? While she was waiting to be let in to Mrs. Griffiths she amused herself by wandering about the house, dropping a little tear here and there as she went along, and trying to think that it amused her to see so many yards of damask and stair-carpeting, all exactly alike, so many acres of chintz of the same pattern.

"Mr. Griffiths desired me to say that this tower room was to be made ready for you to sit in, ma'am," said the respectful butler, meeting her and opening a door. "It has not been used before." And he gave her the key, to which a label was affixed, with "MISS BARLY'S ROOM" written upon it, in the house-keeper's scrawling handwriting.

Belle gave a little shriek of admiration. It was a square room, with four windows, overlooking the gardens, the distant park, and the broad, cheerful road which ran past the house. An ivy screen had been trained over one of the windows, roses were clustering in garlands round the deep, sill casements. There was an Indian carpet, and pretty silk curtains, and comfortable chintz chairs and sofas, upon which beautiful birds were flying and lilies wreathing. There was an old-fashioned-looking piano, too, and a great book-case filled with books and music. "They certainly treat me in the most magnificent way," thought Belle, sinking down upon the sofa in the window which overlooked the rose-garden, and inhaling a delicious breath of fragrant air. "They can't mean to be very unkind." Belle, who was a little curious, it must be confessed, looked at everything, made secret notes in her mind, read the titles of the books, examined the china, discovered a balcony in her turret. There was a little writing-table, too, with paper and pens and inks of various colors, which especially pleased her. A glass cup of cut roses had been placed upon it, and two dear little green books, in one of which some-one had left a paper-cutter.

The first was a book of fairy tales, from which I hope the good fairy editress[5] will forgive me for stealing a sentence or two.

The other little green book was called the *Golden Treasury;*[6] and when Belle took it up, it opened where the paper-cutter had been left, at the seventh page, and some one had scored the sonnet there. Belle read it, and somehow, as she read, the tears in her eyes started afresh.

---

5. **good fairy editress** a probable compliment to Dinah Mulock Craik and her *Fairy Book* (1863)

6. **Golden Treasury** Francis Turner Palgrave's *Golden Treasury of the Best Songs and Lyrical Poems in the English Language* first appeared in 1861; the two verses cited are the opening lines of Shakespeare's sonnet 57 and of Burns's "O My Love's Like a Red, Red Rose."

> "Being your slave, what should I do but tend
> Upon the hours and times of your desire?"

it began. "To——" had been scrawled underneath; and then the letter following the "To" erased. Belle blinked her eyes over it, but could make nothing out. A little further on she found another scoring, —

> "Oh, my love's like a red, red rose
> That's newly sprung in June!
> Oh, my love's like the melody
> That's sweetly played in tune!"

and this was signed with a G.

"Love! That is not for me; but I wish I had a slave," thought poor Belle, hanging her head over the book as it lay open in her lap, "and that he was clever enough to tell me what my father is doing at this minute." She could imagine it for herself, alas! without any magic interference. She could see the dreary little cottage, her poor old father wearily returning alone. She nearly broke down at the thought, but some one knocked at the door at that instant, and she forced herself to be calm as one of the servants came in with a telegram. Belinda tore open her telegram in some alarm and trembling terror of bad news from home; and then smiled a sweet, loving smile of relief. The telegram came from Guy. It was dated from his office. "Your father desires me to send word that he is safe home. He sends his love. I have been to D. on business, and travelled down with him."

Belinda could not help saying to herself that Mr. Griffiths was very kind to have thought of her. His kindness gave her courage to meet his mother.

It was not very much that she had to do; but whatever it was she accomplished well and thoroughly, as was her way. Whatever the girl put her hand to she put her whole heart to at the same time. Her energy, sweetness, and good spirits cheered the sick woman and did her infinite good. Mrs. Griffiths took a great fancy to her, and liked to have her about her. Belle lunched with her the first day. She had better dine down below, Mrs. Griffiths said; and when dinner-time came the girl dressed herself, smoothed her yellow curls, and went shyly down the great staircase into the dining-room. It must be confessed that she glanced a little curiously at the table, wondering whether she was to dine alone or in company. This problem was soon solved; a side-door burst open, and Guy made his appearance, looking shy and ashamed of it as he came up and shook hands with her.

"Miss Belinda," said he, "will you allow me to dine with you?"

"You must do as you like," said Belinda, quickly, starting back.

"Not at all," said Mr. Griffiths. "It is entirely as you shall decide. If you don't like my company, you need only say so. I shall not be offended. Well, shall we dine together?"

"Oh, certainly," laughed Belinda, confused in her turn.

So the two sat down to dine together. For the first time in his life Guy thought the great room light enough and bright and comfortable. The gold and silver plate didn't seem to crush him, nor the draperies to suffocate, nor the great columns ready to fall upon him. There was Belinda picking her grapes and playing with the sugar-plums. He could hardly believe it possible. His poor old heart gave great wistful thumps (if such a thing is possible) at the sound of her voice. She had lost much of her shyness, and they were talking of anything that came into their heads. She had been telling him about Myrtle Cottage, and the spiders there, and looking up, laughing, she was surprised to see him staring at her very sadly and kindly. He turned away abruptly, and began to help himself to all sorts of things out of the silver dishes.

"It's very good of you," Guy said, looking away, "to come and brighten this dismal house, and to stay with a poor suffering woman and a great uncouth fellow like myself."

"But you are both so very kind," said Belinda, simply. "I shall never forget—"

"Kind!" cried Guy, very roughly. "I behaved like a brute to you and your father yesterday. I am not used to ladies' society. I am stupid and shy and awkward."

"If you were very stupid," said Belle, smiling, "you would not have said that, Mr. Griffiths. Stupid people always think themselves charming."

When Guy said good-night immediately after dinner, as usual, he sighed again, and looked at her with such kind and melancholy eyes that Belle felt an odd affection and compassion for him. "I never should have thought it possible to like him so much," thought the girl, as she slowly went along the passage to Mrs. Griffiths' door.

It was an odd life this young creature led in the great silent, stifling house, with uncouth Guy for her playfellow, the sick woman's complaints and fancies for her duty in life. The silence of it all, its very comfort and splendidness, oppressed Belinda more at times than a simpler and more busy life. But the garden was an endless pleasure and refreshment, and she used to stroll about, skim over the terraces and walks, smell the roses, feed the birds and the goldfishes. Sometimes I have stood at my window, watching the active figure flitting by in and out under the trellis, fifteen times round the pond, thirty-two times along the terrace walk. Belle was obliged to set herself tasks, or she would have got tired sometimes of wandering about by herself. All this time she never thought of Guy except as a curious sort of companion; any thought of sentiment had never once occurred to her.

VI

One day that Belle had been in the garden longer than usual, she remembered a note for Mrs. Griffiths that she had forgotten to write, and springing up the steps into the hall, on the way, with some roses in her apron, she suddenly almost ran up against Guy, who had come home earlier than usual. The girl stood blushing and looking more charming that ever. The young fellow stood quite still, too, looking with such expressive and admiring glances that Belinda blushed deeper still, and made haste to escape to her room. Presently the gong sounded, and there was no help for it, and she had to go down again. Guy was in the dining-room as polite and as shy as usual, and Belinda gradually forgot the passing impression. The butler put the dessert on the table and left them, and when she had finished her fruit Belinda got up to say good-by. As she was leaving the room she heard Guy's footsteps following. She stopped short. He came up to her. He looked very pale, and said suddenly, in a quick, husky voice, —

"Belle, will you marry me?"

Poor Belinda opened her gray eyes full in his face. She could hardly believe she had heard aright. She was startled, taken aback, but she followed her impulse of the moment, and answered gravely, —

"No, Guy."

He wasn't angry or surprised. He had known it all along, poor fellow, and expected nothing else. He only sighed, looked at her once again, and then went away out of the room.

Poor Belle! she stood there where he had left her, —the lights burned, the great table glittered, the curtains waved. It was like a strange dream. She clasped her hands together, and then suddenly ran and fled away up to her own room, —frightened, utterly puzzled, bewildered, not knowing what to do or to whom to speak. It was a comfort to be summoned as usual to read to Mrs. Griffiths. She longed to pour out her story to the poor lady, but she dreaded agitating her. She read as she was bid. Once she stopped short, but her mistress impatiently motioned her to go on. She obeyed, stumbling and tumbling over the words before her, until there came a knock at the door, and, contrary to his custom, Guy entered the room. He looked very pale, poor fellow, and sad and subdued.

"I wanted to see you, Miss Belinda," he said aloud, "and to tell you that I hope this will make no difference, and that you will remain with us as if nothing had happened. You warned me, mamma, but I could not help myself. It's my own fault. Good-night. That is all I had to say."

Belle turned wistfully to Mrs. Griffiths. The thin hand was impatiently twisting the coverlet.

"Of course,—who would have anything to say to him? Foolish fellow!" she muttered, in her indistinct way. "Go on, Miss Barly."

"Oh, but tell me first, ought I to remain here?" Belle asked, imploringly.

"Certainly, unless you are unhappy with us," the sick woman answered, peevishly.

Mrs. Griffiths never made any other allusion to what had happened. I think the truth was that she did not care very much for anything outside the doors of her sickroom. Perhaps she thought her son had been over-hasty, and that in time Belinda might change her mind. To people lying on their last sick-beds, the terrors, anxieties, longings of life seem very curious and strange. They seem to forget that they were once anxious, hopeful, eager themselves, as they lie gazing at the awful veil which will so soon be withdrawn from before their fading eyes.

A sort of constraint came between Guy and Belinda at first, but it wore away by degrees. He often alluded to his proposal, but in so hopeless and gentle a way that she could not be angry; still she was disquieted and unhappy. She felt that it was a false and awkward position. She could not bear to see him looking ill and sad, as he did at times, with great black rings under his dark eyes. It was worse still when she saw him brighten up with happiness at some chance word she let fall now and then,—speaking inadvertently of home, as he did, or of the roses next year. He must not mistake her. She could not bear to pain him by hard words, and yet sometimes she felt it was her duty to speak them. One day she met him in the street, on her way back to the house. The roll of the passing carriage-wheels gave Guy confidence, and, walking by her side, he began to say,—

"Now I never know what delightful surprise may not be waiting for me at every street corner. Ah, Miss Belle, my whole life might be one long dream of wonder and happiness, if . . ."

"Don't speak like this ever again; I shall go away," said Belle, interrupting, and crossing the road, in her agitation, under the very noses of two omnibus horses. "I wish I could like you enough to marry you. I shall always love you enough to be your friend; please don't talk of anything else."

Belle said this in a bright, brisk, imploring, decided way, and hoped to have put an end to the matter. That day she came to me and told her little story. There were almost as many reasons for her staying as for her leaving, the poor child thought. I could not advise her to go, for the assistance that she was able to send home was very valuable. Guy laughed, and utterly refused to accept a sixpence of her salary. Mrs. Griffiths evidently wanted her; Guy, poor fellow, would have given all he had to keep her, as we all knew too well.

Circumstance orders events sometimes, when people themselves, with all their powers and knowledge of good and of evil, are but passive instruments in the hands of fate. News came that Mr. Barly was ill, and little Belinda, with an anxious face, and a note in her trembling hand, came into Mrs. Griffiths' room one day to say she must go to him directly.

"Your father is ill," wrote Anna. "Circumstances demand your immediate return to him."

Guy happened to be present, and, when Belle left the room, he followed her out into the passage.

"You are going!" he said.

"I don't know what Anna means by circumstances, but papa is ill, and wants me," said Belinda, almost crying.

"And I want you," said Guy; "but that don't matter, of course. Go,—go, since you wish it."

After all, perhaps it was well she was going, thought Belle, as she went to pack up her boxes. Poor Guy's sad face haunted her. She seemed to carry it away in her box with her other possessions.

It would be difficult to describe what he felt, poor fellow, when he came upon the luggage standing ready corded in the hall, and he found that Belle had taken him at his word. He was so silent a man, so self-contained, so diffident of his own strength to win her love in time, so unused to the ways of the world and of women, that he could be judged by no ordinary rule. His utter despair and bewilderment would have been laughable almost, if they had not been so genuine. He paced about the garden with hasty, uncertain footsteps, muttering to himself as he went along, and angrily cutting at the rose-hedges. "Of course she must go, since she wished it; of course she must—of course, of course. What would the house be like when she was gone?" For an instant a vision of a great dull vault without warmth, or light, or color, or possible comfort anywhere, rose before him. He tried to imagine what his life would be if she never came back into it; but as he stood still, trying to seize the picture, it seemed to him that it was a thing not to be imagined or thought of. Wherever he looked he saw her, everywhere and in everything. He had imagined himself unhappy; now he discovered that for the last few weeks, since little Belinda had come, he had basked in the summer she had brought, and found new life in the sunshine of her presence. Of an evening he had come home eagerly from his daily toil looking to find her. When he left early in the morning, he would look up with kind eyes at her windows as he drove away. Once, early one morning, he had passed her near the lodge-gate, standing in the shadow of the great aspen-tree, and making way for the horses to go by. Belle was holding back the clean, stiff folds of her pink muslin dress; she looked up with that peculiar blink of her gray eyes, smiled and nodded her bright head, and shrunk away from the horses. Every morning Guy used to look under the tree after that to see if she were there by chance, even if he had parted from her but a minute before. Good, stupid old fellow! he used to smile to himself at his own foolishness. One of his fancies about her was that Belinda was a bird who would fly away some day, and perch up in the branches of one of the great trees, far, far beyond his reach. And now was this fancy coming true? was she going—leaving him—flying away where he could not follow her? He gave an inarticulate sound of mingled anger and sorrow and tenderness, which relieved his heart, but which puzzled Belle herself, who was coming down the garden-walk to meet him.

"I was looking for you, Mr. Griffiths," said Belle. "Your mother wants to speak to you. I, too, wanted to ask you something," the girl went on, blushing. "She is kind enough to wish me to come back. . . . But—"

Belle stopped short, blushed up, and began pulling at the leaves sprouting on either side of the narrow alley. When she looked up after a minute, with one of her quick, short-sighted glances, she found that Guy's two little brown eyes were fixed upon her steadily.

"Don't be afraid that I shall trouble you," he said, reddening. "If you knew—if you had the smallest conception what your presence is to me, you would come back. I think you would."

Miss Barly didn't answer, but blushed up again and walked on in silence, hanging her head to conceal the two bright tears which had come into her eyes. She was sorry, so very sorry. But what could she do? Guy had walked on to the end of the rose-garden, and Belle had followed. Now, instead of turning towards the house, he had come out into the bright-looking kitchen-garden, with its red brick walls hung with their various draperies of lichen and mosses, and garlands of clambering fruit. Four little paths led up to the turf-carpet which had been laid down in the center of the garden. Here a fountain plashed with a tranquil fall of waters upon water; all sorts of sweet kitchen-herbs, mint and thyme and parsley, were growing along the straight-cut beds. Birds were pecking at the nets along the walls; one little sparrow that had been drinking at the fountain flew away as they approached. The few bright-colored straggling flowers caught the sunlight and reflected it in sparks like the water.

The master of this pleasant place put out his great, clumsy hand, and took hold of Belle's soft, reluctant fingers.

"Ah, Belle," he said, "is there no hope for me? Will there never be any chance?"

"I wish with all my heart there was a chance," said poor Belle, pulling away her hand impatiently. "Why do you wound and pain me by speaking again and again of what is far best forgotten? Dear Mr. Griffiths, I will marry you to-morrow, if you desire it," said the girl, with a sudden impulse, turning pale and remembering all that she owed to his forbearance and gentleness; "but please, please don't ask it." She looked so frightened and desperate that poor Guy felt that this was worse than anything, and sadly shook his head.

"Don't be afraid," he said. "I don't want to marry you against your will, or keep you here. Yes, you shall go home, and I will stop here alone, and cut my throat if I find I cannot bear the place without you. I am only joking. I dare say I shall do very well," said Griffiths, with a sigh; and he turned away and began stamping off in his clumsy way.

Then he suddenly stopped and looked back. Belle was standing in the sunshine with her face hidden in her hands. She was so puzzled, and sorry, and hopeless, and mournful. The only thing she could do was to cry, poor child, —and by some instinct Griffiths guessed that she was crying; he knew it, —his heart melted with pity. The poor fellow came back trembling. "My dearest," he said, "don't cry. What a brute I am to make you cry! Tell me anything in the whole world I can do to make you happy."

"If I could only do anything for you," said Belle, "that would make me happier."

"Then come back, my dear," said Guy, "and don't fly away yet forever, as you threatened just now. Come back and cheer up my mother, and make tea and a little sunshine for me, until—until some confounded fellow comes and carries you off," said poor Griffiths.

"Oh, that will never be. Yes, I'll come," said Belle, earnestly. "I'll go home for a week and come back; indeed I will."

"Only let me know," said Mr. Griffiths, "and my mother will send the carriage for you. Shall we say a week?" he added, anxious to drive a hard bargain.

"Yes," said Belinda, smiling; "I'll write and tell you the day."

Nothing would induce Griffiths to order the carriage until after dinner, and it was quite late at night when Belle got home.

VII

Poor little Myrtle Cottage looked very small and shabby as she drove up in the darkness to the door. A brilliant illumination streamed from all the windows. Martha rubbed her elbows at the sight of the gorgeous equipage. Fanny came to the door surprised, laughing, giggling, mysterious. Everything looked much as usual, except that a large and pompous-looking gentleman was sitting on the drawing-room sofa, and beside him Anna, with a huge ring on her fourth finger, attempting to blush as Belle came into the room. Belle saw that she was not wanted, and ran upstairs to her father, who was better, and sitting in the arm-chair by his bedside. The poor old man nearly cried with delight and surprise, held out both his shaking hands to her, and clung tenderly to the bright young daughter. Belle sat beside him, holding his hand, asking him a hundred questions, kissing his wrinkled face and cheeks, and telling him all that had happened. Mr. Barly, too, had news to give. The fat gentleman downstairs, he told Belle, was no other than Anna's old admirer, the doctor, of whom mention has been made. He had re-proposed the day before, and was now sitting on the sofa on probation. Fanny's prospects, too, seemed satisfactory. "She assures me," said Mr. Barly, "that young Ogden is on the point of coming forward. An old man like me, my dear, is naturally anxious to see his children settled in life and comfortably provided for. I don't know who would be good enough for my Belinda. Not that awkward lout of a Griffiths. No, no; we must look out better than that."

"O papa, if you knew how good and how kind he is!" said Belle, with a sudden revulsion of feeling; but she broke off abruptly, and spoke of something else.

The other maid, who had already gone to bed the night before when Belle arrived at the cottage, gave a loud shriek when she went into the room next morning and found some one asleep in the bed. Belle awoke, laughed and explained, and asked her to bring up her things.

"Bring'em hup?" said the girl. "What all them 'ampers that's come by the cart? No, miss, that's more than me and Martha have the strength for. I should crick my back if I were to attempt for to do such a thing."

"Hampers,—what hampers?" Belle asked; but when she went down she found the little passage piled with cases, flowers, and game and preserves, and some fine old port for Mr. Barly, and some roses for Belle. As Belinda came downstairs, in her fresh morning dress, Anna, who had been poking about and examining the various packages, looked up with offended dignity.

"I think, considering that I am mistress here," said she, "these hampers should have been directed to me, instead of to you, Belinda. Mr. Griffiths strangely forgets. Indeed, I fear that you too are wanting in any great sense of ladylike propriety."

"Prunes, prism, propriety," said Belle, gayly. "Never mind, dear Anna; he's sent the things for all of us. Mr. Griffiths certainly never meant me to drink two dozen bottles of port wine in a week."

"You are evading the question," said Anna, "I have been wishing to talk to you for some time past,—come into the dining-room, if you please."

It seems almost impossible to believe, and yet I cannot help fearing that out of sheer spite and envy Anna Barly had even then determined that if she could prevent it, Belinda should never go back to Castle Gardens again, but remain in the cottage. The sight of the pretty things which had been given her there, all the evidences which told of the esteem and love in which she was held, maddened the foolish woman. I can give no other reason for the way in which she opposed Belinda's return to Mrs. Griffiths. "Her duty is at home," said Anna. "I myself shall be greatly engaged with Thomas,"—so she had already learnt to call Dr. Robinson. "Fanny also is preoccupied; Belinda must remain."

When Belle demurred and said that for the next few weeks she would like to return as she had promised, and stay until Mrs. Griffiths was suited with another companion, Anna's indignation rose and overpowered her dignity. Was it *her* sister who was so oblivious of the laws of society, propriety, modesty? Anna feared that Belinda had not reflected upon the strange appearance her conduct must have to others, to the Ogdens, to them all. What was the secret attraction which took her back? Anna said she had rather not inquire, and went on with her oration. "Unmaidenly,—not to be thought of,—the advice of those whose experience might be trusted"—does one

not know the rigmarole by heart? When even the father, who had been pre-
viously talked to, sided with his eldest daughter, when Thomas, who was
also called into the family conclave, nodded his head in an ominous manner,
poor little Belinda, frightened, shaken, undecided, almost promised that she
would do as they desired; and as she promised, the thought of poor Guy's
grief and wistful, haggard face came before her, and her poor little heart
ached and sank at the thought. But not even Belinda, with all her courage,
could resist the decision of so much experience, or Anna's hints and innuen-
does, or, more insurmountable than all the rest, a sudden shyness and consciousness which had come over the poor little maiden, who turned crimson
with shame and annoyance.

Belinda had decided as she was told,—had done as her conscience bid
her,—and yet there was but little satisfaction in this duty accomplished. For
about half an hour she went about feeling like a heroine, and then without
any reason or occasion, it seemed to her that the mask had come off her
face, that she had discovered herself to be a traitoress, that she had betrayed and abandoned her kindest friends; she called herself a selfish, ungrateful wretch, she wondered what Guy would think of her; she was out of
temper, out of spirits, out of patience with herself, and the click of the blind
swinging in the draft was unendurable. The complacent expression of Anna's
handsome face put her teeth on edge. When Fanny tumbled over the
footstool with a playful shriek, to everybody's surprise Belinda burst out
crying.

Those few days were endless, slow, dull, unbearable,—every second
brought its pang of regret and discomfort and remorse. It seemed to Belinda
that her ears listened, her mouth talked, her eyes looked at the four walls
of the cottage, at the furze on the common, at the faces of her sisters, with
a sort of mechanical effort. As if she were acting her daily life, not living it
naturally and without effort. Only when she was with her father did she feel
unconstrained; but even then there was an unexpressed reproach in her
heart like a dull pain that she could not quiet. And so the long days lagged.
Although Dr. Robinson enlivened them with his presence, and the Ogdens
drove up to carry Fanny off to the happy regions of Capulet Square (E. for
Elysium Anna I think would have docketed the district), to Belinda those
days seemed slow, and dark, and dim, and almost hopeless at times.

On the day on which Belinda was to have returned, there came a letter
to me telling her story plainly enough. "I must not come back, my dearest
Miss Williamson," she wrote. "I am going to write to Mrs. Griffiths and
dear, kind Mr. Guy to-morrow to tell them so. Anna does not think it is right.

Papa clings to me and wants me, now that both my sisters are going to leave him. How often I shall think of you all,—of all your goodness to me, of the beautiful roses, and my dear little room! Do you think Mr. Guy would let me take one or two books as a remembrance—Hume's *History of England,* Porteous's *Sermons,* and *Essays on Reform?* I should like to have something to remind me of you all, and to look at sometimes, since they say I am not to see you all again. Good-by, and thank you and Mrs. H. a thousand, thousand times. Your ever, ever affectionate BELINDA. P.S. Might I also ask for that little green volume of the *Golden Treasury* which is up in the tower-room?"

This was what Guy had feared all along. Once she was gone, he knew by instinct she would never come back. I hardly know how it fared with the poor fellow all this time. He kept out of our way, and would try to escape me; but once by chance I met him, and I was shocked by the change which had come over him. I had my own opinion, as we all have at times. H. and I had talked it over,—for old women are good for something, after all, and can sometimes play a sentimental part in life as well as young ones. It seemed to us impossible that Belinda should not relent to so much goodness and unselfishness, and come back again some day, never to go any more. We knew enough of Anna Barly to guess the part *she* had played, nor did we despair of seeing Belinda among us once more. But some one must help her; she could not reach us unassisted; and so I told Mrs. Griffiths, who had remarked upon her son's distress and altered looks.

"If you will lend us the carriage," I said, "either H. or I will go over to Dumbleton to-morrow, and I doubt not that we shall bring her."

H. went. She told me about it afterwards. Anna was fortunately absent. Mr. Barly was downstairs, and H. was able to talk to him a little bit before Belinda came down. The poor old man always thought as he was told to think, and since his illness he was more uncertain and broken than ever. He was dismayed when H. told him in her decided way that he was probably sacrificing two people's happiness for life by his ill-timed interference. When at last Belinda came down, she looked almost as ill as Griffiths himself. She rushed into H.'s arms with a scream of delight, and eagerly asked a hundred questions. "How were they all—what were they all doing?"

H. was very decided. Everybody was very ill and wanted Belinda back. "Your father says he can spare you very well," said she. "Why not come back with me this afternoon, if only for a time? It is your duty," H. continued, in her dry way. "You should not leave them in this uncertainty."

"Go my child; pray go," urged Mr. Barly.

And at last Belinda consented shyly, nothing loth.

H. began to question her when she had got her safe in the carriage. Belinda said she had not been well. She could not sleep, she said. She had had bad dreams. She blushed and confessed that she had dreamed of Guy lying dead in the kitchen-garden. She had gone about the house trying—indeed she had tried—to be cheerful and busy as usual, but she felt unhappy, ungrateful. "Oh, what a foolish girl I am!" she said.

All the lights were burning in the little town, the west was glowing and reflected in the river, the boats trembled and shot through the shiny waters, and the people were out upon the banks, as they crossed the bridge again on their way from Dumbleton. Belle was happier, certainly, but crying from agitation.

"Have I made him miserable, poor fellow? Oh, I think I shall blame myself all my life," said she, covering her face with her hands. "O H.! H.! what shall I do?"

H. dryly replied that she must be guided by circumstances, and, when they reached Castle Gardens, kissed her and set her down at the great gate, while she herself went home in the carriage.

It was all twilight by this time among the roses. Belinda met the gate-keeper, who touched his hat and told her his master was in the garden; and so, instead of going into the house, she flitted away towards the garden, crossed the lawns, and went in and out among the bowers and trellises looking for him,—frightened by her own temerity at first, gaining courage by degrees. It was so still, so sweet, so dark; the stars were coming out in the evening sky, a meteor went flashing from east to west, a bat flew across her path; all the scent hung heavy in the air. Twice Belinda called out timidly, "Mr. Griffiths, Mr. Griffiths!" but no one answered. Then she remembered her dream in sudden terror, and hurried into the kitchen-garden to the fountain where they had parted.

What had happened? Some one was lying on the grass. Was this her dream? was it Guy? was he dead? had she killed him? Belinda ran up to him, seized his hand, and called him Guy—dear Guy; and Guy, who had fallen asleep from very weariness and sadness of heart, opened his eyes to hear himself called by the voice he loved best in the world; while the sweetest eyes, full of tender tears, were gazing anxiously into his ugly face. Ugly? Fairy tales have told us this at least, that ugliness and dulness do not exist for those who truly love. Had she ever thought him rough, uncouth, unlovable? Ah! she had been blind in those days; she knew better now. As they walked back through the twilight garden that night, Guy said humbly, —

"I shan't do you any credit, Belinda; I can only love you."

"Only!"

She didn't finish her sentence; but he understood very well what she meant.

MARIA LOUISA MOLESWORTH

The Brown Bull of Norrowa

I

"Delicate, strong, and white,
Hurrah for the magic thread!
The warp and the woof come right."
CHILD WORLD.

They were not to be surprised![1] Both the children remembered that, and yet it was a little difficult to avoid being so.

At first all they saw was just another white room, a small one, and with a curious pointed window in one corner. But when the doors were fully opened there was more to be seen. In the first place, at the opposite corner, was a second window exactly like the other, and in front of this window a spinning-wheel placed, and before this spinning-wheel sat, on a white chair, a white-haired lady.

She was spinning busily. She did not look up as the children came in. She seemed quite absorbed in her work. So the children stood and gazed at her, and the cats stood quietly in front, the right-hand one before Hugh, the left-hand one before Jeanne, not seeming, of course, the least surprised. Whether I should call the white-haired lady an "old" lady or not, I really do not know. No doubt she was old, as we count old, but yet, except for her hair, she did not look so. She was very small, and she was dressed entirely in white, and her hands were the prettiest little things you ever saw. But as

1. **not to be surprised** Jeanne and Hugh, the child protagonists who are on one of the dream journeys in Molesworth's *The Tapestry Room* (1879), were warned not to show surprise by the white cats guarding the door they must enter to meet the lady who has been waiting for them "not above three hundred years."

she did not look up, Hugh and Jeanne could not at first judge of her face. They stood staring at her for some minutes without speaking. At last, as they were not allowed to be surprised, and indeed felt afraid of being reproached with bad manners by the cats if they made any remarks at all, it began, especially for Jeanne, to grow stupid.

She gave Hugh a little tug.

"Won't you speak to her?" she whispered, very, *very* softly.

Instantly both cats lifted their right paws.

"You see," replied Hugh, looking at Jeanne reproachfully, "they're getting angry."

On this the cats wheeled right round and looked at the children.

"I don't care," said Jeanne, working herself up. "I don't care. It's not our fault. They said she was waiting for us, and they made us come in."

"'*She* is the cat,' so I've been told," said a soft voice suddenly. And 'don't care;' something was once spun about 'don't care,' I think."

Immediately the two cats threw themselves on the ground, apparently in an agony of grief.

"*She* the cat," they cried. "Oh what presumption! And who said 'don't care'? Oh dear! oh dear! who would have thought of such a thing?"

The lady lifted her head, and looked at the cats and the children. There was a curious expression on her face, as if she had just awakened. Her eyes were very soft blue, softer and dreamier than Hugh's, and her mouth, even while it smiled, had a rather sad look. But the look of her whole face was very—I can't find a very good word for it. It seemed to ask you questions, and yet to know more about you than you did yourself. It was impossible not to keep looking at her once you had begun.

"Hush, cats," were the next words she said. "Don't be silly; it's nearly as bad as being surprised."

Immediately the cats sat up in their places again, as quiet and dignified as if they had not been at all put about, and Jeanne glanced at Hugh as much as to say, "Aren't you glad she has put them down a little?"

Then the lady looked over the cats to the children.

"It is quite ready," she said; "the threads are all straight."

What could they say? They had not the least idea what she meant, and they were afraid of asking. Evidently the white lady was of the same opinion as the cats as to the rudeness of being surprised; very probably asking questions would be considered still ruder.

Jeanne was the first to pick up courage.

"Madame," she said, "I don't mean to be rude, but I *am* so thirsty. It's with flying, I think, for we're not accustomed to it."

"Why did you not say so before?" said the lady. "I can give you anything you want. It has all been ready a long time. Will you have snow water or milk?"

"Milk, please," said Jeanne.

The lady looked at the cats.

"Fetch it," she said quietly. The cats trotted off, they opened the door as before, but left it open this time, and in another moment they returned, carrying between them a white china tray, on which were two cups of beautiful rich-looking milk. They handed them to the children, who each took one and drank it with great satisfaction. Then the cats took away the cups and tray, and returned and sat down as before.

The lady smiled at the children.

"Now," she said, "are you ready?"

She had been so kind about the milk that Hugh this time took courage.

"We are *very* sorry," he said, "but we really don't understand what it is you would like us to do."

"Do?" said the lady. "Why, you have nothing to do but to listen. Isn't that what you came for? To hear some of the stories I spin?"

The children opened their eyes—with pleasure it is to be supposed rather than surprise—for the white lady did not seem at all annoyed.

"Oh!" said they, both at once. "Is *that* what you're spinning? Stories!"

"Of course," said the lady. "Where did you think they all come from?—all the stories down there?" She pointed downwards in the direction of the stair and the great hall. "Why, here I have been for—no, it would frighten you to tell you how long, by your counting, I have been up here at my spinning. I spin the round of the clock at this window, then I turn my wheel—to get the light, you see—and spin the round again at the other. If you saw the tangle it comes to me in! And the threads I send down! It is not *often* such little people as you come up here themselves, but it does happen sometimes. And there is plenty ready for you—all ready for the wheel."

"How wonderful!" said Hugh. "And oh!" he exclaimed, "I suppose sometimes the threads get twisted again when you have to send them down such a long way, and that's how stories get muddled sometimes."

"Just so," said the white lady. "My story threads need gentle handling, and sometimes people seize them roughly and tear and soil them, and then of course they are no longer pretty. But listen now. What will you have? The first in the wheel is a very, very old fairy story. I span it for your great-great-grandmothers; shall I spin it again for you?"

"Oh, please," said both children at once.

"Then sit down on the floor and lean your heads against my knees," said the lady. "Shut your eyes and listen. That is all you have to do. Never mind the cats, they will be quite quiet."

Hugh and Jeanne did as she told them. They leaned their heads, the smooth black one of the little girl, the fair-haired curly one of the boy, on the lady's white robe. You can hardly imagine how soft and pleasant it was to the touch. A half-sleepy feeling came over them; they shut their eyes and did not feel inclined to open them again. But they did not really go to sleep; the fairy lady began to work the wheel, and through the soft whirr came the sound of a voice—whether it was the voice of the lady or of the wheel they could not tell. And this was the old, old story the wheel spun for them.

"Listen, children," it began.

"We are listening," said Jeanne, rather testily. "You needn't say that again."

"Hush, Jeanne," said Hugh; "you'll stop the story if you're not quiet."

"Listen, children," said the voice again. And Jeanne was quite quiet.

"Once on a time—a very long time ago—in a beautiful castle there lived a beautiful Princess. She was young and sweet and very fair to see. And she was the only child of her parents, who thought nothing too rare or too good for her. At her birth all the fairies had given her valuable gifts—no evil wishes had been breathed over her cradle. Only the fairy who had endowed her with good sense and ready wit had dropped certain words, which had left some anxiety in the minds of her parents.

"'She will need my gifts,' the fairy had said. 'If she uses them well, they and these golden balls will stand her in good need.'

"And as she kissed the baby she left by her pillow three lovely golden balls, at which, as soon as the little creature saw them, she smiled with pleasure, and held out her tiny hands to catch them.

"They were of course balls of fairy make—they were small enough for the little Princess at first to hold in her baby hands, but as she grew they grew, till, when she had reached her sixteenth year, they were the size of an orange. They were golden, but yet neither hard nor heavy, and nothing had power to dint or stain them. And all through her babyhood and child-hood, and on into her girlhood, they were the Princess's favourite toy. They were never away from her, and by the time she had grown to be a tall and beautiful girl, with constant practice she had learnt to catch them as cleverly as an Indian juggler. She could whiz them all three in the air at a time, and never let one drop to the ground. And all the people about grew used to seeing their pretty Princess, as she wandered through the gardens and woods near the castle, throwing her balls in the air as she walked, and catching them again without the slightest effort.

"And remembering the words of the fairy who had given them, naturally her father and mother were pleased to see her love for the magic gift, and every one about the palace was forbidden to laugh at her, or to say that it was babyish for a tall Princess to play so much with a toy that had amused her as an infant.

"She was not a silly Princess at all. She was clever at learning, and liked it, and she was sensible and quick-witted and very brave. So no one was inclined to laugh at her pretty play, even if they had not been forbidden to do so. And she was so kind-hearted and merry, that if ever in her rambles she met any little children who stared at her balls with wondering eyes, she would make her ladies stop, while she threw the balls up in the air, higher and yet higher, ever catching them again as they flew back, and laughed with pleasure to see the little creatures' delight in her skill.

"She was such a happy Princess that the bright balls seemed like herself—ready to catch every ray of sunshine and make it prisoner. And till she had reached her sixteenth year no cloud had come over her brightness. About this time she noticed that the king, her father, began to look anxious and grave, and messengers often came in haste to see him from far-off parts of his kingdom. And once or twice she overheard words dropped which she could not understand, except that it was evident some misfortune was at hand. But in their desire to save their daughter all sorrow, the king and queen had given orders that the trouble which had come to the country was not to be told her; so the Princess could find out nothing even by questioning her ladies or her old nurse, who hitherto had never refused to tell her anything she wanted to know.

"One day when she was walking about the gardens, playing as usual with her golden balls, she came upon a young girl half hidden among the shrubs, crying bitterly. The Princess stopped at once to ask her what was the matter, but the girl only shook her head and went on weeping, refusing to answer.

"'I dare not tell you, Princess,' she said. 'I dare not. You are good and kind, and I do not blame you for my misfortunes. If you knew all, you would pity me.'

"And that was all she would say.

"She was a pretty girl, about the same age and height as the Princess, and the Princess, after speaking to her, remembered that she had sometimes seen her before.

"'You are the daughter of the gardener, are you not?' she inquired.

"'Yes,' said the girl. 'My father is the king's gardener. But I have been away with my grandmother. They only sent for me yesterday to come home—and—and—oh, I was to have been married next week to a young shepherd, who has loved me since my childhood!'

"And with this the girl burst into fresh weeping, but not another word would she say.

"Just then the Princess's governess, who had been a little behind—for sometimes in playing with her balls the Princess ran on faster—came up to where the two young girls were talking together. When the governess saw who the Princess's companion was she seemed uneasy.

"'What has she been saying to you, Princess?' she asked eagerly. 'It is the gardener's daughter, I see.'

"'Yes,' said the Princess. 'She is the gardener's daughter, and she is in some great trouble. That is all I know, for she will tell me nothing but that she was to have been married next week, and then she weeps. I wish I knew what her sorrow is, for, perhaps, I could be of use to her. I would give her all my money if it would do her any good,' and the Princess looked ready to cry herself. But the girl only shook her head. 'No Princess,' she said; 'it would do me no good. It is not your fault; but oh, it is very hard on me!'

"The governess seemed very frightened and spoke sharply to the girl, reproving her for annoying the Princess with her distress. The Princess was surprised, for all her ladies hitherto had, by the king and queen's desire, encouraged her to be kind and sympathising to those in trouble, and to do all she could to console them. But as she had also been taught to be very obedient, she made no remonstrance when her governess desired her to leave the girl and return to the castle. But all that day the Princess remained silent and depressed. It was the first time a shadow had come near her happiness.

"The next morning when she awoke the sun was shining brilliantly. It was a most lovely spring day. The Princess's happy spirits seemed all to have returned. She said to herself that she would confide to the queen her mother her concern about the poor girl that she had seen, and no doubt the queen would devise some way of helping her. And the thought made her feel so light-hearted that she told her attendants to fetch her a beautiful white dress trimmed with silver, which had been made for her but the day before. To her surprise the maidens looked at each other in confusion. At last one replied that the queen had not been pleased with the dress and had sent it away, but that a still more beautiful one trimmed with gold should be ready by that evening. The Princess was perplexed; she was not so silly as to care about the dress, but it seemed to her very strange that her mother should not admire what she had thought so lovely a robe. But still more surprised was she at a message which was brought to her, as soon as she was dressed, from the king and queen, desiring her to remain in her own rooms the whole of that day without going out, for a reason that should afterwards be explained to her. She made no objection, as she was submissive and obedient to her parents' wishes, but she found it strange and sad to spend that beautiful spring day shut up in her rooms, more especially as in her favourite boudoir, a turret chamber which overlooked the castle courtyard, she found the curtains drawn closely, as if it were night, and was told by her governess that this too was by the king's orders; the Princess was requested not to look out of the windows. She grew at this a little impatient.

"'I am willing to obey my parents,' she said, 'but I would fain they trusted me, for I am no longer a child. Some misfortune is threatening us, I feel, and it is concealed from me, as if I could be happy or at rest if sorrow is hanging over my dear parents or the nation.'

"But no explanation was given to her, and all that day she sat in her darkened chamber playing sadly with her golden balls and thinking deeply to herself about the mystery. And towards the middle of the day sounds of excitement reached her from the courtyard beneath. There seemed a running to and fro, a noise of horses and of heavy feet, and now and then faint sounds of weeping.

"'Goes the king a hunting to-day?' she asked her ladies. 'And whose weeping is it I hear?'

"But the ladies only shook their heads without speaking.

"By the evening all seemed quiet. The Princess was desired to join her parents as usual, and the white and golden robe was brought to her to wear. She put it on with pleasure, and said to herself there could after all be no terrible misfortune at hand, for if so there would not be the signs of rejoicing she observed as she passed through the palace. And never had her parents been more tender and loving. They seemed to look at her as if never before they had known how they treasured her, and the Princess was so touched by these proofs of their affection that she could not make up her mind to trouble them by asking questions which they might not wish to answer.

"The next day everything went on as usual in the palace, and it seemed to the Princess that there was a general feeling as if some great danger was safely passed. But this happiness did not last long; about three days later, again a messenger, dusty and wearied with riding fast and hard, made his appearance at the castle; and faces grew gloomy, and the king and queen were evidently overwhelmed with grief. Yet nothing was told to the Princess.

"She wandered out about the gardens and castle grounds, playing as usual with her balls, but wondering sadly what meant this mysterious trouble. And as she was passing the poultry-yard, she heard a sound which seemed to suit her thoughts—some one was crying sadly. The Princess turned to see who it was. This time too it was a young girl about her own age, a girl whom she knew very well by sight, for she was the daughter of the queen's henwife, and the Princess had often seen her driving the flocks of turkeys or geese to their fields, or feeding the pretty cocks and hens which the queen took great pride in.

"'What is the matter, Bruna?' said the Princess, leaning over the gate. 'Have the rats eaten any of the little chickens, or has your mother been scolding you for breaking some eggs?'

"'Neither, Princess,' said the girl among her sobs. 'The chickens are never eaten, and my mother seldom scolds me. My trouble is far worse than that, but I dare not tell it to you—to you of all people in the world.'

"And the Princess's governess, who just then came up, looked again very frightened and uneasy.

"'Princess, Princess,' she said, 'what a habit you are getting of talking to all these foolish girls. Come back to the palace at once with me.'

"'I have often talked to Bruna before,' said the Princess gently, 'and I never was blamed for doing so. She is a pretty girl, and I have known her all my life. Some one said she was betrothed to one of my father's huntsmen, and I would like to ask if it is true. Perhaps they are too poor to marry, and it may be for that she is weeping.'

"Bruna heard what the Princess said, and wept still more violently. 'Ah, yes, it is true!' she said, 'but never, never shall I now be married to him.'

"But the Princess's governess would not let her wait to ask more. She hurried her back to the castle, and the Princess—more sure than ever that some mysterious trouble was in question—could get no explanation.

"She did not see the king and queen that night, and the next morning a strange thing happened—her white and golden robe was missing. And all that her attendants could tell her was that it had been taken away by the queen's orders.

"'Then,' said the Princess, 'there is some sad trouble afloat which is hidden from me.'

"And when she went to her turret room, and found, as before, that the windows were all closed, so that she could not see out, she sat down and cried with distress and anxiety.

"And, again, about mid-day, the same confused noises were to be heard. A sound of horses and people moving about in the courtyard, a tramping of heavy feet, and through all a faint and smothered weeping. The Princess could bear her anxiety no longer. She drew back the curtains, and unfastened the shutters, and leaned out. From her window she could clearly see the courtyard. It was, as she suspected, filled with people; rows of soldiers on horseback lined the sides, and in front, on the steps, the king and queen were standing looking at a strange object. It was an enormous bull: never had the Princess seen such a bull. He was dark brown in colour, and pawed the ground in front of him impatiently, and on his back was seated a young girl whom the Princess gazed at with astonishment. She really thought for a moment it was herself, and that she was dreaming! For the girl was dressed in the Princess's own white and golden robe, and her face could not be seen, for it was covered with a thick veil, and numbers of women and servants standing about were weeping bitterly. And so, evidently, was the girl herself. Then the great bull gave another impatient toss, the girl seized his horns to keep herself from falling, and off he set, with a terrible rush: and a great shout, half of fear, half of rejoicing, as seeing him go, rose from the people about.

"Just at this moment the Princess heard some one approaching her room. She hastily drew the curtains, and sat down playing with her balls, as if she had seen nothing.

"She said not a word to any one, but she had her own thoughts, and that evening she was sent for to her father and mother, who, as usual, received her with caresses and every sign of the tenderest affection. And several days passed quietly, but still the Princess had her own thoughts.

"And one evening when she was sitting with her mother, suddenly the king entered the room in the greatest trouble, and not seeing the Princess, for it was dusk, he exclaimed,

"'It has failed again. The monster is not to be deceived. He vows he will not cease his ravages till he gets the real Princess, our beloved daughter.

He has appeared again, and is more infuriated than ever, tearing up trees by the roots, destroying the people's houses, tramping over their fields, and half killing all the country with terror. What is to be done? The people say they can endure it no longer. The girl Bruna was found bruised and bleeding by the wayside a long way from this, and she gives the same account as the gardener's daughter of the monster's rage at finding he had been deceived.'

"The queen had tried to prevent the king's relating all this, but he was too excited to notice her hints, and, indeed, after the first few words, the Princess had heard enough. She started from her seat and came forward. And when he saw her, the king threw up his hands in despair. But the Princess said quietly, 'Father, you must tell me the whole.'

"So they had to tell her the whole. For many weeks past the terrible monster she had seen in the courtyard had been filling the country with fear. He had suddenly appeared at a distant part of the kingdom—having come, it was said, from a country over the sea named 'Norrowa'[2]—and had laid it waste, for though he did not actually kill or devour, he tore down trees, trampled crops, and terrified every one that came in his way, as the king had said. And when begged to have mercy and to return to his own country, he roared out with a voice between the voice of a man and the bellow of a bull, that he would leave them in peace once the king gave him his daughter in marriage.

"Messenger after messenger had been sent to the palace to entreat for assistance. Soldiers in numbers had been despatched to seize the monster and imprison him. But it was no use—he was not to be caught. Nothing would content him but the promise of the Princess; and as it was of course plain that he was not a common bull, but a creature endowed with magical power, the country-people's fear of him was unbounded. They threatened to rise in revolution unless some means were found of ridding them of their terrible visitor. Then the king called together the wisest of his counsellors, and finding force of no avail, they determined to try cunning. The giving the Princess was not to be thought of, but a pretty girl about her age and size— the gardener's daughter, the same whom the Princess had found weeping over her fate—was chosen, dressed in one of her royal mistress's beautiful robes, and a message sent to the bull that his request was to be granted. He came. All round, the castle was protected by soldiers, though they well knew their power against him was nothing. The king and queen, feigning to

2. **a country . . . named 'Norrowa'** Norway

weep over the loss of their daughter, themselves presented to him the false Princess.

"She was mounted on his back, and off he rushed with her—up hill, down dale, by rocky ground and smooth, across rivers and through forests he rushed, said the girl, faster and faster, till at last, as evening fell, he came to a stand and spoke to her for the first time.

"'What time of day must it be by this, king's daughter?' he said.

"The girl considered for a moment. Then, forgetting her pretended position, she replied thoughtlessly,

"'It must be getting late. About the time that my father gathers the flowers to adorn the king's and queen's supper table.'

"'Throw thee once, throw thee twice, throw thee *thrice*,' roared the bull, each time shaking the girl roughly, and the last time flinging her off his back. 'Shame on thee, gardener's daughter, and thou wouldst call thyself a true Princess.'

"And with that he left her bruised and frightened out of her wits on the ground, and rushed off by himself whither she knew not. And it was not till two days later that the unfortunate gardener's daughter found her way home, glad enough, one may be sure, to be again there in safety.

"In the meantime the ravages and terrors caused by the terrible bull had begun again, and, as before, messengers came incessantly to the king entreating him to find some means of protecting his unfortunate subjects. And the king and queen were half beside themselves with anxiety. Only one thing they were determined on—nothing must be told to the Princess.

II

"And she
Told them an old-world history."
MATTHEW ARNOLD.[3]

"'She is so courageous,' said the queen, 'there is no knowing what she might not do.'

3. **Matthew Arnold** Given the Scottish source of her tale, Molesworth leaves out the word "Breton" in the lines from Arnold's poem "Tristram and Iseult" (III.36–37) she here quotes. That she identifies herself with Arnold's characterization of Iseult of Brittany as a deserted mother who beguiles her children with stories "gleaned from Breton grandames" is also evident from her decision to go to the same poem for the epigraph on the book's title-page: "What tale did Iseult to the children say, / Under the hollies, that winter bright?" (III.150–52).

"'She is so kind-hearted,' said the king; 'she might imagine it her duty to sacrifice herself to our people.'

"And the poor king and queen wept copiously at the mere thought, and all the ladies and attendants of the Princess were ordered on no account to let a breath of the terrible story be heard by her. Yet, after all, it so happened that her suspicions were aroused afresh by the sight this time of the weeping Bruna. For nothing else could be suggested than again to try to deceive the monster; and Bruna, a still prettier girl than the gardener's daughter, was this time chosen to represent the Princess. But all happened as before. The brown bull rushed off with his prize, the whole day the unfortunate Bruna was shaken on his back, and again, as night began to fall, he stopped at the same spot.

"'What time must it be by this, king's daughter?' he asked.

"Foolish Bruna, thankful to have a moment's rest, answered hastily,

"'O brown bull, it must be getting late, and I am sorely tired. It must be about the time that my mother takes all the eggs that have been laid in the day to the king's kitchen.'

"'Throw thee once, throw thee twice, throw thee *thrice*,' roared the bull, each time shaking the henwife's daughter roughly, at the end flinging her to the ground. 'Shame on thee, thou henwife's daughter, to call thyself a true Princess.'

"And with that off he rushed, furious, and from that day the ravages and the terrors began again, and Bruna found her way home, bruised and weeping, to tell her story.

"This was the tale now related to the Princess, and as she listened a strange look of determination and courage came over her face.

"'There is but one thing to be done,' she said. 'It is childish to attempt to deceive a creature who is evidently not what he seems. Let me go myself, my parents. Trust me to do my best. And, at worst, if I perish, it will be in a good cause. Better it should be so than that our people should be driven from their homes, the whole country devastated, and all its happiness destroyed.'

"The king and queen had no answer to give but their tears. But the Princess remained firm, and they found themselves obliged to do as she directed. A messenger was sent to the monster to inform him, for the third time, that his terms were to be agreed to, and the rest of the day was spent in the palace in weeping and lamentation.

"Only, strange to say, the Princess shed no tears. She seemed as cheerful as usual; she played with her golden balls, and endeavoured to comfort her sorrowful parents, and was so brave and hopeful that in spite of themselves the poor king and queen could not help feeling a little comforted.

"'It is a good sign that she has never left off playing with her balls,' they said to each other. 'Who knows but what the fairy's prediction may be true, and that in some way the balls may be the means of saving her?'

"'They and my wits,' said the Princess, laughing, for she had often been told of the fairy's saying.

"And the king and queen and all the ladies and gentlemen of the court looked at her in astonishment, admiring her courage, but marvelling at her having the spirit to laugh at such a moment.

"The next morning, at the usual time, the terrible visitor made his appearance. He came slowly up to the castle courtyard and stood at the great entrance, tossing his enormous head with impatience. But he was not kept waiting long; the doors were flung open, and at the top of the flight of steps leading down from them appeared the young Princess, pale but resolute, her fair hair floating over her shoulders, her golden balls flashing as she slowly walked down the steps, tossing them as she went. And, unlike the false princesses, she was dressed entirely in black, without a single jewel or ornament of any kind—nothing but her balls, and her hair caught the sunlight as she passed. There were no soldiers this time, no crowd of weeping friends; the grief of the king and queen was now too real to be shown, and the Princess had asked that there should be no one to see her go.

"The brown bull stood still as a lamb for her to mount, and then at a gentle pace he set off. The Princess had no need to catch hold of his horns to keep herself from falling, his step was so even. And all along as she rode she threw her balls up softly in the air, catching them as they fell. But the brown bull spoke not a word.

"On and on they went; the sun rose high in the heavens and poured down on the girl's uncovered head the full heat of his rays. But just as she began to feel it painfully, they entered a forest, where the green shade of the summer trees made a pleasant shelter. And when they came out from the forest again on the other side the sun was declining; before long he had sunk below the horizon, evening was at hand. And as before, the brown bull stopped.

"'King's daughter,' he said, in a voice so gentle, though deep, that the Princess started with surprise, 'what hour must it be by this? Tell me, king's daughter, I pray.'

"'Brown bull,' replied the Princess, without a moment's hesitation, for those who have nothing to conceal are fearless and ready; 'brown bull, it is getting late. By now must the king and queen, my father and mother, be sitting down to their solitary supper and thinking of me, for at this hour I was used to hasten to them, throwing my pretty balls as I went.'

"'I thank thee, thou true Princess,' said the bull in the same tone, and he hastened on.

"And ere long the night fell, and the poor Princess was so tired and sleepy, that without knowing it her pretty head drooped lower and lower, and at last she lay fast asleep on the bull's broad back, her fair head resting between his horns.

"She slept so soundly that she did not notice when he stopped, only she had a strange dream. Some one lifted her gently and laid her on a couch, it seemed to her, and a kind voice whispered in her ear, 'Good-night, my fair Princess.'

"But it must have been a dream, she said to herself. How could a bull have arms to lift her, or how could a rough, ferocious creature like him be so gentle and kind? It must have been a dream, for when she awoke she saw the great monster standing beside her on his four legs as usual; yet it was strange, for she found herself lying on a delicious mossy couch, and the softest and driest moss had been gathered together for a pillow, and beside her a cup of fresh milk and a cake of oaten bread were lying for her break-fast. How had all this been done for her? she asked herself, as she ate with a very good appetite, for she had had no food since the morning before. She began to think the bull not so bad after all, and to wonder if it was to Fairy-land he was going to take her. And as she thought this to herself she threw her balls, which were lying beside her, up into the air, and the morning sun caught their sparkle and seemed to send it dancing back again on to her bright fair hair. And a sudden fancy seized her.

"'Catch,' she said to the bull, throwing a ball at him as she spoke. He tossed his head, and to her surprise the ball was caught on one of his horns.

"'Catch,' she said again, and he had caught the second.

"'Catch,' a third time. The great creature caught it in his mouth like a dog, and brought it gently to the Princess and laid it at her feet. She took it and half timidly stroked his head; and no one who had seen the soft pathetic look which crept into his large round eyes would have believed in his being the cruel monster he had been described. He did not speak, he seemed without the power to do so now, but by signs he made the Princess under-stand it was time to continue their journey, and she mounted his back as before.

"All that day the bull travelled on, but the Princess was now getting ac-customed to her strange steed, and felt less tired and frightened. And when

The Brown Bull of Norrowa

the sun grew hot the bull was sure to find a sheltered path, where the trees shaded her from the glare, and when the road was rough he went the more slowly, that she should not be shaken.

"Late in the evening the Princess heard a far-off rushing sound, that as they went seemed to grow louder and louder.

"'What is that, brown bull?' she asked, feeling somehow a little frightened.

"The brown bull raised his head and looked round him. Yes, the sun had sunk, he might speak. And in the same deep voice he answered,

"'The sea, king's daughter, the sea that is to bear you and me to my country of Norrowa.'

"'And how shall we cross it, brown bull?' she said.

"'Have no fear,' he replied. 'Lay down your head and shut your eyes, and no harm will come near you.'

"The Princess did as he bade her. She heard the roar of the waves come nearer and nearer, a cold wind blew over her face, and she felt at last that her huge steed had plunged into the water, for it splashed on to her hand, which was hanging downwards, and then she heard him, with a gasp and a snort, strike out boldly. The Princess drew herself up on the bull's back as closely as she could; she had no wish to get wet. But she was not frightened. She grew accustomed to the motion of her great steed's swimming, and as she kept her eyes fast shut she did not see how near she was to the water, and felt as if in a peaceful dream. And after a while the feeling became reality, for she fell fast asleep and dreamt she was in her little turret chamber, listening to the wind softly blowing through the casement.

"When she awoke she was alone. She was lying on a couch, but this time not of moss, but of the richest and softest silk. She rubbed her eyes and looked about her. Was she in her father's castle? Had her youth and her courage softened the monster's heart, and made him carry her back again to her happy home? For a moment she thought it must be so; but no, when she looked again, none of the rooms in her old home were so beautiful as this one where she found herself. Not even her mother's great saloon, which she had always thought so magnificent, was to be compared with it. It was not very large, but it was more like Fairyland than anything she had ever dreamt of. The loveliest flowers were trained against the walls, here and there fountains of delicately scented waters refreshed the air, the floor was covered with carpets of the richest hues and the softest texture. There were birds singing among the flowers, gold and silver fish sporting in the marble basins—it was a perfect fairy's bower. The Princess sat up and looked about her. There was no one to be seen, not a sound but the dropping of the fountains and the soft chatter of the birds. The Princess admired it all exceedingly, but she was very hungry, and as her long sleep had completely refreshed her, she felt no longer inclined to lie still. So she crossed the room to where a curtain was hanging, which she thought perhaps concealed a door. She drew aside the curtain, the door behind was already open; she found herself in a second room, almost as beautiful as the first, and lighted in the same way with coloured lamps hanging from the roof. And to her great delight, before her was a table already laid for supper with every kind of delicious fruit and bread, and cakes, and everything that a young Princess could desire. She was so hungry that she at once sat down to the table, and then she perceived to her surprise that it was laid for two!

"'Can the bull be coming to sup with me?' she said to herself, half laughing at the idea. And she added aloud, 'Come if you like, Mr. Bull; I find your house very pretty, and I thank you for your hospitality.'

"And as she said the words, a voice which somehow seemed familiar to her, replied,

"'I thank you, gracious Princess, for your permission. Without it I could not have entered your presence as I do now,' and looking up, she saw, coming in by another door that she had not noticed, a most unexpected visitor.

"It was not the bull, it was a young Prince such as our pretty Princess, who was not without her daydreams, like other young girls, had sometimes pictured to herself as coming on a splendid horse, with his followers around him in gallant attire, to ask her of her parents. He was well made and manly, with a bright and pleasant expression, and dressed, of course, to perfection. The Princess glanced at her plain black robe in vexation, and her fair face flushed.

"'I knew not,' she began. 'I thought I should see no one but the brown bull.'

"The Prince laughed merrily. He was in good spirits naturally, as any one would be who, after being forced for ten years to wear a frightful and hideous disguise, and to behave like a rough and surly bull, instead of like a well-born gentleman, should suddenly find himself in his own pleasant person again.

"'I *was* the bull,' he said, 'but you, Princess, have transformed me. How can I ever show you my gratitude?'

"'You owe me none,' said the Princess gently. 'What I did was to save my parents and their people. If it has served you in good stead, that for me is reward enough. But,' she added, 'I wish I had brought some of my pretty dresses with me. It must look so rude to you to have this ugly black one.'

"The Prince begged her not to trouble herself about such a trifle—to him she was beautiful as the day in whatever attire she happened to be. And then they ate their supper with a good appetite, though it seemed strange to the Princess to be quite without attendants, sitting alone at table with a young man whom she had never seen before.

"And after supper a new idea struck her.

"'Catch,' she said, drawing the first ball out of the little pocket in the front of her dress, where she always carried her balls, and flinging it across the table to the Prince with her usual skill, not breaking a glass or bending a leaf of the flowers with which the dishes were adorned.

"In an instant the Prince had caught it, and as she sent off the second, crying again 'Catch,' he returned her the first, leaving his hand free for the third.

"'Yes,' said the Princess, after continuing this game for a little while. 'Yes, I see that you are a true Prince,' for strange to say, he was as skilful at her game as she was herself.

"And they played with her balls for a long time throwing them higher and higher without ever missing, and laughing with pleasure, like two merry children.

"Then suddenly the Prince started from his seat, and his face grew sad and grave.

"'I must go,' he said; 'my hour of liberty is over.'

"'Go?'' said the Princess in surprise and distress, for she had found the Prince a very pleasant companion. 'You must go? and leave me alone here?'

"She looked as if she were going to cry, and the Prince looked as if he were going to cry too.

"'Alas, Princess!' he said, 'in my joy for the moment, I had almost forgotten my sad fate;' and then he went on to explain to her that for many years past he had been under a fairy spell, the work of an evil fairy who had vowed to revenge herself on his parents for some fancied insult to her. He had been forced to take the form of a bull and to spread terror wherever he went; and the power of this spell was to continue till he should meet with a beautiful Princess who of her own free will would return with him to his country and treat him with friendliness, both of which conditions had been now fulfilled.

"'Then all is right!' exclaimed the Princess joyfully. 'Why should you look so sad?'

"'Alas! no,' repeated the Prince, 'the spell is but partly broken. I have only power to regain my natural form for three hours every evening after sunset. And for three years more must it be so. Then, if your goodness continues so long, all will indeed be right. But during that time it will be necessary for you to live alone, except for the three hours I can pass with you, in this enchanted palace of mine. No harm will befall you, all your wants will be supplied by invisible hands; but for a young and beautiful Princess like you, it will be a sad trial, and one that I feel I have no right to ask your consent to.'

"'And can nothing be done?' said the Princess, 'nothing to shorten your endurance of the spell?'

"'Nothing,' said the Prince, sadly. 'Any effort to do so would only cause fearful troubles. I drop my hated skin at sunset, but three hours later I must resume it.'

"He glanced towards the corner of the room where, though the Princess had not before observed it, the brown bull's skin lay in a heap.

"'Hateful thing!' said the Princess, clenching her pretty hands, 'I would like to burn it.'

"The Prince grew pale with fright. 'Hush! Princess,' he said. 'Never breathe such words. Any rash act would have the most fearful consequences.'

"'What?' said the Princess, curiously.

"The Prince came nearer her and said in a low voice, 'For *me* they would be such. In such a case I might too probably never see you more.'

"The Princess blushed. Considering that he had spent ten years as a bull, it seemed to her that the Prince's manners were really not to be found fault with, and she promised him that she would consider the matter over, and by the next evening tell him her decision.

"She felt rather inclined to cry when she found herself again quite alone in the great strange palace, for she was only sixteen, even though so brave and cheerful. But still she had nothing whatever to complain of. Not a wish was formed in her heart but it was at once fulfilled, for this power was still the Prince's. She found, in what was evidently intended for her dressing-room, everything a young Princess could possibly desire in the shape of dresses, each more lovely than the others; shoes of silk or satin, exquisitely embroidered to suit her various costumes; laces and shawls, ribbons and feathers, and jewels of every conceivable kind in far greater abundance than so sensible a young lady found at all necessary. But believing all these pretty things to be provided to please her by the Prince's desire, she endeavoured to amuse herself with them, and found it rather interesting for the first time in her life to have to choose for herself. Her breakfasts and dinners, and everything conceivable in the shape of delicate and delicious food, appeared whenever she wished for anything of the kind; invisible hands opened the windows and shut the doors, lighted the lamps when the evening closed in, arranged her long fair hair more skilfully than any mortal maid, and brushed it softly when at night she wished to have it unfastened. Books in every language to interest her, for the Princess had been well taught, appeared on the tables, also materials for painting and for embroidery, in which she was very clever. Altogether it was impossible to complain, and the next day passed pleasantly enough, though it must be confessed the young Princess often found herself counting the hours till it should be that of sunset.

"Punctual to the moment the Prince made his appearance, but to his guest's distress he seemed careworn and anxious.

"'Has some new misfortune threatened you?' she asked.

"'No,' replied the Prince, 'but I have to-day scarcely been able to endure my anxiety to learn your decision. Never in all these terrible years has my suffering been greater, never have I so loathed the hideous disguise in which I am compelled to live.'

"Tears filled the Princess's eyes. Had anything been wanting to decide her, the deep pity which she now felt for the unfortunate Prince would have done so.

"'I *have* decided!' she exclaimed. 'Three years will soon pass, and I shall be well able to amuse myself with all the charming things with which I am surrounded. Besides, I shall see you every day, and the looking forward to that will help to cheer me.'

"It would be impossible to tell the Prince's delight. He became at once as gay and lively as the day before. The Princess and he had supper together, and amused themselves afterwards with the enchanted balls, and the evening passed so quickly that the Princess could hardly believe more than one hour instead of three had gone, when he started up, saying his time was over. It was sad to see him go, forced, through no fault of his own, to return to his hated disguise; but still it was with a lightened heart that the poor brown bull went tramping about during the next one-and-twenty hours.

"And on her side the Princess's lonely hours were cheered by the thought that she was to be the means of freeing him from the power of the terrible spell, for all that she saw of him only served to increase her sympathy and respect.

"So time went on. The Princess got more and more accustomed to her strange life, and every day more attached to the Prince, who on his side could not do enough to prove to her his gratitude. For many weeks he never failed to enter her presence the instant the sun had sunk below the horizon, and the three hours they spent together made amends to both for the loneliness of the rest of the day. And whenever the Princess felt inclined to murmur, she renewed her patience and courage by the thought of how much harder to bear was the Prince's share of the trial. She was allowed to remain in peaceful security, and to employ her time in pleasant and interesting ways; while he was forced to rove the world as a hateful monster, shunned by any of the human race whom he happened to meet, constantly exposed to fatigue and privation.

"Sometimes they spent a part of the evening in the beautiful gardens surrounding the palace. There, one day, as sunset was approaching, the Princess had betaken herself to wait the Prince's arrival, when a sad shock met her. It was past the usual hour of his coming. Several times she had wandered up and down the path by which he generally approached the castle, tossing her balls as she went, for more than once he had seen their glitter from a distance, and known by it that she was waiting. But this evening she waited and watched in vain, and at last, a strange anxiety seizing her, she turned towards the castle to see if possibly he had entered from the other side, and was hurrying back when a low moan reached her ears, causing her heart for an instant almost to leave off beating with terror.

III

"'And happy they ever lived after'—
Yes, that was the end of the tale."

"The Princess collected her courage, and turned in the direction of the sound. It seemed to come from a little thicket of close-growing bushes near which she had been passing. For a minute or two she could distinguish nothing, but another moan guided her in the right direction, and there, to her horror and distress, she saw the poor Prince lying on the ground, pale and death-like. At first she thought he was without consciousness, but when she hastened up to him with a cry, he opened his eyes.

"'Ah!' he said, faintly; 'I never thought I should have escaped alive. How good of you to have come to seek for me, Princess; otherwise I might have died here without seeing you again.'

"'But you must not die,' said the Princess, weeping; 'can nothing be done for you?'

"He tried to sit up, and when the Princess had fetched him some water from one of the numerous springs in the garden, he seemed better. But his right arm was badly injured.

"'How did it happen?' asked the Princess. 'I thought no mortal weapon had power to hurt you. That has been my only consolation through these lonely days of waiting.'

"'You are right,' replied the Prince; 'as a bull nothing can injure me, but in my own form I am in no way magically preserved. All day long I have been chased by hunters, who saw in me, I suppose, a valuable prize. I was terrified of the hour of sunset arriving and finding me far from home. I used my utmost endeavour to reach this in time, but, alas! I was overcome with fatigue, from which no spell protects me. At the entrance to these gardens I saw the sun disappear, and I fell exhausted, just as an arrow struck my right arm[4] at the moment of my transformation. All I could do was to crawl in among these bushes, and here I have lain, thankful to escape from my persecutors, and most thankful to the happy thought, Princess, which brought you this way.'

"The Princess, her eyes still full of tears, helped him to the palace, where she bound up his arm and tended him carefully, for, young as she was, she had learnt many useful acts of this kind in her father's castle. The wound was not a very serious one; the Prince was suffering more from exhaustion and fatigue.

"'If I could spend a day or two here in peace,' he said sadly, 'I should quickly recover. But alas! that is impossible. I must submit to my cruel fate. But this night I must confine my wanderings to the forests in this neighbourhood, where perhaps, I may be able to hide from the huntsmen, who, no doubt, will be watching for me.'

"He sighed heavily, and the Princess's heart grew very sad.

"'I have little more than an hour left,' he said.

"'Yes,' said the Princess, 'sleep if you can; I will not disturb you.'

4. **an arrow struck my right arm** The Prince's wounding by huntsmen is the first of Molesworth's many radical alterations of the traditional account of the ensuing separation of the two lovers. The personal meanings are inescapable: she blamed her own separation from Major Molesworth on his irrational behavior after the head-wound he suffered in the Crimean war.

"And when she saw that he had fallen asleep she went into the other room, where in a corner lay the bull's skin, which the Prince had dragged behind him from the spot where it had fallen off as the sun sank.

"The Princess looked at it with a fierce expression, very different to the usual gentle look in her pretty eyes.

"'Hateful thing!' she said, giving it a kick with her little foot; 'I wonder how I could get rid of you. Even if the Prince did risk never seeing me again, I am not sure but that it would be better for him than to lead this dreadful life.'

"And as her fancy pictured her poor Prince forced in this monstrous disguise to wander about all night tired and shelterless, her indignation rose beyond her control. She forgot where she was, she forgot the magic power that surrounded her, she forgot everything except her distress and anxiety.

"'Hateful thing!' she repeated, giving the skin another kick; 'I wish you were burnt to cinders.'

"Hardly had she said the words when a sudden noise like a clap of thunder shook the air; a flash of lightning seemed to glance past her and alight on the skin, which in an instant shrivelled up to a cinder like a burnt glove. Too startled at first to know whether she should rejoice or not, the Princess gazed at her work in bewilderment, when a voice of anguish, but, alas! a well-known voice, made her turn round. It was the Prince, hastening from the palace with an expression half of anger half of sorrowful reproach on his face.

"'O Princess, Princess,' he cried, 'what have you done? But a little more patience and all might have been well. And now I know not if I shall ever see you again.'

"'O Prince, forgive me, I did not mean it,' sobbed the poor Princess. 'I *will* see you again, and all shall yet be well.'

"'Seek for me across the hill of ice and the sea of glass,' said the Prince; but almost before the words had passed his lips a second thunderclap, louder and more terrific than the first, was heard. The Princess sank half fainting on the ground. When she again opened her eyes, Prince, palace, everything had disappeared. She was alone, quite alone, on a barren moorland, night coming on, and a cold cutting wind freezing the blood in her veins. And she was clothed in the plain black dress with which she had made her strange journey riding on the brown bull.

"It must be a dream, she thought, a terrible dream, and she shut her eyes again. But no, it was no dream, and soon her courage revived, and she began to ask herself what she should do.

"'Seek me beyond the hill of ice and the sea of glass,' the Prince had said; and she rose up to begin her weary journey. As she rose her hand came in contact with something hard in the folds of her dress; it was her golden balls. With the greatest delight she took them out of her pocket and looked at them. They were as bright and beautiful as ever, and the fairy's prophecy returned to the Princess's mind.

"'With my balls and my ready wit I shall yet conquer the evil powers that are against my poor Prince,' she said to herself cheerfully. 'Courage! all will be well.'"

"But there were sore trials to go through in the first place. The Princess set off on her journey. She had to walk many weary miles across the moor, the cold wind blowing in her face, the rough ground pricking her tender feet. But she walked on and on till at last the morning broke and she saw a road before her, bordered on one side by a forest of trees, for she had reached the extreme edge of the moor. She had gone but a little way when she came to a small and miserable hovel, from which issued feeble sounds of distress. The Princess went up to the door and looked in—a very old woman sat huddled up in a corner weeping and lamenting herself.

"'What is the matter, my friend?' asked the Princess.

"'Matter enough,' replied the old woman. 'I cannot light my fire, and I am bitterly cold. Either the sticks are wet, or the strength has gone out of my poor old arms.'

"'Let me help you,' said the Princess. 'My arms are strong enough.'

"She took the sticks and arranged them cleverly in the fireplace, and just as she was choosing two of the driest to rub together to get a light, one of her balls dropped out of her pocket. It fell on to the piled-up wood, and immediately a bright flame danced up the chimney. The Princess picked up her ball and put it back in her pocket, cheered and encouraged by this proof of their magic power. The old woman came near to the fire, and stretched out her withered hands to the blaze.

"'What can I do for you, my pretty lady,' she said, 'in return for your good nature?'

"'Give me a cup of milk to refresh me for my journey,' said the Princess. 'And perhaps, too, you can tell me something about my journey. Are the hill of ice and the sea of glass anywhere in this neighborhood?'

"The old woman smiled and nodded her head two or three times.

"'Seven days must you travel,' she said, 'before you see them. At the foot of the hill of ice lies the sea of glass. No mortal foot unaided has ever crossed the one or ascended the other. Here, take these shoes—with them you can safely walk over the sea of glass, and with this staff you can mount the hill of ice,' and as she spoke she handed to the Princess a pair of curiously carved wooden shoes and a short sharp-pointed stick. The Princess took them gratefully, and would have thanked the old woman, whom she now knew to be a fairy, but she stopped her. "'Think not,' she said, 'that your difficulties will be over when you have reached the summit of the hill of ice. But all I can do for you more is to give you this nut, which you must open in your moment of sorest perplexity.'

"And as the Princess held out her hand for the nut the old woman had disappeared.

"But refreshed and encouraged the Princess left the cottage, carrying with her her three gifts, and prepared to face all the perils of her journey with an undaunted heart.

"It would be impossible to describe all she went through during the seven days which passed before she reached the sea of glass. She saw some strange and wonderful sights, for in those days the world was very different from what it is now. She was often tired and hungry, thankful for a cup of milk or crust of bread from those she happened to meet on the way. But her courage never failed her, and at last, on the morning of the eighth day, she saw shining before her in the sunlight the great silent sea of glass of which she had been told.

"It would have been hopeless to attempt to cross it without fairy aid, for it was polished more brightly than any mirror, and so hard that no young Princess's bones could have borne a fall on its cruel surface. But with the magic shoes there was less than no difficulty, for no sooner had the Princess slipped her feet into them than they turned into skates, and very wonderful skates, for they possessed the power of enabling their wearer to glide along with the greatest swiftness. The Princess had never skated in her life, and she was delighted.

"'Next to flying,' she said to herself, 'nothing could be pleasanter,' and she was almost sorry when her skim across the sea of glass was over, and she found herself at the foot of the hill of ice.

"She looked upwards with something like despair. It was a terrible ascent to attempt, for the mountain was all but straight, so steep were its sides of hard, clear, sparkling ice. The Princess looked at her feet, the magic shoes had already disappeared; she looked at the staff she still held in her hand— how could a stick help her up such a mountain? and half impatiently, half hopelessly, she threw it from her. Instantly it stretched itself out, growing wider and wider, with notches in the wood expanding, till it had taken the shape of a roughly-made ladder of irregular steps, hooked on to the ice by the sharp spike at its end, and the Princess, ashamed of her discouragement, mounted up the steps without difficulty, and as she reached the top one, of itself the ladder pushed up before her, so that she could mount straight up without hesitation.

"She stepped forward bravely. It took a long time, even though she had the fairy aid, and by the time she reached the top of the hill night had fallen, and but for the light of the stars, she would not have known where to step. A long plain stretched before her—no trees or bushes even broke the wide expanse. There was no shelter of any kind, and the Princess found herself obliged to walk on and on, for the wind was very cold, and she dared not let herself rest. This night and the next day were the hardest part of all the journey, and seemed even more so, because the Princess had hoped that the sea of glass and the hill of ice were to be the worst of her difficulties. More than once she was tempted to crack the nut, the last of the old woman's presents, but she refrained, saying to herself she might yet be in greater need, and she walked on and on, though nearly dead with cold and fatigue, till late in the afternoon. Then at last, far before her still, she saw gleaming the lights of a city, and, encouraged by the sight, she gathered her courage together and pressed on, till, at the door of a little cottage at the outskirts of the town, she sank down with fatigue. An old woman, with a kind face, came out of the house and invited her to enter and rest.

"'You look sorely tired, my child,' she said. 'Have you travelled far?'

"'Ah yes!' replied the poor Princess, 'very far. I am nearly dead with fatigue;' and indeed she looked very miserable. Her beautiful fair hair was all tumbled and soiled, her poor little feet were scratched and blistered, her black dress torn and draggled—she looked far more like a beggar-maiden than like a princess. But yet, her pretty way of speaking and gentle manners showed she was not what she seemed, and when she had washed her face and combed her hair, the old woman looked at her with admiration.

"'Tis a pity you have not a better dress,' she said, 'for then you could have gone with me to see the rejoicings in the town for the marriage of our Prince.'

"'Is your Prince to be married to-day?' asked the Princess.

"'No, not to-day—to-morrow,' said the old woman. 'But the strange thing is that it is not yet known who is to be his bride. The Prince has only lately returned to his home, for, for many years, he has been shut up by a fairy spell in a beautiful palace in the north, and now that the spell is broken and he is restored to his parents, they are anxious to see him married. But he must still be under a spell of some kind, they say, for though he has all that heart can wish, he is ever sad and silent, and as if he were thinking of something far away. And he has said that he will marry no princess but one who can catch three golden balls at a time, as if young princesses were brought up to be jugglers! Nevertheless, all the princesses far and wide have been practising their best at catching balls, and to-morrow the great feasts are to begin, and she who catches best is to be chosen out of all the princesses as the bride of our Prince.'

"The poor Princess listened with a beating heart to the old woman's talk. There could be no doubt as to who the Prince of this country was.

"'I have come but just in time,' she said to herself, and then she rose, and thanking her hostess for her kindness, said she must be going.

"'But where are you going, you poor child?' said the old woman. 'You look far too tired to go farther, and for two or three days all these rejoicings will make the country unpleasant for a young girl to travel through alone. Stay with me till you are rested.'

"The Princess thanked her with tears in her eyes for her kindness. 'I have nothing to reward you with,' she said, 'but some day I may be able to do so,' and then she thankfully accepted her offer.

"'And to-morrow,' said the old woman, 'you must smarten yourself up as well as you can, and then we shall go out to see the gay doings.'

"But the Princess lay awake all night thinking what she should do to make herself known to her faithful Prince.

"The next day the old woman went out early to hear all about the festivities. She came back greatly excited.

"'Come quickly,' she said. 'The crowd is so great that no one will notice your poor clothes. And, indeed, among all the pretty girls there will be none prettier than you,' she added, looking admiringly at the Princess, who had arranged her beautiful hair and brushed her soiled dress, and who looked sweeter than ever now that she was rested and refreshed. 'There are three princesses who have come to the feast,' she went on, 'the first from the south, the second from the east, the third from the west, each more beautiful than another, the people say. The trial of the golden balls is to be in the great hall of the palace, and a friend of mine has promised me a place at one of the windows which overlook it, so that we can see the whole;' and the Princess, feeling as if she were in a dream, rose up to accompany the old woman, her balls and her precious nut in her pocket.

"They made their way through the crowd and placed themselves at the window, as the old woman had said. The Princess looked down at the great hall below, all magnificently decorated and already filled with spectators. Suddenly the trumpet sounded, and the Prince in whose honour was all the rejoicing entered. At sight of him—her own Prince indeed, but looking so strangely pale and sad that she would hardly have recognised him—the Princess could not restrain a little cry.

"'What is it?' said the old woman.

"'A passer-by trod on my foot,' said the Princess, fearful of attracting attention. And the old woman said no more, for at this moment another blast of trumpets announced the arrival of the princesses, who were to make the trial of the balls. The first was tall and dark, with raven tresses and brilliant, flashing eyes. She was dressed in a robe of rich maize colour, and as she took her place on the dais she looked round her, as if to say, 'Who can compete with me in beauty or in skill?' And she was the Princess of the south.

"The second was also tall, and her hair was of a deep rich brown, and her eyes were sparkling and her cheeks rosy. She was dressed in bright pink, and laughed as she came forward, as if sure of herself and her attractions. And she was the Princess of the east.

"The third moved slowly, and as if she cared little what was thought of her, so confident was she of her pre-eminence. She wore a blue robe, and her face was pale and her eyes cold, though beautiful. And her hair had a reddish tinge, but yet she too was beautiful. And she was the Princess of the west.

"The Prince bowed low to each, but no smile lit up his grave face, and his glance rested but an instant on each fair Princess as she approached.

"'Are these ladies all?' he asked, in a low voice, as if expecting yet more. And when the answer came, 'Yes, these are all,' a still deeper melancholy settled on his face, and he seemed indifferent to all about him.

"Then the trial began. The Prince had three golden balls, one of which he offered to each Princess. They took them, and each threw one back to him. Then one after another, as quick as lightning, he threw all three to the yellow Princess. She caught them all and threw them back; again he returned them, but the first only, reached her hand, the second and third fell to the ground, and with another low bow the Prince turned from her, and her proud face grew scarlet with anger. The pink Princess fared no better. She was laughing so, as if to show her confidence, that she missed the third ball, even at the first throw, and when the Prince turned also from her she laughed again, though this time her laughter was not all mirth. Then the cold blue Princess came forward. She caught the balls better, but at the third throw, one of them rising higher than the others, she would not trouble herself to stretch her arm out farther, so it fell to the ground, and as the Prince turned from her likewise, a great silence came over the crowd.

"Suddenly a cry arose. 'A fourth Princess,' the people shouted, and the old woman up at the window was so eager to see the new-comer that she did not notice that her companion had disappeared. She had watched the failure of the two first Princesses, then seeing what was coming she had quietly made her way through the crowd to a hidden corner behind the great pillars of the hall. There, her hands trembling with eagerness, she drew forth from the magic nut, which she had cracked with her pretty teeth, a wonderful fairy robe of spotless white. In an instant her black dress was thrown to her feet, and the white garment, which fitted her as if by magic, had taken its place. Never was Princess dressed in such a hurry, but never was toilette more successful. And as the cry arose of 'A fourth Princess' she made her way up the hall. From one end to the other she came, rapidly making her way through the crowd, which cleared before her in surprise and admiration, for as she walked she threw before her, catching them ever as she went, her golden balls. Her fair hair floated on her shoulders, her white robe gleamed like snow, her sweet face, flushed with hope and eagerness, was like that of a happy child, her eyes saw nothing but the one figure standing at the far end of the hall, the figure of the Prince, who, as the cry reached his ears, started forward with a hope he hardly dared encourage, holding out his hands as she came nearer and yet nearer in joyfulness of welcome.

"But she waved him back—then, taking her place where the other Princees had stood, she threw her balls, one, two, three; in an instant they were caught by the Prince, and returned to her like flashes of lightning over and over again, never failing, never falling, as if attached by invisible cords, till at last a great cry arose from the crowds, and the Prince led forward, full in the view of the people, his beautiful bride, his true Princess.

"Then all her troubles were forgotten, and every one rejoiced, save perhaps the three unsuccessful Princesses, who consoled themselves by saying there was magic in it, and so possibly there was. But there is more than one kind of magic, and some kinds, it is to be hoped, the world will never be without. And messengers were sent to summon to the wedding the father and mother of the Princess, who all this time had been in doubt and anxiety as to the fate of their dear child. And the kind old woman who had sheltered her in her poverty and distress was not forgotten."

The voice stopped—for a minute or two the children sat silent, not sure if they were to hear anything else. Strangely enough, as the story went on, it seemed more and more as if it were Marcelline's voice[5] that was telling it, and at last Hugh looked up to see if it was still the white lady, whose knee his head was resting on. Jeanne too looked up at the same moment, and both children gave a little cry of surprise. The white lady had disappeared, and it was indeed Marcelline who was in her place. The white room, the white chairs, the white cats, the spinning-wheel, and the pointed windows, had all gone, and instead there was old Marcelline with her knitting-needles gently clicking in a regular way, that somehow to Hugh seemed mixed up with his remembrance of the soft whirr of the wheel, her neatly frilled cap round her face, and her bright dark eyes smiling down at the children. Hugh felt so sorry and disappointed that he shut his eyes tight and tried to go on dreaming, if indeed dreaming it was. But it was no use. He leant his face against Marcelline's soft white apron and tried to fancy it the fairy lady's fairy robe; but it was no use. He had to sit up and look about him.

"Well," said Marcelline, "and didn't you like the story?"

Hugh looked at Jeanne. It couldn't be a dream then—there *had* been a story, for if he had been asleep, of course he couldn't have heard it. He said nothing, however—he waited to see what Jeanne would say. Jeanne tossed back her head impatiently.

"Of course I liked it," she said. "It's a beautiful story. But, Marcelline, how did you turn into yourself—*was* it you all the time? Why didn't you leave us with the white lady?"

Hugh was so pleased at what Jeanne said that he didn't mind a bit about Marcelline having taken the place of the white lady. Jeanne was the same as he was—that was all he cared about. He jumped up eagerly—they were in Jeanne's room, close to the fire, and both Jeanne and he had their little red flannel dressing-gowns on.

"How did these come here?" he said, touching the sleeve of his own one.

"Yes," said Jeanne. "And where are our wings, if you please, Mrs. Marcelline?"

Marcelline only smiled.

"I went to fetch you," she said, "and of course I didn't want you to catch cold on the way back."

But that was *all* they could get her to say, and then she carried them off to bed, and they both slept soundly till morning.

5. **Marcelline's voice** the children's nurse presumably has been nearby all during their sleep

JULIANA HORATIA EWING

Amelia and the Dwarfs

My godmother's grandmother knew a good deal about the fairies. *Her* grandmother had seen a fairy rade[1] on a Roodmas Eve,[2] and she herself could remember a copper vessel of a queer shape which had been left by the elves on some occasion at an old farm-house among the hills. The following story came from her, and where she got it I do not know. She used to say it was a pleasant tale, with a good moral in the inside of it. My godmother often observed that a tale without a moral was like a nut without a kernel, not worth the cracking. (We called fireside stories "cracks" in our part of the country.) This is the tale.

AMELIA

A couple of gentlefolk once lived in a certain part of England. (My godmother never would tell me the name either of the place or the people, even if she knew it. She said one ought not to expose one's neighbors' failings more than there was due occasion for.) They had an only child, a daughter, whose name was Amelia. They were an easy-going, good-humored couple; "rather soft," my godmother said, but she was apt to think anybody "soft" who came from the southern shires, as these people did. Amelia, who had been born farther north, was by no means so. She had a strong, resolute will, and a clever head of her own, though she was but a child. She had a

---

"Amelia and the Dwarfs" first appeared in two installments in the February and March 1870 issues of *Aunt Judy's Magazine;* the story was reprinted in the same year in *The Brownies and Other Tales.*

1. **rade** revels
2. **Roodmas Eve** the evening before the holiday celebrating the exaltation of the Cross (September 14)

way of her own too, and had it very completely. Perhaps because she was an only child, or perhaps because they were so easy-going, her parents spoiled her. She was, beyond question, the most tiresome little girl in that or any other neighborhood. From her baby days her father and mother had taken every opportunity of showing her to their friends, and there was not a friend who did not dread the infliction. When the good lady visited her acquaintances, she always took Amelia with her, and if the acquaintances were fortunate enough to see from the windows who was coming, they used to snatch up any delicate knick-knacks, or brittle ornaments lying about, and put them away, crying, "What is to be done? Here comes Amelia!"

When Amelia came in, she would stand and survey the room, whilst her mother saluted her acquaintance; and if anything struck her fancy, she would interrupt the greetings to draw her mother's attention to it, with a twitch of her shawl, "Oh, look, mamma, at that funny bird in the glass case!" or perhaps, "Mamma, mamma! There's a new carpet since we were here last;" for, as her mother said, she was "a very observing child."

Then she would wander round the room, examining and fingering everything, and occasionally coming back with something in her hand to tread on her mother's dress, and break in upon the ladies' conversation with— "Mamma! mamma! What's the good of keeping this old basin? It's been broken and mended, and some of the pieces are quite loose now. I can feel them:" or—addressing the lady of the house—"That's not a real ottoman in the corner. It's a box covered with chintz. I know, for I've looked."

Then her mamma would say, reprovingly, "My *dear* Amelia!"

And perhaps the lady of the house would beg, "Don't play with that old china, my love; for though it is mended, it is very valuable;" and her mother would add, "My dear Amelia, you must not."

Sometimes the good lady said, "You *must* not." Sometimes she tried— "You must *not*." When both these failed, and Amelia was balancing the china bowl on her finger ends, her mamma would get flurried, and when Amelia flurried her, she always rolled her r's, and emphasized her words, so that it sounded thus:

"My dear-r-r-r-Ramelia! You MUST NOT."

At which Amelia would not so much as look round, till perhaps the bowl slipped from her fingers, and was smashed into unmendable fragments. Then her mamma would exclaim, "Oh, dear-r-r-r, oh dear-r-Ramelia!" and the lady of the house would try to look as if it did not matter, and when Amelia and her mother departed, would pick up the bits, and pour out her complaints to her lady friends, most of whom had suffered many such damages at the hands of this "very observing child."

When the good couple received their friends at home, there was no escaping from Amelia. If it was a dinner party, she came in with the dessert, or perhaps sooner. She would take up her position near some one, generally the person most deeply engaged in conversation, and either lean heavily against him or her, or climb on to his or her knee, without being invited. She would break in upon the most interesting discussion with her own little childish affairs, in the following style—

"I've been out to-day. I walked to the town. I jumped across three brooks. Can you jump? Papa gave me sixpence to-day. I am saving up my money to be rich. You may cut me an orange; no, I'll take it to Mr. Brown, he peels it with a spoon and turns the skin back. Mr. Brown! Mr. Brown! Don't talk to mamma, but peel me an orange, please. Mr. Brown! I'm playing with your finger-glass."

And when the finger-glass full of cold water had been upset on to Mr. Brown's shirt-front, Amelia's mamma would cry—"Oh dear, oh dear-r-Ramelia!" and carry her off with the ladies to the drawing-room.

Here she would scramble on to the ladies' knees, or trample out the gathers of their dresses, and fidget with their ornaments, startling some luckless lady by the announcement "I've got your bracelet undone at last!" who would find one of the divisions broken open by force, Amelia not understanding the working of a clasp.

Or perhaps two young lady friends would get into a quiet corner for a chat. The observing child was sure to spy them, and run on to them, crushing their flowers and ribbons, and crying—"You two want to talk secrets, I know. I can hear what you say. I'm going to listen, I am. And I shall tell, too." When perhaps a knock at the door announced the nurse to take Miss Amelia to bed, and spread a general rapture of relief.

Then Amelia would run to trample and worry her mother, and after much teasing, and clinging, and complaining, the nurse would be dismissed, and the fond mamma would turn to the lady next to her, and say with a smile—"I suppose I must let her stay up a little. It is such a treat to her, poor child!"

But it was no treat to the visitors.

Besides tormenting her fellow-creatures, Amelia had a trick of teasing animals. She was really fond of dogs, but she was still fonder of doing what she was wanted not to do, and of worrying everything and everybody about her. So she used to tread on the tips of their tails, and pretend to give them biscuit, and then hit them on the nose, besides pulling at those few, long, sensitive hairs which thin-skinned dogs wear on the upper lip.

Now Amelia's mother's acquaintances were so very well-bred and amiable, that they never spoke their minds to either the mother or the daughter about what they endured from the latter's rudeness, wilfulness, and powers of destruction. But this was not the case with the dogs, and they expressed their sentiments by many a growl and snap. At last one day Amelia was tormenting a snow-white bull-dog (who was certainly as well-bred and as amiable as any living creature in the kingdom), and she did not see that even his patience was becoming worn out. His pink nose became crimson with increased irritation, his upper lip twitched over his teeth, behind which he was rolling as many warning Rs as Amelia's mother herself. She finally held out a bun towards him, and just as he was about to take it, she snatched it away and kicked him instead. This fairly exasperated the bull-dog, and as Amelia would not let him bite the bun, he bit Amelia's leg.

Her mamma was so distressed that she fell into hysterics, and hardly knew what she was saying. She said the bull-dog must be shot for fear he should go mad, and Amelia's wound must be done with a red-hot poker for fear *she* should go mad (with hydrophobia).[3] And as of course she couldn't bear the pain of this, she must have chloroform, and she would most probably die of that; for as one in several thousands dies annually under chloroform, it was evident that her chance of life was very small indeed.[4] So, as the poor lady said, "Whether we shoot Amelia and burn the bull-dog—at least I mean shoot the bull-dog and burn Amelia with a red-hot poker—or leave it alone; and whether Amelia or the bull-dog has chloroform or bears it without—it seems to be death or madness everyway!"

And as the doctor did not come fast enough, she ran out without her bonnet to meet him, and Amelia's papa, who was very much distressed too, ran after her with her bonnet. Meanwhile the doctor came in by another way, found Amelia sitting on the dining-room floor with the bull-dog, and crying bitterly. She was telling him that they wanted to shoot him, but that they should not, for it was all her fault and not his. But she did not tell him that she was to be burnt with a red-hot poker, for she thought it might hurt

3. **hydrophobia** rabies

4. **one . . . indeed** Chloroform was first introduced as an anesthetic in the 1840s. Margaret Gatty, Ewing's mother, had it administered to herself to set an example for people who remained as fearful (and ignorant) as Amelia's mother.

his feelings. And then she wept afresh, and kissed the bull-dog, and the bull-dog kissed her with his red tongue, and rubbed his pink nose against her, and beat his own tail much harder on the floor than Amelia had ever hit it. She said the same things to the doctor, but she told him also that she was willing to be burnt without chloroform if it must be done, and if they would spare the bull-dog. And though she looked very white, she meant what she said.

But the doctor looked at her leg, and found it was only a snap, and not a deep wound; and then he looked at the bull-dog, and saw that so far from looking mad, he looked a great deal more sensible than anybody in the house. So he only washed Amelia's leg and bound it up, and she was not burnt with the poker, neither did she get hydrophobia; but she had got a good lesson on manners, and thenceforward she always behaved with the utmost propriety to animals, though she tormented her mother's friends as much as ever.

Now although Amelia's mamma's acquaintances were too polite to complain before her face, they made up for it by what they said behind her back. In allusion to the poor lady's ineffectual remonstrances, one gentleman said that the more mischief Amelia did, the dearer she seemed to grow to her mother. And somebody else replied that however dear she might be as a daughter, she was certainly a very *dear* friend, and proposed that they should send in a bill for all the damage she had done in the course of the year, as a round robin to her parents at Christmas. From which it may be seen that Amelia was not popular with her parents' friends, as (to do grown-up people justice) good children almost invariably are.

If she was not a favorite in the drawing-room, she was still less so in the nursery, where, besides all the hardships naturally belonging to attendance on a spoilt child, the poor nurse was kept, as she said, "on the continual go" by Amelia's reckless destruction of her clothes. It was not fair wear and tear, it was not an occasional fall in the mire, or an accidental rent or two during a game at "Hunt the Hare," but it was constant wilful destruction, which nurse had to repair as best she might. No entreaties would induce Amelia to "take care" of anything. She walked obstinately on the muddy side of the road when nurse pointed out the clean parts, kicking up the dirt with her feet; if she climbed a wall she never tried to free her dress if it had caught; on she rushed, and half a skirt might be left behind for any care she had in the matter. "They must be mended," or, "They must be washed," was all she thought about it.

"You seem to think things clean and mend themselves, Miss Amelia," said poor nurse one day.

"No, I don't," said Amelia, rudely. "I think you do them; what are you here for?"

But though she spoke in this insolent and unladylike fashion, Amelia really did not realize what the tasks were which her carelessness imposed on other people. When every hour of nurse's day had been spent in struggling to keep her wilful young lady regularly fed, decently dressed, and moderately well-behaved (except, indeed, those hours when her mother was fighting the same battle downstairs); and when at last, after the hardest struggle of all, she had been got to bed not more than two hours later than her appointed time, even then there was no rest for nurse. Amelia's mamma could at least lean back in her chair and have a quiet chat with her husband, which was not broken in upon every two minutes, and Amelia herself was asleep; but nurse must sit up for hours wearing out her eyes by the light of a tallow candle,[5] in fine-darning great, jagged and most unnecessary holes in Amelia's muslin dresses. Or perhaps she had to wash and iron clothes for Amelia's wear next day. For sometimes she was so very destructive, that toward the end of the week she had used up all her clothes and had no clean ones to fall back upon.

Amelia's meals were another source of trouble. She would not wear a pinafore; if it had been put on, she would burst the strings, and perhaps in throwing it away knock her plate of mutton broth over the tablecloth and her own dress. Then she fancied first one thing and then another; she did not like this or that; she wanted a bit cut here and there. Her mamma used to begin by saying, "My dear-r-r-Ramelia, you must not be so wasteful," and she used to end by saying, "The dear child has positively no appetite;" which seemed to be a good reason for not wasting any more food upon her; but with Amelia's mamma it only meant that she might try a little cutlet and tomato sauce when she had half finished her roast beef, and that most of the cutlet and all the mashed potato might be exchanged for plum tart and custard; and that when she had spooned up the custard and played with the paste, and put the plum stones on the tablecloth, she might be tempted with a little Stilton cheese and celery, and exchange that for anything that caught her fancy in the dessert dishes.

The nurse used to say, "Many a poor child would thank God for what you waste every meal time, Miss Amelia," and to quote a certain good old say-

---

5. **tallow candle** candles made out of animal fat were inferior to wax candles

ing, "Waste not want not." But Amelia's mamma allowed her to send away on her plates what would have fed another child, day after day.

UNDER THE HAYCOCKS

It was summer, and haytime. Amelia had been constantly in the hayfield, and the haymakers had constantly wished that she had been anywhere else. She mislaid the rakes, nearly killed herself and several other persons with a fork, and overturned one haycock[6] after another as fast as they were made. At tea time it was hoped that she would depart, but she teased her mamma to have tea brought into the field, and her mamma said, "The poor child must have a treat sometimes," and so it was brought out.

After this she fell off the haycart, and was a good deal shaken, but not hurt. So she was taken indoors, and the haymakers worked hard and cleared the field, all but a few cocks which were left till the morning.

The sun set, the dew fell, the moon rose. It was a lovely night. Amelia peeped from behind the blinds of the drawing-room windows, and saw four haycocks, each with a deep shadow reposing at its side. The rest of the field was swept clean, and looked pale in the moonshine. It was a lovely night.

"I want to go out," said Amelia. "They will take away those cocks before I can get at them in the morning, and there will be no more jumping and tumbling. I shall go out and have some fun now."

"My dear Amelia, you must not," said her mamma; and her papa added, "I won't hear of it." So Amelia went upstairs to grumble to nurse; but nurse only said, "Now, my dear Miss Amelia, do go quietly to bed, like a dear love. The field is all wet with dew. Besides, it's a moonlight night, and who knows what's abroad? You might see the fairies—bless us and sain us![7]—and what not. There's been a magpie hopping up and down near the house all day, and that's a sign of ill luck."

"I don't care for magpies," said Amelia; "I threw a stone at that one to-day."

And she left the nursery, and swung downstairs on the rail of the banisters. But she did not go into the drawing-room; she opened the front door and went out into the moonshine.

It was a lovely night. But there was something strange about it. Everything looked asleep, and yet seemed not only awake but watching. There was not a sound, and yet the air seemed full of half sounds. The child was

6. **haycocks** conical stacks of hay
7. **sain** making the sign of the cross to ward off evil influences

quite alone, and yet at every step she fancied some one behind her, on one side of her, somewhere, and found it only a rustling leaf or a passing shadow. She was soon in the hayfield, where it was just the same; so that when she fancied that something green was moving near the first haycock she thought very little of it, till, coming closer, she plainly perceived by the moonlight a tiny man dressed in green, with a tall, pointed hat, and very, very long tips to his shoes, tying his shoestring with his foot on a stubble stalk. He had the most wizened of faces, and when he got angry with his shoe, he pulled so wry a grimace that it was quite laughable. At last he stood up, stepping carefully over the stubble, went up to the first haycock, and drawing out a hollow grass stalk blew upon it till his cheeks were puffed like footballs. And yet there was no sound, only a half-sound, as of a horn blown in the far distance, or in a dream. Presently the point of a tall hat, and finally just such another little weazened face poked out through the side of the haycock.

"Can we hold revel here to-night?" asked the little green man.

"That indeed you cannot," answered the other; "we have hardly room to turn round as it is, with all Amelia's dirty frocks."

"Ah, bah!" said the dwarf; and he walked on to the next haycock, Amelia cautiously following.

Here he blew again, and a head was put out as before; on which he said—

"Can we hold revel here to-night?"

"How is it possible?" was the reply, "when there is not a place where one can so much as set down an acorn cup, for Amelia's broken victuals."

"Fie! fie!" said the dwarf, and went on to the third, where all happened as before; and he asked the old question—

"Can we hold revel here to-night?"

"Can you dance on glass and crockery sherds?" inquired the other. "Amelia's broken gimcracks are everywhere."

"Pshaw!" snorted the dwarf, frowning terribly; and when he came to the fourth haycock he blew such an angry blast that the grass stalk split into seven pieces. But he met with no better success than before. Only the point of a hat came through the hay, and a feeble voice piped in tones of depression—"The broken threads[8] would entangle our feet. It's all Amelia's fault. If we could only get hold of her!"

"If she's wise, she'll keep as far from these haycocks as she can," snarled the dwarf, angrily; and he shook his fist as much as to say, "If she did come, I should not receive her very pleasantly."

---

8. **threads** their source will become evident later in the story

Now with Amelia, to hear that she had better not do something, was to make her wish at once to do it; and as she was not at all wanting in courage, she pulled the dwarf's little cloak, just as she would have twitched her mother's shawl, and said (with that sort of snarly whine in which spoilt children generally speak), "Why shouldn't I come to the haycocks if I want to? They belong to my papa, and I shall come if I like. But you have no business here."

"Nightshade and hemlock!"[9] ejaculated the little man, "you are not lacking in impudence. Perhaps your Sauciness is not quite aware how things are distributed in this world?" saying which he lifted his pointed shoes and began to dance and sing—

> "All under the sun belongs to men,
> And all under the moon to the fairies,
> So, so, so! Ho, ho, ho!
> All under the moon to the fairies."

As he sang "Ho, ho, ho!" the little man turned head over heels; and though by this time Amelia would gladly have got away, she could not, for the dwarf seemed to dance and tumble round her, and always to cut off the chance of escape; whilst numberless voices from all around seemed to join in the chorus, with—

> "So, so, so! Ho, ho, ho!
> All under the moon to the fairies."

"And now," said the little man, "to work! And you have plenty of work before you, so trip on, to the first haycock."

"I shan't!" said Amelia.

"On with you!" repeated the dwarf.

"I won't!" said Amelia.

But the little man, who was behind her, pinched her funny-bone with his lean fingers, and, as everybody knows, that is agony; so Amelia ran on, and tried to get away. But when she went too fast, the dwarf trod on her heels with his long-pointed shoe, and if she did not go fast enough, he pinched her funny-bone. So for once in her life she was obliged to do as she was told. As they ran, tall hats and wizened faces were popped out on all sides of the haycocks, like blanched almonds on a tipsy cake; and whenever the dwarf

9. **hemlock** both nightshade and hemlock are highly poisonous plants but also can be used medicinally as strong sedatives or narcotics

pinched Amelia, or trod on her heels, they cried "Ho, ho, ho!" with such horrible contortions as they laughed, that it was hideous to behold.

"Here is Amelia!" shouted the dwarf when they reached the first hay-cock.

"Ho, ho, ho!" laughed all the others, as they poked out here and there from the hay.

"Bring a stock," [10] said the dwarf; on which the hay was lifted, and out ran six or seven dwarfs, carrying what seemed to Amelia to be a little girl like herself. And when she looked closer, to her horror and surprise the figure was exactly like her—it was her own face, clothes, and everything.

"Shall we kick it into the house?" said the goblins.

"No," said the dwarf; "lay it down by the haycock. The father and mother are coming to seek her now."

When Amelia heard this she began to shriek for help; but she was pushed into the haycock, where her loudest cries sounded like the chirruping of a grasshopper.

It was really a fine sight to see the inside of the cock.

Farmers do not like to see flowers in a hayfield, but the fairies do. They had arranged all the buttercups, &c., in patterns on the haywalls; bunches of meadowsweet swung from the roof like censers, [11] and perfumed the air; and the ox-eye daisies which formed the ceiling gave a light like stars. But Amelia cared for none of this. She only struggled to peep through the hay, and she did see her father and mother and nurse come down the lawn, fol-lowed by the other servants, looking for her. When they saw the stock they ran to raise it with exclamations of pity and surprise. The stock moaned faintly, and Amelia's mamma wept, and Amelia herself shouted with all her might.

"What's that?" said her mamma. (It is not easy to deceive a mother.)

"Only the grasshoppers, my dear," said papa. "Let us get the poor child home."

The stock moaned again, and the mother said, "Oh dear! Oh dear-r-Ramelia!" and followed in tears.

"Rub her eyes," said the dwarf; on which Amelia's eyes were rubbed with some ointment, and when she took a last peep, she could see that the stock

10. **stock** a primordial shape that can assume a living form; since the word is derived from "stump" or "tree trunk," it is also used to describe a senseless person as well as a wooden idol

11. **censers** receptacles for perfume or incense

was nothing but a hairy imp with a face like the oldest and most grotesque of apes. [12]

"—— and send her below;" said the dwarf. On which the field opened, and Amelia was pushed underground.

She found herself on a sort of open heath, where no houses were to be seen. Of course there was no moonshine, and yet it was neither daylight nor dark. There was as the light of early dawn, and every sound was at once clear and dreamy, like the first sounds of the day coming through the fresh air before sunrise. Beautiful flowers crept over the heath, whose tints were constantly changing in the subdued light; and as the hues changed and blended, the flowers gave forth different perfumes. All would have been charming but that at every few paces the paths were blocked by large clothes-baskets full of dirty frocks. And the frocks were Amelia's. Torn, draggled, wet, covered with sand, mud, and dirt of all kinds, Amelia recognized them.

"You've got to wash them all," said the dwarf, who was behind her as usual; "that's what you've come down for—not because your society is particularly pleasant. So the sooner you begin the better."

"I can't," said Amelia (she had already learnt that "I won't" is not an answer for every one); "send them up to nurse, and she'll do them. It is her business."

"What nurse can do she has done, and now it's time for you to begin," said the dwarf. "Sooner or later the mischief done by spoilt children's wilful disobedience comes back on their own hands. Up to a certain point we help them, for we love children, and we are wilful ourselves. But there are limits to everything. If you can't wash your dirty frocks, it is time you learnt to do so, if only that you may know what the trouble is you impose on other people. *She* will teach you."

The dwarf kicked out his foot in front of him, and pointed with his long toe to a woman who sat by a fire made upon the heath, where a pot was suspended from crossed poles. It was like a bit of a gipsy encampment, and the woman seemed to be a real woman, not a fairy—which was the case, as Amelia afterwards found. She had lived underground for many years, and was the dwarfs' servant.

And this was how it came about that Amelia had to wash her dirty frocks.

12. **apes** In *The Origin of Species* Darwin noted: "In the case of strongly marked races [there is evidence] that all are descended from a single wild stock."

Let any little girl try to wash one of her dresses; not to half wash it, not to leave it stained with dirty water, but to wash it quite clean. Let her then try to starch and iron it—in short, to make it look as if it had come from the laundress—and she will have some idea of what poor Amelia had to learn to do. There was no help for it. When she was working she very seldom saw the dwarfs; but if she were idle or stubborn, or had any hopes of getting away, one was sure to start up at her elbow and pinch her funny-bone, or poke her in the ribs, till she did her best. Her back ached with stooping over the wash-tub; her hands and arms grew wrinkled with soaking in hot soap-suds, and sore with rubbing. Whatever she did not know how to do, the woman of the heath taught her. At first, whilst Amelia was sulky, the woman of the heath was sharp and cross; but when Amelia became willing and obedient, she was good-natured, and even helped her.

The first time that Amelia felt hungry she asked for some food.

"By all means," said one of the dwarfs; "there is plenty down here which belongs to you;" and he led her away till they came to a place like the first, except that it was covered with plates of broken meats; all the bits of good meat, pie, pudding, bread and butter, &c., that Amelia had wasted before-time.

"I can't eat cold scraps like these," said Amelia turning away.

"Then what did you ask for food for before you were hungry?" screamed the dwarf, and he pinched her and sent her about her business.

After a while she became so famished that she was glad to beg humbly to be allowed to go for food; and she ate a cold chop and the remains of a rice pudding with thankfulness. How delicious they tasted! She was surprised herself at the good things she had rejected. After a time she fancied she would like to warm up some of the cold meat in a pan, which the woman of the heath used to cook her own dinner in, and she asked for leave to do so.

"You may do anything you like to make yourself comfortable, if you do it yourself," said she; and Amelia, who had been watching her for many times, became quite expert in cooking up the scraps.

As there was no real daylight underground, so also there was no night. When the old woman was tired she lay down and had a nap, and when she thought that Amelia had earned a rest, she allowed her to do the same. It was never cold, and it never rained, so they slept on the heath among the flowers.

They say that "It's a long lane that has no turning," and the hardest tasks come to an end some time, and Amelia's dresses were clean at last; but then a more wearisome work was before her. They had to be mended. Amelia

Amelia and the Dwarfs

looked at the jagged rents made by the hedges; the great gaping holes in front where she had put her foot through; the torn tucks and gathers. First she wept, then she bitterly regretted that she had so often refused to do her sewing at home that she was very awkward with her needle. Whether she ever would have got through this task alone is doubtful, but she had by this time become so well-behaved and willing that the old woman was kind to her, and, pitying her blundering attempts, she helped her a great deal; whilst Amelia would cook the old woman's victuals, or repeat stories and pieces of poetry to amuse her.

"How glad I am that I ever learnt anything!" thought the poor child; "everything one learns seems to come in useful some time."

At last the dresses were finished.

"Do you think I shall be allowed to go home now?" Amelia asked of the woman of the heath.

"Not yet," said she; "you have got to mend the broken gimcracks next."

"But when I have done all my tasks," Amelia said; "will they let me go then?"

"That depends," said the woman, and she sat silent over the fire; but Amelia wept so bitterly, that she pitied her and said—"Only dry your eyes, for the fairies hate tears, and I will tell you all I know and do the best for you I can. You see, when you first came you were—excuse me!—such an unlicked cub; such a peevish, selfish, wilful, useless, and ill-mannered little miss, that neither the fairies nor anybody else were likely to keep you any longer than necessary. But now you are such a willing, handy, and civil little thing, and so pretty and graceful withal, that I think it is very likely that they will want to keep you altogether. I think you had better make up your mind to it. They are kindly little folk, and will make a pet of you in the end."

"Oh, no, no!" moaned poor Amelia; "I want to be with my mother, my poor dear mother! I want to make up for being a bad child so long. Besides, surely that 'stock,' as they called her, will want to come back to her own people."

"As to that," said the woman, "after a time the stock will affect mortal illness, and will then take possession of the first black cat she sees, and in that shape leave the house, and come home. But the figure that is like you will remain lifeless in the bed, and will be duly buried. Then your people, believing you to be dead, will never look for you, and you will always remain here. However, as this distresses you so, I will give you some advice. Can you dance?"

"Yes," said Amelia; "I did attend pretty well to my dancing lessons. I was considered rather clever about it."

"At any spare moments you find," continued the woman, "dance, dance all your dances, and as well as you can. The dwarfs love dancing."

"And then?" said Amelia.

"Then, perhaps some night they will take you up to dance with them in the meadows above ground."

"But I could not get away. They would tread on my heels—oh! I could never escape them."

"I know that," said the woman; "your only chance is this. If ever, when dancing in the meadows, you can find a four-leaved clover, hold it in your hand and wish to be at home. Then no one can stop you. Meanwhile I advise you to seem happy, that they may think you are content, and have forgotten the world. And dance, above all, dance!"

And Amelia, not to be behindhand, began then and there to dance some pretty figures on the heath. As she was dancing the dwarf came by.

"Ho, ho!" said he, "you can dance, can you?"

"When I am happy, I can," said Amelia, performing several graceful movements as she spoke.

"What are you pleased about now?" snapped the dwarf, suspiciously.

"Have I not reason?" said Amelia. "The dresses are washed and mended."

"Then up with them!" returned the dwarf. On which half a dozen elves popped the whole lot into a big basket and kicked them up into the world, where they found their way to the right wardrobes somehow.

As the woman of the heath had said, Amelia was soon set to a new task. When she bade the old woman farewell, she asked if she could do nothing for her if ever she got at liberty herself.

"Can I do nothing to get you back to your old home?" Amelia cried, for she thought of others now as well as herself.

"No, thank you," returned the old woman; "I am used to this, and do not care to return. I have been here a long time—how long I do not know; for as there is neither daylight nor dark we have no measure of time—long, I am sure, very long. The light and noise up yonder would now be too much for me. But I wish you well, and, above all, remember to dance!"

The new scene of Amelia's labors was a more rocky part of the heath, where grey granite boulders served for seats and tables, and sometimes for workshops and anvils, as in one place, where a grotesque and grimy old dwarf sat forging rivets to mend china and glass. A fire in the hollow of the boulder served for a forge, and on the flatter part was his anvil. The rocks were covered in all directions with the knick-knacks, ornaments, &c., that Amelia had at various times destroyed.

"If you please, sir," she said to the dwarf, "I am Amelia."

The dwarf left off blowing at his forge and looked at her.

"Then I wonder you're not ashamed of yourself," said he.

"I am ashamed of myself," said poor Amelia, "very much ashamed. I should like to mend these things if I can."

"Well, you can't say more than that," said the dwarf, in a mollified tone, for he was a kindly little creature; "bring that china bowl here, and I'll show you how to set to work."

Poor Amelia did not get on very fast, but she tried her best. As to the dwarf, it was truly wonderful to see how he worked. Things seemed to mend themselves at his touch, and he was so proud of his skill, and so particular, that he generally did over again the things which Amelia had done after her fashion. The first time he gave her a few minutes in which to rest and amuse herself, she held out her little skirt, and began one of her prettiest dances.

"Rivets and trivets!" shrieked the little man, "How you dance! It is charming! I say it is charming! On with you! Fa, la fa! La, fa la! It gives me the fidgets in my shoe points to see you!" and forthwith down he jumped, and began capering about.

"I am a good dancer myself," said the little man. "Do you know the 'Hop, Skip, and a Jump' dance?"

"I do not think I do," said Amelia.

"It is much admired," said the dwarf, "when I dance it;" and he thereupon tucked up the little leathern apron in which he worked, and performed some curious antics on one leg.

"That is the Hop," he observed, pausing for a moment. "The Skip is thus. You throw out your left leg as high and as far as you can, and as you drop on the toe of your left foot you fling out the right leg in the same manner, and so on. This is the Jump," with which he turned a somersault and disappeared from view. When Amelia next saw him he was sitting cross legged on his boulder.

"Good, wasn't it?" he said.

"Wonderful!" Amelia replied.

"Now it's your turn again," said the dwarf.

But Amelia cunningly replied—"I'm afraid I must go on with my work."

"Pshaw!" said the little tinker. "Give me your work. I can do more in a minute than you in a month, and better to boot. Now dance again."

"Do you know this?" said Amelia, and she danced a few paces of a polka mazurka. [13]

"Admirable!" cried the little man. "Stay"—and he drew an old violin from behind the rock; "now dance again, and mark the time well, so that I may catch the measure, and then I will accompany you."

Which accordingly he did, improvising a very spirited tune, which had, however, the peculiar subdued and weird effect of all the other sounds in this strange region.

"The fiddle came from up yonder," said the little man. "It was smashed to atoms in the world and thrown away. But ho, ho, ho! There is nothing that I cannot mend, and a mended fiddle is an amended fiddle. It improves the tone. Now teach me that dance, and I will patch up all the rest of the gimcracks. Is it a bargain?"

"By all means," said Amelia; and she began to explain the dance to the best of her ability.

"Charming! charming!" cried the dwarf. "We have no such dance ourselves. We only dance hand in hand, and round and round, when we dance together. Now I will learn the step, and then I will put my arm round your waist and dance with you."

Amelia looked at the dwarf. He was very smutty, [14] and old, and weazened. Truly, a queer partner! But "handsome is that handsome does;" and he had done her a good turn. So when he had learnt the step, he put his arm round Amelia's waist and they danced together. His shoe points were very much in the way, but otherwise he danced very well.

Then he set to work on the broken ornaments, and they were all very soon "as good as new." But they were not kicked up into the world, for, as the dwarfs said, they would be sure to break on the road. So they kept them and used them; and I fear that no benefit came from the little tinker's skill to Amelia's mamma's acquaintance in this matter.

"Have I any other tasks?" Amelia inquired.

"One more," said the dwarfs; and she was led farther on to a smooth mossy green, thickly covered with what looked like bits of broken thread.

13. **polka mazurka** a lively Polish dance, popular in England since the 1830s
14. **smutty** soiled, rather than obscene

One would think it had been a milliner's work-room from the first invention of needles and thread.

"What are these?" Amelia asked.

"They are the broken threads of all the conversations you have interrupted," was the reply; "and pretty dangerous work it is to dance here now, with threads getting round one's shoe points. Dance a hornpipe in a herringnet, and you'll know what it is!"

Amelia began to pick up the threads, but it was tedious work. She had cleared a yard or two, and her back was aching terribly, when she heard the fiddle and the mazurka behind her; and looking round she saw the old dwarf, who was playing away, and making the most hideous grimaces as his chin pressed the violin.

"Dance, my lady, dance!" he shouted.

"I do not think I can," said Amelia; "I am so weary with stooping over my work."

"Then rest a few minutes," he answered, "and I will play you a jig. A jig is a beautiful dance, such life, such spirit! So!"

And he played faster and faster, his arm, his face, his fiddle-bow all seemed working together; and as he played, the threads danced themselves into three heaps.

"That is not bad, is it?" said the dwarf; "and now for our own dance," and he played the mazurka. "Get the measure well into your head. "Lâ, la fã lâ! Lâ, la fã lâ! So!"

And throwing away his fiddle, he caught Amelia round the waist, and they danced as before. After which, she had no difficulty in putting the three heaps of thread into a basket.

"Where are these to be kicked to?" asked the young goblins.

"To the four winds of heaven," said the old dwarf. "There are very few drawing room conversations worth putting together a second time. They are not like old china bowls."

BY MOONLIGHT

Thus Amelia's tasks were ended; but not a word was said of her return home. The dwarfs were now very kind, and made so much of her that it was evident that they meant her to remain with them. Amelia often cooked for them, and she danced and played with them, and never showed a sign of discontent; but her heart ached for home, and when she was alone she would bury her face in the flowers and cry for her mother.

One day she overheard the dwarfs in consultation.

"The moon is full to-morrow," said one—("Then I have been a month down here," thought Amelia; "it was full moon that night")—"shall we dance in the Mary Meads?"

"By all means," said the old tinker dwarf; "and we will take Amelia, and dance my dance."

"Is it safe?" said another.

"Look how content she is," said the old dwarf, "and, oh! how she dances; my feet tickle at the bare thought."

"The ordinary run of mortals do not see us," continued the objector; "but she is visible to any one. And there are men and women who wander in the moonlight, and the Mary Meads[15] are near her old home."

"I will make her a hat of touchwood,"[16] said the old dwarf, "so that even if she is seen it will look like a will-o'-the-wisp [17] bobbing up and down. If she does not come, I will not. I must dance my dance. You do not know what it is! We two alone move together with a grace which even here is remarkable. But when I think that up yonder we shall have attendant shadows echoing our movements, I long for the moment to arrive."

"So be it," said the others; and Amelia wore the touchwood hat, and went up with them to the Mary Meads.

Amelia and the dwarf danced the mazurka, and their shadows, now as short as themselves, then long and gigantic, danced beside them. As the moon went down, and the shadows lengthened, the dwarf was in raptures.

"When one sees how colossal one's very shadow is," he remarked, "one knows one's true worth. You also have a good shadow. We are partners in the dance, and I think we will be partners for life. But I have not fully considered the matter, so this is not to be regarded as a formal proposal." And he continued to dance, singing, "Lâ, la fã, lâ, lâ, la, fã, lâ." It was highly admired.

The Mary Meads lay a little below the house where Amelia's parents lived, and once during the night her father, who was watching by the sick bed of the stock, looked out of the window.

"How lovely the moonlight is!" he murmured; "but, dear me! there is a

15. **Mary Meads** meadowlands, perhaps an earlier site for the festival of Virgin Mary

16. **touchwood** kindling material made out of either rotting wood or dried mushrooms

17. **will-o'-the-wisp** *ignis fatuus,* a light seen in swamps or damp marshes, probably caused by the gaseous combustion of rotting organisms

will-o'-the-wisp yonder. I had no idea the Mary Meads were so damp." Then he pulled the blind down and went back into the room.

As for poor Amelia, she found no four-leaved clover, and at cockcrow they all went underground.

"We will dance on Hunch Hill to-morrow," said the dwarfs.

All went as before; not a clover plant of any kind did Amelia see, and at cockcrow the revel broke up.

On the following night they danced in the hayfield. The old stubble was now almost hidden by green clover. There was a grand fairy dance—a round dance, which does not mean, as with us, a dance for two partners, but a dance where all join hands and dance round and round in a circle with appropriate antics. Round they went, faster and faster, the pointed shoes now meeting in the centre like the spokes of a wheel, now kicked out behind like spikes, and then scamper, caper, hurry! They seemed to fly, when suddenly the ring broke at one corner, and nothing being stronger than its weakest point, the whole circle were sent flying over the field.

"Ho, ho, ho!" laughed the dwarfs, for they are good humored little folk, and do not mind a tumble.

"Ha, ha, ha!" laughed Amelia, for she had fallen with her fingers on a four-leaved clover.

She put it behind her back, for the old tinker dwarf was coming up to her, wiping the mud from his face with his leathern apron.

"Now for our dance!" he shrieked. "And I have made up my mind—partners now and partners always. You are incomparable. For three hundred years I have not met with your equal."

But Amelia held the four-leaved clover above her head, and cried from her very heart—"I want to go home!"

The dwarf gave a hideous yell of disappointment, and at this instant the stock came stumbling head over heels into the midst, crying—"Oh! the pills, the powders, and the draughts! oh, the lotions and embrocations! oh, the blisters, the poultices, and the plasters! men may well be so short-lived!"

And Amelia found herself in bed in her own home.

AT HOME AGAIN

By the side of Amelia's bed stood a little table, on which were so many big bottles of medicine, that Amelia smiled to think of all the stock must have had to swallow during the month past. There was an open Bible on it too, in which Amelia's mother was reading, whilst tears trickled slowly down her pale cheeks. The poor lady looked so thin and ill, so worn with sorrow and watching, that Amelia's heart smote her, as if some one had given her a sharp blow.

"Mamma, mamma! Mother, my dear, dear mother!"

The tender, humble, loving tone of voice was so unlike Amelia's old imperious snarl, that her mother hardly recognized it; and when she saw Amelia's eyes full of intelligence instead of the delirium of fever, and that (though older and thinner and rather pale) she looked wonderfully well, the poor worn-out lady could hardly restrain herself from falling into hysterics for very joy.

"Dear mamma, I want to tell you all about it," said Amelia, kissing the kind hand that stroked her brow.

But it appeared that the doctor had forbidden conversation; and though Amelia knew it would do her no harm, she yielded to her mother's wish and lay still and silent.

"Now, my love, it is time to take your medicine."

But Amelia pleaded—"Oh, mamma, indeed I don't want any medicine. I am quite well, and would like to get up."

"Ah, my dear child!" cried her mother, "what I have suffered in inducing you to take your medicine, and yet see what good it has done you."

"I hope you will never suffer any more from my wilfulness," said Amelia; and she swallowed two tablespoonfuls of a mixture labelled, "To be well shaken before taken," without even a wry face.

Presently the doctor came.

"You're not so very angry at the sight of me to-day my little lady, eh?" he said.

"I have not seen you for a long time," said Amelia "but I know you have been here, attending a stock who looked like me. If your eyes had been touched with fairy ointment, however, you would have been aware that it was a fairy imp, and a very ugly one, covered with hair. I have been living in terror lest it should go back underground in the shape of a black cat. However, thanks to the four-leaved clover, and the old woman of the heath, I am at home again."

On hearing this rhodomontade,[18] Amelia's mother burst into tears, for she thought the poor child was still raving with fever. But the doctor smiled pleasantly, and said—"Ay, ay, to be sure," with a little nod, as one should

18. **rhodomontade** boasting talk

say, "We know all about it;" and laid two fingers in a casual manner on Amelia's wrist.

"But she is wonderfully better, madam," he said afterwards to her mamma; "the brain has been severely tried, but she is marvellously improved: in fact, it is an effort of nature, a most favorable effort, and we can but assist the rally; we will change the medicine." Which he did, and very wisely assisted nature with a bottle of pure water flavored with tincture of roses.

"And it was so very kind of him to give me his directions in poetry," said Amelia's mamma; "for I told him my memory, which is never good, seemed going completely, from anxiety, and if I had done anything wrong just now, I should never have forgiven myself. And I always found poetry easier to remember than prose,"—which puzzled everybody, the doctor included, till it appeared that she had ingeniously discovered a rhyme in his orders

> "To be kept cool and quiet,
> With light nourishing diet."

Under which treatment Amelia was soon pronounced to be well.

She made another attempt to relate her adventures, but she found that not even the nurse would believe in them.

"Why you told me yourself I might meet with the fairies," said Amelia, reproachfully.

"So I did, my dear," nurse replied, "and they say that it's that put it into your head. And I'm sure what you say about the dwarfs and all is as good as a printed book, though you can't think that ever I would have let any dirty clothes store up like that, let alone your frocks, my dear. But for pity sake, Miss Amelia, don't go on about it to your mother, for she thinks you'll never get your senses right again, and she has fretted enough about you, poor lady; and nursed you night and day till she is nigh worn out. And anybody can see you've been ill, miss, you've grown so, and look paler and older like. Well, to be sure, as you say, if you'd been washing and working for a month in a place without a bit of sun, or a bed to lie on, and scraps to eat, it would be enough to do it; and many's the poor child that has to, and gets worn and old before her time. But, my dear, whatever you think, give in to your mother; you'll never repent giving in to your mother, my dear, the longest day you live."

So Amelia kept her own counsel. But she had one confidant.

When her parents brought the stock home on the night of Amelia's visit to the haycocks, the bull-dog's conduct had been most strange. His usual good-humor appeared to have been exchanged for incomprehensible fury, and he was with difficulty prevented from flying at the stock, who on her part showed an anger and dislike fully equal to his.

Finally the bull-dog had been confined in the stable where he remained the whole month, uttering from time to time such howls, with his snub nose in the air, that poor nurse quite gave up hope of Amelia's recovery.

"For indeed, my dear, they do say that a howling dog is a sign of death, and it was more than I could abear."

But the day after Amelia's return, as nurse was leaving the room with a tray which had carried some of the light nourishing diet ordered by the doctor, she was knocked down, tray and all, by the bull-dog, who came tearing into the room, dragging a chain and dirty rope after him, and nearly choked by the desperate efforts which had finally effected his escape from the stable. And he jumped straight on to the end of Amelia's bed, where he lay, *thudding* with his tail, and giving short whines of ecstasy. And as Amelia begged that he might be left, and as it was evident that he would bite any one who tried to take him away, he became established as chief nurse. When Amelia's meals were brought to the bedside on a tray, he kept a fixed eye on the plates, as if to see if her appetite were improving. And he would even take a snack himself, with an air of great affability.

And when Amelia told him her story, she could see by his eyes, and his nose, and his ears, and his tail, and the way he growled whenever the stock was mentioned, that he knew all about it. As, on the other hand, he had no difficulty in conveying to her by sympathetic whines the sentiment "Of course I would have helped you if I could; but they tied me up, and this disgusting old rope has taken me a month to worry through."

So, in spite of the past, Amelia grew up good and gentle, unselfish and considerate for others. She was unusually clever, as those who have been with the "Little People" are said always to be.

And she became so popular with her mother's acquaintances that they said—"We will no longer call her Amelia, for it was a name we learnt to dislike, but we will call her Amy, that is to say, 'Beloved.'"

✳

"And did my godmother's grandmother believe that Amelia had really been with the fairies, or did she think it was all fever ravings?"

"That, indeed, she never said, but she always observed that it was a pleasant tale with a good moral, which was surely enough for anybody."

Part Two

SUBVERSIONS

✳

The five stories in this section no longer rely on preexisting sources, but turn from the rituals of folklore to the idiosyncrasies of fantasy. More openly than the preceding group, they aim to subvert all generic ties, exulting in imaginative freedom. But their startling wildness in no way marks a retreat from literary tradition. Initially, these fantasies seem almost inaccessible compared to the realism of Victorian fiction written for adults. Even the moralism that dominated so much of nineteenth-century English and American children's literature seems greatly in abeyance. Yet the very strangeness of these five stories licenses their authors to engage—sometimes over the heads of child readers—in a steady, and occasionally even angry, dialogue with the assumptions of many of their literary contemporaries.

The first two stories in this section, Christina Rossetti's "Nick," and Juliana Ewing's "Christmas Crackers," dare to mock the hypocrisies of a revered Victorian legend, Charles Dickens's *A Christmas Carol.* Rossetti and Ewing twist the socialization of Dickens's crusty miser, Ebenezer Scrooge, into less therapeutic enchantments. In *A Christmas Carol,* purposeful spirits guide Scrooge on a clearly mapped conversion to fellowship. The guiding spirits in "Nick" and "Christmas Crackers" verge on the sadistic, even the satanic. They bring pain to mortals, as Dickens's Christmas spirits do, but their ministrations have no consoling moral rationale.

Scrooge refuses to love his neighbors for good business reasons: economic doctrine blots out human bonds. Rossetti's Nick simply hates: he has a bad soul, not bad beliefs. His envy and discontent are inherent, not aberrant. Nick's motiveless and compulsive ill-will should disturb adults as well as children, though it suits the uncontrolled hostility of children as Rossetti seems to perceive them in *Speaking Likenesses,* the triad of stories reproduced in part 4. In "Nick," hate cannot be expelled as easily as in *A Christmas Carol.* Its tenacity mocks the ease with which chastened isolates like Scrooge learn to love.

The transformations of magic terrify Nick as they do Scrooge, externalizing his evil wishes; like Scrooge, the enchanted misanthrope journeys through images of his own festering heart. Nick's conversion to neighborliness, though, does not contain even the pretense of fellowship; he is simply browbeaten into benevolence. His salvation is submission: "Finally, Nick was never again heard to utter a wish." This bleak conclusion, repeated with variations in so much literature by women, is in contrast to the beatific consequence of Scrooge's haunted Christmas Eve, which makes him "as good a friend, as good a master, and as good a man, as the good old city knew." But, Rossetti's revision makes us wonder, is not the "good" Scrooge—a word Dickens repeats so remorselessly that it begins to lose its meaning— equally bullied by spirits into altruism? Rossetti's refusal to be edifying, the utter absence of sympathy or love from her tale, exposes the punitive structure within Dickens's moral positivism. "Nick" is, among other things, a revelation of the sadistic skeleton of *A Christmas Carol* and the society that loved it. By paring her world to anger and abuse, Rossetti exposes the violent underside, not only of wickedness, but of submissive virtue.

This bleak parable, with its dark parody of a beloved secular myth, may seem wildly inappropriate for children of any age. But Rossetti's notion of the child differs from both Victorian stereotypes and our own assumptions of what constitutes childhood. Her *Speaking Likenesses,* with its unremitting violence, its trove of denied wishes, would probably be considered equally unsuitable by guardians of innocence today, but *Speaking Likenesses* does at least feature children, acknowledging their frequent unhappiness if it does not console them. Nick, a repellent adult, offers children nothing to identify with. No memories of a lonely childhood soften him; no Tiny Tim lights his progress.

Rossetti's story challenges a series of nostrums Victorian adults questioned at their peril: the virtue of economic paternalism, the immorality of individuality, the evil of the solitary imagination, the salvation of engulfment by family life. Childhood innocence was so unquestioned that Christina Rossetti could safely make her children's tales the repository of a ruthless skepticism adult literature did not tolerate. At the end of *A Christmas Carol,* Scrooge is saved by carrying a child on his shoulder. Middle-class readers preferred to see children as emblems of grace for adults. They chose not to

examine the violence—in books, in social institutions, and in family life—
their sentimental evasions inflicted on actual children.

There is no room in "Nick" for the gregarious rituals of a Victorian family
Christmas. But Juliana Ewing's "Christmas Crackers" evokes, in a unique
and haunting way, the mystic melancholy underlying the holiday which Dickens's readers were conditioned to regard as overflowing with food and jolly
fellowship. Despite the normalcy with which Dickens describes it, a Victorian Christmas must have been a weird occasion. Although it institutionalized family reunions, its climax relied on the surreal transformations and
subversive cross-dressing of the annual Christmas pantomime.

Above all, Christmas was the season of ghosts and ghost stories: *A
Christmas Carol* introduces us to only the most famous of the many dead
released from their graves at a season supposedly celebrating a nativity. At
Christmas, wholesome sociability carried the germs of transgressive release; a holy birthday party was also a pagan day of the dead. Pervaded by
loss and longing, "Christmas Crackers" is a rare evocation of the occult confusion, the tinge of demonism, that underlay the institutionalized fun of a
middle-class Victorian Christmas.

No Saint Nicholas presides over Ewing's story. There is no spirit of any
Christmas past, present, or to come. Instead there is a mocking, "grotesque-looking" tutor who has "been all over the world," and whose only
analogue lies not in religion, but in Gothic fiction: he reminds one astute
young lady of Drosselmeier, the perverse presiding genius of E. T. A. Hoffmann's "The Nut-cracker and the King of Mice" (one of several of Hoffmann's tales ably translated from the German by Major Alexander Ewing,
the writer's husband). The tutor's resemblance to "Godpapa Drosselmeier"
is deliberate. This sardonic practitioner of strange arts, with his indetermi-
nate, vaguely foreign origin, is, one would think, the unlikeliest possible
stage manager of a British family Christmas.

Even before the tutor distributes his crackers, Dickensian family bliss is
mocked in the fatuous moralizing of a conceited young visitor trying to impress the daughter of the house: "To-night he spoke of Christmas, of time-
honored custom and old association; and what he said would have made a
Christmas article for a magazine of the first class. He poured scorn on the
cold nature that could not, and the affectation that would not, appreciate the
domestic festivities of this sacred season. What, he asked, could be more
delightful, more perfect, than such a gathering as this, of the family circle
round the Christmas hearth?" In case we miss the irony, Ewing makes the

young man's hypocrisy blatant: "He spoke with feeling, and it may be said with disinterested feeling, for he had not joined his family circle himself this Christmas, and there was a vacant place by the hearth of his own home."

So much for the family circle round the Christmas hearth. The young man's facile hypocrisy calls its satisfactions into question; the tutor's incendiary gift dissipates them utterly. Like Nick's shape changes, each cracker makes a wish come true for a limited time. This seductive gratification exposes the secret desires and repressed epiphanies of all its members. With the exception of the sentimental visitor, the men in the group dream of travel and excitement. The women dream painful refractions of their lives; the subservient young widow, who "had always given up everything" to her demanding husband and spoiled son, sees herself as a Blue Beard's wife. Like Nick's wishes, the tutor's hallucinogenic Christmas gift provides fantasies that expose the violence and insufficiency of domestic reality.

Half friend and half destroyer, the tutor releases the discontent buried in that supposed center of happiness, the domestic hearth. This thoroughly pagan occasion concludes with an ironic moral, a pious Christmas hymn that has nothing to do with the action. A more appropriate moral might come from Florence Nightingale's *Cassandra,* an enraged attack on the suppressions of middle-class family life: "Awake, ye women, all that sleep, awake! If this domestic life were so very good, would your young men wander away from it, your maidens think of something else?" Given the chance, all the family members in "Christmas Crackers" wander away or think of something else. Like her own tutor, Ewing gives cozy readers a subversive gift, one "a Christmas article for a magazine of the first class" would never sanction. Her crackers bring them to momentary awareness of their own discontent.

As with "Nick," it is difficult to imagine an appropriate child reader for "Christmas Crackers," even though Ewing's tale first appeared, as did many of her stories, in *Aunt Judy's Magazine,* the girl's "magazine of the first class" edited by her mother, Margaret Gatty. (Its appearance, in the December 1869 and January 1870 issues, and hence at a season of Christmas and New Year festivities, makes this supposed children's story an even more daring affront to an official Victorian morality.) The chief child in Ewing's circle is poor Master MacGreedy, who is too repellent for any child to identify with, though adults who were exhorted at all costs to love boys might furtively recognize this spoiled little devourer. Unlike Reginald, who tells his own life in Ewing's "A Flat Iron For a Farthing," and unlike Jackanapes, her most famous boy hero, Master MacGreedy is presented without the slightest tinge of affection. Nor is there any of the interest Ewing showed, in the case of Amelia's adventures underground (the last offering in part 1), in a bratty child's psychology or redemption.

Frances Hodgson Burnett and E. Nesbit are as impious as Christina Rossetti and Juliana Ewing, but they do seem to believe in child readers, if not in adult fantasies about their innocence. Burnett delegates much of her own anger to Jem, whose waking rage at her Aunt Hetty the story of "Behind the White Brick" then sets out to exorcise in the dreamland to which the girl is transported. Although the story ends conventionally with a nurturing mother's return and the provision of a "beautiful scarlet and gold book" to replace the "little blue covered volume" burned by the ill-tempered aunt, Jem's sojourn in the chimneyland behind the white brick unleashes powerfully anarchic energies.

Jem expects the overly feminine dreamchild Flora to act as her guide as she enters a "delightful" room that even sports a "cage full of love-birds" (an icon used as ironically in Hitchcock's famous film *The Birds*). But the dreamer soon strays into more disturbing spaces. The soothing tones of gentle Flora are replaced by the "shrill little voice" of a very different "hostess." In Baby, Jem must confront her own anger. She is surprised that her infant sister has become almost as eloquent in denouncing perceived "wrongs" as that more famous baby-turned-instant-adult, Mary Shelley's wronged and outraged creature. Equipped, not just with the rhetorical weapons of sarcasm but also with two rows of sharp teeth and a shark-like disposition, this once-innocuous crib dweller aggressively turns on all comers, including the genial Mr. S. C., that archetypal dispenser of Christmas gifts.

Like Ewing's "Christmas Crackers," this tale, first published in the American children's magazine named after Santa Claus himself, *St. Nicholas,* offers a sly dissent from Christmas paternalism. Jem is ashamed to admit that she has become a Scrooge-like unbeliever. To mitigate her guilt, she is willing to revert to a belief in the rosy-cheeked little gentleman who rewards good girls who nurture their crippled dolls just as good women might later minister to their crippled boys and crippled husbands (a Burnett leitmotif that stems from her personal life and which became embedded in her masterpiece, *The Secret Garden*). When S. C., Esquire exhorts Jem to continue to believe in him, she is overcome by his benevolism: "How kind he is!" she tells Baby. But Baby remains steadfast to the end. She is unwilling to capitulate by softening her view of the figure who had warned her against becoming too independent.

Earlier, Baby fearlessly challenged this miniaturized version of a Father Christmas, whom Dickens had still cast as a mighty giant. When the acerbic toddler informs him that she insists on having her "rights respected up here," she puts him on the defensive. He may chuckle and rub his hands in amusement, but his need to discredit her suggests his eagerness to put down other unnamed (and ungendered) folk who also impress him as making too big "a fuss about their rights." Burnett, whose uneasy reviewers often wanted to be reassured that she was not a dreaded "New Woman" insisting on universal suffrage and other rights, clearly uses Baby as a safe stand-in for positions she is not prepared to have the maturing Jemima, her mother's gem, adopt. Yet her wonderful ability to identify herself with the impotent fury of infants still unable, linguistically, to convey their wants to those who call them "cross" makes the irate Baby a perfect vehicle for the expression of emotions forbidden to a Victorian lady.

In fact, this tiny nonconformist is even licensed to question a more sacrosanct institution than Christmas when she boldly declares that her mother was "mean" in wishing for a better-tempered baby. Such sacrilege, however, is more than the waking Jem can bear. Like Carroll's Alice, she needs to reject the subversive projections she has animated. If Alice feels compelled to repudiate first the sadism of the Queen of Hearts and then the anarchism of the Red Queen, Jem represses the self that was Baby.

In responding to the endings of both Alice books, however, Burnett also implies that Jem's acquiescence in her mother's definition of what looks "real" remains unsatisfactory. After carefully attending to Alice's narrative, her older sister tried to bridge the realities of dream and domestication. In "Behind the White Brick," however, the mother to whom Jem wants to tell her dream remains uninterested in any account of transgressive wonderlands. She thinks that by simply replacing one book with another she can remove all disturbances and reassert the primacy of her own domestic reality. After her own return from a realm beyond a fireplace, the Looking-Glass Alice maintained her relation to the kitten she had transformed into her agent. The awakened Jem, however, denies all kinship with Baby. Deprived of the power of speech she so briefly enjoyed in Jem's dream, the baby has now reverted to wordless screaming. Once again confined to the crib, she remains unattended by either mother or older sister.

In Nesbit's "Melisande: or, Long and Short Division" and "Fortunatus Rex & Co.," two of her *Nine Unlikely Tales For Children* (1901), impiety assumes the form of impishness. The bourgeois adaptations of feudal fairy tales are carried to burlesque extremes. Kings now become laissez faire entrepreneurs, either as merchants who market a daughter's over-abundant hair as their kingdom's "staple export" or as obsessive housing developers who ravage the green countryside Nesbit invokes as an antidote to the excesses of capitalism. A cofounder of the Fabian Socialist movement, Nesbit was also a critic of imperialism, which she persistently identified with male domination. After Melisande, in the first of these two tales, grows into a giantess large enough to tower over the invading armies of a "neighbouring King," she refuses to wield her new powers to imperialistic or even vengeful ends. Not only does she fail to retaliate by subjugating her foes but she also makes sure to spare every enemy soldier and sailor. And, when an even larger fleet "of warships, and gunboats, and torpedo boats" returns to renew the attack, instead of drowning this Armada, she merely picks up her island country in order to carry it to a safer part of the world.

Still, in both "Melisande" and "Fortunatus Rex & Co.," Nesbit's satire is primarily directed at those male narratives which appropriate or reconstruct female materials. It is no coincidence, therefore, that "Melisande" should totally recast "Rapunzel." Nesbit departs from the Grimms by downplaying the might they had invested exclusively in their story's female villain, the wicked enchantress, "die alte Frau Gothel." In her retelling, the curse of the bad fairy Malevola—Frau Gothel's counterpart—is quickly neutralized by a spare wish which Melisande's father saved after receiving it as a wedding gift from his vacationing fairy godmother, Fortuna F. It is not Malevola's curse of baldness, therefore, but the superabundance of hair Melisande is granted that causes her discomforts far greater than Rapunzel had to endure.

"Rapunzel" had dramatized a contest between the crone who wants to protect her ward's virginity and the young prince who becomes the naive girl's seducer. The maiden's long hair is a mark of the passivity which the tale ultimately upholds as a properly "feminine" attribute, an emphasis still endorsed by Bruno Bettelheim in *The Uses of Enchantment* (pp. 131–32). Both Rapunzel's female guardian and her male seducer use it as a ladder to scale into the privacy of her chamber. When cut off and used by the wily Frau Gothel, the tresses allow her to render the Prince as impotent as Rapunzel, until Rapunzel's tears eventually redeem him.

In Nesbit's handling, however, it is the heroine Melisande (whose name comes from the Teutonic word for "strength") who becomes the unwitting recipient of the power the Grimms had bestowed on Frau Gothel. That power results from the well-meaning but often misguided efforts of those who have Melisande's best interests at heart: her parents, her suitor, and the Fairy Fortuna, who ultimately helps all parties to restore balance. Nesbit thus dispenses with the crude sexual struggle the Grimms had dramatized. By alternately allowing Melisande her gigantic strands of hair and a distention in size so cosmic that the princess eventually worries about knocking her head against the stars, Nesbit has a good-natured laugh at the two major male fabulists for children of the Victorian era, George MacDonald and Lewis Carroll.

MacDonald was the creator of the mighty giantess North Wind whose over-abundant hair allowed the illustrator Arthur Hughes to reflect his own pre-Raphaelite fascination with female energy in drawings as powerful as those he later fashioned for Christina Rossetti's *Speaking Likenesses* (see pp. 326–59, below, as well as Hughes' illustration for "The Brown Bull of Norrowa" on p. 89, above). And before Tenniel gave Carroll's Alice the well-controlled hairdo of a prim little Victorian girl, Carroll himself drew her as a tiny pre-Raphaelite heroine whose unruly locks completely filled the interior of the White Rabbit's house. Nesbit (who signified her modernity by wearing hair that was bobbed short) makes sure to remind her child readers that she is mocking earlier stereotypes of females magnified by male desire. Crying when she is at her tiniest, Alice almost drowns in the pool created by the tears she shed as a giant. The crying Melisande, already "too large to get indoors," starts a flood that threatens to drown normal-sized humans; eager to spare others, she wisely remembers "her 'Alice in Wonderland,' and stopped crying at once." With tongue in cheek, Nesbit here converts Carroll's fantasy into a utilitarian text. A recollection of Alice's restraint in weeping, Nesbit pretends, might be as useful in preventing growing princesses from hurting others as a knowledge in "long and short division" can be for those overwhelmed by rampant multiplication tables. (She also twits Carroll, the mathematician-turned-author-of-children's-books, when she has Prince Florizel become as tiny and as inaudible as the friendly but impotent Gnat in *Through the Looking-Glass.*)

The humor in "Fortunatus Rex & Co." is subtler and more complex than in "Melisande," even though some of Nesbit's targets are quite similar. Here too, modern geopolitics are deliciously mocked. When the male magician, whose upper half Miss Robinson has concealed within the terrestrial globe in her classroom, pleads for release, his auditors confuse his directions with jingoistic demands. The invisible voice hopes that his princely rescuers will "Open up Africa!," "Or cut through the Isthmus of Panama," or "Cut up China!" Such aspirations well fit the "hungry-looking" practitioner of blackmail and black magic who had earlier tried to feed off his rival's newly gained wealth. But the six princes assume that they are being asked to colonize the globe, and protest that they have no such imperialist ambitions, neither having been brought up "in the exploring trade" nor educated as engineers. Such ventures, however, pose no problem for King Fortunatus, who becomes one of the "largest speculative builders in the world," a profession which, as the narrator helpfully translates, involves cutting up "pretty woods and fields" into "ugly" squares, brick houses, and little streets. Great fortunes, the narrator explains, can be made "by turning beautiful things into ugly ones."

As the figure who counters the greed of both King Fortunatus and the magician, Miss Fitzroy Robinson would seem to be cast in the role of Good Fairy played much more indirectly and unobtrusively, in "Melisande" by "Fortuna F." But despite her superior powers of magic, Miss Robinson is also a fraud who thrives on exploiting the illusions of others. Though little actual teaching goes on at her permissive educational establishment, she has so impressed "all the really high-class kings" with her phony credentials that they "were only too pleased to be permitted to pay ten thousand pounds a year for their daughters' education." Pedagogy is less important to Miss Robinson than her investment "in land," the countryside she eventually restores to its greenness, as a real-life Beatrix Potter was able to do from the proceeds of her children's books.

Indeed, it is not too far-fetched to see the fraudulent teacher as an analogue to the writer who produces "unlikely tales" that wealthy parents may buy for their children without a closer scrutiny of their subtext. The narrator and Miss Robinson, after all, collaborate in the art of deception. Joint concealers of plots and meaning, as well as of princesses and rival male enchanters, they craft a story based on suppression and ellipsis. Just as Miss Robinson dupes King Fortunatus into accepting the loss of his favorite daughter Daisy (Nesbit's own childhood nickname) so does the unnamed "little old woman" get the better of him in a trade he thinks is to his advantage. He is not only unaware that the two figures are one and the same, but also fails to grasp that he is actually being enlisted to help Miss Robinson restore the dreamchild he has tried to replace as a builder of sterile structures.

Nesbit's empathy with Miss Robinson is evident. A composite of all the pompous schoolmistresses of Nesbit's youth, of the mother who vainly tried to run the educational establishment her dead husband had set up, of the single women forced to eke out a living by writing pious children's books, and, as suggested, of Nesbit herself as a self-conscious, self-ironizing dispenser of money-making fictions, this lady in her "middle age" is more than a match for the rapacious magician who vainly tries to ruin her reputation. It is her understanding of conventions, however, more than her mastery of magic, that constitutes her greatest strength. The "references" she draws upon are as varied as Nesbit's own. She dazzles the king with a "delightful parlor full of the traces of the refining touch of a woman's hand"; she receives him with a demeanor that is at once dignified and deferential. Her artifice is impeccable, down to the handsome gown she wears for the occasion, an elegant Cinderella's attire "neatly made of sackcloth—with an ingenious trimming of small cinders sown on gold braid—and some larger-sized cinders dangled by silken threads from the edge of her lace cap." Nesbit's parodic references to fairy tale conventions show how far the *kunst-märchen* had moved by the turn of the century. Even the convention in which an aged crone turns into a blooming beauty (still used by MacDonald in a story like "Princess Daylight") is ironically undercut: "While she was speaking the old woman got younger and younger, till as she spoke the last words she was quite young, not more than fifty-five. And it was Miss Fitzroy Robinson!"

Yet it would be a mistake to read "Fortunatus Rex & Co." as nothing more than a burlesque. Some of the mysticism that enters into Nesbit's later *The Story of the Amulet* (1906) already makes a tentative appearance in this story written in the last year of Queen Victoria's reign. In *The Story of the Amulet,* a belief in transmigration as well as in numerological permutations Nesbit had found in the work of female theosophists such as Blavatsky and Besant are enlisted in the wishful restoration of an order that might go beyond materialism, competition, and gender-struggle (Knoepflmacher 1987). Just as the green light of the female *ankh,* or amulet, brings a glimpse of a primal world unsullied by power struggles, so does Miss Robinson want to extend her greening powers beyond the orchard where she preserves her seven wards. Though humor predominates in "Fortunatus Rex & Co.," the story also expresses the same yearning for a female domain that shapes *Mopsa the Fairy,* the fantasy novel reprinted in part 3 of this collection.

CHRISTINA ROSSETTI

Nick

There dwelt in a small village, not a thousand miles from Fairyland, a poor man, who had no family to labour for or friend to assist. When I call him poor, you must not suppose he was a homeless wanderer, trusting to charity for a night's lodging; on the contrary, his stone house, with its green verandah and flower-garden, was the prettiest and snuggest in all the place, the doctor's only excepted. Neither was his store of provisions running low: his farm supplied him with milk, eggs, mutton, butter, poultry, and cheese in abundance; his fields with hops and barley for beer, and wheat for bread; his orchard with fruit and cider; and his kitchen-garden with vegetables and wholesome herbs. He had, moreover, health, an appetite to enjoy all these good things, and strength to walk about his possessions. No, I call him poor because, with all these, he was discontented and envious. It was in vain that his apples were the largest for miles around, if his neighbour's vines were the most productive by a single bunch; it was in vain that his lambs were fat and thriving, if some one else's sheep bore twins: so, instead of enjoying his own prosperity, and being glad when his neighbours prospered too, he would sit grumbling and bemoaning himself as if every other man's riches were his poverty. And thus it was that one day our friend Nick leaned over Giles Hodge's gate, counting his cherries.

'Yes,' he muttered, 'I wish I were sparrows to eat them up, or a blight to kill your fine trees altogether.'

The words were scarcely uttered when he felt a tap on his shoulder, and looking round, perceived a little rosy woman, no bigger than a butterfly, who

"Nick" is the shortest of eight stories Rossetti collected in *Commonplace and Other Short Stories* (1870).

139

held her tiny fist clenched in a menacing attitude. She looked scornfully at him, and said: 'Now listen, you churl, you! henceforward you shall straightway become everything you wish; only mind, you must remain under one form for at least an hour.' Then she gave him a slap in the face, which made his cheek tingle as if a bee had stung him, and disappeared with just so much sound as a dewdrop makes in falling.

Nick rubbed his cheek in a pet, pulling wry faces and showing his teeth. He was boiling over with vexation, but dared not vent it in words lest some unlucky wish should escape him. Just then the sun seemed to shine brighter than ever, the wind blew spicy from the south; all Giles's roses looked redder and larger than before, while his cherries seemed to multiply, swell, ripen. He could refrain no longer, but, heedless of the fairy-gift he had just received, exclaimed, 'I wish I were sparrows eating—' No sooner said than done: in a moment he found himself a whole flight of hungry birds, pecking, devouring, and bidding fair to devastate the envied cherry-trees. But honest Giles was on the watch hard by; for that very morning it had struck him he must make nets for the protection of his fine fruit. Forthwith he ran home, and speedily returned with a revolver furnished with quite a marvellous array of barrels. Pop, bang—pop, bang! he made short work of the sparrows, and soon reduced the enemy to one crestfallen biped with broken leg and wing, who limped to hide himself under a holly-bush. But though the fun was over, the hour was not; so Nick must needs sit out his allotted time. Next a pelting shower came down, which soaked him through his torn, ruffled feathers; and then, exactly as the last drops fell and the sun came out with a beautiful rainbow, a tabby cat pounced upon him. Giving himself up for lost, he chirped in desperation, 'O, I wish I were a dog to worry you!' Instantly— for the hour was just passed—in the grip of his horrified adversary, he turned at bay, a savage bull-dog. A shake, a deep bite, and poor puss was out of her pain. Nick, with immense satisfaction, tore her fur to bits, wishing he could in like manner exterminate all her progeny. At last, glutted with vengeance, he lay down beside his victim, relaxed his ears and tail, and fell asleep.

Now that tabby-cat was the property and special pet of no less a personage than the doctor's lady; so when dinner-time came, and not the cat, a general consternation pervaded the household. The kitchens were searched, the cellars, the attics; every apartment was ransacked; even the watch-dog's kennel was visited. Next the stable was rummaged, then the hay-loft; lastly, the bereaved lady wandered disconsolately through her own private garden into the shrubbery, calling 'Puss, puss,' and looking so intently up the trees as not to perceive what lay close before her feet. Thus it was that, unawares, she stumbled over Nick, and trod upon his tail.

Up jumped our hero, snarling, biting, and rushing at her with such blind fury as to miss his aim. She ran, he ran. Gathering up his strength, he took a flying-leap after his victim; her foot caught in the spreading root of an oak tree, she fell, and he went over her head, clear over, into a bed of stinging-nettles. Then she found breath to raise that fatal cry, 'Mad dog!' Nick's blood curdled in his veins; he would have slunk away if he could; but already a stout labouring-man, to whom he had done many an ill turn in the time of his humanity, had spied him, and, bludgeon in hand, was preparing to give chase. However, Nick had the start of him, and used it too; while the lady, far behind, went on vociferating, 'Mad dog, mad dog!' inciting doctor, servants, and vagabonds to the pursuit. Finally, the whole village came pouring out to swell the hue and cry.

The dog kept ahead gallantly, distancing more and more the asthmatic doctor, fat Giles, and, in fact, all his pursuers except the bludgeon-bearing labourer, who was just near enough to persecute his tail. Nick knew the magic hour must be almost over, and so kept forming wish after wish as he ran,—that he were a viper only to get trodden on, a thorn to run into some one's foot, a man-trap in the path, even the detested bludgeon to miss its aim and break. This wish crossed his mind at the propitious moment; the bull-dog vanished, and the labourer, overreaching himself, fell flat on his face, while his weapon struck deep into the earth, and snapped.

A strict search was instituted after the missing dog, but without success. During two whole days the village children were exhorted to keep indoors and beware of dogs; on the third an inoffensive bull pup was hanged, and the panic subsided.

Meanwhile the labourer, with his shattered stick, walked home in silent wonder, pondering on the mysterious disappearance. But the puzzle was beyond his solution; so he only made up his mind not to tell his wife the whole story till after tea. He found her preparing for that meal, the bread and cheese set out, and the kettle singing softly on the fire. 'Here's something to make the kettle boil, mother,' said he, thrusting our hero between the bars and seating himself; 'for I'm mortal tired and thirsty.'

Nick crackled and blazed away cheerfully, throwing out bright sparks, and lighting up every corner of the little room. He toasted the cheese to a nicety, made the kettle boil without spilling a drop, set the cat purring with comfort, and illuminated the pots and pans into splendour. It was provocation enough to be burned; but to contribute by his misfortune to the well-being of his tormentors was still more aggravating. He heard, too, all their remarks and wonderment about the supposed mad-dog, and saw the doctor's lady's own maid bring the labourer five shillings as a reward for his exertions. Then followed a discussion as to what should be purchased with the gift, till at last it was resolved to have their best window glazed with real glass. The prospect of their grandeur put the finishing-stroke to Nick's indignation. Sending up a sudden flare, he wished with all his might that he were fire to burn the cottage.

Forthwith the flame leaped higher than ever flame leaped before. It played for a moment about a ham, and smoked it to a nicety; then, fastening on the woodwork above the chimney-corner, flashed full into a blaze. The labourer ran for help, while his wife, a timid woman, with three small children, overturned two pails of water on the floor, and set the beer-tap running. This done, she hurried, wringing her hands, to the door, and threw it wide open. The sudden draught of air did more mischief than all Nick's malice, and fanned him into quite a conflagration. He danced upon the rafters, melted a pewter-pot and a pat of butter, licked up the beer, and was just making his way towards the bedroom, when through the thatch and down the chimney came a rush of water. This arrested his progress for the moment; and before he could recover himself, a second and a third discharge from the enemy completed his discomfiture. Reduced ere long to one blue flame, and entirely surrounded by a wall of wet ashes, Nick sat and smouldered; while the goodnatured neighbours did their best to remedy the mishap, — saved a small remnant of beer, assured the labourer that his landlord was certain to do the repairs, and observed that the ham would eat 'beautiful.'

Our hero now had leisure for reflection. His situation precluded all hope of doing further mischief; and the disagreeable conviction kept forcing itself upon his mind that, after all, he had caused more injury to himself than to any of his neighbours. Remembering, too, how contemptuously the fairy woman had looked and spoken, he began to wonder how he could ever have expected to enjoy her gift. Then it occurred to him, that if he merely studied his own advantage without trying to annoy other people, perhaps his persecutor might be propitiated; so he fell to thinking over all his acquaintances, their fortunes and misfortunes; and, having weighed well their several claims on his preference, ended by wishing himself the rich old man who lived in a handsome house just beyond the turnpike. In this wish he burned out.

The last glimmer had scarcely died away, when Nick found himself in a bed hung round with faded curtains, and occupying the centre of a large room. A night-lamp, burning on the chimney-piece, just enabled him to discern a few shabby old articles of furniture, a scanty carpet, and some writing materials on a table. These objects looked somewhat dreary; but for his comfort he felt an inward consciousness of a goodly money-chest stowed away under his bed, and of sundry precious documents hidden in a secret cupboard in the wall.

So he lay very cosily, and listened to the clock ticking, the mice squeaking, and the housedog barking down below. This was, however, but a drowsy occupation; and he soon bore witness to its somniferous influence by sinking into a fantastic dream about his money-chest. First, it was broken open, then shipwrecked, then burned; lastly, some men in masks, whom he knew instinctively to be his own servants, began dragging it away. Nick started up, clutched hold of something in the dark, found his last dream true, and the next moment was stretched on the floor—lifeless, yet not insensible—by a heavy blow from a crowbar.

The men now proceeded to secure their booty, leaving our hero where he fell. They carried off the chest, broke open and ransacked the secret closet, overturned the furniture, to make sure that no hiding-place of treasure escaped them, and at length, whispering together, left the room. Nick felt quite discouraged by his ill success, and now entertained only one wish—that he were himself again. Yet even this wish gave him some anxiety; for he feared that if the servants returned and found him in his original shape they might take him for a spy, and murder him in downright earnest. While he lay thus cogitating two of the men reappeared, bearing a shutter and some tools. They lifted him up, laid him on the shutter, and carried him out of the room, down the back-stairs, through a long vaulted passage, into the open air. No word was spoken; but Nick knew they were going to bury him.

An utter horror seized him, while, at the same time, he felt a strange consciousness that his hair would not stand on end because he was dead. The men set him down, and began in silence to dig his grave. It was soon ready to receive him; they threw the body roughly in, and cast upon it the first shovelful of earth.

But the moment of deliverance had arrived. His wish suddenly found vent in a prolonged unearthly yell. Damp with night dew, pale as death, and shivering from head to foot, he sat bolt upright, with starting, staring eyes and chattering teeth. The murderers, in mortal fear, cast down their tools, plunged deep into a wood hard by, and were never heard of more.

Under cover of night Nick made the best of his way home, silent and pondering. Next morning he gave Giles Hodge a rare tulip-root, with full directions for rearing it; he sent the doctor's wife a Persian cat twice the size of her lost pet; the labourer's cottage was repaired, his window glazed, and his beer-barrel replaced by unknown agency; and when a vague rumour reached the village that the miser was dead, that his ghost had been heard bemoaning itself, and that all his treasures had been carried off, our hero was one of the few persons who did not say, 'And served him right, too.'

Finally, Nick was never again heard to utter a wish.[1]

1. **never again to utter a wish** Rossetti's flat closure bears comparison with the elaborate last paragraph of *A Christmas Carol:* "He had no further intercourse with Spirits, but lived upon the Total Abstinence Principle. . . ."

JULIANA HORATIA EWING

Christmas Crackers

A FANTASIA

It was Christmas-eve in an old-fashioned country-house, where Christmas was being kept with old-fashioned form and custom. It was getting late. The candles swaggered in their sockets, and the yule log glowed steadily like a red-hot coal.

"The fire has reached his heart," said the tutor: "he is warm all through. How red he is! He shines with heat and hospitality like some warmhearted old gentleman when a convivial evening is pretty far advanced. To-morrow he will be as cold and grey as the morning after a festival, when the glasses are being washed up, and the host is calculating his expenses. Yes! you know it is so;" and the tutor nodded to the yule log as he spoke; and the log flared and crackled in return, till the tutor's face shone like his own. He had no other means of reply.

The tutor was grotesque-looking at any time. He was lank and meagre, with a long body and limbs, and high shoulders. His face was smooth-shaven, and his skin like old parchment stretched over high cheek-bones and lantern jaws; but in their hollow sockets his eyes gleamed with the changeful lustre of two precious gems. In the ruddy firelight they were like rubies, and when he drew back into the shade they glared green like the eyes of a cat. It must not be inferred from the tutor's presence this evening that there were no Christmas holidays in this house. They had begun some days before; and if the tutor had had a home to go to, it is to be presumed that he would have gone.

"Christmas Crackers" first appeared in two installments in the December 1869 and January 1870 issues of *Aunt Judy's Magazine;* it was reprinted in *The Brownies and Other Tales* in 1870.

As the candles got lower, and the log flared less often, weird lights and shades, such as haunt the twilight, crept about the room. The tutor's shadow, longer, lanker, and more grotesque than himself, mopped and mowed upon the wall beside him. The snapdragon[1] burnt blue, and as the raisin-hunters stirred the flaming spirit, the ghastly light made the tutor look so hideous that the widow's little boy was on the eve of howling, and spilled the raisins he had just secured. (He did not like putting his fingers into the flames, but he hovered near the more adventurous schoolboys, and collected the raisins that were scattered on the table by the hasty *grabs* of braver hands.)

The widow was a relative of the house. She had married a Mr. Jones, and having been during his life his devoted slave, had on his death transferred her allegiance to his son. The late Mr. Jones was a small man with a strong temper, a large appetite, and a taste for drawing-room theatricals. So Mrs. Jones had called her son Macready;[2] "for," she said, "his poor papa would have made a fortune on the stage, and I wish to commemorate his talents. Besides, Macready sounds better with Jones than a commoner Christian name would do."

But his cousins called him MacGreedy.

"The apples of the enchanted garden were guarded by dragons. Many knights went after them. One wished for the apples, but he did not like to fight the dragons."

It was the tutor who spoke from the dark corner by the fireplace. His eyes shone like a cat's, and MacGreedy felt like a half-scared mouse, and made up his mind to cry. He put his right fist into one eye, and had just taken it out, and was about to put his left fist into the other, when he saw that the tutor was no longer looking at him. So he made up his mind to go on with the raisins, for one can have a peevish cry at any time, but plums are not scattered broadcast every day. Several times he had tried to pocket them, but just at the moment the tutor was sure to look at him, and in his fright he dropped the raisins, and never could find them again. So this time he resolved to eat them then and there. He had just put one into his mouth when the tutor leaned forward, and his eyes, glowing in the firelight, met MacGreedy's, who had not even the presence of mind to shut his mouth, but remained spellbound, with a raisin in his cheek.

---

1. **snapdragon** A Victorian Christmas custom that dared children to fish hot raisins out of a bowl of flaming brandy and to pop them into the player's mouth.

2. **Macready** William Charles Macready (1793–1873) was a successful Shakespearian actor and stage manager.

Flicker, flack! The schoolboys stirred up snapdragon again, and with the blue light upon his features the tutor made so horrible a grimace that MacGreedy swallowed the raisin with a start. He had bolted it whole, and it might have been a bread pill for any enjoyment he had of the flavor. But the tutor laughed aloud. He certainly was an alarming object, pulling those grimaces in the blue brandy glare; and unpleasantly like a picture of Bogy himself with horns and a tail, in a juvenile volume upstairs. True, there were no horns to speak of among the tutor's grizzled curls, and his coat seemed to fit as well as most people's on his long back, so that unless he put his tail in his pocket, it is difficult to see how he could have had one. But then (as Miss Letitia said) "With dress one can do anything and hide anything." And on dress Miss Letitia's opinion was final.

Miss Letitia was a cousin. She was dark, high-colored, glossy-haired, stout, and showy. She was as neat as a new pin, and had a will of her own. Her hair was firmly fixed by bandoline, her garibaldis by an arrangement which failed when applied to those of the widow, and her opinions by the simple process of looking at everything from one point of view. Her *forte* was dress and general ornamentation; not that Miss Letitia was extravagant—far from it. If one may use the expression, she utilized for ornament a hundred bits and scraps that most people would have wasted. But, like other artists, she saw everything through the medium of her own art. She looked at birds with an eye to hats, and at flowers with reference to evening parties. At picture exhibitions and concerts she carried away jacket patterns and bonnets in her head, as other people make mental notes of an aerial effect, or a bit of fine instrumentation. An enthusiastic horticulturist once sent Miss Letitia a cut specimen of a new flower. It was a lovely spray from a lately imported shrub. A botanist would have pressed it—an artist must have taken its portrait—a poet might have written a sonnet in praise of its beauty. Miss Letitia twisted a piece of wire round its stem, and fastened it on to her black lace bonnet. It came on the day of a review, when Miss Letitia had to appear in a carriage, and it was quite a success. As she said to the widow, "It was so natural that no one could doubt its being Parisian."

"What a strange fellow that tutor is!" said the visitor. He spoke to the daughter of the house, a girl with a face like a summer's day, and hair like a ripe cornfield rippling in the sun. He was a fine young man, and had a youth's taste for the sports and amusements of his age. But lately he had changed. He seemed to himself to be living in a higher, nobler atmosphere than hitherto. He had discovered that he was poetical—he might prove to be a genius. He certainly was eloquent, he could talk for hours, and did so—to the young lady with the sunshiny face. They spoke on the highest subjects, and what a listener she was! So intelligent and appreciative, and with such an exquisite *pose* of the head—it must inspire a block of wood merely to see such a creature in a listening attitude. As to our young friend, he poured forth volumes; he was really clever, and for her he became eloquent. To-night he spoke of Christmas, of time-honored custom and old association; and what he said would have made a Christmas article for a magazine of the first class. He poured scorn on the cold nature that could not, and the affectation that would not, appreciate the domestic festivities of this sacred season. What, he asked, could be more delightful, more perfect, than such a gathering as this, of the family circle round the Christmas hearth? He spoke with feeling, and it may be said with disinterested feeling, for he had not joined his family circle himself this Christmas, and there was a vacant place by the hearth of his own home.

"He is strange," said the young lady (she spoke of the tutor in answer to the above remark); "but I am very fond of him. He has been with us so long he is like one of the family; though we know as little of his history as we did on the day he came."

"He looks clever," said the visitor. (Perhaps that is the least one can say for a fellow-creature who shows a great deal of bare skull, and is not otherwise good-looking.)

"He is clever," she answered, "wonderfully clever; so clever and so odd that sometimes I fancy he is hardly 'canny.' There is something almost supernatural about his acuteness and his ingenuity, but they are so kindly used; I wonder he has not brought out any playthings for us tonight."

"Playthings?" inquired the young man.

"Yes; on birthdays or festivals like this he generally brings something out of those huge pockets of his. He has been all over the world, and he produces Indian puzzles, Japanese flower-buds that bloom in hot water, and German toys with complicated machinery, which I suspect him of manufacturing himself. I call him Godpapa Drosselmayer, after that delightful old fellow in Hoffman's tale of the Nut Cracker."[3]

"What's that about crackers?" inquired the tutor, sharply, his eyes changing color like a fire opal.

"I am talking of *Nussknacker und Mausekönig*," laughed the young lady.

3. **Nut Cracker** E. T. A. Hoffmann (1776–1822) first published "Nussknacker und Mausekönig" in an 1818 Christmas collection of children's stories; until the 1984 version by Ralph Manheim and Maurice Sendak, the best English translation of the story was that by Ewing's husband, Alexander Ewing (1830–1895).

"Crackers do not belong to Christmas; fireworks come on the 5th of November."

"Tut, tut!" said the tutor; "I always tell your ladyship that you are still a tomboy at heart, as when I first came, and you climbed trees and pelted myself and my young students with horse-chestnuts. You think of crackers to explode at the heels of timorous old gentlemen in a November fog; but I mean bonbon crackers, colored crackers, dainty crackers—crackers for young people with mottoes of sentiment"—(here the tutor shrugged his high shoulders an inch or two higher, and turned the palms of his hands outwards with a glance indescribably comical)—"crackers with paper prodigies, crackers with sweetmeats—*such* sweetmeats!" He smacked his lips with a grotesque contortion, and looked at Master MacGreedy, who choked himself with his last raisin, and forthwith burst into tears.

The widow tried in vain to soothe him with caresses, he only stamped and howled the more. But Miss Letitia gave him some smart smacks on the shoulders to cure his choking fit, and as she kept up the treatment with vigor, the young gentleman was obliged to stop and assure her that the raisin had "gone the right way" at last. "If he were my child," Miss Letitia had been known to observe, with that confidence which characterizes the theories of those who are not parents, "I would &c. &c. &c.;" in fact, Miss Letitia thought she would have made a very different boy of him as, indeed, I believe she would.

"Are crackers all that you have for us, sir?" asked one of the two schoolboys, as they hung over the tutor's chair. They were twins, grand boys, with broad, good-humored faces, and curly wigs, as like as two puppy dogs of the same breed. They were only known apart by their intimate friends, and were always together, romping, laughing, snarling, squabbling, huffing and helping each other against the world. Each of them owned a wiry terrier, and in their relations to each other the two dogs (who were marvellously alike) closely followed the example of their masters.

"Do you not care for crackers, Jim?" asked the tutor.

"Not much, sir. They do for girls: but, as you know, I care for nothing but military matters. Do you remember that beautiful toy of yours—'The Besieged City?' Ah! I liked that. Look out, Tom! you're shoving my arm. Can't you stand straight, man?"

"R-r-r-r—r-r, snap!"

Tom's dog was resenting contact with Jim's dog on the hearthrug. There was a hustle among the four, and then they subsided.

"The Besieged City was all very well for you, Jim," said Tom, who meant to be a sailor; "but please to remember that it admitted of no attack from the sea; and what was there for me to do? Ah, sir! you are so clever, I often think you could help me to make a swing with ladders instead of single ropes, so that I could run up and down the rigging whilst it was in full go."

"That would be something like your fir-tree prank, Tom," said his sister. "Can you believe," she added, turning to the visitor, "that Tom lopped the branches of a tall young fir-tree all the way up, leaving little bits for foothold, and then climbed up it one day in an awful storm of wind, and clung on at the top, rocking backwards and forwards? And when papa sent word for him to come down, he said parental authority was superseded at sea by the rules of the service. It was a dreadful storm, and the tree snapped very soon after he got safe to the ground."

"Storm!" sneered Tom, "a capful of wind. Well, it did blow half a gale at the last. But oh! it was glorious!"

"Let us see what we can make of the crackers," said the tutor—and he pulled some out of his pocket. They were put in a dish upon the table, for the company to choose from; and the terriers jumped and snapped, and tumbled over each other, for they thought that the plate contained eatables. Animated by the same idea, but with quieter steps, Master MacGreedy also approached the table.

"The dogs are noisy," said the tutor, "too noisy. We must have quiet— peace and quiet." His lean hand was once more in his pocket, and he pulled out a box, from which he took some powder, which he scattered on the burning log. A slight smoke now rose from the hot embers, and floated into the room. Was the powder one of those strange compounds that act upon the brain? Was it a magician's powder? Who knows? With it came a sweet, subtle fragrance. It was strange—every one fancied he had smelt it before, and all were absorbed in wondering what it was, and where they had met with it. Even the dogs sat on their haunches with their noses up, sniffing in a speculative manner.

"It's not lavender," said the grandmother, slowly, "and it's not rosemary. There is a something of tansy in it (and a very fine tonic flavor too, my dears, though it's *not* in fashion now.) Depend upon it, it's a potpourri, and from an excellent receipt, sir"—and the old lady bowed courteously toward the tutor. "My mother made the best potpourri in the county, and it was very much like this. Not quite, perhaps, but much the same, much the same."

The grandmother was a fine old gentlewoman "of the old school," as the phrase is. She was very stately and gracious in her manners, daintily neat in her person, and much attached to the old parson of the parish, who now sat

Christmas Crackers

near her chair. All her life she had been very proud of her fine stock of fair linen, both household and personal; and for many years past had kept her own graveclothes ready in a drawer. They were bleached as white as snow, and lay amongst bags of dried lavender and potpourri. Many times had it seemed likely that they would be needed, for the old lady had had severe illnesses of late, when the good parson sat by her bedside, and read to her of the coming of the Bridegroom, and of that "fine linen clean and white," which is "the righteousness of the saints." It was of that drawer, with its lavender and potpourri bags, that the scented smoke had reminded her.

"It has rather an overpowering odor," said the old parson; "it is suggestive of incense. I am sure I once smelt something like it in the Church of the Nativity at Bethlehem. It is very delicious."

The parson's long residence in his parish had been marked by one great holiday. With the savings of many years he had performed a pilgrimage to the Holy Land; and it was rather a joke against him that he illustrated a large variety of subjects by reference to his favorite topic, the holiday of his life.

"It smells of gunpowder," said Jim, decidedly, "and something else. I can't tell what."

"Something one smells in a seaport town," said Tom.

"Can't be very delicious then," Jim retorted.

"It's not *quite* the same," piped the widow "but it reminds me very much of an old bottle of attar of roses that was given to me when I was at school, with a copy of verses, by a young gentleman who was brother to one of the pupils. I remember Mr. Jones was quite annoyed when he found it in an old box, where I am sure I had not touched it for ten years or more; and I never spoke to him but once, on Examination Day (the young gentleman, I mean). And it's like—yes it's certainly like a hair-wash Mr. Jones used to use. I've forgotten what it was called, but I know it cost fifteen shillings a bottle; and Macready threw one over a few weeks before his dear papa's death, and annoyed him extremely."

Whilst the company were thus engaged, Master MacGreedy took advantage of the general abstraction to secure half a dozen crackers to his own share; he retired to a corner with them, where he meant to pick them quietly to pieces by himself. He wanted the gay paper, and the motto, and the sweetmeats; but he did not like the report of the cracker. And then what he did want, he wanted all to himself.

"Give us a cracker," said Master Jim, dreamily.

The dogs, after a few dissatisfied snorts, had dropped from their sitting posture, and were lying close together on the rug, dreaming, and uttering short commenting barks and whines at intervals. The twins were now reposing lazily at the tutor's feet, and did not feel disposed to exert themselves even so far as to fetch their own bonbons.

"There's one," said the tutor, taking a fresh cracker from his pocket. One end of it was of red and gold paper, the other of transparent green stuff with silver lines. The boys pulled it.

✳

The report was louder than Jim had expected.

"The firing has begun," he murmured, involuntarily; "steady, steady!" these last words were to his horse, who seemed to be moving under him, not from fear but from impatience. What had been the red and gold paper of the cracker was now the scarlet and gold lace of his own cavalry uniform. He knocked a speck from his sleeve, and scanned the distant ridge, from which a thin line of smoke floated solemnly away, with keen, impatient eyes. Were they to stand inactive all the day?

Presently the horse erects his head. His eyes sparkle—he pricks his sensitive ears—his nostrils quiver with a strange delight. It is the trumpet! Fan farrâ! Fan farrâ! The brazen voice speaks—the horses move—the plumes wave—the helmets shine. On a summer's day they ride slowly, gracefully, calmly down a slope, to Death or Glory. Fan farrâ! Fan farrâ! Fan farrâ!

✳

Of all this Master Tom knew nothing. The report of the cracker seemed to him only an echo in his brain of a sound that had been in his ears for thirty-six weary hours. The noise of a heavy sea beating against the ship's side in a gale. It was over now, and he was keeping the midnight watch on deck, gazing upon the liquid green of the waves, which heaving and seething after storm, were lit with phosphoric light, and as the ship held steadily on her course, poured past at the rate of twelve knots an hour in a silvery stream. Faster than any ship can sail his thoughts travelled home; and as old times came back to him, he hardly knew whether what he looked at was the phosphor-lighted sea, or green gelatine paper barred with silver. And did the tutor speak? Or was it the voice of some sea monster sounding in his ears?

"The spirits of the storm have gone below to make their report. The treasure gained from sunk vessels has been reckoned, and the sea is illuminated in honor of the spoil."

✺

The visitor now took a cracker and held it to the young lady. Her end was of the white paper with a raised pattern; his of dark-blue gelatine with gold stars. It snapped, the bonbon dropped between them, and the young man got the motto. It was a very bald one—

> "My heart is thine.
> Wilt thou be mine?"

He was ashamed to show it to her. What could be more meagre? One could write a hundred better couplets "standing on one leg," as the saying is. He was trying to improvise just one for the occasion, when he became aware that the blue sky over his head was dark with the shades of night, and lighted with stars. A brook rippled near with a soothing monotony. The evening wind sighed through the trees, and wafted the fragrance of the sweet bay-leaved willow toward him, and blew a stray lock of hair against his face. Yes! *She* also was there, walking beside him, under the scented willow bushes. Where, why, and whither he did not ask to know. She was with him—with him; and he seemed to tread on the summer air. He had no doubt as to the nature of his own feelings for her, and here was such an opportunity for declaring them as might never occur again. Surely now, if ever, he would be eloquent! Thoughts of poetry clothed in words of fire must spring unbidden to his lips at such a moment. And yet somehow he could not find a single word to say. He beat his brains, but not an idea would come forth. Only that idiotic cracker motto, which haunted him with its meagre couplet.

> "My heart is thine.
> Wilt thou be mine?"

Meanwhile they wandered on. The precious time was passing. He must at least make a beginning.

"What a fine night it is!" he observed. But, oh dear! That was a thousand times balder and more meagre than the cracker motto; and not another word could he find to say. At this moment the awkward silence was broken by a voice from a neighboring copse. It was a nightingale singing to his mate. There was no lack of eloquence, and of melodious eloquence, there. The song was as plaintive as old memories, and as full of tenderness as the eyes of the young girl were full of tears. They were standing still now, and with her graceful head bent she was listening to the bird. He stooped his head near hers, and spoke with a simple natural outburst almost involuntary.

"Do you ever think of old times? Do you remember the old house, and the fun we used to have? and the tutor? whom you pelted with horse-chestnuts when you were a little girl? And those cracker bonbons, and the motto *we* drew—

> 'My heart is thine.
> Wilt thou be mine?'"

She smiled, and lifted her eyes ("blue as the sky, and bright as the stars," he thought) to his, and answered "Yes."

Then the bonbon motto was avenged, and there was silence. Eloquent, perfect, complete, beautiful silence! Only the wind sighed through the fragrant willows, the stream rippled, the stars shone, and in the neighboring copse the nightingale sang, and sang, and sang.

✺

When the white end of the cracker came into the young lady's hand, she was full of admiration for the fine raised pattern. As she held it between her fingers it suddenly struck her that she had discovered what the tutor's fragrant smoke smelt like. It was like the scent of orange-flowers, and had certainly a soporific effect upon the senses. She felt very sleepy, and as she stroked the shiny surface of the cracker she found herself thinking it was very soft for paper, and then rousing herself with a start, and wondering at her own folly in speaking thus of the white silk in which she was dressed, and of which she was holding up the skirt between her finger and thumb, as if she were dancing a minuet.

"It's grandmamma's eggshell brocade!" she cried. "Oh, grandmamma! Have you given it to me? That lovely old thing! But I thought it was the family wedding-dress, and that I was not to have it till I was a bride."

"And so you are, my dear. And a fairer bride the sun never shone on," sobbed the old lady, who was kissing and blessing her, and wishing her, in the words of the old formula—

> "Health to wear it,
> Strength to tear it,
> And money to buy another."

"There is no hope for the last two things, you know," said the young girl; "for I am sure that the flag that braved a thousand years was not half so strong as your brocade; and as to buying another, there are none to be bought in these degenerate days."

The old lady's reply was probably very gracious, for she liked to be complimented on the virtues of old things in general, and of her eggshell brocade in particular. But of what she said her granddaughter heard nothing. With the strange irregularity of dreams, she found herself, she knew not how, in the old church. It was true. She was a bride, standing there with old friends and old associations thick around her, on the threshold of a new life. The sun shone through the stained glass of the windows, and illuminated the brocade, whose old-fashioned stiffness so became her childish beauty, and flung a thousand new tints over her sunny hair, and drew so powerful a fragrance from the orange blossom with which it was twined, that it was almost overpowering. Yes! It was too sweet—too strong. She certainly would not be able to bear it much longer without losing her senses. And the service was going on. A question had been asked of her, and she must reply. She made a strong effort, and said "Yes," simply and very earnestly, for it was what she meant. But she had no sooner said it than she became uneasily conscious that she had not used the right words. Some one laughed. It was the tutor, and his voice jarred and disturbed the dream, as a stone troubles the surface of still water. The vision trembled, and then broke, and the young lady found herself still sitting by the table and fingering the cracker paper, whilst the tutor chuckled and rubbed his hands by the fire, and his shadow scrambled on the wall like an ape upon a tree. But her "Yes" had passed into the young man's dream without disturbing it, and he dreamt on.

⁂

It was a cracker like the preceding one that the grandmother and the parson pulled together. The old lady had insisted upon it. The good rector had shown a tendency to low spirits this evening, and a wish to withdraw early. But the old lady did not approve of people "shirking" (as boys say) either their duties or their pleasures; and to keep a "merry Christmas" in a family circle that had been spared to meet in health and happiness, seemed to her to be both the one and the other.

It was his sermon for next day which weighed on the parson's mind. Not that he was behind-hand with that part of his duties. He was far too methodical in his habits for that, and it had been written before the bustle of Christmas week began. But after preaching Christmas sermons from the same pulpit for thirty-five years, he felt keenly how difficult it is to awaken due interest in subjects that are so familiar, and to give new force to lessons so often repeated. So he wanted a quiet hour in his own study before he went to rest, with the sermon that did not satisfy him, and the subject that should be so heart-stirring and ever new, —the Story of Bethlehem.

He consented, however, to pull one cracker with the grandmother, though he feared the noise might startle her nerves, and said so.

"Nerves were not invented in my young days," said the old lady, firmly; and she took her part in the ensuing explosion without so much as a wink.

As the crackers snapped, it seemed to the parson as if the fragrant smoke from the yule log were growing denser in the room. Through the mist from time to time the face of the tutor loomed large, and then disappeared. At last the clouds rolled away, and the parson breathed clear air. Clear, yes, and how clear! This brilliant freshness, these intense lights and shadows, this mildness and purity in the night air—

"It is not England," he muttered, "it is the East. I have felt no air like this since I breathed the air of Palestine."

Over his head, through immeasurable distances, the dark-blue space was lighted by the great multitude of the stars, whose glittering ranks have in that atmosphere a distinctness and glory unseen with us. Perhaps no scene of beauty in the visible creation has proved a more hackneyed theme for the poet and the philosopher than a starry night. But not all the superabundance of simile and moral illustration with which the subject has been loaded can rob the beholder of the freshness of its grandeur or the force of its teaching; that noblest and most majestic vision of the handiwork of GOD on which the eye of man is here permitted to rest.

As the parson gazed he became conscious that he was not alone. Other eyes beside his were watching the skies to-night. Dark, profound, patient, eastern eyes, used from the cradle to the grave to watch and wait. The eyes of stargazers and dream-interpreters; men who believed the fate of empires to be written in shining characters on the face of heaven, as the "Mene, Mene,"[4] was written in fire on the walls of the Babylonian palace. The old parson was one of the many men of real learning and wide reading who pursue their studies in the quiet country parishes of England, and it was with the keen interest of intelligence that he watched the group of figures that lay near him.

"Is this a vision of the past?" he asked himself. "There can be no doubt as to these men. They are star-gazers, magi, and, from their dress and

---

4. **Mene Mene** the words ("he is numbered") appeared on the wall of Belshazar's palace to warn him of the destruction of Babylon (Daniel 5:25)

bearing, men of high rank, perhaps 'teachers of a higher wisdom' in one of the purest philosophies of the old heathen world. When one thinks," he pursued, "of the intense interest, the eager excitement which the student of history finds in the narrative of the past as unfolded in dusty records written by the hand of man, one may realize how absorbing must have been that science which professed to unveil the future, and to display to the eyes of the wise the fate of dynasties written with the finger of GOD amid the stars."

The dark-robed figures were so still that they might almost have been carved in stone. The air seemed to grow purer and purer; the stars shone brighter and brighter; suspended in ether the planets seemed to hang like lamps. Now a shooting meteor passed athwart the sky, and vanished behind the hill. But not for this did the watchers move; in silence they watched on— till, on a sudden, how and whence the parson knew not, across the shining ranks of that immeasurable host, whose names and number are known to GOD alone, there passed in slow but obvious motion one brilliant solitary star—a star of such surpassing brightness that he involuntarily joined in the wild cry of joy and greeting with which the Men of the East now prostrated themselves with their faces to the earth.

He could not understand the language in which, with noisy clamor and gesticulation, they broke their former profound and patient silence, and greeted the portent for which they had watched. But he knew now that these were the Wise Men of the Epiphany, and that this was the Star of Bethlehem. In his ears rang the energetic simplicity of the Gospel narrative, "When they saw the Star, they rejoiced with exceeding great joy."

With exceeding great joy! Ah! happy magi, who (more blest than Balaam the son of Beor),[5] were faithful to the dim light vouchsafed to you; the Gentile church may well be proud of your memory. Ye travelled long and far to bring royal offerings to the King of the Jews, with a faith not found in Israel. Ye saw him whom prophets and kings had desired to see, and were glad. Wise men indeed, and wise with the highest wisdom, in that ye suffered yourselves to be taught of GOD.

Then the parson prayed that if this were indeed a dream he might dream on; might pass, if only in a vision, over the hill, following the footsteps of the magi, whilst the Star went before them, till he should see it rest above that city, which, little indeed among the thousands of Judah, was yet the birthplace of the Lord's Christ.

5. **Balaam the son of Beor** the necromancer who blesses rather than curses the Israelite invaders in Numbers 23–25

"Ah!" he almost sobbed, "let me follow! On my knees let me follow into the house and see the Holy Child. In the eyes of how many babies I have seen mind and thought far beyond their powers of communication, every mother knows. But if at times, with a sort of awe, one sees the immortal soul shining through the prison bars of helpless infancy, what, oh! what must it be to behold the Godhead veiled in flesh through the face of a little child!"

The parson stretched out his arms, but even with the passion of his words the vision began to break. He dared not move for fear it should utterly fade, and as he lay still and silent, the wise men roused their followers, and led by the Star, the train passed solemnly over the distant hills.

Then the clear night became clouded with fragrant vapor, and with a sigh the parson awoke.

✳

When the cracker snapped and the white end was left in the grandmother's hand, she was astonished to perceive (as she thought) that the white lace veil which she had worn over her wedding bonnet was still in her possession, and that she was turning it over in her fingers. "I fancied I gave it to Jemima when her first baby was born," she muttered dreamily. It was darned and yellow, but it carried her back all the same, and recalled happy hours with wonderful vividness. She remembered the post-chaise and the postilion. "He was such a pert little fellow, and how we laughed at him! He must be either dead or a very shaky old man by now," said the old lady. She seemed to smell the scent of meadowsweet that was so powerful in a lane through which they drove; and how clearly she could see the clean little country inn where they spent the honeymoon! She seemed to be there now, taking off her bonnet and shawl, in the quaint clean chamber, with the heavy oak rafters, and the jasmine coming in at the window, and glancing with pardonable pride at the fair face reflected in the mirror. But as she laid her things on the patchwork coverlet, it seemed to her that the lace veil became fine white linen, and was folded about a figure that lay in the bed; and when she looked round the room again everything was draped in white—white blinds hung before the windows, and even the old oak chest and the press were covered with clean white cloths, after the decent custom of the country; whilst from the church tower without the passing bell tolled slowly. She had not seen the face of the corpse, and a strange anxiety came over her to count the strokes of the bell, which tell if it is a man, woman, or child who has passed away. One, two, three, four, five, six, seven! No more. It was a woman, and when she looked on the face of the dead she saw her own. But even as she looked the fair linen of the grave clothes became the buoyant drapery of another figure, in whose face she found a strange recognition of the lineaments of the dead with all the loveliness of the bride. But ah! more, much more! On that face there was a beauty not doomed to wither, before those happy eyes lay a future unshadowed by the imperfections of earthly prospects, and the folds of that robe were white as no fuller on earth can white them. The window curtain parted, the jasmine flowers bowed their heads, the spirit passed from the chamber of death, and the old lady's dream was ended.

✳

Miss Letitia had shared a cracker with the widow. The widow squeaked when the cracker went off, and then insisted upon giving up the smart paper and everything to Miss Letitia. She had always given up everything to Mr. Jones, she did so now to Master MacGreedy, and was quite unaccustomed to keep anything for her own share. She did not give this explanation herself, but so it was.

The cracker that thus fell into the hands of Miss Letitia was one of those new-fashioned ones that have a paper pattern of some article of dress wrapped up in them instead of a bonbon. This one was a paper bonnet made in the latest *mode*—of green tissue paper; and Miss Letitia stuck it on the top of her chignon with an air that the widow envied from the bottom of her heart. She had not the gift of "carrying off" her clothes. But to the tutor, on the contrary, it seemed to afford the most extreme amusement; and as Miss Letitia bowed gracefully hither and thither in the energy of her conversation with the widow, the green paper fluttering with each emphasis, he fairly shook with delight, his shadow dancing like a maniac beside him. He had scattered some more powder on the coals, and it may have been that the smoke got into her eyes, and confused her ideas of color, but Miss Letitia was struck with a fervid and otherwise unaccountable admiration for the paper ends of the cracker, which were most unusually ugly. One was of a sallowish salmon-color, and transparent, the other was of brick-red paper with a fringe. As Miss Letitia turned them over, she saw, to her unspeakable delight, that there were several yards of each material, and her peculiar genius instantly seized upon the fact that in the present rage for double skirts there might be enough of the two kinds to combine into a fashionable dress.

It had never struck her before that a dirty salmon went well with brick red. "They blend so becomingly, my dear," she murmured; "and I think the under skirt will sit well, it is so stiff."

The widow did not reply. The fumes of the tutor's compound made her sleepy, and though she nodded to Miss Letitia's observations, it was less from appreciation of their force, than from inability to hold up her head. She was dreaming uneasy, horrible dreams, light nightmares; in which from time to time there mingled expressions of doubt and dissatisfaction which fell from Miss Letitia's lips. "Just half a yard short—no gores—false hem" (and the melancholy reflection that) "flounces take so much stuff." Then the tutor's face kept appearing and vanishing with horrible grimaces through the mist. At last the widow fell fairly asleep, and dreamed that she was married to the Blue Beard of nursery annals, and that on his return from his memorable journey he had caught her in the act of displaying the mysterious cupboard to Miss Letitia. As he waved his scimitar over her head, he seemed unaccountably to assume the form and features of the tutor. In her agitation the poor woman could think of no plea against his severity, except that the cupboard was already crammed with the corpses of his previous wives, and that there was no room for her. She was pleading this argument when Miss Letitia's voice broke in upon her dream with decisive accent:

"There's enough for two bodies."

The widow shrieked and awoke.

"High and low," explained Miss Letitia. "My dear, what *are* you screaming about?"

"I am very sorry indeed," said the widow; "I beg your pardon, I'm sure, a thousand times. But since Mr. Jones's death I have been so nervous, and I had such a horrible dream. And, oh dear! oh dear!" she added, "what is the matter with my precious child? Macready, love, come to your mamma, my pretty lamb."

Ugh! ugh! There were groans from the corner where Master Mac-Greedy sat on his crackers as if they were eggs, and he hatching them. He had only touched one, as yet, of the stock he had secured. He had picked it to pieces, had avoided the snap, and had found a large comfit like an egg with a rough shell inside. Every one knows that the goodies in crackers are not of a very superior quality. There is a large amount of white lead in the outside thinly disguised by a shabby flavor of sugar. But that outside once disposed of, there lies an almond at the core. Now an almond is a very delicious thing in itself, and doubly nice when it takes the taste of white paint and chalk out of one's mouth. But in spite of all the white lead and sugar and chalk through which he had sucked his way, MacGreedy could not come to the almond. A dozen times had he been on the point of spitting out the delusive sweetmeat; but just as he thought of it he was sure to feel a bit of hard rough edge, and thinking he had gained the kernel at last, he held valiantly on. It only proved to be a rough bit of sugar, however, and still the interminable coating melted copiously in his mouth; and still the clean, fragrant almond evaded his hopes. At last with a groan he spat the seemingly undiminished bonbon on to the floor, and turned as white and trembling as an arrowroot blancmange. [6]

In obedience to the widow's entreaties the tutor opened a window, and tried to carry MacGreedy to the air; but that young gentleman utterly refused to allow the tutor to approach him, and was borne howling to bed by his mamma.

With the fresh air the fumes of the fragrant smoke dispersed, and the company roused themselves.

"Rather oppressive, eh?" said the master of the house, who had had his dream too, with which we have no concern.

The dogs had had theirs also, and had testified to the same in their sleep by low growls and whines. Now they shook themselves, and rubbed against each other, growling in a warlike manner through their teeth, and wagging peaceably with their little stumpy tails.

The twins shook themselves and fell to squabbling as to whether they had been to sleep or no; and, if either, which of them had given way to that weakness.

Miss Letitia took the paper bonnet from her head with a nervous laugh, and after looking regretfully at the cracker papers put them in her pocket.

The parson went home through the frosty night. In the village street he heard a boy's voice singing two lines of the Christmas hymn—

> "Trace we the Babe Who hath redeemed our loss
> From the poor Manger to the bitter Cross;"

and his eyes filled with tears.

The old lady went to bed and slept in peace.

"In all the thirty-five years we have been privileged to hear you, sir," she told the rector next day after service, "I never heard such a Christmas sermon before."

The visitor carefully preserved the blue paper and the cracker motto. He

---

6. **blancmange** a whitish, jelly-like dessert

came down early next morning to find the white half to put with them. He did not find it, for the young lady had taken it the night before.

The tutor had been in the room before him, wandering round the scene of the evening's festivities.

The yule log lay black and cold upon the hearth, and the tutor nodded to it. "I told you how it would be," he said; "but never mind, you have had your day, and a merry one too." In the corner lay the heap of crackers which Master MacGreedy had been too ill to remember when he retired. The tutor pocketed them with a grim smile.

As to the comfit, it was eaten by one of the dogs, who had come down earliest of all. He swallowed it whole, so whether it contained an almond or not, remains a mystery to the present time.

FRANCES HODGSON BURNETT

Behind the White Brick

It began with Aunt Hetty's being out of temper, which, it must be confessed, was nothing new. At its best, Aunt Hetty's temper was none of the most charming, and this morning it was at its worst. She had awakened to the consciousness of having a hard day's work before her, and she had awakened late, and so everything had gone wrong from the first. There was a sharp ring in her voice when she came to Jem's bedroom door and called out, "Jemima, get up this minute!"

Jem knew what to expect when Aunt Hetty began a day by calling her "Jemima." It was one of the poor child's grievances that she had been given such an ugly name. In all the books she had read, and she had read a great many, Jem never had met a heroine who was called Jemima. But it had been her mother's favourite sister's name, and so it had fallen to her lot. Her mother always called her "Jem," or "Mimi," which was much prettier, and even Aunt Hetty only reserved Jemima for unpleasant state occasions.

It was a dreadful day to Jem. Her mother was not at home, and would not be until night. She had been called away unexpectedly, and had been obliged to leave Jem and the baby to Aunt Hetty's mercies.

So Jem found herself busy enough. Scarcely had she finished doing one thing, when Aunt Hetty told her to begin another. She wiped dishes and picked fruit and attended to the baby;[1] and when baby had gone to sleep, and everything else seemed disposed of, for a time, at least, she was so tired that she was glad to sit down.

First published in *St. Nicholas Magazine* in 1879, "Behind the White Brick" was later collected in *Little St. Elizabeth and Other Stories* (1890).

1. **the baby** The chores Jem must perform make her a very different child than Ewing's Amelia; there seem to be no servants in *this* American middle-class family.

164

And then she thought of the book she had been reading the night before—a certain delightful story book, about a little girl whose name was Flora, and who was so happy and rich and pretty and good that Jem had likened her to the little princesses one reads about, to whose christening feast every fairy brings a gift.

"I shall have time to finish my chapter before dinner-time comes," said Jem, and she sat down snugly in one corner of the wide, old fashioned fireplace.

But she had not read more than two pages before something dreadful happened. Aunt Hetty came into the room in a great hurry—in such a hurry, indeed, that she caught her foot in the matting and fell, striking her elbow sharply against a chair, which so upset her temper that the moment she found herself on her feet she flew at Jem.

"What!" she said, snatching the book from her, "reading again, when I am running all over the house for you?" And she flung the pretty little blue covered volume into the fire.

Jem sprang to rescue it with a cry, but it was impossible to reach it; it had fallen into a great hollow of red coal, and the blaze caught it at once.

"You are a wicked woman!" cried Jem, in a dreadful passion, to Aunt Hetty. "You are a wicked woman."

Then matters reached a climax. Aunt Hetty boxed her ears, pushed her back on her little footstool, and walked out of the room.

Jem hid her face on her arms and cried as if her heart would break. She cried until her eyes were heavy, and she thought she should be obliged to go to sleep. But just as she was thinking of going to sleep, something fell down the chimney and made her look up. It was a piece of mortar, and it brought a good deal of soot with it. She bent forward and looked up to see where it had come from. The chimney was so very wide that this was easy enough. She could see where the mortar had fallen from the side and left a white patch.

"How white it looks against the black!" said Jem; "it is like a white brick among the black ones. What a queer place a chimney is! I can see a bit of the blue sky, I think."

And then a funny thought came into her fanciful little head. What a many things were burned in the big fireplace and vanished in smoke or tinder up the chimney! Where did everything go? There was Flora, for instance— Flora who was represented on the frontispiece—with lovely, soft, flowing hair, and a little fringe on her pretty round forehead, crowned with a circlet of daisies, and a laugh in her wide-awake round eyes. Where was she by this time? Certainly there was nothing left of her in the fire. Jem almost began to cry again at the thought.

"It was too bad," she said. "She was so pretty and funny, and I did like her so."

I daresay it scarcely will be credited by unbelieving people when I tell them what happened next, it was such a very singular thing, indeed.

Jem felt herself gradually lifted off her little footstool.

"Oh!" she said, timidly, "I feel very light." She did feel light, indeed. She felt so light that she was sure she was rising gently in the air.

"Oh," she said again, "how—how very light I feel! Oh, dear. I'm going up the chimney!"

It was rather strange that she never thought of calling for help, but she did not. She was not easily frightened; and now she was only wonderfully astonished, as she remembered afterwards. She shut her eyes tight and gave a little gasp.

"I've heard Aunt Hetty talk about the draught drawing things up the chimney, but I never knew it was as strong as this," she said.

She went up, up, up, quietly and steadily, and without any uncomfortable feeling at all; and then all at once she stopped, feeling that her feet rested against something solid. She opened her eyes and looked about her, and there she was, standing right opposite the white brick, her feet on a tiny ledge.

"Well," she said, "this is funny."

But the next thing that happened was funnier still. She found that, without thinking what she was doing, she was knocking on the white brick with her knuckles, as if it was a door and she expected somebody to open it. The next minute she heard footsteps, and then a sound, as if someone was drawing back a little bolt.

"It is a door," said Jem, "and somebody is going to open it."

The white brick moved a little, and some more mortar and soot fell; then the brick moved a little more, and then it slid aside and left an open space.

"It's a room!" cried Jem. "There's a room behind it!"

And so there was, and before the open space stood a pretty little girl, with long lovely hair and a fringe on her forehead. Jem clasped her hands in amazement. It was Flora herself, as she looked in the picture, and Flora stood laughing and nodding.

"Come in," she said. "I thought it was you."

"But how can I come in through such a little place?" asked Jem.

"Oh, that is easy enough," said Flora. "Here, give me your hand."

Jem did as she told her, and found that it was easy enough. In an instant she had passed through the opening, the white brick had gone back to its place, and she was standing by Flora's side in a large room—the nicest room she had ever seen. It was big and lofty and light, and there were all kinds of delightful things in it—books and flowers and playthings and pictures, and in one corner a great cage full of lovebirds.

"Have I ever seen it before?" asked Jem, glancing slowly round.

"Yes," said Flora; "you saw it last night—in your mind. Don't you remember it?"

Jem shook her head.

"I feel as if I did, but—"

"Why," said Flora, laughing, "it's my room, the one you read about last night."

"So it is," said Jem. "But how did you come here?"

"I can't tell you that; I myself don't know. But I am here, and so"—rather mysteriously—"are a great many other things."

"Are they?" said Jem, very much interested. "What things? Burned things? I was just wondering—"

"Not only burned things," said Flora, nodding. "Just come with me and I'll show you something."

She led the way out of the room and down a little passage with several doors in each side of it, and she opened one door and showed Jem what was on the other side of it. That was a room, too, and this time it was funny as well as pretty. Both floor and walls were padded with rose colour, and the floor was strewn with toys. There were big soft balls, rattles, horses, woolly dogs, and a doll or so; there was one low cushioned chair and a low table.

"You can come in," said a shrill little voice behind the door, "only mind you don't tread on things."

"What a funny little voice!" said Jem, but she had no sooner said it than she jumped back.

The owner of the voice, who had just come forward, was no other than Baby.

"Why," exclaimed Jem, beginning to feel frightened. "I left you fast asleep in your crib."

"Did you?" said Baby, somewhat scornfully. "That's just the way with you grown-up people. You think you know everything, and yet you haven't discretion enough to know when a pin is sticking into one. You'd know soon enough if you had one sticking into your own back."

"But I'm not grown up," stammered Jem; "and when you are at home you can neither walk nor talk. You're not six months old."

"Well, miss," retorted Baby, whose wrongs seemed to have soured her disposition somewhat, "you have no need to throw that in my teeth; you were not six months old, either, when you were my age."

Jem could not help laughing.

"You haven't got any teeth," she said.

"Haven't I?" said Baby, and she displayed two beautiful rows with some haughtiness of manner. "When I am up here," she said, "I am supplied with the modern conveniences, and that's why I never complain. Do I ever cry when I am asleep? It's not falling asleep I object to, it's falling awake."

"Wait a minute," said Jem. "Are you asleep now?"

"I'm what you call asleep. I can only come here when I'm what you call asleep. Asleep, indeed! It's no wonder we always cry when we have to fall awake."

"But we don't mean to be unkind to you," protested Jem, meekly.

She could not help thinking baby was very severe.

"Don't mean!" said Baby. "Well, why don't you think more, then? How would you like to have all the nice things snatched away from you, and all the old rubbish packed off on you, as if you hadn't any sense? How would you like to have to sit and stare at things you wanted, and not to be able to reach them, or, if you did reach them, have them fall out of your hand, and roll away in the most unfeeling manner? And then be scolded and called 'cross!' It's no wonder we are bald. You'd be bald yourself. It's trouble and worry that keep us bald until we can begin to take care of ourselves; I had more hair than this at first, but it fell off, as well it might. No philosopher ever thought of that, I suppose!"

"Well," said Jem, in despair, "I hope you enjoy yourself when you are here?"

"Yes, I do," answered Baby. "That's one comfort. There is nothing to knock my head against, and things have patent stoppers on them, so that they can't roll away, and everything is soft and easy to pick up."

There was a slight pause after this, and Baby seemed to cool down.

"I suppose you would like me to show you round?" she said.

"Not if you have any objection," replied Jem, who was rather subdued.

"I would as soon do it as not," said Baby. "You are not as bad as some people, though you do get my clothes twisted when you hold me."

Upon the whole, she seemed rather proud of her position. It was evident she quite regarded herself as hostess. She held her small bald head very high indeed, as she trotted on before them. She stopped at the first door she came to, and knocked three times. She was obliged to stand upon tiptoe to reach the knocker.

"He's sure to be at home at this time of year," she remarked. "This is the busy season."

"Who's 'he'?" inquired Jem.

But Flora only laughed at Miss Baby's consequential air.

"S. C.,[2] to be sure," was the answer, as the young lady pointed to the door-plate, upon which Jem noticed, for the first time, "S. C." in very large letters.

The door opened, apparently without assistance, and they entered the apartment.

"Good gracious!" exclaimed Jem, the next minute "Good*ness* gracious!"

She might well be astonished. It was such a long room that she could not see to the end of it, and it was piled up from floor to ceiling with toys of every description, and there was such bustle and buzzing in it that it was quite confusing. The bustle and buzzing arose from a very curious cause, too,—it was the bustle and buzz of hundreds of tiny men and women who were working at little tables no higher than mushrooms,—the pretty tiny women cutting out and sewing, the pretty tiny men sawing and hammering, and all talking at once. The principal person in the place escaped Jem's notice at first; but it was not long before she saw him,—a little old gentleman, with a rosy face and sparkling eyes, sitting at a desk, and writing in a book almost as big as himself. He was so busy that he was quite excited, and had been obliged to throw his white fur coat and cap aside, and he was at work in his red waistcoat.

"Look here, if you please," piped Baby. "I have brought someone to see you."

When he turned round, Jem recognized him at once.

"Eh! Eh!" he said. "What! What! Who's this, Tootsicums?"

Baby's manner became very acid indeed.

"I shouldn't have thought you would have said that, Mr. Claus," she remarked. "I can't help myself down below, but I generally have my rights respected up here. I should like to know what sane godfather or godmother

2. **S. C.** "Sinter Klaas," a mispronunciation of the Dutch name for Saint Nicholas or "San Nicolaas," led to the American naming of the figure of Father Christmas. Santa's jolly image was fixed by the cartoonist Thomas Nast in the Christmas issue of *Harper's Weekly* in 1862.

would give one the name of 'Tootsicums' in one's baptism. They are bad enough, I must say; but I never heard of any of them calling a person 'Tootsicums.'"

"Come, come!" said S. C., chuckling comfortably and rubbing his hands. "Don't be too dignified,—it's a bad thing. And don't be too fond of flourishing your rights in people's faces,—that's the worst of all, Miss Midget. Folks who make such a fuss about their rights turn them into wrongs sometimes."

The he turned suddenly to Jem.

"You are the little girl from down below," he said.

"Yes, sir," answered Jem. "I'm Jem, and this is my friend Flora,—out of the blue book."

"I'm happy to make her acquaintance," said S. C., "and I'm happy to make yours. You are a nice child, though a trifle peppery. I'm very glad to see you."

"I'm very glad indeed to see you, sir," said Jem. "I wasn't quite sure—"

But there she stopped, feeling that it would be scarcely polite to tell him that she had begun of late years to lose faith in him.

But S. C. only chuckled more comfortably than ever and rubbed his hands again.

"Ho, ho!" he said. "You know who I am, then?"

Jem hesitated a moment, wondering whether it would not be taking a liberty to mention his name without putting "Mr." before it; then she remembered what Baby had called him.

"Baby called you 'Mr. Claus,' sir," she replied; "and I have seen pictures of you."

"To be sure," said S. C. "S. Claus, Esquire, of Chimneyland. How do you like me?"

"Very much," answered Jem,; "very much, indeed, sir."

"Glad of it! Glad of it! But what was it you were going to say you were not quite sure of?"

Jem blushed a little.

"I was not quite sure that—that you were true, sir. At least I have not been quite sure since I have been older."

S. C. rubbed the bald part of his head and gave a little sigh.

"I hope I have not hurt your feelings, sir," faltered Jem, who was a very kind hearted little soul.

"Well, no," said S. C. "Not exactly. And it is not your fault either. It is natural, I suppose; at any rate, it is the way of the world. People lose their belief in a great many things as they grow older; but that does not make the

"Eh! Eh!" he said. "What! What! Who's this, Tootsicums?"

things not true, thank goodness! and their faith often comes back after a while. But, bless me!" he added, briskly, "I'm moralizing, and who thanks a man for doing that? Suppose—"

"Black eyes or blue, sir?" said a tiny voice close to them.

Jem and Flora turned round, and saw it was one of the small workers who was asking the question.

"Whom for?" inquired S. C.

"Little girl in the red brick house at the corner," said the workwoman; "name of Birdie."

"Excuse me a moment," said S. C. to the children, and he turned to the big book and began to run his fingers down the pages in a business-like manner. "Ah! here she is!" he exclaimed at last. "Blue eyes, if you please, Thistle, and golden hair. And let it be a big one. She takes good care of them."

"Yes, sir," said Thistle; "I am personally acquainted with several dolls in her family. I go to parties in her dolls' house sometimes when she is fast asleep at night, and they all speak very highly of her. She is most attentive to them when they are ill. In fact, her pet doll is a cripple, with a stiff leg."

She ran back to her work and S. C. finished his sentence.

"Suppose I show you my establishment," he said. "Come with me."

It really would be quite impossible to describe the wonderful things he showed them. Jem's head was quite in a whirl before she had seen one-half of them, and even Baby condescended to become excited.

"There must be a great many children in the world, Mr. Claus," ventured Jem.

"Yes, yes, millions of 'em; bless 'em," said S. C., growing rosier with delight at the very thought. "We never run out of them, that's one comfort. There's a large and varied assortment always on hand. Fresh ones every year, too, so that when one grows too old there is a new one ready. I have a place like this in every twelfth chimney. Now it's boys, now it's girls, always one or t'other; and there's no end of playthings for them, too, I'm glad to say. For girls, the great thing seems to be dolls. Blitzen! what comfort they *do* take in dolls! but the boys are for horses and racket."

They were standing near a table where a worker was just putting the finishing touch to the dress of a large wax doll, and just at that moment, to Jem's surprise, she set it on the floor, upon its feet, quite coolly.

"Thank you," said the doll, politely.

Jem quite jumped.

"You can join the rest now and introduce yourself," said the worker.

The doll looked over her shoulder at her train.

"It hangs very nicely," she said. "I hope it's the latest fashion."

"Mine never talked like that," said Flora. "My best one could only say 'Mamma,' and it said it very badly, too."

"She was foolish for saying it at all," remarked the doll, haughtily. "We don't talk and walk before ordinary people; we keep our accomplishments for our own amusement, and for the amusement of our friends. If you should chance to get up in the middle of the night, some time, or should run into the room suddenly some day, after you have left it, you might hear—but what is the use of talking to human beings?"

"You know a great deal, considering you are only just finished," snapped Baby, who really was a Tartar.

"I was FINISHED," retorted the doll. "I did not begin life as a baby!" very scornfully.

"Pooh!" said Baby. "We improve as we get older."

"I hope, so, indeed," answered the doll. "There is plenty of room for improvement." And she walked away in great state.

S. C. looked at Baby and then shook his head. "I shall not have to take very much care of you," he said, absent-mindedly. "You are able to take pretty good care of yourself."

"I hope I am," said Baby, tossing her head.

S. C. gave his head another shake.

"Don't take too good care of yourself," he said. "That's a bad thing, too."

He showed them the rest of his wonders, and then went with them to the door to bid them good-bye.

"I am sure we are very much obliged to you, Mr. Claus," said Jem, gratefully. "I shall never again think you are not true, sir."

S. C. patted her shoulder quite affectionately.

"That's right," he said. "Believe in things just as long as you can, my dear. Good-bye until Christmas Eve. I shall see you then, if you don't see me."

He must have taken quite a fancy to Jem, for he stood looking at her, and seemed very reluctant to close the door, and even after he had closed it, and they had turned away, he opened it a little again to call to her.

"Believe in things as long as you can, my dear."

"How kind he is!" exclaimed Jem, full of pleasure.

Baby shrugged her shoulders.

"Well enough in his way," she said, "but rather inclined to prose and be old-fashioned."

Jem looked at her, feeling rather frightened, but she said nothing.

Baby showed very little interest in the next room she took them to.

"I don't care about this place," she said, as she threw open the door. "It has nothing but old things in it. It is the Nobody-knows-where room."

She had scarcely finished speaking before Jem made a little spring and picked something up.

"Here's my old strawberry pincushion!" she cried out. And then, with another jump and another dash at two or three other things, "And here's my old fairy-book! And here's my little locket I lost last summer! How did they come here?'

"They went Nobody-knows-where," said Baby.

"And this is it."

"But cannot I have them again?" asked Jem.

"No," answered Baby. "Things that go to Nobody-know-where stay there."

"Oh!" sighed Jem, "I am so sorry."

"They are only old things," said Baby.

"But I like my old things," said Jem. "I love them. And there is mother's needle case. I wish I might take that. Her dead little sister gave it to her, and she was so sorry when she lost it."

"People ought to take better care of their things," remarked Baby.

Jem would have liked to stay in this room and wander about among her old favourites for a long time, but Baby was in a hurry.

"You'd better come away," she said. "Suppose I was to have to fall awake and leave you?"

The next place they went into was the most wonderful of all.

"This is the Wish room,"said Baby. "Your wishes come here—yours and mother's and Aunt Hetty's and father's and mine. When did you wish that?"

Each article was placed under a glass shade, and labeled with the words and name of the wishes. Some of them were beautiful, indeed; but the tall shade Baby nodded at when she asked her question was truly alarming, and caused Jem a dreadful pang of remorse. Underneath it sat Aunt Hetty, with her mouth stitched up so that she could not speak a word, and beneath the stand was a label bearing these words, in large black letters—

"I wish Aunt Hetty's mouth was sewed up. Jem."

"Oh, dear!" cried Jem, in great distress. "How it must have hurt her! How unkind of me to say it! I wish I hadn't wished it. I wish it would come undone."

She had no sooner said it than her wish was gratified. The old label disappeared and a new one showed itself, and there sat Aunt Hetty, looking herself again, and even smiling.

Jem was grateful beyond measure, but Baby seemed to consider her weak minded.

"It served her right," she said.

But when, after looking at the wishes at that end of the room, they went to the other end, her turn came. In one corner stood a shade with a baby under it, and the baby was Miss Baby herself, but looking as she very rarely looked; in fact, it was the brightest, best tempered baby one could imagine.

"I wish I had a better tempered baby. Mother," was written on the label.

Baby became quite red in the face with anger and confusion.

"That wasn't here the last time I came," she said. "And it is right down mean in mother!"

This was more than Jem could bear.

"It wasn't mean," she said. "She couldn't help it. You know you are a cross baby—everybody says so."

Baby turned two shades redder.

"Mind your own business,"she retorted. "It was mean; and as to that silly little thing being better than I am," turning up her small nose, which was quite turned up enough by Nature—"I must say I don't see anything so very grand about her. So, there!"

She scarcely condescended to speak to them while they remained in the Wish room, and when they left it, and went to the last door in the passage, she quite scowled at it.

"I don't know whether I shall open it at all," she said.

"Why not?" asked Flora. "You might as well."

"It is the Lost Pin room," she said. "I hate pins."

She threw the door open with a bang, and then stood and shook her little fist viciously. The room was full of pins, stacked solidly together. There were hundreds of them—thousands—millions, it seemed.

"I'm glad they *are* lost!" she said. "I wish there were more of them there."

"I didn't know there were so many pins in the world," said Jem.

"Pooh!" said Baby. "Those are only the lost ones that have belonged to our family."

After this they went back to Flora's room and sat down, while Flora told Jem the rest of her story.

"Oh!" sighed Jem, when she came to the end. "How delightful it is to be here! Can I never come again?"

"In one way you can," said Flora. "When you want to come, just sit down and be as quiet as possible, and shut your eyes and think very hard about it. You can see everything you have seen to-day, if you try."

"Then I shall be sure to try," Jem answered. She was going to ask some other question but Baby stopped her.

"Oh! I'm falling awake," she whimpered, crossly, rubbing her eyes. "I'm falling awake again."

And then, suddenly, a very strange feeling came over Jem. Flora and the pretty room seemed to fade away, and, without being able to account for it at all, she found herself sitting on her little stool again, with a beautiful scarlet and gold book on her knee, and her mother standing by laughing at her amazed face. As to Miss Baby, she was crying as hard as she could in her crib.

"Mother!" Jem cried out, "have you really come home so early as this, and—and," rubbing her eyes in great amazement, "how did I come down?"

"Don't I look as if I was real?" said her mother, laughing and kissing her. "And doesn't your present look real? I don't know how you came down, I'm sure. Where have you been?"

Jem shook her head very mysteriously. She saw that her mother fancied she had been asleep, but she herself knew better.

"I know you wouldn't believe it was true if I told you," she said; "I have been

BEHIND THE WHITE BRICK."

E. NESBIT

Melisande

OR, LONG AND SHORT DIVISION

When the Princess Melisande was born, her mother, the Queen, wished to have a christening party, but the King put his foot down and said he would not have it.

"I've seen too much trouble come of christening parties," said he. "However carefully you keep your visiting-book, some fairy or other is sure to get left out, and you know what *that* leads to. Why, even in my own family, the most shocking things have occurred. The Fairy Malevola was not asked to my great-grandmother's christening—and you know all about the spindle and the hundred years' sleep." [1]

"Perhaps you're right," said the Queen. "My own cousin by marriage forgot some stuffy old fairy or other when she was sending out the cards for her daughter's christening, and the old wretch turned up at the last moment, and the girl drops toads out of her mouth to this day."

"Just so. And then there was that business of the mouse and the kitchen-maids," said the King; "we'll have no nonsense about it. I'll be her godfather, and you shall be her godmother, and we won't ask a single fairy; then none of them can be offended."

"Unless they all are," said the Queen.

And that was exactly what happened. When the King and the Queen and the baby got back from the christening the parlourmaid met them at the door, and said—

"Melisande" and "Fortunatus Rex," the next selection, were the fifth and sixth stories in Nesbit's *Nine Unlikely Tales* (1901).

1. **the hundred years' sleep** an allusion to "Sleeping Beauty"

"Please, your Majesty, several ladies have called. I told them you were not at home, but they all said they'd wait."

"Are they in the parlour?" asked the Queen.

"I've shown them into the Throne Room, your Majesty," said the parlourmaid. "You see, there are several of them."

There were about seven hundred. The great Throne Room was crammed with fairies, of all ages and of all degrees of beauty and ugliness— good fairies and bad fairies, flower fairies and moon fairies, fairies like spiders and fairies like butterflies—and as the Queen opened the door and began to say how sorry she was to have kept them waiting, they all cried, with one voice, "Why didn't you ask *me* to your christening party?"

"I haven't had a party," said the Queen, and she turned to the King and whispered, "I told you so." This was her only consolation.

"You've had a christening," said the fairies, all together.

"I'm very sorry," said the poor Queen, but Malevola pushed forward and said, "Hold your tongue," most rudely.

Malevola is the oldest, as well as the most wicked, of the fairies. She is deservedly unpopular, and has been left out of more christening parties than all the rest of the fairies put together.

"Don't begin to make excuses," she said, shaking her finger at the Queen. "That only makes your conduct worse. You know well enough what happens if a fairy is left out of a christening party. We are all going to give our christening presents *now*. As the fairy of highest social position, I shall begin. The Princess shall be bald."

The Queen nearly fainted as Malevola drew back, and another fairy, in a smart bonnet with snakes in it, stepped forward with a rustle of bats' wings. But the King stepped forward too.

"No you don't!" said he. "I wonder at you, ladies, I do indeed. How can you be so unfairylike? Have none of you been to school—have none of you studied the history of your own race? Surely you don't need a poor, ignorant King like me to tell you that this is *no go?*"

"How dare you?" cried the fairy in the bonnet, and the snakes in it quivered as she tossed her head. "It is my turn, and I say the Princess shall be—"

The King actually put his hand over her mouth.

"Look here," he said; "I won't have it. Listen to reason—or you'll be sorry afterwards. A fairy who breaks the traditions of fairy history goes out—you know she does—like the flame of a candle. And all tradition shows that only *one* bad fairy is ever forgotten at a christening party and the good ones are always invited; so either this is not a christening party, or else you were all invited except one, and, by her own showing, that was Malevola. It nearly always is. Do I make myself clear?"

Several of the better-class fairies who had been led away by Malevola's influence murmured that there was something in what His Majesty said.

"Try it, if you don't believe me," said the King; "give your nasty gifts to my innocent child—but as sure as you do, out you go, like a candle-flame. Now, then, will you risk it?"

No one answered, and presently several fairies came up to the Queen and said what a pleasant party it had been, but they really must be going. This example decided the rest. One by one all the fairies said goodbye and thanked the Queen for the delightful afternoon they had spent with her.

"It's been quite too lovely," said the lady with the snake-bonnet; "*do* ask us again soon, dear Queen. I shall be so *longing* to see you again, and the *dear* baby," and off she went, with the snake-trimming quivering more than ever.

When the very last fairy was gone the Queen ran to look at the baby—she tore off its Honiton lace cap and burst into tears. For all the baby's downy golden hair came off with the cap, and the Princess Melisande was as bald as an egg.

"Don't cry, my love," said the King. "I have a wish lying by, which I've never had occasion to use. My fairy godmother gave it me for a wedding present, but since then I've had nothing to wish for!"

"Thank you, dear," said the Queen, smiling through her tears.

"I'll keep the wish till baby grows up," the King went on. "And then I'll give it to her, and if she likes to wish for hair she can."

"Oh, won't you wish for it *now?*" said the Queen, dropping mixed tears and kisses on the baby's round, smooth head.

"No, dearest. She may want something else more when she grows up. And besides, her hair may grow by itself."

But it never did. Princess Melisande grew up as beautiful as the sun and as good as gold, but never a hair grew on that little head of hers. The Queen sewed her little caps of green silk, and the Princess's pink and white face looked out of these like a flower peeping out of its bud. And every day as she grew older she grew dearer, and as she grew dearer she grew better, and as she grew more good she grew more beautiful.

Now, when she was grown up the Queen said to the King—

"My love, our dear daughter is old enough to know what she wants. Let her have the wish."

So the King wrote to his fairy godmother and sent the letter by a butter-fly. He asked if he might hand on to his daughter the wish the fairy had given him for a wedding present.

"I have never had occasion to use it," said he, "though it has always made me happy to remember that I had such a thing in the house. The wish is as good as new, and my daughter is now of an age to appreciate so valuable a present."

To which the fairy replied by return of butterfly: —

"DEAR KING, —Pray do whatever you like with my poor little present. I had quite forgotten it, but I am pleased to think that you have treasured my humble keepsake all these years.

"Your affectionate godmother,

"FORTUNA F."

So the King unlocked his gold safe with the seven diamond-handled keys that hung at his girdle, and took out the wish and gave it to his daughter.

And Melisande said: "Father, I will wish that all your subjects should be quite happy."

But they were that already, because the King and Queen were so good. So the wish did not go off.

So then she said: "Then I wish them all to be good."

But they were that already, because they were happy. So again the wish hung fire.

Then the Queen said: "Dearest, for my sake, wish what I tell you."

"Why, of course I will," said Melisande. The Queen whispered in her ear, and Melisande nodded. Then she said, aloud—

"I wish I had golden hair a yard long, and that it would grow an inch every day, and grow twice as fast every time it was cut, and—"

"Stop," cried the King. And the wish went off, and the next moment the Princess stood smiling at him through a shower of golden hair.

"Oh, how lovely," said the Queen. "What a pity you interrupted her, dear; she hadn't finished."

"What was the end?" asked the King.

"Oh," said Melisande, "I was only going to say, 'and twice as thick.'"

"It's a very good thing you didn't," said the King. "You've done about enough." For he had a mathematical mind, and could do the sums about the grains of wheat on the chess-board, and the nails in the horse's shoes, in his Royal head without any trouble at all.

"Why, what's the matter?" asked the Queen.

"You'll know soon enough," said the King. "Come, let's be happy while we may. Give me a kiss, little Melisande, and then go to nurse and ask her to teach you how to comb your hair."

"I know," said Melisande, "I've often combed mother's."

"Your mother has beautiful hair," said the King; "but I fancy you will find your own less easy to manage."

And, indeed, it was so. The Princess's hair began by being a yard long, and it grew an inch every night. If you know anything at all about the simplest sums you will see that in about five weeks her hair was about two yards long. This is a very inconvenient length. It trails on the floor and sweeps up all the dust, and though in palaces, of course, it is all gold-dust, still it is not nice to have it in your hair. And the Princess's hair was growing an inch every night. When it was three yards long the Princess could not bear it any longer—it was so heavy and so hot—so she borrowed nurse's cutting-out scissors and cut it all off, and then for a few hours she was comfortable. But the hair went on growing, and now it grew twice as fast as before; so that in thirty-six days it was as long as ever. The poor Princess cried with tiredness; when she couldn't bear it any more she cut her hair and was comfortable for a very little time. For the hair now grew four times as fast as at first, and in eighteen days it was as long as before, and she had to have it cut. Then it grew eight inches a day, and the next time it was cut it grew sixteen inches a day, and then thirty-two inches and sixty-four inches and a hundred and twenty-eight inches a day, and so on, growing twice as fast after each cutting, till the Princess would go to bed at night with her hair clipped short, and wake up in the morning with yards and yards and yards of golden hair flowing all about the room, so that she could not move without pulling her own hair, and nurse had to come and cut the hair off before she could get out of bed.

"I wish I was bald again," sighed poor Melisande, looking at the little green caps she used to wear, and she cried herself to sleep o' nights between the golden billows of the golden hair. But she never let her mother see her cry, because it was the Queen's fault, and Melisande did not want to seem to reproach her.

When first the Princess's hair grew her mother sent locks of it to all her Royal relations, who had them set in rings and brooches. Later, the Queen was able to send enough for bracelets and girdles. But presently so much hair was cut off that they had to burn it. Then when autumn came all the crops failed; it seemed as though all the gold of harvest had gone into the Princess's hair. And there was a famine. Then Melisande said—

"It seems a pity to waste all my hair; it does grow so very fast. Couldn't we stuff things with it, or something, and sell them, to feed the people?"

So the King called a council of merchants, and they sent out samples of the Princess's hair, and soon orders came pouring in; and the Princess's hair became the staple export of that country. They stuffed pillows with it, and they stuffed beds with it. They made ropes of it for sailors to use, and curtains for hanging in Kings' palaces. They made haircloth of it, for hermits, and other people who wished to be uncomfy. But it was so soft and silky that it only made them happy and warm, which they did not wish to be. So the hermits gave up wearing it, and, instead, mothers bought it for their little babies, and all well-born infants wore little shirts of Princess-haircloth.

And still the hair grew and grew. And the people were fed and the famine came to an end.

Then the King said: "It was all very well while the famine lasted—but now I shall write to my fairy godmother and see if something cannot be done."

So he wrote and sent the letter by a skylark, and by return of bird came this answer—

"Why not advertise for a competent Prince? Offer the usual reward."

So the King sent out his heralds all over the world to proclaim that any respectable Prince with proper references should marry the Princess Melisande if he could stop her hair growing.

Then from far and near came trains of Princes anxious to try their luck, and they brought all sorts of nasty things with them in bottles and round wooden boxes. The Princess tried all the remedies, but she did not like any of them, and she did not like any of the Princes, so in her heart she was rather glad that none of the nasty things in bottles and boxes made the least difference to her hair.

The Princess had to sleep in the great Throne Room now, because no other room was big enough to hold her and her hair. When she woke in the morning the long high room would be quite full of her golden hair, packed tight and thick like wool in a barn. And every night when she had had the hair cut close to her head she would sit in her green silk gown by the window and cry, and kiss the little green caps she used to wear, and wish herself bald again.

It was as she sat crying there on Midsummer Eve that she first saw Prince Florizel.

He had come to the palace that evening, but he would not appear in her

Trains of Princes Bringing Nasty Things in Bottles and Round Wooden Boxes

presence with the dust of travel on him, and she had retired with her hair
borne by twenty pages before he had bathed and changed his garments and
entered the reception-room.

Now he was walking in the garden in the moonlight, and he looked up and
she looked down, and for the first time Melisande, looking on a Prince,
wished that he might have the power to stop her hair from growing. As for
the Prince, he wished many things, and the first was granted him. For he
said—

"You are Melisande?"

"And you are Florizel?"

"There are many roses round your window," said he to her, "and none
down here."

She threw him one of three white roses she held in her hand. Then he
said—

"White rose trees are strong. May I climb up to you?"

"Surely," said the princess.

So he climbed up to the window.

"Now," said he, "if I can do what your father asks, will you marry me?"

"My father has promised that I shall," said Melisande, playing with the
white roses in her hand.

"Dear Princess," said he, "your father's promise is nothing to me. I want
yours. Will you give it to me?"

"Yes," said she, and gave him the second rose.

"I want your hand."

"Yes," she said.

"And your heart with it."

"Yes," said the Princess, and she gave him the third rose.

"And a kiss to seal the promise."

"Yes," said she.

"And a kiss to go with the hand."

"Yes," she said.

"And a kiss to bring the heart."

"Yes," said the Princess, and she gave him the three kisses.

"Now," said he, when he had given them back to her, "to-night do not go
to bed. Stay by your window, and I will stay down here in the garden and
watch. And when your hair has grown to the filling of your room call to me,
and then do as I tell you."

"I will," said the Princess.

So at dewy sunrise the Prince, lying on the turf beside the sun-dial, heard her voice—

"Florizel! Florizel! My hair has grown so long that it is pushing me out of the window."

"Get out on to the window-sill," said he, "and twist your hair three times round the great iron hook that is there."

And she did.

Then the Prince climbed up the rose bush with his naked sword in his teeth, and he took the Princess's hair in his hand about a yard from her head and said—

"Jump!"

The Princess jumped, and screamed, for there she was hanging from the hook by a yard and a half of her bright hair; the Prince tightened his grasp of the hair and drew his sword across it.

Then he let her down gently by her hair till her feet were on the grass, and jumped down after her.

They stayed talking in the garden till all the shadows had crept under their proper trees and the sun-dial said it was breakfast time.

Then they went in to breakfast, and all the Court crowded round to wonder and admire. For the Princess's hair had not grown.

"How did you do it?" asked the King, shaking Florizel warmly by the hand.

"The simplest thing in the world," said Florizel, modestly. "You have always cut the hair off the Princess. *I* just cut the Princess off the hair."

"Humph!" said the King, who had a logical mind. And during breakfast he more than once looked anxiously at his daughter. When they got up from breakfast the Princess rose with the rest, but she rose and rose and rose, till it seemed as though there would never be an end of it. The Princess was nine feet high.

"I feared as much," said the King, sadly. "I wonder what will be the rate of progression. You see," he said to poor Florizel, "when we cut the hair off *it* grows—when we cut the Princess off *she* grows. I wish you had happened to think of that!"

The Princess went on growing. By dinnertime she was so large that she had to have her dinner brought out into the garden because she was too large to get indoors. But she was too unhappy to be able to eat anything. And she cried so much that there was quite a pool in the garden, and several pages were nearly drowned. So she remembered her "Alice in Wonderland,"[2] and stopped crying at once. But she did not stop growing. She grew bigger and bigger and bigger, till she had to go outside the palace gardens and sit on the common, and even that was too small to hold her comfortably, for every hour she grew twice as much as she had done the hour before. And nobody knew what to do, nor where the Princess was to sleep. Fortunately, her clothes had grown with her, or she would have been very cold indeed, and now she sat on the common in her green gown, embroidered with gold, looking like a great hill covered with gorse in flower.

You cannot possibly imagine how large the Princess was growing, and her mother stood wringing her hands on the castle tower, and the Prince Florizel looked on broken-hearted to see his Princess snatched from his arms and turned into a lady as big as a mountain.

The King did not weep or look on. He sat down at once and wrote to his fairy godmother, asking her advice. He sent a weasel with the letter, and by return of weasel he got his own letter back again, marked "Gone away. Left no address."

It was now, when the kingdom was plunged into gloom, that a neighbouring King took it into his head to send an invading army against the island where Melisande lived. They came in ships and they landed in great numbers, and Melisande looking down from her height saw alien soldiers marching on the sacred soil of her country.

"I don't mind so much now," said she, "if I can really be of some use this size."

And she picked up the army of the enemy in handfuls and double-handfuls, and put them back into their ships, and gave a little flip to each transport ship with her finger and thumb, which sent the ships off so fast that they never stopped till they reached their own country, and when they arrived there the whole army to a man said it would rather be courtmartialled a hundred times over than go near the place again.

Meantime Melisande, sitting on the highest hill on the island, felt the land trembling and shivering under her giant feet.

"I do believe I'm getting too heavy," she said, and jumped off the island into the sea, which was just up to her ankles. Just then a great fleet of warships and gunboats and torpedo boats came in sight, on their way to attack the island.

Melisande could easily have sunk them all with one kick, but she did not

2. **"Alice in Wonderland"** The nine-foot Alice sheds "gallons of tears" at the start of chapter two.

The Princess Grew So Big that She Had to Go and Sit on the Common

like to do this because it might have drowned the sailors, and besides, it might have swamped the island.

So she simply stooped and picked the island as you would pick a mushroom—for, of course, all islands are supported by a stalk underneath—and carried it away to another part of the world. So that when the warships got to where the island was marked on the map they found nothing but sea, and a very rough sea it was, because the Princess had churned it all up with her ankles as she walked away through it with the island.

When Melisande reached a suitable place, very sunny and warm, and with no sharks in the water, she set down the island; and the people made it fast with anchors, and then every one went to bed, thanking the kind fate which had sent them so great a Princess to help them in their need, and calling her the saviour of her country and the bulwark of the nation.

But it is poor work being the nation's bulwark and your country's saviour when you are miles high, and have no one to talk to, and when all you want is to be your humble right size again and to marry your sweetheart. And when it was dark the Princess came close to the island, and looked down, from far up, at her palace and her tower and cried, and cried, and cried. It does not matter how much you cry into the sea, it hardly makes any difference, however large you may be. Then when everything was quite dark the Princess looked up at the stars.

"I wonder how soon I shall be big enough to knock my head against them," said she.

And as she stood star-gazing she heard a whisper right in her ear. A very little whisper, but quite plain.

"Cut off your hair!" it said.

Now, everything the Princess was wearing had grown big along with her, so that now there dangled from her golden girdle a pair of scissors as big as the Malay Peninsula, together with a pin-cushion the size of the Isle of Wight, and a yard measure that would have gone round Australia.

And when she heard the little, little voice, she knew it, small as it was, for the dear voice of Prince Florizel, and she whipped out the scissors from her gold case and snip, snip, snipped all her hair off, and it fell into the sea. The coral insects got hold of it at once and set to work on it, and now they have made it into the biggest coral reef in the world; but that has nothing to do with the story.

Then the voice said, "Get close to the island," and the Princess did, but she could not get very close because she was so large, and she looked up again at the stars and they seemed to be much farther off.

The Princess in One Scale and Her Hair in the Other

Then the voice said, "Be ready to swim," and she felt something climb out of her ear and clamber down her arm. The stars got farther and farther away, and next moment the Princess found herself swimming in the sea, and Prince Florizel swimming beside her.

"I crept on to your hand when you were carrying the island," he explained, when their feet touched the sand and they walked in through the shallow water, "and I got into your ear with an ear-trumpet. You never noticed me because you were so great then."

"Oh, my dear Prince," cried Melisande, falling into his arms, "you have saved me. I am my proper size again."

So they went home and told the King and Queen. Both were very, very happy, but the King rubbed his chin with his hand, and said—

"You've certainly had some fun for your money, young man, but don't you see that we're just where we were before? Why, the child's hair is growing already."

And indeed it was.

Then once more the King sent a letter to his godmother. He sent it by a flying-fish, and by return of fish came the answer—

"Just back from my holidays. Sorry for your troubles. Why not try scales?"

And on this message the whole Court pondered for weeks.

But the Prince caused a pair of gold scales to be made, and hung them up in the palace gardens under a big oak tree. And one morning he said to the Princess—

"My darling Melisande, I must really speak seriously to you. We are getting on in life. I am nearly twenty: it is time that we thought of being settled. Will you trust me entirely and get into one of those gold scales?"

So he took her down into the garden, and helped her into the scale, and she curled up in it in her green and gold gown, like a little grass mound with buttercups on it.

"And what is going into the other scale?" asked Melisande.

"Your hair," said Florizel. "You see, when your hair is cut off you it grows, and when you are cut off your hair you grow—oh, my heart's delight, I can never forget how you grew, never! But if, when your hair is no more than you, and you are no more than your hair, I snip the scissors between you and it, then neither you nor your hair can possibly decide which ought to go on growing."

"Suppose *both* did," said the poor Princess, humbly.

"Impossible," said the Prince, with a shudder; "there are limits even to Malevola's malevolence. And, besides, Fortuna said 'Scales.' Will you try it?"

"I will do whatever you wish," said the poor Princess, "but let me kiss my father and mother once, and Nurse, and you, too, my dear, in case I grow large again and can kiss nobody any more."

So they came one by one and kissed the Princess.

Then the nurse cut off the Princess's hair, and at once it began to grow at a frightful rate.

The King and Queen and nurse busily packed it, as it grew, into the other scale, and gradually the scale went down a little. The Prince stood waiting between the scales with his drawn sword, and just before the two were equal he struck. But during the time his sword took to flash through the air the Princess's hair grew a yard or two, so that at the instant when he struck the balance was true.

"You are a young man of sound judgment," said the King, embracing him, while the Queen and the nurse ran to help the Princess out of the gold scale.

The scale full of golden hair bumped down on to the ground as the Princess stepped out of the other one, and stood there before those who loved her, laughing and crying with happiness, because she remained her proper size, and her hair was not growing any more.

She kissed her Prince a hundred times, and the very next day they were married. Every one remarked on the beauty of the bride, and it was noticed that her hair was quite short—only five feet five and a quarter inches long—just down to her pretty ankles. Because the scales had been ten feet ten and a half inches apart, and the Prince, having a straight eye, had cut the golden hair exactly in the middle!

E. NESBIT

Fortunatus Rex & Co.

There was once a lady who found herself in middle life with but a slight income. Knowing herself to be insufficiently educated to be able to practise any other trade or calling, she of course decided, without hesitation, to enter the profession of teaching. She opened a very select Boarding School for Young Ladies. The highest references were given and required. And in order to keep her school as select as possible, Miss Fitzroy Robinson had a brass plate fastened on to the door, with an inscription in small polite lettering. (You have, of course, heard of the "polite letters." Well, it was with these that Miss Fitzroy Robinson's door-plate was engraved.)

"SELECT BOARDING ESTABLISHMENT FOR THE
DAUGHTERS OF RESPECTABLE MONARCHS."

A great many kings who were not at all respectable would have given their royal ears to be allowed to send their daughters to this school, but Miss Fitzroy Robinson was very firm about references, and the consequence was that all the really high-class kings were only too pleased to be permitted to pay ten thousand pounds a year for their daughters' education. And so Miss Fitzroy Robinson was able to lay aside a few pounds as a provision for her old age. And all the money she saved was invested in land.

Only one monarch refused to send his daughter to Miss Fitzroy Robinson, on the ground that so cheap a school could not be a really select one, and it was found out afterwards that his references were not at all satisfactory.

There were only six boarders, and of course the best masters were engaged to teach the royal pupils everything which their parents wished them to learn, and as the girls were never asked to do lessons except when they felt quite inclined, they all said it was the nicest school in the world, and cried at the very thought of being taken away. Thus it happened that the six pupils were quite grown up and were just becoming parlour boarders when events began to occur. Princess Daisy, the daughter of King Fortunatus, the ruling sovereign, was the only little girl in the school.

Now it was when she had been at school about a year, that a ring came at the front door-bell, and the maid-servant came to the schoolroom with a visiting card held in the corner of her apron—for her hands were wet because it was washing-day.

"A gentleman to see you, Miss," she said; and Miss Fitzroy Robinson was quite fluttered because she thought it might be a respectable monarch, with a daughter who wanted teaching.

But when she looked at the card she left off fluttering, and said, "Dear me!" under her breath, because she was very genteel. If she had been vulgar like some of us she would have said "Bother!" and if she had been more vulgar than, I hope, any of us are, she might have said "Drat the man!" The card was large and shiny and had gold letters on it. Miss Fitzroy Robinson read:–

Chevalier Doloro De Lara
Professor of Magic (white)
and the Black Art.
Pupils instructed at their own residences.
No extras.
Special terms for Schools. Evening Parties
attended.

Miss Fitzroy Robinson laid down her book—she never taught without a book—smoothed her yellow cap and her grey curls and went into the front parlour to see her visitor. He bowed low at sight of her. He was very tall and hungry-looking, with black eyes, and an indescribable mouth.

"It is indeed a pleasure," said he, smiling so as to show every one of his thirty-two teeth—a very polite, but very difficult thing to do—"it is indeed a pleasure to meet once more my old pupil."

"The pleasure is mutual, I am sure," said Miss Fitzroy Robinson. If it is sometimes impossible to be polite and truthful at the same moment, that is not my fault, nor Miss Fitzroy Robinson's.

"I have been travelling about," said the Professor, still smiling immeasurably, "increasing my stock of wisdom. Ah, dear lady—we live and learn, do we not? And now I am really a far more competent teacher than when I had the honour of instructing you. May I hope for an engagement as Professor in your Academy?

"I have not yet been able to arrange for a regular course of Magic," said the schoolmistress; "it is a subject in which parents, especially royal ones, take but too little interest."

"It was your favourite study," said the professor.

"Yes—but—well, no doubt some day—"

"But I want an engagement *now*," said he, looking hungrier than ever; "a thousand pounds for thirteen lessons to—*you*, dear lady."

"It's quite impossible," said she, and she spoke firmly, for she knew from history how dangerous it is for a Magician to be allowed anywhere near a princess. Some harm almost always comes of it.

"Oh, very well!" said the Professor.

"You see my pupils are all princesses," she went on, "they don't require the use of magic, they can get all they want without it."

"Then it's '*No*'?" said he.

"It's 'No thank you kindly,' " said she.

Then, before she could stop him, he sprang past her out at the door, and she heard his boots on the oilcloth of the passage. She flew after him just in time to have the schoolroom door slammed and locked in her face.

"Well, I never!" said Miss Fitzroy Robinson. She hastened to the top of the house and hurried down the schoolroom chimney, which had been made with steps, in case of fire or other emergency. She stepped out of the grate on to the schoolroom hearthrug just one second too late. The seven Princesses were all gone, and the Professor of Magic stood alone among the ink-stained desks, smiling the largest smile Miss Fitzroy Robinson had seen yet.

"Oh, you naughty, bad, wicked man, you!" said she, shaking the school ruler at him.

✳

The next day was Saturday, and the King of the country called as usual to take his daughter Daisy[1] out to spend her half holiday. The servant who opened the door had a coarse apron on and cinders in her hair, and the King thought it was sackcloth and ashes, and said so a little anxiously, but the girl

---

1. **Daisy** Edith Nesbit's own nickname as a child

said, "No, I've only been a-doing of the kitchen range—though, for the matter of that—but you'd best see missus herself."

So the King was shown into the best parlour where the tasteful wax-flowers were, and the antimacassars and water-colour drawings executed by the pupils, and the wool mats which Miss Fitzroy Robinson's bed-ridden aunt made so beautifully. A delightful parlour full of the traces of the refining touch of a woman's hand.

Miss Fitzroy Robinson came in slowly and sadly. Her gown was neatly made of sackcloth—with an ingenious trimming of small cinders sewn on gold braid—and some larger-sized cinders dangled by silken threads from the edge of her lace cap.

The King saw at once that she was annoyed about something. "I hope I'm not too early," said he.

"Your Majesty," she answered, "not at all. You are always punctual, as stated in your references. Something has happened. I will not aggravate your misfortunes by breaking them to you. Your daughter Daisy, the pride and treasure of our little circle, has disappeared. Her six royal companions are with her. For the present all are safe, but at the moment I am unable to lay my hand on any one of the seven."

The King sat down heavily on part of the handsome walnut and rep suite (ladies' and gentlemen's easy-chairs, couch and six occasional chairs) and gasped miserably. He could not find words. But the schoolmistress had written down what she was going to say on a slate and learned it off by heart, so she was able to go on fluently.

"Your Majesty, I am not wholly to blame—hang me if I am—I mean hang me if you must; but first allow me to have the honour of offering to you one or two explanatory remarks."

With this she sat down and told him the whole story of the Professor's visit, only stopping exactly where I stopped when I was telling it to you just now.

The King listened, plucking nervously at the fringe of a purple and crimson antimacassar.

"I never *was* satisfied with the Professor's methods," said Miss Fitzroy Robinson sadly; "and I always had my doubts as to his moral character, doubts now set at rest for ever. After concluding my course of instruction with him some years ago I took a series of lessons from a far more efficient master, and thanks to those lessons, which were, I may mention, extremely costly, I was mercifully enabled to put a spoke in the wheel of the unprincipled ruffian—"

"Did you save the Princess?" cried the King.

"No; but I can if your Majesty and the other parents will leave the matter entirely in my hands."

"It's rather a serious matter," said the King; "my poor little Daisy—"

"I would ask you," said the schoolmistress with dignity, "not to attach too much importance to this event. Of course it is regrettable, but unpleasant accidents occur in all schools, and the consequences of them can usually be averted by the exercise of tact and judgment."

"I ought to hang you, you know," said the King doubtfully.

"No doubt," said Miss Fitzroy Robinson, "and if you do you'll never see your Daisy again. Your duty as a parent—yes—and your duty to me—conflicting duties are very painful things."

"But can I trust you?"

"I may remind you," said she, drawing herself up so that the cinders rattled again, "that we exchanged satisfactory references at the commencement of our business relations."

The King rose. "Well, Miss Fitzroy Robinson," he said, "I have been entirely satisfied with Daisy's progress since she has been in your charge, and I feel I cannot do better than leave this matter entirely in your able hands."

The schoolmistress made him a curtsey, and he went back to his marble palace a broken-hearted monarch, with his crown all on one side and his poor, dear nose red with weeping.

The select boarding establishment was shut up.

Time went on and no news came of the lost Princesses.

The King found but little comfort in the fact that his other child, Prince Denis, was still spared to him. Denis was all very well and a nice little boy in his way, but a boy is not a girl.[2]

The Queen was much more broken-hearted than the King, but of course she had the housekeeping to see to and the making of the pickles and preserves and the young Prince's stockings to knit, so she had not much time for weeping, and after a year she said to the King—

"My dear, you ought to do something to distract your mind. It's unkinglike to sit and cry all day. Now, do make an effort; do something useful, if it's only opening a bazaar or laying a foundation stone."

2. **not a girl** a dig at the preference of Carroll, Ruskin, and all those other Victorian males who idealized little girls

"I am frightened of bazaars," said the King; "they are like bees—they buzz and worry; but foundation stones—" And after that he began to sit and think sometimes, without crying, and to make notes on the backs of old envelopes. So the Queen felt that she had not spoken quite in vain.

A month later the suggestion of foundation stones bore fruit.

The King floated a company, and Fortunatus Rex & Co. became almost at once the largest speculative builders in the world.

Perhaps you do not know what a speculative builder is. I'll tell you what the King and his Co. did, and then you will know.

They bought all the pretty woods and fields they could get and cut them up into squares, and grubbed up the trees and the grass and put streets there and lamp-posts and ugly little yellow brick houses, in the hopes that people would want to live in them. And curiously enough people did. So the King and his Co. made quite a lot of money.

It is curious that nearly all the great fortunes are made by turning beautiful things into ugly ones. Making beauty out of ugliness is very ill-paid work.

The ugly little streets crawled further and further out of the town, eating up the green country like greedy yellow caterpillars, but at the foot of the Clover Hill they had to stop. For the owner of Clover Hill would not sell any land at all—for any price that Fortunatus Rex & Co. could offer. In vain the solicitors of the Company called on the solicitors of the owner, wearing their best cloaks and swords and shields, and took them out to lunch and gave them nice things to eat and drink. Clover Hill was not for sale.

At last, however, a little old woman all in grey called at the Company's shining brass and mahogany offices and had a private interview with the King himself.

"I am the owner of Clover Hill," said she, "and you may build on all its acres except the seven at the top and the fifteen acres that go round that seven, and you must build me a high wall round the seven acres and another round the fifteen—of *red* brick, mind; none of your cheap yellow stuff—and you must make a brand new law that any one who steals my fruit is to be hanged from the tree he stole it from. That's all. What do you say?"

The king said "Yes," because since his trouble he cared for nothing but building, and his royal soul longed to see the green Clover Hill eaten up by yellow brick caterpillars with slate tops. He did not at all like building the two red brick walls, but he did it.

Now, the old woman wanted the walls and the acres to be this sort of shape—

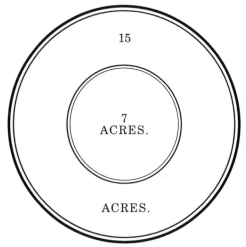

But it was such a bother getting the exact amount of ground into the two circles that all the surveyors tore out their hair by handfuls, and at last the King said, "Oh bother! Do it this way," and drew a plan on the back of an old Act of Parliament. So they did, and it was like this—

			1	2
13	14	15	I	3
12	II	III	IV	4
11	V	VI	VII	5
10	9	8	7	6

The old lady was very vexed when she found that there was only one wall between her orchard and the world, as you see was the case at the corner where the two 1's and the 15 meet; but the King said he couldn't afford to build it all over again and that she'd got her two walls as she had said. So she had to put up with it. Only she insisted on the King's getting her a fierce bull-dog to fly at the throat of any one who should come over the wall at that weak point where the two 1's join on to the 15. So he got her a stout bull-dog whose name was Martha, and brought it himself in a jewelled leash.

"Martha will fly at any one who is not of kingly blood," said he. "Of course she wouldn't dream of biting a royal person; but, then, on the other hand, royal people don't rob orchards."

So the old woman had to be contented. She tied Martha up in the unprotected corner of her inner enclosure and then she planted little baby apple trees and had a house built and sat down in it and waited.

And the King was almost happy. The creepy, crawly yellow caterpillars ate up Clover Hill—all except the little green crown on the top, where the apple trees were and the two red brick walls and the little house and the old woman.

The poor Queen went on seeing to the jam and the pickles and the blanket washing and the spring cleaning, and every now and then she would say to her husband—

"Fortunatus, my love, do you *really* think Miss Fitzoy Robinson is trustworthy? Shall we ever see our Daisy again?"

And the King would rumple his fair hair with his hands till it stuck out like cheese straws under his crown, and answer—

"My dear, you must be patient; you know we had the very highest references."

Now one day the new yellow brick town the King had built had a delightful experience. Six handsome Princes on beautiful white horses came riding through the dusty little streets. The housings of their chargers shone with silver embroidery and gleaming glowing jewels, and their gold armour flashed so gloriously in the sun that all the little children clapped their hands, and the Princes' faces were so young and kind and handsome that all the old women said: "Bless their pretty hearts!"

Now, of course, you will not need to be told that these six Princes were looking for the six grown-up Princesses who had been so happy at the Select Boarding Establishment. Their six Royal fathers, who lived many years' journey away on the other side of the world, and had not yet heard that the Princesses were mislaid, had given Miss Fitzroy Robinson's address to these Princes, and instructed them to marry the six Princesses without delay, and bring them home.

But when they got to the Select Boarding Establishment for the Daughters of Respectable Monarchs, the house was closed, and a card was in the window, saying that this desirable villa residence was to be let on moderate terms, furnished or otherwise. The wax fruit under the glass shade still showed attractively through the dusty panes. The six Princes looked through the window by turns. They were charmed with the furniture, and the refining touch of a woman's hand drew them like a magnet. They took the house, but they had their meals at the Palace by the King's special invitation.

King Fortunatus told the Princes the dreadful story of the disappearance of the entire Select School; and each Prince swore by his sword-hilt and his honour that he would find out the particular Princess that he was to marry, or perish in the attempt. For, of course, each Prince was to marry one Princess, mentioned by name in his instructions, and not one of the others.

The first night that the Princes spent in the furnished house passed quietly enough, so did the second and the third and the fourth, fifth and sixth, but on the seventh night, as the Princes sat playing spilikins in the schoolroom, they suddenly heard a voice that was not any of theirs. It said, "Open up Africa!"

The Princes looked here, there, and everywhere—but they could see no one. They had not been brought up to the exploring trade, and could not have opened up Africa if they had wanted to.

"Or cut through the Isthmus of Panama," said the voice again.

Now, as it happened, none of the six Princes were engineers. They confessed as much.

"Cut up China, then!" said the voice, desperately.

"It's like the ghost of a Tory newspaper,"[3] said one of the Princes.

And then suddenly they knew that the voice came from one of the pair of globes which hung in frames at the end of the schoolroom. It was the terrestrial globe.

"I'm inside," said the voice; "I can't get out. Oh, cut the globe—anywhere—and let me out. But the African route is most convenient."

Prince Primus opened up Africa with his sword, and out tumbled half a Professor of Magic.

"My other half's in there," he said, pointing to the Celestial globe. "Let my legs out, do—"

But Prince Secundus said, "Not so fast," and Prince Tertius said, "Why were you shut up?"

"I was shut up for as pretty a bit of parlour-magic as ever you saw in all your born days," said the top half of the Professor of Magic.

---

3. **Tory newspaper** Tories had advocated even more territorial concessions from China as a retaliation against the so-called Boxer rebellion of 1900.

"Oh, you were, were you?" said Prince Quartus; "well, your legs aren't coming out just yet. We want to engage a competent magician. You'll do."

"But I'm not all here," said the Professor.

"Quite enough of you," said Prince Quintus.

"Now look here," said Prince Sextus; "we want to find our six Princesses. We can give a very good guess as to how they were lost; but we'll let bygones be bygones. You can tell us how to find them, and after our weddings we'll restore your legs to the light of day."

"This half of me feels so faint," said the half Professor of Magic.

"What are we to do?" said all the Princes, threateningly; "if you don't tell us, you shall never have a leg to stand on."

"Steal apples," said the half Professor, hoarsely, and fainted away.

They left him lying on the bare boards between the inkstained desks, and off they went to steal apples. But this was not so easy. Because Fortunatus Rex & Co. had built, and built, and built, and apples do not grow freely in those parts of the country which have been "opened up" by speculative builders.

So at last they asked the little Prince Denis where he went for apples when he wanted them. And Denis said—

"The old woman at the top of Clover Hill has apples in her seven acres, and in her fifteen acres, but there's a fierce bulldog in the seven acres, and I've stolen all the apples in the fifteen acres myself."

"We'll try the seven acres," said the Princes.

"Very well," said Denis; "You'll be hanged if you're caught. So, as I put you up to it, I'm coming too, and if you won't take me, I'll tell. So there!"

For Denis was a most honourable little Prince, and felt that you must not send others into danger unless you go yourself, and he would never have stolen apples if it had not been quite as dangerous as leading armies.

So the Princes had to agree, and the very next night Denis let himself down out of his window by a knotted rope made of all the stockings his mother had knitted for him, and the grown-up Princes were waiting under the window, and off they all went to the orchard on the top of Clover Hill.

They climbed the wall at the proper corner, and Martha, the bulldog, who was very well-bred, and knew a Prince when she saw one, wagged her kinked tail respectfully and wished them good luck.

The Princes stole over the dewy orchard grass and looked at tree after tree: there were no apples on any of them.

Only at last, in the very middle of the orchard there was a tree with a copper trunk and brass branches, and leaves of silver. And on it hung seven beautiful golden apples.

So each Prince took one of the golden apples, very quietly, and off they went, anxious to get back to the half-Professor of Magic, and learn what to do next. No one had any doubt as to the half-Professor having told the truth; for when your legs depend on your speaking the truth you will not willingly tell a falsehood.

They stole away as quietly as they could, each with a gold apple in his hand, but as they went Prince Denis could not resist his longing to take a bite out of his apple. He opened his mouth very wide so as to get a good bite, and the next moment he howled aloud, for the apple was as hard as stone, and the poor little boy had broken nearly all his first teeth.

He flung the apple away in a rage, and the next moment the old woman rushed out of her house. She screamed. Martha barked. Prince Denis howled. The whole town was aroused, and the six Princes were arrested, and taken under a strong guard to the Tower. Denis was let off, on the ground of his youth, and, besides, he had lost most of his teeth, which is a severe punishment, even for stealing apples.

The King sat in his Hall of Justice next morning, and the old woman and the Princes came before him. When the story had been told, he said—

"My dear fellows, I hope you'll excuse me—the laws of hospitality are strict—but business is business after all. I should not like to have any con-stitutional unpleasantness over a little thing like this; you must all be hanged to-morrow morning."

The Princes were extremely vexed, but they did not make a fuss. They asked to see Denis, and told him what to do.

So Denis went to the furnished house which had once been a Select Boarding Establishment for the Daughters of Respectable Monarchs. The door was locked, but Denis knew a way in, because his sister had told him all about it one holiday. He got up on the roof and walked down the school-room chimney.

There, on the schoolroom floor, lay half a Professor of Magic, struggling feebly, and uttering sad, faint squeals.

"What are we to do now?" said Denis.

"Steal apples," said the half-Professor in a weak whisper. "Do let my legs out. Slice up the Great Bear—or the Milky Way would be a good one for them to come out by."

But Denis knew better.

"Not till we get the lost Princesses," said he, "now, what's to be done?"

"Steal apples I tell you," said the half-Professor, crossly; "seven apples—there—seven kisses. Cut them down. Oh go along with you, do. Leave me to die, you heartless boy. I've got pins and needles in my legs."

Then off ran Denis to the Seven Acre Orchard at the top of Clover Hill, and there were the six Princes hanging to the appletree, and the hangman had gone home to his dinner, and there was no one else about. And the Princes were not dead.

Denis climbed up the tree and cut the Princes down with the penknife of the gardener's boy. (You will often find this penknife mentioned in your German exercises; now you know why so much fuss is made about it.)

The Princes fell to the ground, and when they recovered their wits Denis told them what he had done.

"Oh why did you cut us down?" said the Princes, "we were having such happy dreams."

"Well," said Denis, shutting up the penknife of the gardener's boy, "of all the ungrateful chaps!" And he turned his back and marched off. But they ran quickly after him and thanked him and told him how they had been dreaming of walking arm in arm with the most dear and lovely Princesses in the world.

"Well," said Denis, "it's no use dreaming about *them*. You've got your own registered Princesses to find, and the half-Professor says, 'Steal apples.' "

"There aren't any more to steal," said the Princes—but when they looked there were the gold apples back on the tree just as before.

So once again they each picked one. Denis chose a different one this time. He thought it might be softer. The last time he had chosen the biggest apple—but now he took the littlest apple of all.

"Seven kisses!" he cried, and began to kiss the little gold apple.

Each Prince kissed the apple he held, till the sound of kisses was like the whisper of the evening wind in leafy trees. And, of course, at the seventh kiss each Prince found that he had in his hand not an apple, but the fingers of a lovely Princess. As for Denis, he had got his little sister Daisy, and he was so glad he promised at once to give her his guineapigs and his whole collection of foreign postage stamps.

"What is your name, dear and lovely lady?" asked Prince Primus.

"Sexta," said his Princess. And then it turned out that every single one of the Princes had picked the wrong apple, so that each one had a Princess who was not the one mentioned in his letter of instructions. Secundus had plucked the apple that held Quinta, and Tertius held Quarta, and so on—and everything was as criss-cross-crooked[4] as it possibly could be.

And yet nobody wanted to change.

Then the old woman came out of her house and looked at them and chuckled, and she said—

"You must be contented with what you have."

"We *are*," said all twelve of them, "but what about our parents?"

"They must put up with your choice," said the old woman, "it's the common lot of parents."

"I think you ought to sort yourselves out properly," said Denis; "I'm the only one who's got his right Princess—because I wasn't greedy. I took the smallest."

The tallest Princess showed him a red mark on her arm, where his little teeth had been two nights before, and everybody laughed.

But the old woman said—

"They can't change, my dear. When a Prince has picked a gold apple that has a Princess in it, and has kissed it till she comes out, no other Princess will ever do for him, any more than any other Prince will ever do for her."

While she was speaking the old woman got younger and younger and younger, till as she spoke the last words she was quite young, not more than fifty-five. And it was Miss Fitzroy Robinson!

Her pupils stepped forward one by one with respectful curtsies, and she allowed them to kiss her on the cheek, just as if it was breaking-up day.

Then, all together, and very happily, they went down to the furnished villa that had once been the Select School, and when the half-professor had promised on his honour as a Magician to give up Magic and take to a respectable trade, they took his legs out of the starry sphere, and gave them back to him; and he joined himself together, and went off full of earnest resolve to live and die an honest plumber.

"My talents won't be quite wasted," said he; "a little hanky-panky is useful in most trades."

When the King asked Miss Fitzroy Robinson to name her own reward for restoring the Princesses, she said—

"Make the land green again, your Majesty."

So Fortunatus Rex & Co. devoted themselves to pulling down and carting off the yellow streets they had built. And now the country there is almost

---

4. **as criss-cross-crooked** Although each of the six princes picks a mate other than the one he expected, each marriage is numerologically impeccable, since it always results in same sum total of seven.

as green and pretty as it was before Princess Daisy and the six parlour-boarders were turned into gold apples.

"It was very clever of dear Miss Fitzroy Robinson to shut up that Professor in those two globes," said the Queen; "it shows the advantage of having lessons from the *best* Masters."

"Yes," said the King, "I always say that you cannot go far wrong if you insist on the highest references!"

Part Three

A FANTASY NOVEL
MOPSA THE FAIRY

✳

Jean Ingelow (1820–1897) had, like Christina Rossetti, already achieved a high reputation as a poet before she began to publish children's fiction. Indeed, her 1863 volume, *Poems,* was so favorably reviewed that Rossetti, "aware of a new eminent name having arisen among us," immediately, and deferentially, pronounced Ingelow to be "a formidable rival to most men, and to any woman" (*The Rossetti Macmillan Letters,* 19). Yet the two writers, together with Dora Greenwell, the third major aspirant to the poetic throne vacated by the death of Elizabeth Barrett Browning, became rather friendly competitors. That friendship extended to a nonpoetic contest which may have some bearing on the feverish sewing activities so prominent in the narrative frame of Rossetti's *Speaking Likenesses,* reproduced in part 4. Greenwell once challenged Rossetti and Ingelow to produce a piece of needlework as good as her own. Rossetti declined, but Ingelow gladly complied. She not only sent Greenwell a flowery bag decorated with an intricate pattern "of my own invention," but also promised to tease the third member of the triumvirate for some evidence of such domestic accomplishments: "When I next see Miss Rossetti I shall ask for proof that she can do hemming and sewing" (*Some Recollections,* 163).

The anecdote suggests that, for Ingelow, the skill required to pattern a piece of embroidery may be no less than that required to pattern verses. Both require fierce, if covert, competition in traditional womanly virtues. This competition need not stray beyond domestic space. Although that domestic space, which Victorian culture had assigned to women, may seem sheltered and static, it conceals a competitiveness that is based on the same aggressive energies more overtly displayed in an outer male world of action. It seems significant, in this connection, that *Mopsa the Fairy,* the highly inventive fantasy for children which Ingelow published in 1869, should end with a boy's grateful return to domesticity while the little girl who was his travel companion remains in the innermost heart of a female realm as a powerful ruler of a nation of fairies.

Only the title of *Mopsa the Fairy* allows a reader to anticipate the sharp reversal that takes place in its last chapters. A story that seemed ostensibly centered on the energies of "Captain Jack," the determined little boy who penetrates deeper and deeper in his forays into a series of wonderlands, unexpectedly turns into a female Bildungsroman when Jack becomes displaced by Mopsa. The toddler who was so tiny that Jack easily confined her into one of his pockets now finds that she has been destined to preside as a wise and visionary Fairy Queen over an entire nation. Not only has Mopsa rapidly grown far beyond the size of the race of fairies to which she belongs but she also now outstrips her former protector in maturity, power, and authority. Less and less potent, the sturdy "Captain Jack" is no longer suitable as Mopsa's mate. Although indirectly responsible for her crowning, he has become her decided inferior.

The boy who had singled the sleeping Mopsa out from among her siblings with a prince-like kiss thus finds himself pathetically excluded from her magical domain. In a conscious reversal of the story of "Sleeping Beauty," Ingelow has Mopsa sadly inform Jack that the time has finally come "to give you back your kiss." As soon as that kiss is returned, the thicket that was successfully subdued by the intruding prince in "Sleeping Beauty" vehemently pushes back a boy who yearns to become Queen Mopsa's consort. Mopsa's "fairy castle" rapidly recedes as "spear-like leaves" spring up between it and Jack, forcing him to move back and back until he resignedly accepts his banishment.

Mopsa's prodigious maturation in a female wonderland shatters Jack's expectations. Aware that she no longer requires his protection, he had nonetheless hoped to be allowed to remain her companion. Thrust back into his father's yard, Jack suddenly finds himself repressing all memory of his bizarre adventures. In the drawing-room where he is matter-of-factly greeted by parents who seem never to have missed him, Jack hears his mother read a poem "aloud" to his father. Her voice proves soothing and allows Jack to forget the fairylands he has visited and, above all, to "forget the boy-king," the much-resented clone who had replaced him as Mopsa's consort.

Directed by his mother to "some strawberries on the side-board," Jack is delighted to "find the house just as usual." Like a dutiful little Victorian boy, he goes into his room, says his prayers, climbs "into his little white bed," and "comfortably" falls asleep. He has repressed his acute pain at being separated from Mopsa; indeed, his memories of her have by now altogether faded. Gone, too, are his earlier anger and futile defiance at his banishment from her fantasy world. The boy whose last word in the book is "Mamma!'" no longer resembles the aggressive Captain Jack or Master Jack who had penetrated deeper and deeper into ever more dangerous realms of the female imagination. Instead, he welcomes the security of the parental home. The last paragraph of the novel—a bare two words—ostensibly endorses this quietistic closure. "That's all," says a narrator, seemingly as eager to soothe the child reader as the mother in the book was eager to calm her own child. Yet in their abrupt finality, these last two words also imply that there can be no return to the imaginative worlds Jack has now altogether forgotten.

Neither the narrator nor the mother, however, can forget what Jack, who now admiringly looks up at his father and thinks "what a great thing a man was," is allowed to suppress. Their awareness of division—like that of a Mopsa who has outgrown her onetime playmate—exceeds his by far. And, as adult women, they must—again, like the grown Mopsa—bear the burden that such division entails. Mopsa's pain as she turns away from the ejected Jack is evident to the reader, but not to the boy who assumes that she is "quite content" with her new duties as a fairy queen. Her melancholy at their parting seems deeper than his self-pity. Musing "as if speaking to herself," she notes that Jack can, after all, return to a freer world, at liberty to play again "in his father's garden."

For her part, the girl turned into matriarchal ruler must accept the duties for which she has been destined by "Old Mother Fate." Mopsa is no longer the doll-like toddler Jack both loved and patronized. Her sadness betokens her reluctant acceptance of the powers with which she is now invested. She has too rapidly outgrown her stolid boy protector in order to become herself the protectress of her new subjects. Not blessed, like Jack, with obliviousness, she is condemned to remember the shared childhood from which she, but not he, has egressed. Ingelow here inverts the emphasis of Victorian male writers such as Lewis Carroll, who tried to prevent the growth of a beloved dreamchild into an adult woman. Mopsa has ceased to be a dreamchild well before Jack sinks gratefully into his dreamless bed. Having grown far beyond him in size and in responsibilities, it is she who remains haunted by memories that become the final mark of her superiority to the fearless, but unthinking little boy.

Jack's ability to screen out all consciousness of his loss stems from a capacity for forgetfulness that has been stressed throughout his adventures. As Ingelow implies, Victorian boys who grew into men found it easier to forget what could not be ignored by girls who, by growing into women, became more acutely conscious of an impairment of their former freedom. Their sense of separation from their male playmates was sharpened by a segregation that decreed their confinement, as adults, to a domestic sphere. And their consciousness of that confinement only helped, paradoxically enough, to activate their restless powers of imagination. Jack can compensate for the loss of a female complement by returning to a still nurturing "Mamma." He had begun his adventures, after all, by adopting for himself the maternal role of nurturer: he first fed his plum cake to the fairy nestlings left by their "old mother" and then replaced her as an incubator and carrier. But the good-natured, unimaginative little boy who encounters ever more powerful female figures in his peregrinations finds himself increasingly out of place in their world of fantasy. Femininity lost thus becomes supplanted, in the parental home, by the pater familias who decrees that it is "time this man of ours was in bed."

The narrator and the mother, however, like Mopsa, remain fully aware of the losses involved in a child's growth into an order divided by genders. Ingelow calls her last chapter "Failure." She begins it by having her narrator offer, as an epigraph, a sonnet about the art that stems from the inevitable partings that make all life a "failure." Using the example of Orpheus's separation from Eurydice, she suggests that even though this poet's lyrics have been forgotten he will continue to be remembered for his segregation from Eurydice. He may "win" a contest by his superior artistry, "but few for that his deed recall: / Its power is in the look which costs him all."

Towards the end of this last chapter, the separation of the feminine from the masculine is again dramatized through poetry, a more elliptical form of expression than prose narrative. Ingelow now has Jack's mother read a ballad "about the Shepherd Lady." Why is the mother assigned to recite the last of the poems Ingelow has inserted in the text? Earlier, on hearing his mother read to his father, Jack became aware that her reading was not "like anything that he had heard," in Fairyland. It was at that point that he began to forget all his former adventures. Ingelow here seems to tease the reader with implications that she deliberately veils. Is the mother now inducing a further forgetfulness in her child, by lulling him to sleep, just as the previous enchantresses he had met in fairylands had managed to do? Or is she, conversely, implanting in him a subliminal memory of his own separation from Mopsa?

In either case, Ingelow appears to hint that a seemingly ordinary woman confined to her domestic world can be fully attuned to the extraordinary fairy world that manifested itself to her son when he took upon himself the role of nurturer. The mother whose familiarity Jack finds so reassuring thus may know more than she lets on about the fantastic female realms she is helping him to forget. Her unsurprised look upon his return and her choice of poem suggest that her powers go well beyond the provision of strawberries. Hers is a double role: a comforting presence in the quotidian world, and, at the same time, our last link to a fantasy world ruled by the female imagination. In this sense, this matriarch is Queen Mopsa's everyday counterpart.

The ballad about the Shepherd Lady replays Jack's separation from Mopsa and Orpheus's separation from Eurydice. Charged with the task of tending and feeding a flock left to her by a vanished male lover, the lady also inherits the musical powers of the seductive piper she had first heard "in her sleep." The voices of mother and narrator blend with lyrics this female caretaker "sings when light doth wane." Tennyson's fragile female lyricists—Mariana and the Lady of Shalott—could not bear their severance from the masculine order operating in the world outside the walls in which they were immured. But this lady, though drawn out of her "high tower" like the Lady of Shalott, can wield the shepherd's crook as well as he did. Unlike Mariana, who bewails the absent "he" who "cometh not," the Shepherd Lady is confident that "he will come again." But even without her male complement, she resolutely discharges her task when she leads his sheep. The flock he has deserted has become "*her* flock."

The song of the Shepherd Lady allows Jack's mother to impersonate Mopsa's simultaneous empowerment and sense of loss. The poem thus acts as a last reminder of the subversive texture of *Mopsa the Fairy,* a book full of surprises and unexplained ellipses. The narrative that had started out with Jack as its ostensible hero, the patron of a nameless fairy-child, ends with her eminence as a crowned queen and his abasement and reduction. A story that might well have borne the title of *Captain Jack* turns out to be named after the chubby fairy child who will outgrow him in wisdom and authority. It is precisely Jack's unimaginativeness, his stolidity, that protects him in his forays into the dangerous realms of the fantastic fairylands so persistently identified with a female imagination. And that female imagination, though superior to Jack's, is treated as mercurial and painful, accompanied by a self-aware suffering from which the more easily domesticated boy is exempt.

Ingelow's book is dedicated to a little girl, her younger cousin Janet Holloway. But what starts out so deceptively as a boy's book, promising to feature Jack's adventures in a series of wonderlands, turns out to be in many ways a conscious pendant to Carroll's *Alice's Adventures in Wonderland,* which purported to be—but really wasn't—a girl's book. Its relation to Carroll's text is, in fact, even more overt than that of some of the other fictions gathered in this volume. The echoes and reversals are numerous: whereas Alice falls down, down, down in pursuit of a male white rabbit, Jack shoots up, up, up, propelled out of the hollow tree trunk by the female albatross who dashes "through the hole." Alice is shunned and degraded by most Wonderland creatures; the discomforts she experiences reach their highpoint at the Mad Hatter's Tea Party and their climax at the Kafkaesque trial at the end. Jack, on the other hand, is always received with great awe and respect by fairies who value the material objects carried by any ordinary human boy. His denigration at the end is therefore all the more unexpected. Whereas Alice, increasingly irritated by the indignities she suffers at the hands of Carroll's fantastic agents, wills her exit from Wonderland, Ingelow's Jack refuses to accept his displacement. He cannot understand why he should not be allowed to remain with Mopsa as her consort. Carroll's Alice asserts her superiority by exposing the powerlessness of Wonderland's matriarch, the Queen of Hearts. Ingelow's Jack, however, must be deposited back in his father's garden precisely because there is no place for him in a female Utopia in which even monarchs cannot evade the dictates of Old Mother Fate and her punitive three daughters. Like Alice, Jack forgets his bizarre adventures. But by then he has ceased to be the book's protagonist.

Alice's dream had to be reprocessed by a more mature female figure, her older sister. In *Mopsa the Fairy,* however, it is Mopsa herself who is charged with the task of remembering. Her decision not to forget makes her superior to that other resident of fairyland, the Apple Woman, a human who prefers the adulation of the fairies who flatter her to the memories of a reality full of "cold and poverty." The Apple Woman misses her three sons but cannot bring herself to return to her former world. Painfully hovering, like Mopsa herself, between the human world she has left behind and the fairy world where she is destined to remain, she becomes enslaved by her very superiority to the fairies who feed on her human capacity for emotion.

Mopsa's imprisonment in her own fairy world, however, is far more painful than the Apple Woman's paralysis. For Mopsa has chosen to endow the boy-king with Jack's features in order to make sure that she will never forget the human boy whose kiss sealed her fate. Like the abandoned Shepherd Lady, Mopsa's willingness to carry the burden of memory is a mark of her imaginative superiority. And yet that superiority, as Ingelow so well knew, carries a great price. Ingelow may have inscribed her own yearnings in figures like Mopsa, the Apple Woman, and Jack's mother. Yet by identifying herself as well with the unnostalgic Jack, Ingelow manages to resist the lugubrious sentimentality that marked Lewis Carroll's later work as well as the writings of those women who beatified little boys (Molesworth comes to mind, as well as Ewing). If Jack displays unimaginativeness and dullness, he also exhibits a healthy resistance to nostalgia. The boy who welcomes the strawberries and gladly climbs into his clean bed refuses to be fixated on loss. Since retrogression—a return to Mopsa's Ur-world—becomes impossible, he cheerfully submits to an ordinary world in which growth is much slower than in Mopsa's fairyland.

The "comforts" that Jack finds at the end of *Mopsa* cannot, therefore, be wholly discounted. They must be placed in apposition to the profound discomforts which so many child readers claim to have felt, in Victorian times as well as in our own, on first experiencing the account of Alice's abrupt size changes or on encountering with her such unpleasant creatures as the hideous Duchess or the sadistic Mad Hatter. Indeed, even in the thick of his most grotesque adventures, little Jack is never much disturbed by threats that would have unnerved a more imaginative child. *Mopsa the Fairy* is a highly imaginative work that rewards its hero's lack of imagination.

Ingelow's own imaginative faculties led some American intellectuals to petition Queen Victoria that she succeed Tennyson as England's first female poet laureate. The petition was unsuccessful, much to Ingelow's apparent relief. The poet who professed to value hemming and sewing as much as verse making preferred to lead an unobtrusive life. The closure of *Mopsa the Fairy,* though at odds with the book's extraordinary powers of fantasy, is in keeping with that unobtrusiveness. It is a tribute to Jean Ingelow's art and psychology that she so well understood the simple comforts that close out her decidedly unsimple book. As for the discomforts of her myth-making imagination, she seems to suggest that these are a burden best borne by fairies like Mopsa, whose matriarchal country allows her to outgrow, albeit reluctantly, the pocket of a nice English boy.

JEAN INGELOW

Mopsa the Fairy

CHAPTER ONE

Above the Clouds

✳

'And can this be my own world?
 'Tis all gold and snow,
Save where scarlet waves are hurled
 Down yon gulf below,'
''Tis thy world, 'tis my world,
 City, mead, and shore,
For he that hath his own world
 Hath many worlds more.'[1]

A boy, whom I knew very well, was once going through a meadow which was full of buttercups. The nurse and his baby sister were with him; and when they got to an old hawthorn, which grew in the hedge and was covered with blossom, they all sat down in its shade, and the nurse took out three slices of plum cake, gave one to each of the children and kept one for herself.

While the boy was eating he observed that this hedge was very high and thick, and that there was a great hollow in the trunk of the old thorn tree, and he heard a twittering, as if there was a nest somewhere inside; so he thrust his head in, twisted himself round and looked up.

It was a very great thorn tree, and the hollow was so large that two or

---

1. **'And . . . more'** Ingelow's own verses head chapters 1, 3, 4, 6, 8, 9, 12, and 16.

three boys could have stood upright in it; and when he got used to the dim light in that brown, still place, he saw that a good way above his head there was a nest—rather a curious one too, for it was as large as a pair of blackbirds would have built—and yet it was made of fine white wool and delicate bits of moss; in short, it was like a goldfinch's nest magnified three times.

Just then he thought he heard some little voices cry, 'Jack! Jack!' His baby sister was asleep, and the nurse was reading a story book, so it could not have been either of them who called. 'I must get in here,' said the boy. 'I wish this hole was larger.' So he began to wriggle and twist himself through, and just as he pulled in his last foot he looked up, and three heads which had been peeping over the edge of the nest suddenly popped down again.

'Those heads had no beaks, I am sure,' said Jack, and he stood on tiptoe and poked in one of his fingers. 'And the things have no feathers,' he continued; so, the hollow being rather rugged, he managed to climb up and look in.

His eyes were not used yet to the dim light; but he was sure those things were not birds—no. He poked them, and they took no notice; but when he snatched one of them out of the nest it gave a loud squeak, and said: 'Oh, don't, Jack!' as plainly as possible, upon which he was so frightened that he lost his footing, dropped the thing and slipped down himself. Luckily he was not hurt, nor the thing either; he could see it quite plainly now: it was creeping about like rather an old baby, and had on a little frock and pinafore.

'It's a fairy!' exclaimed Jack to himself. 'How curious! and this must be a fairy's nest. Oh, how angry the old mother will be if this little thing creeps away and gets out of the hole!' So he looked down. 'Oh, the hole is on the other side,' he said; and he turned round, but the hole was not on the other side; it was not on any side; it must have closed up all on a sudden, while he was looking into the nest, for, look whichever way he would, there was no hole at all, excepting a very little one high up over the nest, which let in a very small sunbeam.

Jack was very much astonished, but he went on eating his cake, and was so delighted to see the young fairy climb up the side of the hollow and scramble again into her nest that he laughed heartily; upon which all the nestlings popped up their heads and, showing their pretty white teeth, pointed at the slice of cake.

'Well,' said Jack, 'I may have to stay inside here for a long time, and I have nothing to eat but this cake; however, your mouths are very small, so you shall have a piece'; and he broke off a small piece and put it into the nest, climbing up to see them eat it.

These young fairies were a long time dividing and munching the cake, and before they had finished it began to be rather dark, for a black cloud came over and covered the little sunbeam. At the same time the wind rose and rocked the boughs, and made the old tree creak and tremble. Then there was thunder and rain, and the little fairies were so frightened that they got out of the nest and crept into Jack's pockets. One got into each waistcoat pocket, and the other two were very comfortable, for he took out his hand-kerchief and made room for them in the pocket of his jacket.

It got darker and darker, till at last Jack could only just see the hole, and it seemed to be a very long way off. Every time he looked at it, it was farther off, and at last he saw a thin crescent moon shining through it.

'I am sure it cannot be night yet,' he said; and he took out one of the fattest of the young fairies and held it up towards the hole.

'Look at that,' said he; 'what is to be done now? The hole is so far off that it's night up there, and down here I haven't done eating my lunch.'

'Well,' answered the young fairy, 'then why don't you whistle?'

Jack was surprised to hear her speak in this sensible manner, and in the light of the moon he looked at her very attentively.

'When first I saw you in the nest,' said he, 'you had a pinafore on, and now you have a smart little apron, with lace round it.'

'That is because I am much older now,' said the fairy; 'we never take such a long time to grow up as you do.'

'But your pinafore?' said Jack.

'Turned into an apron, of course,' replied the fairy, 'just as your velvet jacket will turn into a tail-coat when you are old enough.'

'It won't,' said Jack.

'Yes, it will,' answered the fairy, with an air of superior wisdom. 'Don't argue with me; I am older now than you are—nearly grown up in fact. Put me into your pocket again, and whistle as loudly as you can.'

Jack laughed, put her in, and pulled out another. 'Worse and worse,' he said; 'why, this was a boy fairy, and now he has a moustache and a sword, and looks as fierce as possible!'

'I think I heard my sister tell you to whistle?' said this fairy very sternly.

'Yes, she did,' said Jack. 'Well, I suppose I had better do it.' So he whistled very loudly indeed.

'Why did you leave off so soon?' said another of them, peeping out.

'Why, if you wish to know,' answered Jack, 'it was because I thought something took hold of my legs.'

'Ridiculous child,' cried the last of the four, 'how do you think you are ever to get out, if she doesn't take hold of your legs?'

Jack thought he would rather have done a long-division sum than have been obliged to whistle; but he could not help doing it when they told him, and he felt something take hold of his legs again, and then give him a jerk, which hoisted him on to its back, where he sat astride, and wondered whether the thing was a pony; but it was not, for he presently observed that it had a very slender neck, and then that it was covered with feathers. It was a large bird, and he presently found that they were rising towards the hole, which had become so very far off, and in a few minutes she dashed through the hole, with Jack on her back and all the fairies in his pockets.

It was so dark that he could see nothing, and he twined his arms round the bird's neck, to hold on, upon which this agreeable fowl told him not to be afraid, and said she hoped he was comfortable.

'I should be more comfortable,' replied Jack, 'if I knew how I could get home again. I don't wish to go home just yet, for I want to see where we are flying to, but papa and mamma will be frightened if I never do.'

'Oh no,' replied the albatross[2] (for she was an albatross), 'you need not be at all afraid about that. When boys go to Fairyland, their parents never are uneasy about them.'

'Really?' exclaimed Jack.

'Quite true,' replied the albatross.

'And so we are going to Fairyland?' exclaimed Jack. 'How delightful!'

'Yes,' said the albatross; 'the back way, mind; we are only going the back way. You could go in two minutes by the usual route; but these young fairies want to go before they are summoned, and therefore you and I are taking them.' And she continued to fly on in the dark sky for a very long time.

'They seem to be all fast asleep,' said Jack.

'Perhaps they will sleep till we come to the wonderful river,' replied the albatross; and just then she flew with a great bump against something that met her in the air.

'What craft is this that hangs out no light?' said a gruff voice.

'I might ask the same question of you,' answered the albatross sullenly.

---

2. **albatross** sea-bird associated with the imagination ever since Coleridge's "The Rime of the Ancient Mariner" (1798)

'I'm only a poor Will-o'-the-wisp,'[3] replied the voice, 'and you know very well that I have but a lantern to show.' Thereupon a lantern became visible, and Jack saw by the light of it a man who looked old and tired, and he was so transparent that you could see through him, lantern and all.

'I hope I have not hurt you, William,' said the albatross; 'I will light up immediately. Good night.'

'Good night,' answered the Will-o'-the-wisp. 'I am going down as fast as I can; the storm blew me up, and I am never easy excepting in my native swamps.'

Jack might have taken more notice of Will if the albatross had not begun to light up. She did it in this way. First one of her eyes began to gleam with a beautiful green light, which cast its rays far and near, and then, when it was as bright as a lamp, the other eye began to shine, and the light of that eye was red. In short, she was lighted up just like a vessel at sea.

Jack was so happy that he hardly knew which to look at first, there really were so many remarkable things.

'They snore,' said the albatross; 'they are very fast asleep, and before they wake I should like to talk to you a little.'

She meant that the fairies snored, and so they did, in Jack's pockets.

'My name,' continued the albatross, 'is Jenny. Do you think you shall remember that? Because when you are in Fairyland and want someone to take you home again, and call "Jenny," I shall be able to come to you; and I shall come with pleasure, for I like boys better than fairies.'

'Thank you,' said Jack. 'Oh yes, I shall remember your name, it is such a very easy one.'

'If it is in the night that you want me, just look up,' continued the albatross, 'and you will see a green and a red spark moving in the air; you will then call Jenny, and I will come; but remember that I cannot come unless you do call me.'

'Very well,' said Jack; but he was not attending, because there was so much to be seen.

In the first place all the stars excepting a few large ones were gone, and they looked frightened; and as it got lighter one after the other seemed to give a little start in the blue sky and go out. And then Jack looked down and saw, as he thought, a great country covered with very jagged snow mountains with astonishingly sharp peaks. Here and there he saw a very deep

3. **Will-o'-the-wisp** See p. 123, note 17.

lake—at least he thought it was a lake; but while he was admiring the mountains there came an enormous crack between two of the largest, and he saw the sun come rolling up among them, and it seemed to be almost smothered.

'Why those are clouds!' exclaimed Jack. 'And, oh, how rosy they have all turned! I thought they were mountains.'

'Yes, they are clouds,' said the albatross; and then they turned gold colour; and next they began to plunge and tumble, and every one of the peaks put on a glittering crown; and next they broke themselves to pieces and began to drift away. In fact Jack had been out all night, and now it was morning.

CHAPTER TWO

Captain Jack

❋

It has been our lot to sail with many captains, not one of whom is fit to be a patch on your back. *Letter of the Ship's Company of H.M.S.S. 'Royalist' to Captain W. T. Bate.*

All this time the albatross kept dropping down and down like a stone till Jack was quite out of breath, and they fell or flew, whichever you like to call it, straight through one of the great chasms which he had thought were lakes, and he looked down as he sat on the bird's back to see what the world is like when you hang a good way above it at sunrise.

It was a very beautiful sight; the sheep and lambs were still fast asleep on the green hills, and the sea birds were asleep in long rows upon the ledges of the cliffs, with their heads under their wings.

'Are those young fairies awake yet?' asked the albatross.

'As sound asleep as ever,' answered Jack; 'but, Albatross, is not that the sea which lies under us? You are a sea bird, I know, but I am not a sea boy, and I cannot live in the water.'

'Yes, that is the sea,' answered the albatross. 'Don't you observe that it is covered with ships?'

'I see boats and vessels,' answered Jack, 'and all their sails are set, but they cannot sail because there is no wind.'

'The wind never does blow in this great bay,' said the bird; 'and those ships would all lie there becalmed till they dropped to pieces if one of them was not wanted now and then to go up the wonderful river.'

'But how did they come there?' asked Jack.

'Some of them had captains who ill-used their cabin-boys, some were pirate ships and others were going out on evil errands. The consequence was that when they chanced to sail within this great bay they got becalmed; the fairies came and picked all the sailors out and threw them into the water; they then took away the flags and pennons to make their best coats of, threw the ship-biscuits and other provisions to the fishes and set all the sails. Many ships which are supposed by men to have foundered lie becalmed in this quiet sea. Look at those five grand ones with high poops: they are moored close together, they were part of the Spanish Armada; and those open boats with blue sails belonged to the Romans, they sailed with Caesar when he invaded Britain.'

By this time the albatross was hovering about among the vessels, making choice of one to take Jack and the fairies up the wonderful river.

'It must not be a large one,' she said, 'for the river in some places is very shallow.'

Jack would have liked very much to have a fine three-master, all to himself; but then he considered that he did not know anything about sails and rigging, he thought it would be just as well to be contented with whatever the albatross might choose, so he let her set him down in a beautiful little open boat, with a great carved figurehead to it. There he seated himself in great state, and the albatross perched herself on the next bench and faced him.

'You remember my name?' asked the albatross.

'Oh yes,' said Jack; but he was not attending—he was thinking what a fine thing it was to have such a curious boat all to himself.

'That's well,' answered the bird; 'then, in the next place, are those fairies awake yet?'

'No, they are not,' said Jack; and he took them out of his pockets and laid them down in a row before the albatross.

'They are certainly asleep,' said the bird. 'Put them away again, and take care of them. Mind you don't lose any of them, for I really don't know what will happen if you do. Now I have one thing more to say to you, and that is, are you hungry?'

'Rather,' said Jack.

'Then,' replied the albatross, 'as soon as you feel *very* hungry, lie down in the bottom of the boat and go to sleep. You will dream that you see before you a roasted fowl, some new potatoes and an apple pie. Mind you don't eat too much in your dream, or you will be sorry for it when you wake. That is all. Goodbye! I must go.'

Jack put his arms round the neck of the bird and hugged her; then she spread her magnificent wings and sailed slowly away. At first he felt very lonely, but in a few minutes he forgot that, because the little boat began to swim so fast.

She was not sailing, for she had no sail, and he was not rowing, for he had no oars; so I am obliged to call her motion swimming, because I don't know of a better word. In less than a quarter of an hour they passed close under the bows of a splendid three-decker, a seventy-gun ship. The gannets[4] who live in those parts had taken possession of her, and she was so covered with nests that you could not have walked one step on her deck without treading on them. The father birds were aloft in the rigging, or swimming in the warm green sea, and they made such a clamour when they saw Jack that they nearly woke the fairies—nearly, but not quite, for the little things turned round in Jack's pockets, and sneezed, and began to snore again.

Then the boat swam past a fine brig. Some sea fairies had just flung her cargo overboard, and were playing at leapfrog on deck. These were not at all like Jack's own fairies; they were about the same height and size as himself, and they had brown faces, and red flannel shirts and red caps on. A large fleet of the pearly nautilus was collected close under the vessel's lee. The little creatures were feasting on what the sea fairies had thrown overboard, and Jack's boat, in its eagerness to get on, went plunging through them so roughly that several were capsized. Upon this the brown sea fairies looked over, and called out angrily: 'Boat ahoy!' and the boat stopped.

'Tell that boat of yours to mind what she is about,' said the fairy sea-captain to Jack.

Jack touched his cap, and said: 'Yes, sir,' and then called out to his boat: 'You ought to be ashamed of yourself, running down these little live fishing-vessels so carelessly. Go at a more gentle pace.'

So it swam more slowly; and Jack, being by this time hungry, curled himself up in the bottom of the boat and fell asleep.

He dreamt directly about a fowl and some potatoes, and he ate a wing, and then he ate a merrythought, and then somebody said to him that he had

4. **gannets** northern sea birds

better not eat any more, but he did, he ate another wing; and presently an apple pie came, and he ate some of that, and then he ate some more, and then he immediately woke.

'Now that bird told me not to eat too much,' said Jack, 'and yet I have done it. I never felt so full in my life,' and for more than half an hour he scarcely noticed anything.

At last he lifted up his head, and saw straight before him two great brown cliffs, and between them flowed in the wonderful river. Other rivers flow out, but this river flowed in, and took with it far into the land dolphins, swordfish, mullet, sunfish and many other strange creatures; and that is one reason why it was called the magic river, or the wonderful river.

At first it was rather wide, and Jack was alarmed to see what multitudes of soldiers stood on either side to guard the banks and prevent any person from landing.

He wondered how he should get the fairies on shore. However, in about an hour the river became much narrower, and then Jack saw that the guards were not real soldiers, but rose-coloured flamingoes.[5] There they stood in long regiments among the reeds, and never stirred. They are the only foot-soldiers the fairies have in their pay; they are very fierce, and never allow anything but a fairy ship to come up the river.

They guarded the banks for miles and miles, many thousands of them, standing a little way into the water among the flags and rushes; but at last there were no more reeds and no soldier guards, for the stream became narrower, and flowed between such steep rocks that no one could possibly have climbed them.

CHAPTER THREE

Winding-up Time

✻

'Wake, baillie, wake! the crafts are out;
Wake!' said the knight. 'Be quick!
For high street, bystreet, over the town

5. **flamingoes** Carroll's Alice used flamingoes as mallets in the croquet game in which soldiers formed arches

They fight with poker and stick.'
Said the squire, 'A fight so fell was ne'er
   In all thy bailiewick.'
What said the old clock in the tower?
    'Tick, tick, tick!'

'Wake, daughter, wake! the hour draws on;
   Wake!' quoth the dame. 'Be quick!
The meats are set, the guests are coming,
   The fiddler's waxing his stick.'
She said, 'The bridegroom waiting and waiting
   To see thy face is sick.'
What said the new clock in her bower?
    'Tick, tick, tick!'

Jack looked at these hot brown rocks, first on the left bank and then on the right, till he was quite tired; but at last the shore on the right bank became flat, and he saw a beautiful little bay, where the water was still and where grass grew down to the brink.

He was so much pleased at this change that he cried out hastily: 'Oh, how I wish my boat would swim into that bay and let me land!' He had no sooner spoken than the boat altered her course, as if somebody had been steering her, and began to make for the bay as fast as she could go.

'How odd!' thought Jack. 'I wonder whether I ought to have spoken; for the boat certainly did not intend to come into this bay. However, I think I will let her alone now, for I certainly do wish very much to land here.'

As they drew towards the strand the water got so shallow that you could see crabs and lobsters walking about at the bottom. At last the boat's keel grated on the pebbles; and just as Jack began to think of jumping on shore he saw two little old women approaching and gently driving a white horse before them.

The horse had panniers,[6] one on each side; and when his feet were in the water he stood still; and Jack said to one of the old women: 'Will you be so kind as to tell me whether this is Fairyland?'

'What does he say?' asked one old woman of the other.

'I asked if this was Fairyland,' repeated Jack, for he thought the first old woman might have been deaf. She was very handsomely dressed in a red satin gown, and did not look in the least like a washer-woman, though it afterwards appeared that she was one.

6. **panniers** carrying baskets placed on horses or mules

'He says "Is this Fairyland?"' she replied; and the other, who had a blue satin cloak, answered: 'Oh, does he?' and then began to empty the panniers of many small blue and pink and scarlet shirts, and coats, and stockings; and when they had made them into two little heaps they knelt down and began to wash them in the river, taking no notice of him whatever.

Jack stared at them. They were not much taller than himself, and they were not taking the slightest care of their handsome clothes; then he looked at the old white horse, who was hanging his head over the lovely clear water with a very discontented air.

At last the blue washer-woman said: 'I shall leave off now; I've got a pain in my works.'

'Do,' said the other. 'We'll go home and have a cup of tea.' Then she glanced at Jack, who was still sitting in the boat, and said: 'Can you strike?'

'I can if I choose,' replied Jack, a little astonished at this speech. And the red and blue washer-women wrung out the clothes, put them again into the panniers and, taking the old horse by the bridle, began gently to lead him away.

'I have a great mind to land,' thought Jack. 'I should not wonder at all if this is Fairyland. So, as the boat came here to please me, I shall ask it to stay where it is, in case I should want it again.'

So he sprang ashore, and said to the boat: 'Stay just where you are, will you?' and he ran after the old women, calling to them:

'Is there any law to prevent my coming into your country?'

'Wo!' cried the red-coated old woman, and the horse stopped, while the blue-coated woman repeated: 'Any law? No, not that I know of; but if you are a stranger here you had better look out.'

'Why?' asked Jack.

'You don't suppose, do you,' she answered, 'that our Queen will wind up strangers?'

While Jack was wondering what she meant, the other said:

'I shouldn't wonder if he goes eight days. Gee!' and the horse went on.

'No, wo!' said the other.

'No, no. Gee! I tell you,' cried the first.

Upon this, to Jack's intense astonishment, the old horse stopped, and said, speaking through his nose:

'Now, then, which it is to be? I'm willing to gee, and I'm agreeable to wo; but what's a fellow to do when you say them both together?'

'Why, he talks!' exclaimed Jack.

'It's because he's got a cold in his head,' observed one of the washer-women; 'he always talks when he's got a cold, and there's no pleasing him; whatever you say, he's not satisfied. Gee, Boney, do!'

'Gee it is, then,' said the horse, and began to jog on.

'He spoke again!' said Jack, upon which the horse laughed, and Jack was quite alarmed.

'It appears that your horses don't talk?' observed the blue-coated woman.

'Never,' answered Jack; 'they can't.'

'You mean they won't,' observed the old horse; and though he spoke the words of mankind it was not in a voice like theirs. Still Jack felt that his was just the natural tone for a horse, and that it did not arise only from the length of his nose. 'You'll find out some day, perhaps,' he continued, 'whether horses can talk or not.'

'Shall I?' said Jack very earnestly.

'They'll TELL,' proceeded the white horse. 'I wouldn't be you when they tell how you've used them.'

'Have you been ill used?' said Jack, in an anxious tone.

'Yes, yes, of course he has,' one of the women broke in; 'but he has come here to get all right again. This is a very wholesome country for horses; isn't it, Boney?'

'Yes,' said the horse.

'Well, then, jog on, there's a dear,' continued the old woman. 'Why, you will be young again soon, you know—young, and gamesome, and hand-some; you'll be quite a colt by and by, and then we shall set you free to join your companions in the happy meadows.'

The old horse was so comforted by this kind speech that he pricked up his ears and quickened his pace considerably.

'He was shamefully used,' observed one washer-woman. 'Look at him, how lean he is! You can see all his ribs.'

'Yes,' said the other, as if apologizing for the poor old horse. 'He gets low-spirited when he thinks of all he has gone through; but he is a vast deal better already than he was. He used to live in London; his master always carried a long whip to beat him with, and never spoke civilly to him.'

'London!' exclaimed Jack. 'Why, that is my country. How did the horse get here?'

'That's no business of yours,' answered one of the women. 'But I can tell you he came because he was wanted, which is more than you are.'

'You let him alone,' said the horse in a querulous tone. 'I don't bear any malice.'

'No; he has a good disposition, has Boney,' observed the red old woman. 'Pray, are you a boy?'

'Yes,' said Jack.

'A real boy, that wants no winding up?' inquired the old woman.

'I don't know what you mean,' answered Jack; 'but I am a real boy, certainly.'

'Ah!' she replied. 'Well, I thought you were, by the way Boney spoke to you. How frightened you must be! I wonder what will be done to all your people for driving, and working, and beating so many beautiful creatures to death every year that comes? They'll have to pay for it some day, you may depend.'

Jack was a little alarmed, and answered that he had never been unkind himself to horses, and he was glad that Boney bore no malice.

'They worked him, and often drove him about all night in the miserable streets, and never let him have so much as a canter in a green field,' said one of the women; 'but he'll be all right now, only he has to begin at the wrong end.'

'What do you mean?' said Jack.

'Why, in this country', answered the old woman, 'they begin by being terribly old and stiff, and they seem miserable and jaded at first, but by degrees they get young again, as you heard me reminding him.'

'Indeed,' said Jack; 'and do you like that?'

'It has nothing to do with me,' she answered. 'We are only here to take care of all the creatures that men have ill used. While they are sick and old, which they are when first they come to us—after they are dead, you know—we take care of them, and gradually bring them up to be young and happy again.'

'This must be a very nice country to live in then,' said Jack.

'For horses it is,' said the old lady significantly.

'Well,' said Jack, 'it does seem very full of haystacks certainly, and all the air smells of fresh grass.'

At this moment they came to a beautiful meadow, and the old horse stopped and, turning to the blue-coated woman, said: 'Faxa, I think I could fancy a handful of clover.' Upon this Faxa snatched Jack's cap off his head, and in a very active manner jumped over a little ditch, and gathering some clover, presently brought it back full, handing it to the old horse with great civility.

'You shouldn't be in such a hurry,' observed the old horse; 'your weights will be running down some day, if you don't mind.'

'It's all zeal,' observed the red-coated woman.

Just then a little man, dressed like a groom, came running up, out of breath. 'Oh, here you are, Dow!' he exclaimed to the red-coated woman. 'Come along, will you? Lady Betty wants you; it's such a hot day, and nobody, she says, can fan her so well as you can.'

The red-coated woman, without a word, went off with the groom, and Jack thought he would go with them, for this Lady Betty could surely tell him whether the country was called Fairyland, or whether he must get into his boat and go farther. He did not like either to hear the way in which Faxa and Dow talked about their works and their weights; so he asked Faxa to give him his cap, which she did, and he heard a curious sort of little ticking noise as he came close to her, which startled him.

'Oh, this must be Fairyland, I am sure,' thought Jack, 'for in my country our pulses beat quite differently from that.'

'Well,' said Faxa, rather sharply, 'do you find any fault with the way I go?'

'No,' said Jack, a little ashamed of having listened. 'I think you walk beautifully; your steps are so regular.'

'She's machine-made,' observed the old horse, in a melancholy voice, and with a deep sigh. 'In the largest magnifying glass you'll hardly find the least fault with her chain. She's not like the goods they turn out in Clerkenwell.'

Jack was more and more startled, and so glad to get his cap and run after the groom and Dow to find Lady Betty, that he might be with ordinary human beings again; but when he got up to them he found that Lady Betty was a beautiful brown mare! She was lying in a languid and rather affected attitude, with a load of fresh hay before her, and two attendants, one of whom stood holding a parasol over her head, while the other was fanning her.

'I'm so glad you are come, my good Dow,' said the brown mare. 'Don't you think I am strong enough today to set off for the happy meadows?'

'Well,' said Dow, 'I'm afraid not yet; you must remember that it is no use your leaving us till you have quite got over the effects of the fall.'

Just then Lady Betty observed Jack, and said: 'Take that boy away; he reminds me of a jockey.'

The attentive groom instantly started forward, but Jack was too nimble for him; he ran and ran with all his might, and only wished he had never left the boat. But still he heard the groom behind him; and in fact the groom caught him at last, and held him so fast that struggling was no use at all.

'You young rascal!' he exclaimed, as he recovered breath. 'How you do run! It's enough to break your mainspring.'

'What harm did I do?' asked Jack. 'I was only looking at the mare.'

'Harm!' exclaimed the groom. 'Harm, indeed! Why, you reminded her of a jockey. It's enough to hold her back, poor thing!—and we trying so hard, too, to make her forget what a cruel end she came to in the old world.'

'You need not hold me so tightly,' said Jack. 'I shall not run away again; but,' he added, 'if this is Fairyland, it is not half such a nice country as I expected.'

'Fairyland!' exclaimed the groom, stepping back with surprise. 'Why, what made you think of such a thing? This is only one of the border countries, where things are set right again that people have caused to go wrong in the world. The world, you know, is what men and women call their own home.'

'I know,' said Jack; 'and that's where I came from.' Then, as the groom seemed no longer to be angry, he went on: 'And I wish you would tell me about Lady Betty.'

'She was a beautiful fleet creature, of the racehorse breed,' said the groom; 'and she won silver cups for her master, and then they made her run a steeplechase, which frightened her, but still she won it; and then they made her run another, and she cleared some terribly high hurdles, and many gates and ditches, till she came to an awful one, and at first she would not take it, but her rider spurred and beat her till she tried. It was beyond her powers, and she fell and broke her forelegs. Then they shot her. After she had died that miserable death we had her here, to make her all right again.'

'Is this the only country where you set things right?' asked Jack.

'Certainly not,' answered the groom; 'they lie about in all directions. Why, you might wander for years and never come to the end of this one.'

'I am afraid I shall not find the one I am looking for,' said Jack, 'if your countries are so large.'

'I don't think our world is much larger than yours,' answered the groom. 'But come along; I hear the bell, and we are a good way from the palace.'

Jack, in fact, heard the violent ringing of a bell at some distance; and when the groom began to run, he ran beside him, for he thought he should like to see the palace. As they ran, people gathered from all sides—fields, cottages, mills—till at last there was a little crowd, among whom Jack saw Dow and Faxa, and they were all making for a large house, the wide door of which was standing open. Jack stood with the crowd and peeped in. There was a woman sitting inside upon a rocking-chair, a tall, large woman, with a gold-coloured gown on, and beside her stood a table, covered with things that looked like keys.

'What is that woman doing?' said he to Faxa, who was standing close to him.

'Winding us up, to be sure,' answered Faxa. 'You don't suppose, surely, that we can go for ever?'

'Extraordinary!' said Jack. 'Then are you wound up every evening, like watches?'

'Unless we have misbehaved ourselves,' she answered; 'and then she lets us run down.'

'And what then?'

'What then?' repeated Faxa. 'Why, then we have to stop and stand against a wall, till she is pleased to forgive us, and let our friends carry us in to be set going again.'

Jack looked in, and saw the people pass in and stand close by the woman. One after the other she took by the chin with her left hand, and with her right hand found a key that pleased her. It seemed to Jack that there was a tiny keyhole in the back of their heads, and that she put the key in and wound them up.

'You must take your turn with the others,' said the groom.

'There's no keyhole in my head,' said Jack; 'besides, I do not want any woman to wind me up.'

'But you must do as others do,' he persisted; 'and if you have no keyhole, our Queen can easily have one made, I should think.'

'Make one in my head!' exclaimed Jack. 'She shall do no such thing.'

'We shall see,' said Faxa quietly. And Jack was so frightened that he set off, and ran back towards the river with all his might. Many of the people called to him to stop, but they could not run after him, because they wanted winding up. However, they would certainly have caught him if he had not been very quick, for before he got to the river he heard behind him the footsteps of those who had been first attended to by the Queen, and he had only just time to spring into the boat when they reached the edge of the water.

No sooner was he on board than the boat swung round, and got again into the middle of the stream; but he could not feel safe till not only was there a long reach of water between him and the shore, but till he had gone so far down river that the beautiful bay had passed out of sight and the sun was going down. By this time he began to feel very tired and sleepy; so, having looked at his fairies, and found that they were all safe and fast asleep, he laid down in the bottom of the boat, and fell into a doze, and then into a dream.

CHAPTER FOUR

Bees and other Fellow Creatures

⁂

> The dove laid some little sticks,
>   Then began to coo;
> The gnat took his trumpet up
>   To play the day through;
> The pie chattered soft and long—
>   But that she always does;
> The bee did all he had to do,
>   And only said 'Buzz'.

When Jack at length opened his eyes, he found that it was night, for the full moon was shining; but it was not at all a dark night, for he could see distinctly some black birds that looked like ravens. They were sitting in a row on the edge of the boat.

Now that he had fairies in his pockets he could understand bird-talk, and he heard one of these ravens saying: 'There is no meat so tender; I wish I could pick their little eyes out.'

'Yes,' said another, 'fairies are delicate eating indeed. We must speak Jack fair if we want to get at them.' And she heaved up a deep sigh.

Jack lay still, and thought he had better pretend to be asleep; but they soon noticed that his eyes were open, and one of them presently walked up his leg and bowed, and asked if he was hungry.

Jack said: 'No.'

'No more am I,' replied the raven; 'not at all hungry.' Then she hopped off his leg, and Jack sat up.

'And how are the sweet fairies that my young master is taking to their home?' asked another of the ravens. 'I hope they are safe in my young master's pockets?'

Jack felt in his pockets. Yes, they were all safe; but he did not take any of them out, lest the ravens should snatch at them.

'Eh?' continued the raven, pretending to listen. 'Did this dear young gentleman say that the fairies were asleep?'

'It doesn't amuse me to talk about fairies,' said Jack; 'but if you would explain some of the things in this country that I cannot make out, I should be very glad.'

'What things?' asked the blackest of the ravens.

'Why,' said Jack, 'I see a full moon lying down there among the water-flags, and just going to set, and there is a half-moon overhead plunging among those great grey clouds, and just this moment I saw a thin crescent moon peeping out between the branches of that tree.'

'Well,' said all the ravens at once, 'did the young master never see a crescent moon in the men and women's world?'

'Oh yes,' said Jack.

'Did he never see a full moon?' asked the ravens.

'Yes, of course,' said Jack; 'but they are the same moon. I could never see all three of them at the same time.'

The ravens were very much surprised at this, and one of them said:

'If my young master did not see the moons it must have been because he didn't look. Perhaps my young master slept in a room, and had only one window; if so, he couldn't see all the sky at once.'

'I tell you, Raven,' said Jack, laughing, 'that I KNOW there is never more than one moon in my country, and sometimes there is no moon at all!'

Upon this all the ravens hung down their heads, and looked very much ashamed; for there is nothing that birds hate so much as to be laughed at, and they believed that Jack was saying this to mock them, and that he knew what they had come for. So first one and then another hopped to the other end of the boat and flew away, till at last there was only one left, and she appeared to be out of spirits, and did not speak again till he spoke to her.

'Raven,' said Jack, 'there's something very cold and slippery lying at the bottom of the boat. I touched it just now, and I don't like it at all.'

'It's a water-snake,'[7] said the raven, and she stooped and picked up a long thing with her beak, which she threw out, and then looked over. 'The water swarms with them, wicked, murderous creatures; they smell the young fairies, and they want to eat them.'

Jack was so thrown off his guard that he snatched one fairy out, just to make sure that it was safe. It was the one with the moustache; and, alas! in one instant the raven flew at it, got it out of his hand and pecked off its head before it had time to wake or Jack to rescue it. Then, as she slowly rose, she croaked, and said to Jack: 'You'll catch it for this, my young master!' and she flew to the bough of a tree, where she finished eating the fairy, and threw his little empty coat into the river.

---

7. **water-snake** cf. "The Rime of the Ancient Mariner," lines 272–73

On this Jack began to cry bitterly, and to think what a foolish boy he had been. He was the more sorry because he did not know that poor little fellow's name. But he had heard the others calling by name to their companions, and very grand names they were too. One was Jovinian—he was a very fierce-looking gentleman; the other two were Roxaletta and Mopsa.

Presently, however, Jack forgot to be unhappy, for two of the moons went down, and then the sun rose, and he was delighted to find that however many moons there might be, there was only one sun, even in the country of the wonderful river.

So on and on they went; but the river was very wide and the waves were boisterous. On the right brink was a thick forest of trees, with such heavy foliage that a little way off they looked like a bank, green and smooth and steep; but as the light became clearer Jack could see here and there the great stems, and see creatures like foxes, wild boars and deer come stealing down to drink in the river.

It was very hot here; not at all like the spring weather he had left behind. And as the low sunbeams shone into Jack's face he said hastily, without thinking of what would occur: 'I wish I might land among those lovely glades on the left bank.'

No sooner said than the boat began to make for the left bank, and the nearer they got towards it the more beautiful it became; but also the more stormy were the reaches of water they had to traverse.

A lovely country indeed! It sloped gently down to the water's edge and beautiful trees were scattered over it, soft mossy grass grew everywhere, great old laburnum trees stretched their boughs down in patches over the water, and higher up camellias, almost as large as hawthorns, grew together and mingled their red and white flowers.

The country was not so open as a park—it was more like a half-cleared woodland; but there was a wide space just where the boat was steering for that had no trees, only a few flowering shrubs. Here groups of strange-looking people were bustling about, and there were shrill fifes sounding, and drums.

Farther back he saw rows of booths or tents under the shade of the trees.

In another place some people dressed like gipsies had made fires of sticks just at the skirts of the woodland, and were boiling their pots. Some of these had very gaudy tilted carts, hung all over with goods, such as baskets, brushes, mats, little glasses, pottery and beads.

It seemed to be a kind of fair, to which people had gathered from all parts; but there was not one house to be seen. All the goods were either hung upon the trees or collected in strange-looking tents.

The people were not all of the same race; indeed, he thought the only human beings were the gipsies, for the folks who had tents were no taller than himself.

How hot it was that morning! and as the boat pushed itself into a little creek, and made its way among the beds of yellow and purple iris which skirted the brink, what a crowd of dragon-flies and large butterflies rose from them!

'Stay where you are!' cried Jack to the boat; and at that instant such a splendid moth rose slowly that he sprang on shore after it, and quite forgot the fair and the people in his desire to follow it.

The moth settled on a great red honey-flower, and he stole up to look at it. As large as a swallow, it floated on before him. Its wings were nearly black, and they had spots of gold on them.

When it rose again Jack ran after it, till he found himself close to the rows of tents where the brown people stood; and they began to cry out to him: 'What'll you buy? what'll you buy, sir?' and they crowded about him, so that he soon lost sight of the moth, and forgot everything else in his surprise at the booths.

They were full of splendid things—clocks and musical boxes, strange china ornaments, embroidered slippers, red caps and many kinds of splendid silks and small carpets. In other booths were swords and dirks, glittering with jewels; and the chatter of the people when they talked together was not in a language that Jack could understand.

Some of the booths were square, and evidently made of common canvas, for when you went into them and the sun shone you could distinctly see the threads.

But scattered a little farther on in groups were some round tents which were far more curious. They were open on all sides, and consisted only of a thick canopy overhead, which was supported by one beautiful round pillar in the middle.

Outside, the canopy was white or brownish; but when Jack stood under these tents he saw that they were lined with splendid flutings of brown or pink silk—what looked like silk, at least, for it was impossible to be sure whether these were real tents or gigantic mushrooms.

They varied in size, also, as mushrooms do, and in shape: some were large enough for twenty people to stand under them, and had flat tops with a brown lining; others had dome-shaped roofs; these were lined with pink, and would only shelter six or seven.

The people who sold in these tents were as strange as their neighbours; each had a little high cap on his head, in shape just like a beehive, and it was made of straw, and had a little hole in front. In fact Jack very soon saw bees flying in and out, and it was evident that these people had their honey made on the premises. They were chiefly selling country produce. They had cheeses so large as to reach to their waists, and the women trundled them along as boys do their hoops. They sold a great many kinds of seed too, in wooden bowls, and cakes and good things to eat, such as gilt gingerbread. Jack bought some of this, and found it very nice indeed. But when he took out his money to pay for it the little man looked rather strangely at it, and turned it over with an air of disgust. Then Jack saw him hand it to his wife, who also seemed to dislike it; and presently Jack observed that they followed him about, first on one side, then on the other. At last the little woman slipped her hand into his pocket, and Jack, putting his hand in directly, found his sixpence had been returned.

'Why, you've given me back my money!' he said.

The little woman put her hands behind her. 'I do not like it,' she said; 'it's dirty; at least, it's not new.'

'No, it's not new,' said Jack, a good deal surprised, 'but it is a good sixpence.'

'The bees don't like it,' continued the little woman. 'They like things to be neat and new, and that sixpence is bent.'

'What shall I give you then?' said Jack.

The good little woman laughed and blushed. 'This young gentleman has a beautiful whistle round his neck,' she observed politely, but did not ask for it.

Jack had a dog-whistle, so he took it off and gave it to her.

'Thank you, for the bees,' she said. 'They love to be called home when we've collected flowers for them.'

So she made a pretty little curtsy, and went away to her customers.

There were some very strange creatures also, about the same height as Jack, who had no tents, and seemed there to buy, not to sell. Yet they looked poorer than the other folks and they were also very cross and discontented; nothing pleased them. Their clothes were made of moss, and their mantles of feathers; and they talked in a queer whistling tone of voice, and carried their skinny little children on their backs and on their shoulders.

They were treated with great respect by the people in the tents; and when Jack asked his friend to whom he had given the whistle what they were, and where they got so much money as they had, she replied that they lived over the hills, and were afraid to come in their best clothes. They were rich and powerful at home, and they came shabbily dressed, and behaved humbly, lest their enemies should envy them. It was very dangerous, she said, to fairies to be envied.

Jack wanted to listen to their strange whistling talk, but he could not for the noise and cheerful chattering of the brown folks, and more still for the screaming and talking of parrots.

Among the goods were hundreds of splendid gilt cages, which were hung by long gold chains from the trees. Each cage contained a parrot and his mate, and they all seemed to be very unhappy indeed.

The parrots could talk, and they kept screaming to the discontented women to buy things for them, and trying very hard to attract attention.

One old parrot made himself quite conspicuous by these efforts. He flung himself against the wires of his cage, he squalled, he screamed, he knocked the floor with his beak till Jack and one of the customers came running up to see what was the matter.

'What do you make such a fuss for?' cried the discontented woman. 'You've set your cage swinging with knocking yourself about; and what good does that do? I cannot break the spell and open it for you.'

'I know that,' answered the parrot, sobbing; 'but it hurts my feelings so that you should take no notice of me now that I have come down in the world.'

'Yes,' said the parrot's mate, 'it hurts our feelings.'

'I haven't forgotten you,' answered the woman, more crossly than ever; 'I was buying a measure of maize for you when you began to make such a noise.'

Jack thought this was the queerest conversation he had ever heard in his life, and he was still more surprised when the bird answered:

'I would much rather you would buy me a pocket-handkerchief. Here we are, shut up, without a chance of getting out, and with nobody to pity us; and we can't even have the comfort of crying, because we've got nothing to wipe our eyes with.'

'But at least,' replied the woman, 'you CAN cry now if you please, and when you had your other face you could not.'

'Buy me a handkerchief,' sobbed the parrot.

'I can't afford both,' whined the cross woman, 'and I've paid now for the maize.' So saying, she went back to the tent to fetch her present to the parrots, and as their cage was still swinging Jack put out his hand to steady it for them, and the instant he did so they became perfectly silent, and all the other parrots on that tree, who had been flinging themselves about in their cages, left off screaming and became silent too.

The old parrot looked very cunning. His cage hung by such a long gold chain that it was just on a level with Jack's face, and so many odd things had happened that day that it did not seem more odd than usual to hear him say, in a tone of great astonishment:

'It's a BOY, if ever there was one!'

'Yes,' said Jack, 'I'm a boy.'

'You won't go yet, will you?' said the parrot.

'No, don't,' said a great many other parrots. Jack agreed to stay a little while, upon which they all thanked him.

'I had no notion you were a boy till you touched my cage,' said the old parrot.

Jack did not know how this could have told him, so he only answered: 'Indeed!'

'I'm a fairy,' observed the parrot, in a confidential tone. 'We are imprisoned here by our enemies the gipsies.'

'So we are,' answered a chorus of other parrots.

'I'm sorry for that,' replied Jack. 'I'm friends with the fairies.'

'Don't tell,' said the parrot, drawing a film over his eyes, and pretending to be asleep. At that moment his friend in the moss petticoat and feather cloak came up with a little measure of maize, and poured it into the cage.

'Here, neighbour,' she said; 'I must say goodbye now, for the gipsy is coming this way, and I want to buy some of her goods.'

'Well, thank you,' answered the parrot, sobbing again; 'but I could have wished it had been a pocket-handkerchief.'

'I'll lend you my handkerchief,' said Jack. 'Here!' And he drew it out and pushed it between the wires.

The parrot and his wife were in a great hurry to get Jack's handkerchief. They pulled it in very hastily; but instead of using it they rolled it up into a ball, and the parrot-wife tucked it under her wing.

'It makes me tremble all over,' said she, 'to think of such good luck.'

'I say!' observed the parrot to Jack. 'I know all about it now. You've got some of my people in your pockets—not of my own tribe, but fairies.'

By this Jack was sure that the parrot really was a fairy himself, and he listened to what he had to say the more attentively.

CHAPTER FIVE

The Parrot in his Shawl

✳

> That handkerchief
> Did an Egyptian to my mother give:
> She was a charmer, and could almost read
> The thoughts of people.
> *Othello.*[8]

'That gipsy woman who is coming with her cart,' said the parrot, 'is a fairy too, and very malicious. It was she and others of her tribe who caught us and put us into these cages, for they are more powerful than we. Mind you do not let her allure you into the woods, nor wheedle you or frighten you into giving her any of those fairies.'

'No,' said Jack; 'I will not.'

'She sold us to the brown people,' continued the parrot. 'Mind you do not buy anything of her, for your money in her palm would act as a charm against you.'

'She has a baby,' observed the parrot-wife scornfully.

'Yes, a baby,' repeated the old parrot; 'and I hope by means of that baby to get her driven away, and perhaps get free myself. I shall try to put her in a passion. Here she comes.'

There she was indeed, almost close at hand. She had a little cart; her goods were hung all about it, and a small horse drew it slowly on, and stopped when she got a customer.

Several gipsy children were with her, and as the people came running together over the grass to see her goods, she sang a curious kind of song, which made them wish to buy them.

Jack turned from the parrot's cage as she came up. He had heard her singing a little way off, and now, before she began again, he felt that already her searching eyes had found him out, and taken notice that he was different from the other people.

When she began to sing her selling song he felt a most curious sensation. He felt as if there were some cobwebs before his face, and he put up his hand as if to clear them away. There were no real cobwebs, of course; and

8. *Othello* II.iv.62–66

yet he again felt as if they floated from the gipsy-woman to him, like gossamer threads, and attracted him towards her. So he gazed at her, and she at him, till Jack began to forget how the parrot had warned him.

He saw her baby too, wondered whether it was heavy for her to carry and wished he could help her. I mean, he saw that she had a baby on her arm. It was wrapped in a shawl and had a handkerchief over its face. She seemed very fond of it, for she kept hushing it; and Jack softly moved nearer and nearer to the cart, till the gipsy-woman smiled, and suddenly began to sing:

> 'My good man—he's an old, old man—
>   And my good man got a fall,
> To buy me a bargain so fast he ran
>   When he heard the gipsies call:
>   "Buy, buy brushes,
>   Baskets wrought o' rushes,
>   Buy them, buy them, take them, try them,
>   Buy, dames all."

> 'My old man, he has money and land,
>   And a young, young wife am I.
> Let him put the penny in my white hand
>   When he hears the gipsies cry:
>   "Buy, buy laces,
>   Veils to screen your faces.
>   Buy them, buy them, take and try them,
>   Buy, maids, buy." '

When the gipsy had finished her song Jack felt as if he was covered all over with cobwebs; but he could not move away, and he did not mind them now. All his wish was to please her, and get close to her; so when she said, in a soft wheedling voice: 'What will you please to buy, my pretty gentleman?' he was just going to answer that he would buy anything she recommended, when, to his astonishment and displeasure, for he thought it very rude, the parrot suddenly burst into a violent fit of coughing, which made all the customers stare. 'That's to clear my throat,' he said, in a most impertinent tone of voice; and then he began to beat time with his foot, and sing, or rather scream out, an extremely saucy imitation of the gipsy's song, and all his parrot friends in the other cages joined in the chorus.

> 'My fair lady's a dear, dear lady—
>   I walked by her side to woo.
> In a garden alley, so sweet and shady,

> She answered, "I love not you,
> John, John Brady,"
> Quoth my dear lady,
> "Pray now, pray now, go your way now,
> Do, John, do!" '

At first the gipsy did not seem to know where that mocking song came from, but when she discovered that it was her prisoner, the old parrot, who was thus daring to imitate her, she stood silent and glared at him, and her face was almost white with rage.

When he came to the end of the verse, he pretended to burst into a violent fit of sobbing and crying, and screeched out to his wife: 'Mate! mate! hand up my handkerchief. Oh! oh! it's so affecting, this song is.'

Upon this the other parrot pulled Jack's handkerchief from under her wing, hobbled up and began, with a great show of zeal, to wipe his horny beak with it. But this was too much for the gipsy; she took a large brush from her cart and flung it at the cage with all her might.

This set it violently swinging backwards and forwards, but did not stop the parrot, who screeched out: 'How delightful it is to be swung!' And then he began to sing another verse in the most impudent tone possible, and with a voice that seemed to ring through Jack's head, and almost pierce it.

> 'Yet my fair lady's my own, own lady,
> For I passed another day;
> While making her moan, she sat all alone,
> And thus and thus did she say:
> "John, John Brady,"
> Quoth my dear lady,
> "Do now, do now, once more woo now,
> Pray, John, pray!" '

'It's beautiful!' screeched the parrot-wife. 'And so ap-pro-pri-ate.' Jack was delighted when she managed slowly to say this long word with her black tongue, and he burst out laughing. In the meantime a good many of the brown people came running together, attracted by the noise of the parrots and the rage of the gipsy, who flung at his cage, one after the other, all the largest things she had in her cart. But nothing did the parrot any harm; the more violently this cage swung the louder he sang, till at last the wicked gipsy seized her poor little young baby, who was lying in her arms, rushed frantically at the cage as it flew swiftly through the air towards her and struck at it with the little creature's head. 'Oh, you cruel, cruel woman!' cried Jack, and all the small mothers who were standing near with their skinny children on their shoulders screamed out with terror and indignation; but only for one instant, for the handkerchief flew off that had covered its face, and was caught in the wires of the cage, and all the people saw that it was not a real baby at all,[9] but a bundle of clothes, and its head was a turnip.

Yes, a turnip! You could see that as plainly as possible, for though the green leaves had been cut off, their stalks were visible through the lace cap that had been tied on it.

Upon this all the crowd pressed closer, throwing her baskets, and brushes, and laces, and beads at the gipsy, and calling out: 'We will have none of your goods, you false woman! Give us back our money, or we will drive you out of the fair. You've stuck a stick into a turnip, and dressed it up in baby clothes. You're a cheat! a cheat!'

'My sweet gentlemen, my kind ladies,' began the gipsy; but baskets and brushes flew at her so fast that she was obliged to sit down on the grass and hold up the sham baby to screen her face.

While this was going on Jack felt that the cobwebs which had seemed to float about his face were all gone; he did not care at all any more about the gipsy, and began to watch the parrots with great attention.

He observed that when the handkerchief stuck between the cage wires the parrots caught it, and drew it inside; and then Jack saw the cunning old bird himself lay it on the floor, fold it crosswise like a shawl, and put in on his wife.

Then she jumped upon the perch, and held it with one foot, looking precisely like an old lady with a parrot's head. Then he folded Jack's handkerchief in the same way, put it on and got upon the perch beside his wife, screaming out, in his most piercing tone:

'I like shawls; they're so becoming.'

Now the gipsy did not care at all what those inferior people thought of her, and she was calmly counting out their money, to return it; but she was very desirous to make Jack forget her behaviour, and had begun to smile again, and tell him she had only been joking, when the parrot spoke and, looking up, she saw the two birds sitting side by side, and the parrot-wife was screaming in her mate's ear, though neither of them was at all deaf:

'If Jack lets her allure him into the woods, he'll never come out again. She'll hang him up in a cage, as she did us. I say, how does my shawl fit?'

So saying, the parrot-wife whisked herself round on the perch, and lo! in the corner of the handkerchief were seen some curious letters, marked in

9. **turnip** The baby whom the Duchess flings with similar abandon in *Alice in Wonderland* also turns out to be no real child.

red. When the crowd saw these they drew a little farther off, and glanced at one another with alarm.

'You look charming, my dear; it fits well!' screamed the old parrot in answer. 'A word in your ear: "Share and share alike" is a fine motto.'

'What do you mean by all this?' said the gipsy, rising, and going with slow steps to the cage, and speaking cautiously.

'Jack,' said the parrot, 'do they ever eat handkerchiefs in your part of the country?'

'No, never,' answered Jack.

'Hold your tongue and be reasonable,' said the gipsy, trembling, 'What do you want? I'll do it, whatever it is.'

'But do they never pick out the marks?' continued the parrot. 'Oh, Jack! are you sure they never pick out the marks?'

'The marks?' said Jack, considering. 'Yes, perhaps they do.'

'Stop!' cried the gipsy, as the old parrot make a peck at the strange letters. 'Oh! you're hurting me. What do you want? I say again, tell me what you want, and you shall have it.'

'We want to get out,' replied the parrot; 'you must undo the spell.'

'Then give me my handkerchief,' answered the gipsy, 'to bandage my eyes. I dare not say the words with my eyes open. You had no business to steal it. It was woven by human hands, so that nobody can see through it; and if you don't give it to me, you'll never get out—no, never!'

'Then,' said the old parrot, tossing his shawl off, 'you may have Jack's handkerchief; it will bandage your eyes just as well. It was woven over the water, as yours was.'

'It won't do!' cried the gipsy in terror; 'give me my own.'

'I tell you,' answered the parrot, 'that you shall have Jack's handkerchief; you can do no harm with that.'

By this time the parrots all around had become perfectly silent, and none of the people ventured to say a word, for they feared the malice of the gipsy. She was trembling dreadfully, and her dark eyes, which had been so bright and piercing, had become dull and almost dim; but when she found there was no help for it, she said:

'Well, pass out Jack's handkerchief. I will set you free if you will bring out mine with you.'

'Share and share alike,' answered the parrot; 'You must let all my friends out too.'

'Then I won't let you out,' answered the gipsy. 'You shall come out first, and give me my handkerchief, or not one of their cages will I undo. So take your choice.'

'My friends, then,' answered the brave old parrot; and he poked Jack's handkerchief out to her through the wires.

The wondering crowd stood by to look, and the gipsy bandaged her eyes tightly with the handkerchief; and then, stooping low, she began to murmur something and clap her hands—softly at first, but by degrees more and more violently. The noise was meant to drown the words she muttered; but as she went on clapping, the bottom of cage after cage fell clattering down. Out flew the parrots by hundreds, screaming and congratulating one another; and there was such a deafening din that not only the sound of her spell but the clapping of her hands was quite lost in it.

But all this time Jack was very busy; for the moment the gipsy had tied up her eyes the old parrot snatched the real handkerchief off his wife's shoulders and tied it round her neck. Then she pushed out her head through the wires, and the old parrot called to Jack, and said: 'Pull!'

Jack took the ends of the handkerchief, pulled terribly hard, and stopped. 'Go on! go on!' screamed the old parrot.

'I shall pull her head off,' cried Jack.

'No matter,' cried the parrot; 'no matter—only pull.'

Well, Jack did pull, and he actually did pull her head off! nearly tumbling backward himself as he did it; but he saw what the whole thing meant then, for there was another head inside—a fairy's head.

Jack flung down the old parrot's head and great beak, for he saw that what he had to do was to clear the fairy of its parrot covering. The poor little creature seemed nearly dead, it was so terribly squeezed in the wires. It had a green gown or robe on, with an ermine collar; and Jack got hold of this dress, stripped the fairy out of the parrot feathers, and dragged her through—velvet robe, and crimson girdle, and little yellow shoes. She was very much exhausted, but a kind brown woman took her instantly, and laid her in her bosom. She was a splendid little creature, about half a foot long.

'There's a brave boy!' cried the parrot. Jack glanced round, and saw that not all the parrots were free yet—the gipsy was still muttering her spell.

He returned the handkerchief to the parrot, who put it round his own neck, and again Jack pulled. But oh! what a tough old parrot that was, and how Jack tugged before his cunning head would come off! It did, however, at last; and just as a fine fairy was pulled through, leaving his parrot skin and the handkerchief behind him, the gipsy untied her eyes and saw what Jack had done.

'Give me my handkerchief!' she screamed in despair.

'It's in the cage, gipsy,' answered Jack; 'you can get it yourself. Say your words again.'

But the gipsy's spell would only open places where she had confined fairies, and no fairies were in the cage now.

'No, no, no!' she screamed; 'too late! Hide me! Oh, good people, hide me!'

But it was indeed too late. The parrots had been wheeling in the air, hundreds and hundreds of them, high above her head; and as she ceased speaking she fell shuddering on the ground, drew her cloak over her face, and down they came, swooping in one immense flock, and settled so thickly all over her that she was completely covered; from her shoes to her head not an atom of her was to be seen.

All the people stood gravely looking on. So did Jack, but he could not see much for the fluttering of the parrots, nor hear anything for their screaming voices; but at last he made one of the cross people hear when he shouted to her: 'What are they going to do to the poor gipsy?'

'Make her take her other form,' she replied; 'and then she cannot hurt us while she stays in our country. She is a fairy, as we have just found out, and all fairies have two forms.'

'Oh!' said Jack; but he had no time for more questions.

The screaming, and fighting, and tossing about of little bits of cloth and cotton ceased; a black lump heaved itself up from the ground among the parrots; and as they flew aside an ugly great condor, with a bare neck, spread out its wings and, skimming the ground, sailed slowly away.

'They have pecked her so that she can hardly rise,' exclaimed the parrot fairy. 'Set me on your shoulder, Jack, and let me see the end of it.'

Jack set him there; and his little wife, who had recovered herself, sprang from her friend the brown woman and sat on the other shoulder. He then ran on—the tribe of brown people, and mushroom people, and the feather-coated folks running too—after the great black bird, who skimmed slowly on before them till she got to the gipsy carts, when out rushed the gipsies, armed with poles, milking-stools, spades and everything they could get hold of to beat back the people and the parrots from hunting their relation, who had folded her tired wings and was skulking under a cart with ruffled feathers and a scowling eye.

Jack was so frightened at the violent way in which the gipsies and the other tribes were knocking each other about that he ran off, thinking he had seen enough of such a dangerous country.

As he passed the place where that evil-minded gipsy had been changed he found the ground strewed with little bits of her clothes. Many parrots were picking them up and poking them into the cage where the handkerchief was; and presently another parrot came with a lighted brand, which she had pulled from one of the gipsies' fires.

'That's right,' said the fairy on Jack's shoulder, when he saw his friend push the brand between the wires of what had been his cage, and set the gipsy's handkerchief on fire, and all the bits of her clothes with it. 'She won't find much of herself here,' he observed, as Jack went on. 'It will not be very easy to put herself together again.'

So Jack moved away. He was tired of the noise and confusion; and the sun was just setting as he reached the little creek where his boat lay.

Then the parrot fairy and his wife sprang down, and kissed their hands to him as he stepped on board and pushed the boat off. He saw, when he looked back, that a great fight was still going on; so he was glad to get away, and he wished his two friends goodbye, and set off, the old parrot fairy calling after him: 'My relations have put some of our favourite food on board for you.' Then they again thanked him for his good help, and sprang into a tree, and the boat began to go down the wonderful river.

'This has been a most extraordinary day,' thought Jack; 'the strangest day I have had yet.' And after he had eaten a good supper of what the parrots had brought he felt so tired and sleepy that he lay down in the boat, and presently fell fast asleep. His fairies were sound asleep too in his pockets, and nothing happened of the least consequence; so he slept comfortably till morning.

CHAPTER SIX

The Town with Nobody in it

※

'Master,' quoth the auld hound,
'Where will ye go?'
'Over moss, over muir,

To court my new jo.'
'Master, though the night be merk,
  I'se follow through the snow.

'Court her, master, court her,
  So shall ye do weel;
But and ben she'll guide the house,
  I'se get milk and meal.
Ye'se get lilting while she sits
  With her rock and reel.'

'For, oh! she has a sweet tongue,
  And een that look down,
A gold girdle for her waist,
  And a purple gown.
She has a good word forbye
  Fra a' folk in the town.'

Soon after sunrise they came to a great city, and it was perfectly still. There were grand towers and terraces, wharves, too, and a large market, but there was nobody anywhere to be seen. Jack thought that might be because it was so early in the morning; and when the boat ran itself up against a wooden wharf and stopped, he jumped ashore, for he thought this must be the end of his journey. A delightful town it was, if only there had been any people in it! The market-place was full of stalls, on which were spread toys, baskets, fruit, butter, vegetables and all the other things that are usually sold in a market.

Jack walked about in it. Then he looked in at the open doors of the houses, and at last, finding that they were all empty, he walked into one, looked at the rooms, examined the picture-books, rang the bells and set the musical-boxes going. Then, after he had shouted a good deal, and tried in vain to make someone hear, he went back to the edge of the river where his boat was lying, and the water was so delightfully clear and calm that he thought he would bathe. So he took off his clothes, and folding them very carefully, so as not to hurt the fairies, laid them down beside a haycock[10] and went in, and ran about and paddled for a long time—much longer than there was any occasion for; but then he had nothing to do.

When at last he had finished he ran to the haycock and began to dress himself; but he could not find his stockings, and after looking about for some time he was obliged to put on his clothes without them, and he was going to put his boots on his bare feet when, walking to the other side of the haycock,

10. **haycock** See p. 111, note 6.

he saw a little old woman about as large as himself. She had a pair of spectacles on, and she was knitting.

She looked so sweet tempered that Jack asked her if she knew anything about his stockings.

'It will be time enough to ask for them when you have had your breakfast,' said she. 'Sit down. Welcome to our town. How do you like it?'

'I should like it very much indeed,' said Jack, 'if there was anybody in it.'

'I'm glad of that,' said the woman. 'You've seen a good deal of it; but it pleases me to find that you are a very honest boy. You did not take anything at all. I am honest too.'

'Yes,' said Jack, 'of course you are.'

'And as I am pleased with you for being honest,' continued the little woman. 'I shall give you some breakfast out of my basket.' So she took out a saucer full of honey, a roll of bread and a cup of milk.

'Thank you,' said Jack, 'but I am not a beggar-boy; I have got a half-crown, a shilling, a sixpence and two pence; so I can buy this breakfast of you, if you like. You look very poor.'

'Do I?' said the little woman softly; and she went on knitting, and Jack began to eat the breakfast.

'I wonder what has become of my stockings,' said Jack.

'You will never see them any more,' said the old woman. 'I threw them into the river, and they floated away.'

'Why did you?' asked Jack.

The little woman took no notice; but presently she had finished a beautiful pair of stockings, and she handed them to Jack and said:

'Is that like the pair you lost?'

'Oh no,' said Jack, 'these are much more beautiful stockings than mine.'

'Do you like them as well?' asked the fairy woman.

'I like them much better,' said Jack, putting them on. 'How clever you are!'

'Would you like to wear these', said the woman, 'instead of yours?'

She gave Jack such a strange look when she said this that he was afraid to take them, and answered:

'I shouldn't like to wear them if you think I had better not.'

'Well,' she answered, 'I am very honest, as I told you; and therefore I am obliged to say that if I were you I would not wear those stockings on any account.'

'Why not?' said Jack; for she looked so sweet tempered that he could not help trusting her.

Jack's New Friend

'Why not?' repeated the fairy. 'Why, because when you have those stock-ings on your feet belong to me.'

'Oh!' said Jack. 'Well, if you think that matters, I'll take them off again. Do you think it matters?'

'Yes,' said the fairy woman; 'it matters, because I am a slave, and my master can make me do whatever he pleases, for I am completely in his power. So if he found out that I had knitted those stockings for you he would make me order you to walk into his mill—the mill which grinds the corn for the town; and there you would have to grind and grind till I got free again.'

When Jack heard this he pulled off the beautiful stockings and laid them on the old woman's lap. Upon this she burst out crying as if her heart would break.

'If my fairies that I have in my pocket would only wake', said Jack, 'I would fight your master; for if he is no bigger than you are perhaps I could beat him, and get you away.'

'No, Jack,' said the little woman; 'that would be of no use. The only thing you could do would be to buy me; for my cruel master has said that if ever I am late again he will sell me in the slave-market to the brown people, who work underground. And, though I am dreadfully afraid of my master, I mean to be late today, in hopes (as you are kind, and as you have some money) that you will come to the slave-market and buy me. Can you buy me, Jack, to be your slave?'

'I don't want a slave,' said Jack; 'and, besides, I have hardly any money to buy you with.'

'But it is real money,' said the fairy woman, 'not like what my master has. His money has to be made every week, for if there comes a hot day it cracks, so it never has time to look old, as your half-crown does; and that is how we know the real money, for we cannot imitate anything that is old. Oh, now, now it is twelve o'clock! now I am late again! and though I said I would do it, I am so frightened!'

So saying, the little woman ran off towards the town, wringing her hands, and Jack ran beside her.

'How am I to find your master?' he said.

'Oh, Jack, buy me! buy me!' cried the fairy woman. 'You will find me in the slave-market. Bid high for me. Go back and put your boots on, and bid high.'

Now Jack had nothing on his feet, so he left the poor little woman to run into the town by herself, and went back to put his boots on. They were very uncomfortable, as he had no stockings; but he did not much mind that, and he counted his money. There was the half-crown that his grandmamma had given him on his birthday, there was a shilling, a sixpence, and two pence, besides a silver four-penny-piece which he had forgotten. He then marched into the town; and now it was quite full of people—all of them little men and women about his own height. They thought he was somebody of consequence, and they called out to him to buy their goods. And he bought some stockings, and said: 'What I want to buy now is a slave.'

So they showed him the way to the slave-market, and there whole rows of odd-looking little people were sitting, while in front of them stood the slaves.

Now Jack had observed as he came along how very disrespectful the dogs of that town were to the people. They had a habit of going up to them and smelling at their legs, and even gnawing their feet as they sat before the little tables selling their wares; and what made this more surprising was that the people did not always seem to find out when they were being gnawed. But the moment the dogs saw Jack they came and fawned on him, and two old hounds followed him all the way to the slave-market; and when he took a seat one of them lay down at his feet, and said: 'Master, set your handsome feet on my back, that they may be out of the dust.'

'Don't be afraid of him,' said the other hound; 'he won't gnaw your feet. He knows well enough that they are real ones.'

'Are the other people's feet not real?' asked Jack.

'Of course not,' said the hound. 'They had a feud long ago with the fairies, and they all went one night into a great cornfield which belonged to these enemies of theirs, intending to steal the corn. So they made themselves invisible, as they are always obliged to do till twelve o'clock at noon; but before morning dawn, the wheat being quite ripe, down came the fairies with their sickles, surrounded the field and cut the corn. So all their legs of course got cut off with it, for when they are invisible they cannot stir. Ever since that they have been obliged to make their legs of wood.'

While the hound was telling this story Jack looked about, but he did not see one slave who was in the least like his poor little friend, and he was beginning to be afraid that he should not find her, when he heard two people talking together.

'Good day!' said one. 'So you have sold that good-for-nothing slave of yours?'

'Yes,' answered a very cross-looking old man. 'She was late again this morning, and came to me crying and praying to be forgiven; but I was determined to make an example of her, so I sold her at once to Clink-of-the-Hole, and he has just driven her away to work in his mine.'

Jack, on hearing this, whispered to the hound at his feet: 'If you will guide me to Clink's hole, you shall be my dog.'

'Master, I will do my best,' answered the hound; and he stole softly out of the market, Jack following him.

CHAPTER SEVEN

Half A Crown

✳

So useful it is to have money, heigh ho!
So useful it is to have money!
A. H. CLOUGH.[11]

The old hound went straight through the town, smelling Clink's footsteps, till he came into a large field of barley; and there, sitting against a sheaf, for it was harvest time, they found Clink-of-the-Hole. He was a very ugly little brown man, and he was smoking a pipe in the shade; while crouched near him was the poor little woman, with her hands spread before her face.

'Good day, sir,' said Clink to Jack. 'You are a stranger here, no doubt?'

'Yes,' said Jack; 'I only arrived this morning.'

'Have you seen the town?' asked Clink civilly. 'There is a very fine market.'

'Yes, I have seen the market,' answered Jack. 'I went into it to buy a slave, but I did not see one that I liked.'

'Ah,' said Clink; 'and yet they had some very fine articles.' Here he pointed to the poor little woman, and said: 'Now that's a useful body enough, and I had her very cheap.'

'What did you give for her?' said Jack, sitting down.

11. **Clough** from Clough's *Dipsychus,* act 1, scene iv

'Three pitchers,' said Clink, 'and fifteen cups and saucers, and two shillings in the money of the town.'

'Is their money like this?' said Jack, taking out his shilling.

When Clink saw the shilling he changed colour, and said, very earnestly: 'Where did you get that, dear sir?'

'Oh, it was given me,' said Jack carelessly.

Clink looked hard at the shilling, and so did the fairy woman, and Jack let them look some time, for he amused himself with throwing it up several times and catching it. At last he put it back in his pocket, and then Clink heaved a deep sigh. Then Jack took out a penny, and began to toss that up, upon which, to his great surprise, the little brown man fell on his knees, and said: 'Oh, a shilling and a penny—a shilling and a penny of mortal coin! What would I not give for a shilling and a penny!'

'I don't believe you have got anything to give,' said Jack cunningly. 'I see nothing but that ring on your finger, and the old woman.'

'But I have a great many things at home, sir,' said the brown man, wiping his eyes; 'and besides, that ring would be cheap at a shilling—even a shilling of mortal coin.'

'Would the slave be cheap at a penny?' said Jack.

'Would you give a penny for her, dear sir?' inquired Clink, trembling with eagerness.

'She is honest,' answered Jack; 'ask her whether I had better buy her with this penny.'

'It does not matter what she says,' replied the brown man; 'I would sell twenty such as she is for a penny—a real one.'

'Ask her,' repeated Jack; and the poor little woman wept bitterly, but she said 'No.'

'Why not?' asked Jack; but she only hung down her head and cried.

'I'll make you suffer for this,' said the brown man. But when Jack took out the shilling, and said: 'Shall I buy you with this, slave?' his eyes actually shot out sparks, he was so eager.

'Speak!' he said to the fairy woman; 'and if you don't say "Yes," I'll strike you.'

'He cannot buy me with that,' answered the fairy woman, 'unless it is the most valuable coin he has got.'

The brown man, on hearing this, rose up in a rage, and was just going to strike her a terrible blow, when Jack cried out: 'Stop!' and took out his half-crown.

'Can I buy you with this?' said he; and the fairy woman answered: 'Yes.'

Upon this Clink drew a long breath, and his eyes grew bigger and bigger as he gazed at the half-crown.

'Shall she be my slave for ever, and not yours,' said Jack, 'if I give you this?'

'She shall,' said the brown man. And he made such a low bow as he took the money that his head actually knocked the ground. Then he jumped up; and, as if he was afraid Jack should repent of his bargain, he ran off towards the hole in the hill with all his might, shouting for joy as he went.

'Slave,' said Jack, 'that is a very ragged old apron that you have got, and your gown is quite worn out. Don't you think we had better spend my shilling in buying you some new clothes? You look so very shabby.'

'Do I?' said the fairy woman gently. 'Well, master, you will do as you please.'

'But you know better than I do,' said Jack, 'though you are my slave.'

'You had better give me the shilling, then,' answered the little old woman; 'and then I advise you to go back to the boat, and wait there till I come.'

'What!' said Jack. 'Can you go all the way back into the town again? I think you must be tired, for you know you are so very old.'

The fairy woman laughed when Jack said this, and she had such a sweet laugh that he loved to hear it; but she took the shilling, and trudged off to the town, and he went back to the boat, his hound running after him.

He was a long time going, for he ran a good many times after butterflies, and then he climbed up several trees; and altogether he amused himself for such a long while that when he reached the boat his fairy woman was there before him. So he stepped on board, the hound followed, and the boat immediately began to swim on.

'Why, you have not bought any new clothes!' said Jack to his slave.

'No, master,' answered the fairy woman; 'but I have bought what I wanted.' And she took out of her pocket a little tiny piece of purple ribbon, with a gold-coloured satin edge, and a very small tortoiseshell comb.

When Jack saw these he was vexed, and said: 'What do you mean by being so silly? I can't scold you properly, because I don't know what name to call you by, and I don't like to say "Slave," because that sounds so rude. Why, this bit of ribbon is such a little bit that it's of no use at all. It's not large enough even to make one mitten of.'

'Isn't it?' said the slave. 'Just take hold of it, master, and let us see if it will stretch.'

So Jack did. And she pulled, and he pulled, and very soon the silk had stretched till it was nearly as large as a handkerchief; and then she shook it, and they pulled again. 'This is very good fun,' said Jack; 'why, now it is as large as an apron.'

So she shook it again, and gave it a twitch here and a pat there; and then they pulled again, and the silk suddenly stretched so wide that Jack was very nearly falling overboard. So Jack's slave pulled off her ragged gown and apron, and put it on. It was a most beautiful robe of purple silk, it had a gold border, and it just fitted her.

'That will do,' she said. And then she took out the little tortoiseshell comb, pulled off her cap and threw it into the river. She had a little knot of soft grey hair, and she let it down and began to comb. And as she combed the hair got much longer and thicker, till it fell in waves all about her throat. Then she combed again, and it all turned gold colour, and came tumbling down to her waist; and then she stood up in the boat and combed once more, and shook out the hair, and there was such a quantity that it reached down to her feet, and she was so covered with it that you could not see one bit of her, excepting her eyes, which peeped out, and looked bright and full of tears.

Then she began to gather up her lovely locks; and when she had dried her eyes with them, she said: 'Master, do you know what you have done? Look at me now!' So she threw back the hair from her face, and it was a beautiful young face; and she looked so happy that Jack was glad he had bought her with his half-crown—so glad that he could not help crying, and the fair slave cried too; and then instantly the little fairies woke, and sprang out of Jack's pockets. As they did so, Jovinian cried out: 'Madam, I am your most humble servant'; and Roxaletta said: 'I hope your Grace is well'; but the third got on Jack's knee and took hold of the buttons of his waistcoat, and when the lovely slave looked at her she hid her face and blushed with pretty childish shyness.

'These are fairies,' said Jack's slave; 'but what are you?'

'Jack kissed me,' said the little thing; 'and I want to sit on his knee.'

'Yes,' said Jack, 'I took them out, and laid them in a row, to see if they were safe, and this one I kissed, because she looked such a little dear.'

'Was she not like the others, then?' asked the slave.

'Yes,' said Jack; 'but I liked her the best; she was my favourite.'

Now the instant these three fairies sprang out of Jack's pockets they got very much larger; in fact, they became fully grown—that is to say, they measured exactly one foot one inch in height, which, as most people know, is exactly the proper height for fairies of that tribe. The two who had sprung

These are Fairies, but What are You?

out first were very beautifully dressed. One had a green velvet coat, and a sword, the hilt of which was encrusted with diamonds. The second had a white spangled robe, and the loveliest rubies and emeralds round her neck and in her hair; but the third, the one who sat on Jack's knee, had a white frock and a blue sash on. She had soft, fat arms, and a face just like that of a sweet little child.

When Jack's slave saw this she took the little creature on her knee, and said to her: 'How comes it that you are not like your companions?'

And she answered, in a pretty lisping voice: 'It's because Jack kissed me.'

'Even so it must be,' answered the slave; 'the love of a mortal works changes indeed. It is not often that we win anything so precious. Here, master, let her sit on your knee sometimes, and take care of her, for she cannot now take the same care of herself that others of her race are capable of.'

So Jack let little Mopsa sit on his knee; and when he was tired of admiring his slave, and wondering at the respect with which the other two fairies treated her, and at their cleverness in getting water-lilies for her, and fanning her with feathers, he curled himself up in the bottom of the boat with his own little favourite, and taught her how to play at cat's-cradle.

When they had been playing some time, and Mopsa was getting quite clever at the game, the lovely slave said: 'Master, it is a long time since you spoke to me.'

'And yet,' said Jack, 'there is something that I particularly want to ask you about.'

'Ask it, then,' she replied.

'I don't like to have a slave,' answered Jack; 'and as you are so clever, don't you think you can find out how to be free again?'

'I am very glad you asked me about that,' said the fairy woman. 'Yes, master, I wish very much to be free; and as you were so kind as to give the most valuable piece of real money you possessed in order to buy me, I can be free if you can think of anything that you really like better than that half-crown, and if I can give it you.'

'Oh, there are many things,' said Jack. 'I like going up this river to Fairy-land much better.'

'But you are going there, master,' said the fairy woman; 'you were on the way before I met with you.'

'I like this little child better,' said Jack; 'I love this little Mopsa. I should like her to belong to me.'

'She is yours,' answered the fairy woman; 'she belongs to you already. Think of something else.'

Jack thought again, and was so long about it that at last the beautiful slave said to him: 'Master, do you see those purple mountains?'

Jack turned round in the boat and saw a splendid range of purple mountains, going up and up. They were very great and steep, each had a crown of snow, and the sky was very red behind them, for the sun was going down.

'At the other side of those mountains is Fairyland,' said the slave; 'but if you cannot think of something that you should like better to have than your half-crown I can never enter in. The river flows straight up to yonder steep precipice, and there is a chasm in it which pierces it, and through which the river runs down beneath, among the very roots of the mountains, till it comes out at the other side. Thousands and thousands of the small people will come when they see the boat, each with a silken thread in his hand; but if there is a slave in it not all their strength and skill can tow it through. Look at those rafts on the river; on them are the small people coming up.'

Jack looked, and saw that the river was spotted with rafts, on which were crowded brown fairy sailors, each one with three green stripes on his sleeve, which looked like good-conduct marks. All these sailors were chattering very fast, and the rafts were coming down to meet the boat.

'All these sailors to tow my slave!' said Jack. 'I wonder, I do wonder, what you are?' But the fairy woman only smiled, and Jack went on: 'I have thought of something that I should like much better than my half-crown. I should like to have a little tiny bit of that purple gown of yours with the gold border.'

Then the fairy woman said: 'I thank you, master. Now I can be free.' So she told Jack to lend her his knife, and with it she cut off a very small piece of the skirt of her robe, and gave it to him. 'Now mind,' she said; 'I advise you never to stretch this unless you want to make some particular thing of it, for then it will only stretch to the right size; but if you merely begin to pull it for your own amusement, it will go on stretching and stretching, and I don't know where it will stop.'

CHAPTER EIGHT

A Story

❋

In the night she told a story,
   In the night and all night through,

While the moon was in her glory,
　　And the branches dropped with dew.

'Twas my life she told, and round it
　　Rose the years as from a deep;
In the world's great heart she found it,
　　Cradled like a child asleep.

In the night I saw her weaving
By the misty moonbeam cold,
All the weft her shuttle cleaving
　　With a sacred thread of gold.

Ah! she wept me tears of sorrow,
　　Lulling tears so mystic sweet;
Then she wove my last tomorrow,
　　And her web lay at my feet.

Of my life she made the story:
　　I must weep—so soon 'twas told!
But your name did lend it glory,
　　And your love its thread of gold!

By this time, as the sun had gone down, and none of the moons had risen, it would have been dark but that each of the rafts was rigged with a small mast that had a lantern hung to it.

By the light of these lanterns Jack saw crowds of little brown faces, and presently many rafts had come up to the boat, which was now swimming very slowly. Every sailor in every raft fastened to the boat's side a silken thread; then the rafts were rowed to shore, and the sailors jumped out and began to tow the boat along.

These crimson threads looked no stronger than the silk that ladies sew with, yet by means of them the small people drew the boat along merrily. There were so many of them that they looked like an army as they marched in the light of the lanterns and torches. Jack thought they were very happy, though the work was hard, for they shouted and sang.

The fairy woman looked more beautiful than ever now, and far more stately. She had on a band of precious stones to bind back her hair, and they shone so brightly in the night that her features could be clearly seen.

Jack's little favourite was fast asleep, and the other two fairies had flown away. He was beginning to feel rather sleepy himself, when he was roused by the voice of his free lady, who said to him: 'Jack, there is no one listening now, so I will tell you my story. I am the Fairy Queen!'

Jack opened his eyes very wide, but he was so much surprised that he did not say a word.

'One day, long, long ago,' said the Queen, 'I was discontented with my own happy country. I wished to see the world, so I set forth with a number of the one-foot-one fairies, and went down the wonderful river, thinking to see the world.

'So we sailed down the river till we came to that town which you know of; and there, in the very middle of the stream, stood a tower—a tall tower built upon a rock.

'Fairies are afraid of nothing but other fairies, and we did not think this tower was fairy work, so we left our ship and went up the rock and into the tower, to see what it was like; but just as we had descended into the dungeon keep we heard the gurgling of water overhead, and down came the tower. It was nothing but water enchanted into the likeness of stone, and we all fell down with it into the very bed of the river.

'Of course, we were not drowned, but there we were obliged to lie, for we have no power out of our own element; and the next day the townspeople came down with a net and dragged the river, picked us all out of the meshes, and made us slaves. The one-foot-one fairies got away shortly; but from that day to this, in sorrow and distress, I have had to serve my masters. Luckily my crown had fallen off in the water, so I was not known to be the Queen; but till you came, Jack, I had almost forgotten that I had ever been happy and free, and I had hardly any hope of getting away.'

'How sorry your people must have been,' said Jack, 'when they found you did not come home again.'

'No,' said the Queen; 'they only went to sleep, and they will not wake till tomorrow morning, when I pass in again. They will think I have been absent for a day, and so will the apple-woman. You must not undeceive them; if you do, they will be very angry.'

'And who is the apple-woman?' inquired Jack; but the Queen blushed; and pretended not to hear the question, so he repeated:

'Queen, who is the apple-woman?'

'I've only had her for a very little while,' said the Queen evasively.

'And how long do you think you have been a slave, Queen?' asked Jack.

'I don't know,' said the Queen. 'I have never been able to make up my mind about that.'

And now all the moons began to shine, and all the trees lighted themselves up, for almost every leaf had a glowworm or a firefly on it, and the water was full of fishes that had shining eyes. And now they were close to the steep mountainside; and Jack looked and saw an opening in it, into which the river ran. It was a kind of cave, something like a long, long church with a vaulted roof, only the pavement of it was that magic river, and a narrow towing-path ran on either side.

As they entered the cave there was a hollow murmuring sound, and the Queen's crown became so bright that it lighted up the whole boat; at the same time she began to tell Jack a wonderful story, which he liked very much to hear, but at every fresh thing she said he forgot what had gone before; and at last, though he tried very hard to listen, he was obliged to go to sleep; and he slept soundly and never dreamed of anything till it was morning.

He saw such a curious sight when he woke. They had been going through this underground cavern all night, and now they were approaching its opening on the other side. This opening, because they were a good way from it yet, looked like a lovely little round window of blue and yellow and green glass, but as they drew on he could see far-off mountains, blue sky and a country all covered with sunshine.

He heard singing too, such as fairies make; and he saw some beautiful people, such as those fairies whom he had brought with him. They were coming along the towing-path. They were all lady fairies; but they were not very polite, for as each one came up she took a silken rope out of a brown sailor's hand and gave him a shove which pushed him into the water. In fact the water became filled with such swarms of these sailors that the boat could hardly get on. But the poor little brown fellows did not seem to mind this conduct, for they plunged and shook themselves about, scattering a good deal of spray. Then they all suddenly dived, and when they came up again they were ducks—nothing but brown ducks, I assure you, with green stripes on their wings; and with a great deal of quacking and floundering they all began to swim back again as fast as they could.

Then Jack was a good deal vexed, and he said to himself: 'If nobody thanks the ducks for towing us I will'; so he stood up in the boat and shouted: 'Thank you, ducks; we are very much obliged to you!' But neither the Queen nor these new towers took the least notice, and gradually the boat came out of that dim cave and entered Fairyland, while the river became so narrow that you could hear the song of the towers quite easily; those on the right bank sang the first verse, and those on the left bank answered:

> 'Drop, drop from the leaves of lign aloes,
> O honey-dew! drop from the tree.

Float up through your clear river shallows,
  White lilies, beloved of the bee.

'Let the people, O Queen! say, and bless thee,
  Her bounty drops soft as the dew,
And spotless in honour confess thee,
  As lilies are spotless in hue.

'On the roof stands yon white stork awaking,
  His feathers flush rosy the while,
For, lo! from the blushing east breaking,
  The sun sheds the bloom of his smile.

'Let them boast of thy word, "It is certain;
  We doubt it no more," let them say,
"Than tomorrow that night's dusky curtain
  Shall roll back its folds for the day." '

'Master,' whispered the old hound, who was lying at Jack's feet.

'Well?' said Jack.

'They didn't invent that song themselves,' said the hound; 'the old apple-woman taught it to them—the woman whom they love because she can make them cry.'

Jack was rather ashamed of the hound's rudeness in saying this; but the Queen took no notice. And now they had reached a little landing-place, which ran out a few feet into the river and was strewn thickly with cowslips and violets.

Here the boat stopped, and the Queen rose and got out.

Jack watched her. A whole crowd of one-foot-one fairies came down a garden to meet her, and he saw them conduct her to a beautiful tent with golden poles and a silken covering; but nobody took the slightest notice of him, or of little Mopsa, or of the hound, and after a long silence the hound said: 'Well, master, don't you feel hungry? Why don't you go with the others and have some breakfast?'

'The Queen didn't invite me,' said Jack.

'But do you feel as if you couldn't go?' asked the hound.

'Of course not,' answered Jack; 'but perhaps I may not.'

'Oh yes, master,' replied the hound; 'whatever you *can* do in Fairyland you *may* do.'

'Are you sure of that?' asked Jack.

'Quite sure, master,' said the hound; 'and I am hungry too.'

'Well,' said Jack, 'I will go there and take Mopsa. She shall ride on my shoulder; you may follow.'

So he walked up that beautiful garden till he came to the great tent. A banquet was going on inside. All the one-foot-one fairies sat down the sides of the table, and at the top sat the Queen on a larger chair; and there were two empty chairs, one on each side of her.

Jack blushed; but the hound whispering again: 'Master, whatever you can do you may do,' he came slowly up the table towards the Queen, who was saying as he drew near: 'Where is our trusty and well-beloved, the apple-woman?' And she took no notice of Jack; so, though he could not help feeling rather red and ashamed, he went and sat in the chair beside her with Mopsa still on his shoulder. Mopsa laughed for joy when she saw the feast. The Queen said: 'Oh, Jack, I am so glad to see you!' and some of the one-foot-one fairies cried out: 'What a delightful little creature that is! She can laugh! Perhaps she can also cry!'

Jack looked about, but there was no seat for Mopsa; and he was afraid to let her run about on the floor, lest she should be hurt.

There was a very large dish standing before the Queen; for though the people were small the plates and dishes were exactly like those we use, and of the same size.

This dish was raised on a foot, and filled with grapes and peaches. Jack wondered at himself for doing it, but he saw no other place for Mopsa; so he took out the fruit, laid it round the dish, and set his own little one-foot-one in the dish.

Nobody looked in the least surprised; and there she sat very happily, biting an apple with her small white teeth.

Then, as they brought him nothing to eat, Jack helped himself from some of the dishes before him, and found that a fairy breakfast was very nice indeed.

In the meantime there was a noise outside, and in stumped an elderly woman. She had very thick boots on, a short gown of red print, an orange cotton handkerchief over her shoulders and a black silk bonnet. She was exactly the same height as the Queen—for of course nobody in Fairyland is allowed to be any bigger than the Queen; so, if they are not children when they arrive, they are obliged to shrink.

'How are you, dear?' said the Queen.

'I am as well as can be expected,' answered the apple-woman, sitting down in the empty chair. 'Now, then, where's my tea? They're never ready with my cup of tea.'

Two attendants immediately brought a cup of tea and set it down before the apple-woman, with a plate of bread and butter; and she proceeded to

Landing of the Queen

pour it out into the saucer, and blow it, because it was hot. In so doing her wandering eyes caught sight of Jack and little Mopsa, and she set down the saucer and looked at them with attention.

Now Mopsa, I am sorry to say, was behaving so badly that Jack was quite ashamed of her. First she got out of her dish, took something nice out of the Queen's plate with her fingers and ate it; and then, as she was going back, she tumbled over a melon and upset a glass of red wine, which she wiped up with her white frock; after which she got into her dish again, and there she sat smiling, and daubing her pretty face with a piece of buttered muffin.

'Mopsa,' said Jack, 'you are very naughty; if you behave in this way, I shall never take you out to parties again.'

'Pretty lamb!' said the apple-woman; 'it's just like a child.' And then she burst into tears, and exclaimed, sobbing: 'It's many a long day since I've seen a child. Oh dear! Oh deary me!'

Upon this, to the astonishment of Jack, every one of the guests began to cry and sob too.

'Oh dear! Oh dear!' they said to one another, 'we're crying; we can cry just as well as men and women. Isn't it delightful? What a luxury it is to cry, to be sure!'

They were evidently quite proud of it; and when Jack looked at the Queen for an explanation, she only gave him a still little smile.

But Mopsa crept along the table to the apple-woman, let her take her and hug her, and seemed to like her very much; for as she sat on her knee she patted her brown face with a little dimpled hand.

'I should like vastly well to be her nurse,' said the apple-woman, drying her eyes, and looking at Jack.

'If you'll always wash her, and put clean frocks on her, you may,' said Jack; 'for just look at her—what a figure she is already!'

Upon this the apple-woman laughed for joy, and again everyone else did the same. The fairies can only laugh and cry when they see mortals do so.

CHAPTER NINE

After the Party

✳

Stephano. This will prove a brave kingdom to me,
Where I shall have my music for nothing.
The Tempest.[12]

When breakfast was over the guests got up, one after the other, without taking the least notice of the Queen; and the tent began to get so thin and transparent that you could see the trees and the sky through it. At last it looked only like a coloured mist, with blue and green and yellow stripes, and then it was gone; and the table and all the things on it began to go in the same way. Only Jack, and the apple-woman, and Mopsa were left, sitting on their chairs, with the Queen between them.

Presently the Queen's lips began to move, and her eyes looked straight before her, as she sat upright in her chair. Whereupon the apple-woman snatched up Mopsa and, seizing Jack's hand, hurried him off, exclaiming: 'Come away! Come away! She is going to tell one of her stories; and if you listen you'll be obliged to go to sleep, and sleep nobody knows how long.'

Jack did not want to go to sleep; he wished to go down to the river again and see what had become of his boat, for he had left his cap and several other things in it.

So he parted from the apple-woman—who took Mopsa with her, and said he would find her again when he wanted her at her apple-stall—and went down to the boat, where he saw that his faithful hound was there before him.

'It was lucky, master, that I came when I did,' said the hound, 'for a dozen or so of those one-foot-one fellows were just shoving it off, and you will want it at night to sleep in.'

'Yes,' said Jack; 'and I can stretch the bit of purple silk to make a canopy overhead—a sort of awning—for I should not like to sleep in tents or palaces that are inclined to melt away.'

So the hound with his teeth, and Jack with his hands, pulled and pulled at

12. **The Tempest** III.ii.144–45

the silk till it was large enough to make a splendid canopy, like a tent; and it reached down to the water's edge, and roofed in all the after part of the boat.

So now he had a delightful little home of his own; and there was no fear of its being blown away, for no wind ever blows in Fairyland. All the trees are quite still, no leaf rustles and the flowers lie on the ground exactly where they fall.

After this Jack told the hound to watch his boat, and went himself in search of the apple-woman. Not one fairy was to be seen, any more than if he had been in his own country, and he wandered down the green margin of the river till he saw the apple-woman sitting at a small stall with apples on it, and cherries tied to sticks, and some dry-looking nuts. She had Mopsa on her knee, and had washed her face, and put a beautiful clean white frock on her.

'Where are all the fairies gone to?' asked Jack.

'I never take any notice of that common trash and their doings,' she answered. 'When the Queen takes to telling her stories they are generally frightened, and go and sit in the tops of the trees.'

'But you seem very fond of Mopsa,' said Jack, 'and she is one of them. You will help me to take care of her, won't you, till she grows a little older?'

'Grows!' said the apple-woman, laughing, 'Grows! Why you don't think, surely, that she will ever be any different from what she is now!'

'I thought she would grow up,' said Jack.

'They never change so long as they last,' answered the apple-woman, 'when once they are one-foot-one high.'

'Mopsa,' said Jack, 'come here, and I'll measure you.'

Mopsa came dancing towards Jack, and he tried to measure her, first with a yard measure that the apple-woman took out of her pocket, and then with a stick, and then with a bit of string; but Mopsa would not stand steady, and at last it ended in their having a good game of romps together, and a race; but when he carried her back, sitting on his shoulder, he was sorry to see that the apple-woman was crying again, and he asked her kindly what she did it for.

'It is because,' she answered, 'I shall never see my own country any more, nor any men and women and children, excepting such as by a rare chance stray in for a little while as you have done.'

'I can go back whenever I please,' said Jack. 'Why don't you?'

'Because I came in of my own good will, after I had had fair warning that if I came at all it would end in my staying always. Besides, I don't know that I exactly wish to go home again—I should be afraid.'

'Afraid of what?' asked Jack.

'Why, there's the rain and the cold, and not having anything to eat excepting what you earn. And yet,' said the apple-woman, 'I have three boys of my own at home; one of them must be nearly a man by this time, and the youngest is about as old as you are. If I went home I might find one or more of those boys in jail, and then how miserable I should be.'

'But you are not happy as it is,' said Jack. 'I have seen you cry.'

'Yes,' said the apple-woman; 'but now I live here I don't care about anything so much as I used to do. "May I have a satin gown and a coach?" I asked when first I came. "You may have a hundred and fifty satin gowns if you like," said the Queen, "and twenty coaches with six cream-coloured horses to each." But when I had been here a little time, and found I could have everything I wished for, and change it as often as I pleased, I began not to care for anything; and at last I got so sick of all their grand things that I dressed myself in my own clothes that I came in, and made up my mind to have a stall and sit at it, as I used to do, selling apples. And I used to say to myself: "I have but to wish with all my heart to go home, and I can go, I know that"; but oh dear! oh dear! I couldn't wish enough, for it would come into my head that I should be poor, or that my boys would have forgotten me, or that my neighbours would look down on me, and so I always put off wishing for another day.[13] Now here is the Queen coming. Sit down on the grass and play with Mopsa. Don't let her see us talking together, lest she should think I have been telling you things which you ought not to know.'

Jack looked, and saw the Queen coming slowly towards them, with her hands held out before her, as if it was dark. She felt her way, yet her eyes were wide open, and she was telling her stories all the time.

'Don't you listen to a word she says,' whispered the apple-woman, and then, in order that Jack might not hear what the Queen was talking about, she began to sing.

She had no sooner begun than up from the river came swarms of one-foot-one fairies to listen, and hundreds of them dropped down from the trees. The Queen, too, seemed to attend as they did, though she kept murmuring her story all the time; and nothing that any of them did appeared to surprise the apple-woman—she sang as if nobody was taking any notice at all:

---

13. **and so . . . for another day** The apple-woman's rationale for not wanting to return to her human world bears comparing with the reasons adduced by the captive slave woman in Ewing's "Amelia and the Dwarfs."

'When I sit on market-days amid the comers and the goers,
　　Oh! full oft I have a vision of the days without alloy,
And a ship comes up the river with a jolly gang of towers,
　　And a "pull'e haul'e, pull'e haul'e, yoy! heave, hoy!"

'There is busy talk around me, all about mine ears it hummeth,
　　But the wooden wharves I look on, and a dancing heaving buoy,
For 'tis tidetime in the river, and she cometh—oh, she cometh!
　　With a "pull'e haul'e, pull'e haul'e, yoy! heave, hoy!"

'Then I hear the water washing, never golden waves were brighter,
　　And I hear the capstan creaking—'tis a sound that cannot cloy.
Bring her to, to ship her lading, brig or schooner, sloop or lighter,
　　With a "pull'e haul'e, pull'e haul'e, yoy! heave, hoy!"

'"Will ye step aboard, my dearest? for the high seas lie before us."
　　So I sailed adown the river in those days without alloy.
We are launched! But when, I wonder, shall a sweeter sound float o'er us
　　Than yon "pull'e haul'e, pull'e haul'e, yoy! heave, hoy!"'

As the apple-woman left off singing the Queen moved away, still murmuring the words of her story, and Jack said:

'Does the Queen tell stories of what has happened, or of what is going to happen?'

'Why, of what is going to happen, of course,' replied the woman. 'Anybody could tell the other sort.'

'Because I heard a little of it,' observed Jack. 'I thought she was talking of me. She said: "So he took the measure, and Mopsa stood still for once, and he found she was only one foot high, and she grew a great deal after that. Yes, she can grow."'

'That's a fine hearing, and a strange hearing,' said the apple-woman; 'and what did she mutter next?'

'Of how she heard me sobbing,' replied Jack; 'and while you went on about stepping on board the ship, she said: "He was very good to me, dear little fellow! But Fate is the name of my old mother, and she reigns here.[14] Oh, she reigns! The fatal F is in her name, and I cannot take it out!"'

'Ah!' replied the apple-woman, 'they all say that, and that they are fays, and that mortals call their history fable; they are always crying out for an alphabet without the fatal F.'

---

14. **But Fate . . . reigns here.** The words "fay" and "fairy" actually do derive from the Latin *fata* or fate, a connection Ingelow will exploit in her later characterization of old Mother Fate and her daughters.

'And then she told how she heard Mopsa sobbing too,' said Jack; 'sobbing among the reeds and rushes by the river side.'

'There are no reeds and no rushes either here,' said the apple-woman, 'and I have walked the river from end to end. I don't think much of that part of the story. But you are sure she said that Mopsa was short of her proper height?'

'Yes, and that she would grow; but that's nothing. In my country we always grow.'

'Hold your tongue about your country!' said the apple-woman sharply. 'Do you want to make enemies of them all?'

Mopsa had been listening to this, and now she said: 'I don't love the Queen. She slapped my arm as she went by, and it hurts.'

Mopsa showed her little fat arm as she spoke, and there was a red place on it.

'That's odd too,' said the apple-woman; 'there's nothing red in a common fairy's veins. They have sap in them: that's why they can't blush.'

Just then the sun went down, and Mopsa got up on the apple-woman's lap and went to sleep; and Jack, being tired, went to his boat and lay down under the purple canopy, his old hound lying at his feet to keep guard over him.

The next morning, when he woke, a pretty voice called to him: 'Jack! Jack!' and he opened his eyes and saw Mopsa. The apple-woman had dressed her in a clean frock and blue shoes, and her hair was so long! She was standing on the landing-place, close to him. 'Oh, Jack! I'm so big,' she said. 'I grew in the night; look at me.'

Jack looked. Yes, Mopsa had grown indeed; she had only just reached to his knee the day before, and now her little bright head, when he measured her, came as high as the second button on his waistcoat.

'But I hope you will not go on growing so fast as this,' said Jack, 'or you will be as tall as my mamma is in a week or two—much too big for me to play with.'

CHAPTER TEN

Mopsa Learns her Letters

❊

A——apple-pie.
B——bit it.

'How ashamed I am,' Jack said, 'to think that you don't know even your letters!'

Mopsa replied that she thought that did not signify, and then she and Jack began to play at jumping from the boat on to the bank and back again; and afterwards, as not a single fairy could be seen, they had breakfast with the apple-woman.

'Where is the Queen?' asked Jack.

The apple-woman answered: 'It's not the fashion to ask questions in Fairyland.'

'That's a pity,' said Jack, 'for there are several things that I particularly want to know about this country. Mayn't I even ask how big it is?'

'How big?' said Mopsa—little Mopsa looking as wise as possible. 'Why, the same size as your world, of course.'

Jack laughed. 'It's the same world that you call yours,' continued Mopsa; 'and when I'm a little older I'll explain it all to you.'

'If it's our world,' said Jack, 'why are none of us in it, excepting me and the apple-woman?'

'That's because you've got something in your world that you call TIME,' said Mopsa; 'so you talk about NOW, and you talk about THEN.'

'And don't you?' asked Jack.

'I do if I want to make you understand,' said Mopsa.

The apple-woman laughed, and said: 'To think of the pretty thing talking so queen-like already! Yes, that's right, and just what the grown-up fairies say. Go on, and explain it to him if you can.'

'You know,' said Mopsa, 'that your people say there was a time when there were none of them in the world—a time before they were made. Well, THIS is that time. This IS long ago.'

'Nonsense!' said Jack. 'Then how do I happen to be here?'

'Because,' said Mopsa, 'when the albatross brought you she did not fly

The Apple Woman

with you a long way off, but a long way back—hundreds and hundreds of years. This is your world, as you can see; but none of your people are here, because they are not made yet. I don't think any of them will be made for a thousand years.'

'But I saw the old ships', answered Jack, 'in the enchanted bay.'

'That was a border country,' said Mopsa. 'I was asleep while you went through those countries; but these are the real Fairylands.'

Jack was very much surprised when he heard Mopsa say these strange things; and as he looked at her he felt that a sleep was coming over him, and he could not hold up his head. He felt how delightful it was to go to sleep; and though the apple-woman sprang to him when she observed that he was shutting his eyes, and though he heard her begging and entreating him to keep awake, he did not want to do so; but he let his head sink down on the mossy grass, which was as soft as a pillow, and there under the shade of a Guelder rose tree, [15] that kept dropping its white flowerets all over him, he had this dream.

He thought that Mopsa came running up to him, as he stood by the river, and that he said to her: 'Oh, Mopsa, how old we are! We have lived back to the times before Adam and Eve!'

'Yes,' said Mopsa; 'but I don't feel old. Let us go down the river, and see what we can find.'

So they got into the boat, and it floated into the middle of the river, and then made for the opposite bank, where the water was warm and very muddy, and the river became so very wide that it seemed to be afternoon when they got near enough to see it clearly; and what they saw was a boggy country, green, and full of little rills, but the water—which, as I told you, was thick and muddy—the water was full of small holes! You never saw water with eyelet-holes in it; but Jack did. On all sides of the boat he saw holes moving about in pairs, and some were so close that he looked and saw their lining; they were lined with pink, and they snorted! Jack was afraid, but he considered that this was such a long time ago that the holes, whatever they were, could not hurt him; but it made him start, notwithstanding, when a huge flat head reared itself up close to the boat, and he found that the holes were the nostrils of creatures who kept all the rest of themselves under water.

In a minute or two, hundreds of ugly flat-heads popped up, and the boat danced among them as they floundered about in the water.

15. **Guelder rose tree** white-flowered bush, also called "snowball"

'I hope they won't upset us,' said Jack. 'I wish you would land.'

Mopsa said she would rather not, because she did not like the hairy elephants.

'There are no such things as hairy elephants,' said Jack, in his dream; but he had hardly spoken when out of a wood close at hand some huge creatures, far larger than our elephants, came jogging down to the water. There were forty or fifty of them, and they were covered with what looked like tow. In fact, so coarse was their shaggy hair that they looked as if they were dressed in door-mats; and when they stood still and shook themselves such clouds of dust flew out, as it swept over the river, that it almost stifled Jack and Mopsa.

'Odious!' exclaimed Jack, sneezing. 'What terrible creatures these are!'

'Well,' answered Mopsa, at the other end of the boat (but he could hardly see her for the dust), 'then why do you dream of them?'

Jack had just decided to dream of something else when, with a noise greater than fifty trumpets, the elephants, having shaken out all the dust, came thundering down to the water to bathe in the liquid mud. They shook the whole country as they plunged; but that was not all. The awful river-horses rose up and, with shrill screams, fell upon them, and gave them battle; while up from every rill peeped above the rushes frogs as large as oxen, and with blue and green eyes that gleamed like the eyes of cats.

The frogs' croaking and the shrill trumpeting of the elephants, together with the cries of the river-horses, as all these creatures fought with horn and tusk, and fell on one another, lashing the water into whirlpools, among which the boat danced up and down like a cork, the blinding spray, and the flapping about of great bats over the boat and in it—so confused Jack that Mopsa had spoken to him several times before he answered.

'Oh, Jack!' she said at last; 'if you can't dream any better, I must call the Craken.'

'Very well,' said Jack. 'I'm almost wrapped up and smothered in bats' wings, so call anything you please.'

Thereupon Mopsa whistled softly, and in a minute or two he saw, almost spanning the river, a hundred yards off, a thing like a rainbow, or a slender bridge, or still more like one ring or coil of an enormous serpent; and presently the creature's head shot up like a fountain, close to the boat, almost as high as a ship's mast. It was the Craken;[16] and when Mopsa saw it she began

---

16. **Craken** The sea-monster of Scandinavian mythology was the subject of Tennyson's short poem "The Kraken" (1830).

to cry, and said: 'We are caught in this crowd of creatures, and we cannot get away from the land of dreams. Do help us, Craken.'

Some of the bats that hung to the edges of the boat had wings as large as sails, and the first thing the Craken did was to stoop its lithe neck, pick two or three of them off, and eat them.

'You can swim your boat home under my coils where the water is calm,' the Craken said, 'for she is so extremely old now that if you do not take care she will drop to pieces before you get back to the present time.'

Jack knew it was of no use saying anything to this formidable creature, before whom the river-horses and the elephants were rushing to the shore; but when he looked and saw down the river rainbow behind rainbow—I mean coil behind coil—glittering in the sun, like so many glorious arches that did not reach to the banks, he felt extremely glad that this was a dream, and besides that, he thought to himself: 'It's only a fabled monster.'

'No, it's only a fable to these times,' said Mopsa, answering his thought; 'but in spite of that we shall have to go through all the rings.'

They went under one—silver, green, and blue, and gold. The water dripped from it upon them, and the boat trembled, either because of its great age or because it felt the rest of the coil underneath.

A good way off was another coil, and they went so safely under that that Jack felt himself getting used to Crakens, and not afraid. Then they went under thirteen more. These kept getting nearer and nearer together, but, besides that, the fourteenth had not quite such a high span as the former ones; but there were a great many to come, and yet they got lower and lower.

Both Jack and Mopsa noticed this, but neither said a word. The thirtieth coil brushed Jack's cap off, then they had to stoop to pass under the two next, and then they had to lie down in the bottom of the boat, and they got through with the greatest difficulty; but still before them was another! The boat was driving straight towards it, and it lay so close to the water that the arch it made was only a foot high. When Jack saw it, he called out: 'No! that I cannot bear. Somebody else may do the rest of this dream. I shall jump overboard!'

Mopsa seemed to answer in quite a pleasant voice, as if she was not afraid:

'No, you'd much better wake.' And then she went on: 'Jack! Jack! why don't you wake?'

Than all on a sudden Jack opened his eyes, and found that he was lying quietly on the grass, that little Mopsa really had asked him why he did not wake. He saw the Queen too, standing by, looking at him, and saying to herself: '*I* did not put him to sleep. *I* did not put him to sleep.'

'We don't want any more stories to-day, Queen,' said the apple-woman, in a disrespectful tone, and she immediately began to sing, clattering some tea-things all the time, for a kettle was boiling on some sticks, and she was going to make tea out of doors:

> 'The marten flew to the finch's nest,
>   Feathers, and moss, and a wisp of hay:
> "The arrow it sped to thy brown mate's breast;
>   Low in the broom is thy mate today."
>
> '"Liest thou low, love? low in the broom?
>   Feathers and moss, and a wisp of hay,
> Warm the white eggs till I learn his doom."
>   She beateth her wings, and away, away.
>
> '"Ah, my sweet singer, thy days are told
>   (Feathers and moss, and a wisp of hay)!
> Thine eyes are dim, and the eggs grow cold.
>   O mournful morrow! O dark today!"
>
> 'The finch flew back to her cold, cold nest,
>   Feathers and moss, and a wisp of hay.
> Mine is the trouble that rent her breast,
>   And home is silent, and love is clay.'

Jack felt very tired indeed—as much tired as if he had really been out all day on the river, and gliding under the coils of the Craken. He, however, rose up when the apple-woman called him, and drank his tea, and had some fairy bread with it, which refreshed him very much.

After tea he measured Mopsa again, and found that she had grown up to a higher button. She looked much wiser too, and when he said she must be taught to read she made no objection, so he arranged daisies and buttercups into the forms of the letters, and she learnt nearly all of them that one evening, while crowds of the one-foot-one fairies looked on, hanging from the boughs and sitting in the grass, and shouting out the names of the letters as Mopsa said them. They were very polite to Jack, for they gathered all these flowers for him, and emptied them from their little caps at his feet as fast as he wanted them.

CHAPTER ELEVEN

Good Morning Sister

✻

Sweet is childhood—childhood's over,
        Kiss and part.
Sweet is youth; but youth's a rover—
        So's my heart.
Sweet is rest; but by all showing
        Toil is nigh.
We must go. Alas! the going,
        Say 'goodbye.'

Jack crept under his canopy, went to sleep early that night and did not wake till the sun had risen, when the apple-woman called him, and said breakfast was nearly ready.

The same thing never happens twice in Fairyland, so this time the breakfast was not spread in a tent, but on the river. The Queen had cut off a tiny piece of her robe, the one-foot-one fairies had stretched it till it was very large, and then they had spread it on the water, where it floated and lay like a great carpet of purple and gold. One corner of it was moored to the side of Jack's boat; but he had not observed this, because of his canopy. However, that was now looped up by the apple-woman, and Jack and Mopsa saw what was going on.

Hundreds of swans had been towing the carpet along, and were still holding it with their beaks, while a crowd of doves walked about on it, smoothing out the creases and patting it with their pretty pink feet till it was quite firm and straight. The swans then swam away, and they flew away.

Presently troops of fairies came down to the landing-place, jumped into Jack's boat without asking leave, and so got on to the carpet, while at the same time a great tree which grew on the bank began to push out fresh leaves, as large as fans, and shoot out long branches, which again shot out others, till very soon there was shade all over the carpet—a thick shadow as good as a tent, which was very pleasant, for the sun was already hot.

When the Queen came down the tree suddenly blossomed out with thousands of red and white flowers.

'You must not go on to that carpet,' said the apple-woman; 'let us sit still in the boat, and be served here.' She whispered this as the Queen stepped into the boat.

'Good morning, Jack,' said the Queen. 'Good morning, dear.' This was to the apple-woman; and then she stood still for a moment and looked earnestly at little Mopsa, and sighed.

'Well,' she said to her, 'don't you mean to speak to me?' Then Mopsa lifted up her pretty face and blushed very rosy red, and said, in a shy voice: 'Good morning—sister.'

'I said so!' exclaimed the Queen; 'I said so!' and she lifted up her beautiful eyes, and murmured out: 'What is to be done now?'

'Never mind, Queen dear,' said Jack. 'If it was rude of Mopsa to say that, she is such a little young thing that she does not know better.'

'It was not rude,' said Mopsa, and she laughed and blushed again. 'It was not rude, and I am not sorry.'

As she said this the Queen stepped on to the carpet, and all the flowers began to drop down. They were something like camellias, and there were thousands of them.

The fairies collected them in little heaps. They had no tables and chairs, nor any plates and dishes for this breakfast; but the Queen sat down on the carpet close to Jack's boat, and leaned her cheek on her hand, and seemed to be lost in thought. The fairies put some flowers into her lap, then each took some, and they all sat down and looked at the Queen, but she did not stir.

At last Jack said: 'When is the breakfast coming?'

'This is the breakfast,' said the apple-woman; 'these flowers are most delicious eating. You never tasted anything so good in your life; but we don't begin till the Queen does.'

Quantities of blossoms had dropped into the boat. Several fairies tumbled into it almost head over heels, they were in such a hurry, and they heaped them into Mopsa's lap, but took no notice of Jack, nor of the apple-woman either.

At last, when everyone had waited some time, the Queen pulled a petal off one flower, and began to eat, so everyone else began; and what the apple-woman had said was quite true. Jack knew that he never had tasted anything half so nice, and he was quite sorry when he could not eat any more. So, when everyone had finished, the Queen leaned her arm on the edge of the boat and, turning her lovely face towards Mopsa, said: 'I want to whisper to you, sister.'

'Oh!' said Mopsa. 'I wish I was in Jack's waistcoat pocket again; but I'm so big now.' And she took hold of the two sides of his velvet jacket, and hid her face between them.

'My old mother sent a message last night,' continued the Queen, in a soft, sorrowful voice. 'She is much more powerful than we are.'

'What is the message?' asked Mopsa; but she still hid her face.

So the Queen moved over, and put her lips close to Mopsa's ear, and repeated it: 'There cannot be two queens in one hive.'

'If Mopsa leaves the hive, a fine swarm will go with her,' said the apple-woman. 'I shall, for one; that I shall!'

'No!' answered the Queen. 'I hope not, dear; for you know well that this is my old mother's doing, not mine.'

'Oh!' said Mopsa. 'I feel as if I must tell a story too, just as the Queen does.' But the apple-woman broke out in a very cross voice: 'It's not at all like Fairyland, if you go on in this way, and I would as lief be out of it as in it.' Then she began to sing, that she and Jack might not hear Mopsa's story:

> 'On the rocks by Aberdeen.
> Where the whistlin' wave had been,
> As I wanted and at e'en
> > Was eerie;
> There I saw thee sailing west,
> And I ran with joy opprest—
> Ay, and took out all my best,
> > My dearie.
>
> 'Then I busked mysel' wi' speed,
> And the neighbours cried, "What need?
> 'Tis a lass in any weed
> > Aye bonny!"
> Now my heart, my heart is sair.
> What's the good, though I be fair,
> For thou'lt never see me mair,
> > Man Johnnie!'

While the apple-woman sang Mopsa finished her story; and the Queen untied the fastening which held her carpet to the boat, and went floating upon it down the river.

'Goodbye,' she said, kissing her hand to them. 'I must go and prepare for the deputation.'

So Jack and Mopsa played about all the morning, sometimes in the boat and sometimes on the shore, while the apple-woman sat on the grass, with her arms folded, and seemed to be lost in thought. At last she said to Jack: 'What was the name of the great bird that carried you two here?'

'I have forgotten,' answered Jack. 'I've been trying to remember ever since we heard the Queen tell her first story, but I cannot.'

'I remember,' said Mopsa.

'Tell it then,' replied the apple-woman; but Mopsa shook her head.

'I don't want Jack to go,' she answered.

'I don't want to go, nor that you should,' said Jack.

'But the Queen said, "There cannot be two Queens in one hive," and that means that you are going to be turned out of this beautiful country.'

'The other fairy lands are just as nice,' answered Mopsa. 'She can only turn me out of this one.'

'I never heard of more than one Fairyland,' observed Jack.

'It's my opinion,' said the apple-woman, 'that there are hundreds! And those one-foot-one fairies are such a saucy set that if I were you I should be very glad to get away from them. You've been here a very little while as yet, and you've no notion what goes on when the leaves begin to drop.'

'Tell us,' said Jack.

'Well, you must know,' answered the apple-woman, 'that fairies cannot abide cold weather; so, when the first rime frost comes, they bury themselves.'

'Bury themselves?' repeated Jack.

'Yes, I tell you, they bury themselves. You've seen fairy rings, of course, even in your own country; and here the fields are full of them. Well, when it gets cold a company of fairies forms itself into a circle, and every one digs a little hole. The first that has finished jumps into his hole, and his next neighbour covers him up, and then jumps into his own little hole, and he gets covered up in his turn, till at last there is only one left, and he goes and joins another circle, hoping he shall have better luck than to be last again. I've often asked them why they do that, but no fairy can ever give a reason for anything. They always say that old Mother Fate makes them do it. When they come up again they are not fairies at all, but the good ones are mushrooms, and the bad ones are toadstools.'

'Then you think there are no one-foot-one fairies in the other countries?' said Jack.

'Of course not,' answered the apple-woman; 'all the fairy lands are different. It's only the queens that are alike.'

'I wish the fairies would not disappear for hours,' said Jack. 'They all seem to run off and hide themselves.'

'That's their ways,' answered the apple-woman. 'All fairies are part of their time in the shape of human creatures, and the rest of it in the shape of some animal. These can turn themselves, when they please, to Guinea-fowl. In the heat of the day they generally prefer to be in that form, and they sit among the leaves of the trees.

'A great many are now with the Queen, because there is a deputation coming; but if I were to begin to sing, such a flock of Guinea-hens would gather round that the boughs of the trees would bend with their weight, and they would light on the grass all about so thickly that not a blade of grass would be seen as far as the song was heard.'

So she began to sing, and the air was darkened by great flocks of these Guinea-fowl. They alighted just as she had said, and kept time with their heads and their feet, nodding like a crowd of mandarins; and yet it was nothing but a stupid old song that you would have thought could have no particular meaning for them.

Like A Laverock in the Lift

I

It's we two, it's we two, it's we two for aye,
All the world and we two, and Heaven be our stay.
Like a laverock in the lift, sing, O bonny bride!
All the world was Adam once, with Eve by his side.

II

What's the world, my lass, my love! what can it do?
I am thine, and thou art mine; life is sweet and new.
If the world have missed the mark, let it stand by,
For we two have gotten leave, and once more we'll try.

III

Like a laverock in the lift, sing, O bonny bride!
It's we two, it's we two, happy side by side.
Take a kiss from me thy man; now the song begins:
'All is made afresh for us, and the brave heart wins.'

IV

When the darker days come, and no sun will shine,
Thou shalt dry my tears, lass, and I'll dry thine.
It's we two, it's we two, while the world's away,
Sitting by the golden sheaves on our wedding-day.[17]

17. **Laverock in the Lift** Sky-larks (known as "lavericks" in the North) are noted for their airy acrobatic lifts.

CHAPTER TWELVE

They Run Away from Old Mother Fate

✳

A land that living warmth disowns,
 It meets my wondering ken;
A land where all the men are stones,
 Or all the stones are men.

Before the apple-woman had finished, Jack and Mopsa saw the Queen coming in great state, followed by thousands of the one-foot-one fairies, and leading by a ribbon round its neck a beautiful brown doe. A great many pretty fawns were walking among the fairies.

'Here's the deputation,' said the apple-woman; but as the Guinea-fowl rose like a cloud at the approach of the Queen, and the fairies and fawns pressed forward, there was a good deal of noise and confusion, during which Mopsa stepped up close to Jack and whispered in his ear: 'Remember, Jack, whatever you can do you may do.'

Then the brown doe lay down at Mopsa's feet, and the Queen began:

'Jack and Mopsa, I love you both. I had a message last night from my old mother, and I told you what it was.'

'Yes, Queen,' said Mopsa, 'you did.'

'And now', continued the Queen, 'she has sent this beautiful brown doe from the country beyond the lake, where they are in the greatest distress for a queen, to offer Mopsa the crown; and, Jack, it is fated that Mopsa is to reign there, so you had better say no more about it.'

'I don't want to be a queen,' said Mopsa, pouting; 'I want to play with Jack.'

'You are a queen already,' answered the real Queen; 'at least, you will be in a few days. You are so much grown, even since the morning, that you come up nearly to Jack's shoulder. In four days you will be as tall as I am; and it is quite impossible that anyone of fairy birth should be as tall as a queen in her own country.'

'But I don't see what stags and does can want with a queen,' said Jack.

'They were obliged to turn into deer,' said the Queen, 'when they crossed their own border; but they are fairies when they are at home, and they want Mopsa, because they are always obliged to have a queen of alien birth.'

'If I go,' said Mopsa, 'shall Jack go too?'

'Oh no,' answered the Queen; 'Jack and the apple-woman are my subjects.'

'Apple-woman,' said Jack, 'tell us what you think; shall Mopsa go to this country?'

'Why, child,' said the apple-woman, 'go away from here she must; but she need not go off with the deer, I suppose, unless she likes. They look gentle and harmless; but it is very hard to get at the truth in this country, and I've heard queer stories about them.'

'Have you?' said the Queen. 'Well, you can repeat them if you like; but remember that the poor brown doe cannot contradict them.'

So the apple-woman said: 'I have heard, but I don't know how true it is, that in that country they shut up their queen in a great castle, and cover her with a veil, and never let the sun shine on her; for if by chance the least little sunbeam should light on her she would turn into a doe directly, and all the nation would turn with her, and stay so.'

'I don't want to be shut up in a castle,' said Mopsa.

'But is it true?' asked Jack.

'Well,' said the apple-woman, 'as I told you before, I cannot make out whether it's true or not, for all these stags and fawns look very mild, gentle creatures.'

'I won't go,' said Mopsa; 'I would rather run away.'

All this time the Queen with the brown doe had been gently pressing with the crowd nearer and nearer to the brink of the river, so that now Jack and Mopsa, who stood facing them, were quite close to the boat; and while they argued and tried to make Mopsa come away, Jack suddenly whispered to her to spring into the boat, which she did, and he after her, and at the same time he cried out:

'Now, boat, if you are my boat, set off as fast as you can, and let nothing of fairy birth get on board of you.'

No sooner did he begin to speak than the boat swung itself away from the edge, and almost in a moment it was in the very middle of the river, and beginning to float gently down with the stream.

Now, as I have told you before, that river runs up the country instead of down to the sea, so Jack and Mopsa floated still farther up into Fairyland; and they saw the Queen, and the apple-woman, and all the crowd of fawns and fairies walking along the bank of the river, keeping exactly to the same pace that the boat went; and this went on for hours and hours, so that there seemed to be no chance that Jack and Mopsa could land; and they heard no

They Run Away from Old Mother Fate

voices at all, nor any sound but the baying of the old hound, who could not
swim out to them, because Jack had forbidden the boat to take anything of
fairy birth on board of her.

Luckily the bottom of the boat was full of those delicious flowers that had
dropped into it at breakfast time, so there was plenty of nice food for Jack
and Mopsa; and Jack noticed, when he looked at her towards evening, that
she was now nearly as tall as himself, and that her lovely brown hair floated
down to her ankles.

'Jack,' she said, before it grew dusk, 'will you give me your little purse
that has the silver fourpence in it?'

Now Mopsa had often played with this purse. It was lined with a piece of
pale green silk, and when Jack gave it to her she pulled the silk out, and
shook it, and patted it, and stretched it, just as the queen had done, and it
came into a most lovely cloak, which she tied round her neck. Then she
twisted up her long hair into a coil, and fastened it round her head, and called
to the fireflies which were beginning to glitter on the trees to come, and
they came and alighted in a row upon the coil, and turned into diamonds
directly. So now Mopsa had got a crown and a robe, and she was so beautiful
that Jack thought he should never be tired of looking at her; but it was nearly
dark now, and he was so sleepy and tired that he could not keep his eyes
open, though he tried very hard, and he began to blink, and then he began
to nod, and at last he fell fast asleep, and did not awake till morning.

Then he sat up in the boat, and looked about him. A wonderful country,
indeed!—no trees, no grass, no houses, nothing but red stones and red
sand—and Mopsa was gone. Jack jumped on shore, for the boat had
stopped, and was close to the brink of the river. He looked about for some
time, and at last, in the shadow of a pale brown rock, he found her; and oh!
delightful surprise, the apple-woman was there too. She was saying: 'Oh,
my bones! Dearie, dearie me, how they do ache!' That was not surprising,
for she had been out all night. She had walked beside the river with the
Queen and her tribe till they came to a little tinkling stream, which divides
their country from the sandy land, and there they were obliged to stop; they
could not cross it. But the apple-woman sprang over, and, though the Queen
told her she must come back again in twenty-four hours, she did not appear
to be displeased. Now the Guinea-hens, when they had come to listen, the
day before, to the apple-woman's song, had brought each of them a grain of
maize in her beak, and had thrown it into her apron; so when she got up she
carried it with her gathered up there, and now she had been baking some
delicious little cakes on a fire of dry sticks that the river had drifted down,

and Mopsa had taken a honeycomb from the rock, so they all had a very nice breakfast. And the apple-woman gave them a great deal of good advice, and told them if they wished to remain in Fairyland, and not be caught by the brown doe and her followers, they must cross over the purple mountains.

'For on the other side of those peaks', she said, 'I have heard that fairies live who have the best of characters for being kind and just. I am sure they would never shut up a poor queen in a castle.'

'But the best thing you could do, dear,' she said to Mopsa, 'would be to let Jack call the bird, and make her carry you back to his own country.'

'The Queen is not at all kind,' said Jack; 'I have been very kind to her, and she should have let Mopsa stay.'

'No, Jack, she could not,' said Mopsa; 'but I wish I had not grown so fast, and I don't like to go to your country. I would rather run away.'

'But who is to tell us where to run?' asked Jack.

'Oh,' said Mopsa, 'some of these people.'

'I don't see anybody,' said Jack, looking about him.

Mopsa pointed to a group of stones, and then to another group, and as Jack looked he saw that in shape they were something like people—stone people. One stone was a little like an old man with a mantle over him, and he was sitting on the ground with his knees up nearly to his chin. Another was like a woman with a hood on, and she seemed to be leaning her chin on her hand. Close to these stood something very much like a cradle in shape; and beyond were stones that resembled a flock of sheep lying down on the bare sand, with something that reminded Jack of the figure of a man lying asleep near them, with his face to the ground.

That was a very curious country; all the stones reminded you of people or of animals, and the shadows that they cast were much more like than the stones themselves. There were blocks with things that you might have mistaken for stone ropes twisted round them; but, looking at the shadows, you could see distinctly that they were trees, and that what coiled round were snakes. Then there was a rocky prominence, at one side of which was something like a sitting figure, but its shadow, lying on the ground, was that of a girl with a distaff. Jack was very much surprised at all this; Mopsa was not. She did not see, she said, that one thing was more wonderful than another. All the fairy lands were wonderful, but the men-and-women world was far more so. She and Jack went about among the stones all day, and as the sun got low both the shadows and the blocks themselves became more and more like people, and if you went close you could now see features, very sweet, quiet features, but the eyes were all shut.

By this time the apple-woman began to feel very sad. She knew she would soon have to leave Jack and Mopsa, and she said to Mopsa, as they finished their evening meal: 'I wish you would ask the inhabitants a few questions, dear, before I go, for I want to know whether they can put you in the way of how to cross the purple mountains.'

Jack said nothing, for he thought he would see what Mopsa was going to do; so when she got up, and went towards the shape that was like a cradle he followed, and the apple-woman too. Mopsa went to the figure that sat by the cradle. It was a stone yet, but when Mopsa laid her little warm hand on its bosom it smiled.

'Dear,' said Mopsa, 'I wish you would wake.'

A curious little sound was now heard, but the figure did not move, and the apple-woman lifted Mopsa on to the lap of the statue; then she put her arms round its neck, and spoke to it again very distinctly: 'Dear! why don't you wake? You had better wake now; the baby's crying.'

Jack now observed that the sound he had heard was something like the crying of a baby. He also heard the figure answering Mopsa. It said: 'I am only a stone!'

'Then', said Mopsa, 'I am not a queen yet. I cannot wake her. Take me down.'

'I am not warm,' said the figure; and that was quite true, and yet she was not a stone now which reminded one of a woman, but a woman that reminded one of a stone.

All the west was very red with the sunset, and the river was red too, and Jack distinctly saw some of the coils of rope glide down from the trees and slip into the water; next he saw the stones that had looked like sheep raise up their heads in the twilight, and then lift themselves and shake their woolly sides. At that instant the large white moon heaved up her pale face between two dark blue hills, and upon this the statue put out its feet and gently rocked the cradle.

Then it spoke again to Mopsa: 'What was it that you wished me to tell you?'

'How to find the way over those purple mountains,' said Mopsa.

'You must set off in an hour, then,' said the woman, and she had hardly anything of the stone about her now. 'You can easily find it by night without any guide, but nothing can ever take you to it by day.'

'But we would rather stay a few days in this curious country,' said Jack; 'let us wait at least till tomorrow night.'

The statue at this moment rubbed her hands together as if they still felt cold and stiff. 'You are quite welcome to stay,' she observed; 'but you had better not.'

'Why not?' persisted Jack.

'Father,' said the woman, rising and shaking the figure next to her by the sleeve. 'Wake up!' What had looked like an old man was a real old man now, and he got up and began to gather sticks to make a fire, and to pick up the little brown stones which had been scattered about all day, but which now were berries of coffee; the larger ones, which you might find here and there, were rasped rolls.[18] Then the woman answered Jack: 'Why not? Why, because it's full moon tonight at midnight, and the moment the moon is past the full your Queen, whose country you have just left, will be able to cross over the little stream, and she will want to take you and that other mortal back. She can do it, of course, if she pleases; and we can afford you no protection, for by that time we shall be stones again. We are only people two hours out of the twenty-four.'

'That is very hard,' observed Jack.

'No,' said the women, in a tone of indifference; 'it comes to the same thing, as we live twelve times as long as others do.'

By this time the shepherd was gently driving his flock down to the water, and round fifty little fires groups of people were sitting roasting coffee, while cows were lowing to be milked, and girls with distaffs were coming to them slowly, for no one was in a hurry there. They say in that country that they wish to enjoy their day quietly, because it is so short.

'Can you tell us anything of the land beyond the mountains?' asked Jack.

'Yes,' said the woman. 'Of all fairy lands it is the best; the people are the gentlest and kindest.'

'Then I had better take Mopsa there than down the river?' said Jack.

'You can't take her down the river,' replied the woman; and Jack thought she laughed and was glad of that.

'Why not?' asked Jack. 'I have a boat.'

'Yes, sir,' answered the woman, 'but where is it now?'

18. **rasped rolls** breakfast buns with a rough exterior

CHAPTER THIRTEEN

Melon Seeds

✶

Rosalind. Well, this is the forest of Arden.
Touchstone. Ay, now am I in Arden: the more fool I; when I was at home I
was in a better place; but travellers must be content.

As You Like It. [19]

'Where is it now?' said the stone woman; and when Jack heard that he ran
down to the river, and looked right and looked left. At last he saw his boat—
a mere speck in the distance, it had floated so far.

He called it, but it was far beyond the reach of his voice; and Mopsa, who
had followed him, said:

'It does not signify, Jack, for I feel that no place is the right place for me
but that country beyond the purple mountains, and I shall never be happy
unless we go there.'

So they walked back towards the stone people hand in hand, and the
apple-woman presently joined them. She was crying gently, for she knew
that she must soon pass over the little stream and part with these whom
she called her dear children. Jack had often spoken to her that day about
going home to her own country, but she said it was too late to think of that
now, and she must end her days in the land of Faery.

The kind stone people asked them to come and sit by their little fire; and
in the dusk the woman whose baby had slept in a stone cradle took it up and
began to sing to it. She seemed astonished when she heard that the apple-
woman had power to go home if she could make up her mind to do it; and as
she sang she looked at her with wonder and pity.

> 'Little babe, while burns the west,
> Warm thee, warm thee in my breast;
> While the moon doth shine her best,
>   And the dews distil not.
>
> 'All the land so sad, so fair—
> Sweet its toils are, blest its care.
> Child, we may not enter there!
>   Some there are that will not.

19. ***As You Like It*** II.iv.15–18

'Fain would I thy margins know,
Land of work, and land of snow;
Land of life, whose rivers flow
    On, and on, and stay not.

'Fain would I thy small limbs fold,
While the weary hours are told,
Little babe in cradle cold.
    Some there are that may not.'

'You are not exactly fairies, I suppose?' said Jack. 'If you were, you could go to our country when you pleased.'

'No,' said the woman; 'we are not exactly fairies; but we shall be more like them when our punishment is over.'

'I am sorry you are punished,' answered Jack, 'for you seem very nice, kind people.'

'We were not always kind,' answered the woman; 'and perhaps we are only kind now because we have no time and no chance of being otherwise. I'm sure I don't know about that. We were powerful once, and we did a cruel deed. I must not tell you what it was. We were told that our hearts were all as cold as stones—and I suppose they were—and we were doomed to be stones all our lives, excepting for the two hours of twilight. There was no one to sow the crops, or water the grass, so it all failed, and the trees died, and our houses fell, and our possessions were stolen from us.'

'It is a very sad thing,' observed the apple-woman; and then she said that she must go, for she had a long way to walk before she would reach the little brook that led to the country of her own queen; so she kissed the two children, Jack and Mopsa, and they begged her again to think better of it, and return to her own land. But she said No; she had no heart for work now, and could not bear either cold or poverty.

Then the woman who was hugging her little baby, and keeping it cosy and warm, began to tell Jack and Mopsa that it was time they should begin to run away to the country over the purple mountains, or else the Queen would overtake them and be very angry with them; so, with many promises that they would mind her directions, they set off hand in hand to run; but before they left her they could see plainly that she was beginning to turn again into stone. However, she had given them a slice of melon with the seeds in it. It had been growing on the edge of the river, and was stone in the day-time, like everything else. 'When you are tired,' she said, 'eat the seeds, and they will enable you to go running on. You can put the slice into this little red pot, which has string handles to it, and you can hang it on your arm. While you have it with you it will not turn to stone, but if you lay it down it will, and then it will be useless.'

So, as I said before, Jack and Mopsa set off hand in hand to run; and as they ran all the things and people gradually and softly settled themselves to turn into stone again. Their cloaks and gowns left off fluttering, and hung stiffly; and then they left off their occupations, and sat down, or lay themselves down; and the sheep and cattle turned stiff and stonelike too, so that in a very little while all that country was nothing but red stones and red sand, just as it had been in the morning.

Presently the full moon, which had been hiding behind a cloud, came out, and they saw their shadows, which fell straight before them; so they ran on hand in hand very merrily till the half-moon came up, and the shadows she made them cast fell sideways. This was rather awkward, because as long as only the full moon gave them shadows they had but to follow them in order to go straight towards the purple mountains. Now they were not always sure which were her shadows; and presently a crescent moon came, and still further confused them; also the sand began to have tufts of grass in it; and then, when they had gone a little farther, there were beautiful patches of anemones, and hyacinths, and jonquils, and crown imperials, and they stopped to gather them; and they got among some trees, and then, as they had nothing to guide them but the shadows, and these went all sorts of ways, they lost a great deal of time, and the trees became of taller growth; but they still ran on and on till they got into a thick forest where it was quite dark, and there Mopsa began to cry, for she was tired.

'If I could only begin to be a queen', she said to Jack, 'I could go wherever I pleased. I am not a fairy, and yet I am not a proper queen. Oh, what shall I do? I cannot go any farther.'

So Jack gave her some of the seeds of the melon, though it was so dark that he could scarcely find the way to her mouth, and then he took some himself, and they both felt that they were rested, and Jack comforted Mopsa.

'If you are not a queen yet,' he said, 'you will be by tomorrow morning; for when our shadows danced on before us yours was so very nearly the same height as mine that I could see hardly any difference.'

When they reached the end of that great forest, and found themselves out in all sorts of moonlight, the first thing they did was to laugh—the shadows looked so odd, sticking out in every direction; and the next thing they did was to stand back to back, and put their heels together, and touch their heads together, to see by the shadow which was the taller; and Jack was still the least bit in the world taller than Mopsa; so they knew she was not a queen yet, and they ate some more melon seeds, and began to climb up the mountain.

They climbed till the trees of the forest looked no bigger than gooseberry bushes, and then they climbed till the whole forest looked only like a patch of moss; and then, when they got a little higher, they saw the wonderful river, a long way off, and the snow glittering on the peaks overhead; and while they were looking and wondering how they should find a pass, the moons all went down, one after the other, and, if Mopsa had not found some glow-worms, they would have been quite in the dark again. However, she took a dozen of them, and put them round Jack's ankles, so that when he walked he could see where he was going; and he found a little sheep-path, and she followed him.

Now they had noticed during the night how many shooting stars kept darting about from time to time, and at last one shot close by them, and fell in the soft moss on before. There it lay shining; and Jack, though he began to feel tired again, made haste to it, for he wanted to see what it was like.

It was not what you would have supposed. It was soft and round, and about the colour of a ripe apricot; it was covered with fur, and in fact it was evidently alive, and had curled itself up into a round ball.

'The dear little thing!' said Jack, as he held it in his hand, and showed it to Mopsa. 'How its hearts beats! Is it frightened?'

'Who are you?' said Mopsa to the thing. 'What is your name?'

The little creature made a sound that seemed like 'Wisp'.

'Uncurl yourself, Wisp,' said Mopsa. 'Jack and I want to look at you.'

So Wisp unfolded himself, and showed two little black eyes, and spread out two long filmy wings. He was like a most beautiful bat, and the light he shed out illuminated their faces.

'It is only one of the air fairies,' said Mopsa. 'Pretty creature! It never did any harm, and would like to do us good if it knew how, for it knows that I shall be a queen very soon. Wisp, if you like, you may go and tell your friends and relations that we want to cross over the mountains, and if they can they may help us.'

Upon this Wisp spread out his wings, and shot off again; and Jack's feet were so tired that he sat down and pulled off one of his shoes, for he thought there was a stone in it. So he set the little red jar beside him, and quite forgot what the stone woman had said, but went on shaking his shoe, and buckling it, and admiring the glow-worms round his ankle, till Mopsa said: 'Darling Jack, I am so dreadfully tired! Give me some more melon seeds.'

Then he lifted up the jar, and thought it felt very heavy; and when he put in his hand, jar, and melon, and seeds were all turned to stone together.

They were both very sorry, and they sat still for a minute or two, for they were much too tired to stir; and then shooting stars began to appear in all directions. The fairy bat had told his friends and relations, and they were coming. One fell at Mopsa's feet, another in her lap; more, more, all about, behind, before and over them. And they spread out long filmy wings, some of them a yard long, till Jack and Mopsa seemed to be enclosed in a perfect network of the rays of shooting stars, and they were both a good deal frightened. Fifty or sixty shooting stars, with black eyes that could stare, were enough, they thought, to frighten anybody.

'If we had anything to sit upon', said Mopsa, 'they could carry us over the pass.' She had no sooner spoken than the largest of the bats bit off one of his own long wings, and laid it at Mopsa's feet. It did not seem to matter much to him that he had parted with it, for he shot out another wing directly, just as a comet shoots out a ray of light sometimes when it approaches the sun.

Mopsa thanked the shooting fairy and, taking the wing, began to stretch it, till it was large enough for her and Jack to sit upon. Then all the shooting fairies came round it, took its edges in their mouths and began to fly away with it over the mountains. They went slowly, for Jack and Mopsa were heavy, and they flew very low, resting now and then; but in the course of time they carried the wing over the pass, and half way down the other side. Then the sun came up; and the moment he appeared all their lovely apricot-coloured light was gone, and they only looked like common bats, such as you can see every evening.

They set down Jack and Mopsa, folded up their long wings and hung down their heads.

Mopsa thanked them, and said they had been useful; but still they looked ashamed, and crept into little corners and crevices of the rock, to hide.

CHAPTER FOURTEEN

Reeds and Rushes

❋

'Tis merry, 'tis merry in Fairyland,
    When Fairy birds are singing;
When the court doth ride by their monarch's side,
    With bit and bridle ringing.
                                    WALTER SCOTT.

There were many fruit-trees on that slope of the mountain, and Jack and
Mopsa, as they came down, gathered some fruit for breakfast, and did not
feel very tired, for the long ride on the wing had rested them.

They could not see the plain, for a slight blue mist hung over it; but the
sun was hot already, and as they came down they saw a beautiful bed of high
reeds, and thought they would sit awhile and rest in it. A rill of clear water
ran beside the bed, so when they had reached it they sat down, and began
to consider what they should do next.

'Jack,' said Mopsa, 'did you see anything particular as you came down
with the shooting stars?'

'No, I saw nothing so interesting as they were,' answered Jack. 'I was
looking at them and watching how they squeaked to one another, and how
they had little hooks in their wings, with which they held the large wing that
we sat on.'

'But I saw something,' said Mopsa. 'Just as the sun rose I looked down,
and in the loveliest garden I ever saw, and all among trees and woods, I saw
a most beautiful castle. Oh, Jack! I am sure that castle is the place I am to
live in, and now we have nothing to do but to find it. I shall soon be a queen,
and there I shall reign.'

'Then I shall be king there,' said Jack; 'shall I?'

'Yes, if you can,' answered Mopsa. 'Of course, whatever you can do you
may do. And, Jack, this is a much better fairy country than either the stony
land or the other that we first came to, for this castle is a real place! It will
not melt away. There the people can work, they know how to love each
other: common fairies cannot do that, I know. They can laugh and cry, and I
shall teach them several things that they do not know yet. Oh, do let us
make haste and find the castle!'

So they arose; but they turned the wrong way, and by mistake walked farther and farther in among the reeds, whose feathery heads puffed into Mopsa's face, and Jack's coat was all covered with the fluffy seed.

'This is very odd,' said Jack. 'I thought this was only a small bed of reeds when we stepped into it; but really we must have walked a mile already.'

But they walked on and on, till Mopsa grew quite faint, and her sweet face became very pale, for she knew that the beds of reeds were spreading faster than they walked, and then they shot up so high that it was impossible to see over their heads; so at last Jack and Mopsa were so tired that they sat down, and Mopsa began to cry.

However, Jack was the braver of the two this time, and he comforted Mopsa, and told her that she was nearly a queen, and would never reach her castle by sitting still. So she got up and took his hand, and he went on before, parting the reeds and pulling her after him, till all on a sudden they heard the sweetest sound in the world: it was like a bell, and it sounded again and again.

It was the castle clock, and it was striking twelve at noon.

As it finished striking they came out at the farther edge of the great bed of reeds, and there was the castle straight before them—a beautiful castle, standing on the slope of a hill. The grass all about it was covered with beautiful flowers; two of the taller turrets were overgrown with ivy, and a flag was flying on a staff; but everything was so silent and lonely that it made one sad to look on. As Jack and Mopsa drew near they trod as gently as they could, and did not say a word.

All the windows were shut, but there was a great door in the centre of the building, and they went towards it, hand in hand.

What a beautiful hall! The great door stood wide open, and they could see what a delightful place this must be to live in: it was paved with squares of blue and white marble, and here and there carpets were spread, with chairs and tables upon them. They looked and saw a great dome overhead, filled with windows of coloured glass, and they cast down blue and golden and rosy reflections.

'There is my home that I shall live in,' said Mopsa; and she came close to the door, and they both looked in, till at last she let go of Jack's hand, and stepped over the threshold.

The bell in the tower sounded again more sweetly than ever, and the instant Mopsa was inside there came from behind the fluted columns, which rose up on every side, the brown doe, followed by troops of deer and fawns!

'Mopsa! Mopsa!' cried Jack. 'Come away! come back!' But Mopsa was too much astonished to stir, and something seemed to hold Jack from following; but he looked and looked, till, as the brown doe advanced, the door of the castle closed—Mopsa was shut in, and Jack was left outside.

So Mopsa had come straight to the place she thought she had run away from.

'But I am determined to get her away from those creatures,' thought Jack; 'she does not want to reign over deer.' And he began to look about him, hoping to get in. It was of no use: all the windows in the front of the castle were high, and when he tried to go round, he came to a high wall with battlements. Against some parts of this wall the ivy grew, and looked as if it might have grown there for ages; its stems were thicker than his waist, and its branches were spread over the surface like network; so by means of them he hoped to climb to the top.

He immediately began to try. Oh, how high the wall was! First he came to several sparrows' nests, and very much frightened the sparrows were; then he reached starlings' nests, and very angry the starlings were; but at last, just under the coping, he came to jackdaws' nests, and these birds were very friendly, and pointed out to him the best little holes for him to put his feet into. At last he reached the top, and found to his delight that the wall was three feet thick, and he could walk upon it quite comfortably, and look down into a lovely garden, where all the trees were in blossom, and creepers tossed their long tendrils from tree to tree, covered with puffs of yellow, or bells of white, or bunches and knots of blue or rosy bloom.

He could look down into the beautiful empty rooms of the castle, and he walked cautiously on the wall till he came to the west front, and reached a little casement window that had latticed panes. Jack peeped in; nobody was there. He took his knife and cut away a little bit of lead to let out the pane, and it fell with such a crash on the pavement below that he wondered it did not bring the deer over to look at what he was about. Nobody came.

He put in his hand and opened the latchet, and with very little trouble got down into the room. Still nobody was to be seen. He thought that the room, years ago, might have been a fairies' schoolroom, for it was strewn with books, slates and all sorts of copybooks. A fine soft dust had settled down over everything,—pens, papers and all. Jack opened a copybook: its pages were headed with maxims, just as ours are, which proved that these fairies must have been superior to such as he had hitherto come among. Jack read some of them:

> Turn your back on the light, and you'll follow a shadow.
> The deaf queen Fate has dumb courtiers.

> If the hound is your foe, don't sleep in his kennel.
> That that is, is.

And so on; but nobody came, and no sound was heard, so he opened the door, and found himself in a long and most splendid gallery, all hung with pictures, and spread with a most beautiful carpet, which was as soft and white as a piece of wool, and wrought with a beautiful device. This was the letter M, with a crown and sceptre, and underneath a beautiful little boat, exactly like the one in which he had come up the river. Jack felt sure that this carpet had been made for Mopsa, and he went along the gallery upon it till he reached a grand staircase of oak that was almost black with age, and he stole gently down it, for he began to feel rather shy, more especially as he could now see the great hall under the dome, and that it had a beautiful lady in it, and many other people, but no deer at all.

These fairy people were something like the one-foot-one fairies, but much larger and more like children, and they had very gentle, happy faces, and seemed to be extremely glad and gay. But seated on a couch, where lovely painted windows threw down all sorts of rainbow colours on her, was a beautiful fairy lady, as large as a woman. She had Mopsa in her arms, and was looking down upon her with eyes full of love, while at her side stood a boy, who was exactly and precisely like Jack himself. He had rather long light hair and grey eyes, and a velvet jacket. That was all Jack could see at first, but as he drew nearer the boy turned, and then Jack felt as if he was looking at himself in the glass.

Mopsa had been very tired, and now she was fast asleep, with her head on that lady's shoulder. The boy kept looking at her, and he seemed very happy indeed; so did the lady, and she presently told him to bring Jack something to eat.

It was rather a curious speech that she made to him: it was this:

'Jack, bring Jack some breakfast.'

'What!' thought Jack to himself. 'Has he got a face like mine, and a name like mine too?'

So that other Jack went away, and presently came back with a golden plate full of nice things to eat.

'I know you don't like me,' he said, as he came up to Jack with the plate.

'Not like him?' repeated the lady; 'and pray, what reason have you for not liking my royal nephew?'

'Oh, dame!' exclaimed the boy, and laughed.

The lady, on hearing this, turned pale, for she perceived that she herself had mistaken the one for the other.

'I see you know how to laugh,' said the real Jack. 'You are wiser people than those whom I went to first; but the reason I don't like you is that you are so exactly like me.'

'I am not!' exclaimed the boy. 'Only hear him, dame! You mean, I suppose, that you are so exactly like me. I am sure I don't know what you mean by it.'

'Nor I either,' replied Jack, almost in a passion.

'It couldn't be helped, of course,' said the other Jack.

'Hush! hush!' said the fairy woman. 'Don't wake our dear little Queen. Was it you, my royal nephew, who spoke out last?'

'Yes, dame,' answered the boy, and again he offered the plate; but Jack was swelling with indignation, and he gave the plate a push with his elbow, which scattered the fruit and bread on the ground.

'I won't eat it,' he said; but when the other Jack went and picked it up again, and said: 'Oh yes, do, old fellow; it's not my fault, you know,' he began to consider that it was no use being cross in Fairyland; so he forgave his double, and had just finished his breakfast when Mopsa woke.

CHAPTER FIFTEEN

The Queen's Wand

※

> One, two, three, four; one, two, three, four;
>   'Tis still one, two, three, four.
> Mellow and silvery are the tones,
>   But I wish the bells were more.
> SOUTHEY.

Mopsa woke: she was rather too big to be nursed, for she was the size of Jack, and looked like a sweet little girl of ten years, but she did not always behave like one; sometimes she spoke as wisely as a grown-up woman, and sometimes she changed again and seemed like a child.

Mopsa lifted up her head and pushed back her long hair: her coronet had fallen off while she was in the bed of reeds; and she said to the beautiful dame:

'I am a queen now.'

'Yes, my sweet Queen,' answered the lady, 'I know you are.'

'And you promise that you will be kind to me till I grow up,' said Mopsa, 'and love me, and teach me how to reign?'

'Yes,' repeated the lady; 'and I will love you too, just as if you were a mortal and I your mother.'

'For I am only ten years old yet,' said Mopsa, 'and the throne is too big for me to sit upon; but I am a queen.' And then she paused, and said: 'Is it three o'clock?'

As she spoke the sweet clear bell of the castle sounded three times, and then chimes began to play; they played such a joyous tune that it made everybody sing. The dame sang, the crowd of fairies sang, the boy who was Jack's double sang and Mopsa sang—only Jack was silent—and this was the song:

> 'The prince shall to the chase again,
> The dame has got her face again,
> The king shall have his place again
>   Aneath the fairy dome.
>
> 'And all the knights shall woo again,
> And all the doves shall coo again,
> And all the dreams come true again,
>   And Jack shall go home.'

'We shall see about that!' thought Jack to himself. And Mopsa, while she sang those last words, burst into tears, which Jack did not like to see; but all the fairies were so very glad, so joyous and so delighted with her for having come to be their queen, that after a while she dried her eyes, and said to the wrong boy:

'Jack, when I pulled the lining out of your pocket-book there was a silver fourpence in it.'

'Yes,' said the real Jack, 'and here it is.'

'Is it real money?' asked Mopsa. 'Are you sure you brought it with you all the way from your own country?'

'Yes,' said Jack, 'quite sure.'

'Then, dear Jack,' answered Mopsa, 'will you give it to me?'

'I will,' said Jack, 'if you will send this boy away.'

'How can I?' answered Mopsa, surprised. 'Don't you know what happened when the door closed? Has nobody told you?'

'I did not see anyone after I got into the place,' said Jack. 'There was no one to tell anything—not even a fawn, nor the brown doe. I have only seen down here these fairy people, and this boy, and this lady.'

'The lady is the brown doe,' answered Mopsa; 'and this boy and the fairies were the fawns.' Jack was so astonished at this that he stared at the lady and the boy and the fairies with all his might.

'The sun came shining in as I stepped inside,' said Mopsa, 'and a long beam fell down from the fairy dome across my feet. Do you remember what the apple-woman told us—how it was reported that the brown doe and her nation had a queen whom they shut up, and never let the sun shine on her? That was not a kind or true report, and yet it came from something that really happened.'

'Yes, I remember,' said Jack; 'and if the sun did shine they were all to be turned into deer.'

'I dare not tell you all that story yet,' said Mopsa; 'but, Jack, as the brown doe and all the fawns came up to greet me, and passed by turns into the sunbeam, they took their own forms, every one of them, because the spell was broken. They were to remain in the disguise of deer till a queen of alien birth should come to them against her will. I am a queen of alien birth, and did not I come against my will?'

'Yes, to be sure,' answered Jack. 'We thought all the time that we were running away.'

'If ever you come to Fairyland again,' observed Mopsa, 'you can save yourself the trouble of trying to run away from the old mother.'

'I shall not "come,"' answered Jack, 'because I shall not go—not for a long while, at least. But the boy—I want to know why this boy turned into another ME?'

'Because he is the heir, of course,' answered Mopsa.

'But I don't see that this is any reason at all,' said Jack.

Mopsa laughed. 'That's because you don't know how to argue,' she replied. 'Why, the thing is as plain as possible.'

'It may be plain to you,' persisted Jack, 'but it's no reason.'

'No reason!' repeated Mopsa. 'No reason! when I like you the best of anything in the world, and when I am come here to be queen! Of course, when the spell was broken he took exactly your form on that account; and very right too.'

'But why?' asked Jack.

Mopsa, however, was like other fairies in this respect—that she knew all about Old Mother Fate, but not about causes and reasons. She believed, as we do in this world, that

That that is, is,

but the fairies go further than this; they say:

That that is, is; and when it is, that is the reason that it is.

This sounds like nonsense to us, but it is all right to them.

So Mopsa, thinking she had explained everything, said again:

'And, dear Jack, will you give the silver fourpence to me?'

Jack took it out; and she got down from the dame's knee and took it in the palm of her hand, laying the other palm upon it.

'It will be very hot,' observed the dame.

'But it will not burn me so as really to hurt, if I am a real queen,' said Mopsa.

Presently she began to look as if something gave her pain.

'Oh, it's so hot!' she said to the other Jack; 'so very hot!'

'Never mind, sweet Queen,' he answered; 'it will not hurt you long. Remember my poor uncle and all his knights.'

Mopsa still held the little silver coin; but Jack saw that it hurt her, for two bright tears fell from her eyes; and in another moment he saw that it was actually melted, for it fell in glittering drops from Mopsa's hand to the marble floor, and there it lay as soft as quicksilver.

'Pick it up,' said Mopsa to the other Jack; and he instantly did so, and laid it in her hand again; and she began gently to roll it backwards and forwards between her palms till she had rolled it into a very slender rod, two feet long, and not nearly so thick as a pin; but it did not bend, and it shone so brightly that you could hardly look at it.

Then she held it out towards the real Jack, and said: 'Give this a name.'

'I think it is a—' began the other Jack; but the dame suddenly stopped him. 'Silence, sire! Don't you know that what it is first called that it will be?'

Jack hesitated; he thought if Mopsa was a queen the thing ought to be a sceptre; but it was certainly not at all like a sceptre.

'That thing is a wand,' said he.

'You are a wand,' said Mopsa, speaking to the silver stick, which was glittering now in a sunbeam almost as if it were a beam of light itself. Then she spoke again to Jack:

'Tell me, Jack, what can I do with a wand?'

Again the boy king began to speak, and the dame stopped him, and again Jack considered. He had heard a great deal in his own country about fairy wands, but he could not remember that the fairies had done anything particular with them, so he gave what he thought was true, but what seemed to him a very stupid answer:

'You can make it point to anything that you please.'

The moment he said this, shouts of ecstasy filled the hall, and all the fairies clapped their hands with such hurrahs of delight that he blushed for joy.

The dame also looked truly glad, and as for the other Jack, he actually turned head over heels, just as Jack had often done himself on his father's lawn.

Jack had merely meant that Mopsa could point with the wand to anything that she saw; but he was presently told that what he had meant was nothing, and that his words were everything.

'I can make it point now,' said Mopsa, 'and it will point aright to anything I please, whether I know where the thing is or not.'

Again the hall was filled with those cries of joy, and the sweet childlike fairies congratulated each other with 'The Queen has got a wand—a wand! and she can make it point wherever she pleases!'

Then Mopsa rose and walked towards the beautiful staircase, the dame and all the fairies following. Jack was going too, but the other Jack held him.

'Where is Mopsa going? and why am I not to follow?' inquired Jack.

'They are going to put on her robes, of course,' answered the other Jack.

'I am so tired of always hearing you say "of course,"' answered Jack; 'and I wonder how it is that you always seem to know what is going to be done without being told. However, I suppose you can't help being odd people.'

The boy king did not make a direct answer; he only said: 'I like you very much, though you don't like me.'

'Why do you like me?' asked Jack.

The other opened his eyes wide with surprise. 'Most boys say Sire to me,' he observed; 'at least they used to when there were any boys here. However, that does not signify. Why, of course I like you, because I am so tired of being always a fawn, and you brought Mopsa to break the spell. You cannot think how disagreeable it is to have no hands, and to be all covered with hair. Now look at my hands; I can move them and turn them everywhere, even over my head if I like. Hoofs are good for nothing in comparison: and we could not talk.'

'Do tell me about it,' said Jack. 'How did you become fawns?'

'I dare not tell you,' said the boy; 'and listen—I hear Mopsa.'

Jack looked, and certainly Mopsa was coming, but very strangely, he thought. Mopsa, like all other fairies, was afraid to whisper a spell with her eyes open; so a handkerchief was tied across them, and as she came on she felt her way, holding by the banisters with one hand, and with the other, between her finger and thumb, holding out the silver wand. She felt with her foot for the edge of the first stair; and Jack heard her say: 'I am much older—ah! so much older, now I have got my wand. I can feel sorrow too, and *their* sorrow weighs down my heart.'

Mopsa was dressed superbly in a white satin gown, with a long, long train of crimson velvet which was glittering with diamonds; it reached almost from one end of the great gallery to the other, and had hundreds of fairies to hold it and keep it in its place. But in her hair were no jewels, only a little crown made of daisies, and on her shoulders her robe was fastened with the little golden image of a boat. These things were to show the land she had come from and the vessel she had come in.

So she came slowly, slowly downstairs blindfold, and muttering to her wand all the time.

> 'Though the sun shine brightly,
> Wand, wand, guide rightly.'

So she felt her way down to the great hall. There the wand turned half round in the hall towards the great door, and she and Jack and the other Jack came out on to the lawn in front with all the followers and train-bearers; only the dame remained behind.

Jack noticed now for the first time that, with the one exception of the boy-king, all these fairies were lady-fairies; he also observed that Mopsa, after the manner of fairy queens, though she moved slowly and blindfold, was beginning to tell a story. This time it did not make him feel sleepy. It did not begin at the beginning: their stories never do.

These are the first words he heard, for she spoke softly and very low, while he walked at her right hand, and the other Jack on her left:

'And so now I have no wings. But my thoughts can go up (Jovinian and Roxaletta could not think). My thoughts are instead of wings; but they have dropped with me now, as a lark among the clods of the valley. Wand, do you bend? Yes, I am following, wand.

'And after that the bird said: "I will come when you call me." I have never seen her moving overhead; perhaps she is out of sight. Flocks of birds hover over the world, and watch it high up where the air is thin. There are zones, but those in the lowest zone are far out of sight.

'I have not been up there. I have no wings.

'Over the highest of the birds is the place where angels float and gather the children's souls as they are set free.

'And so that woman told me—(Wand, you bend again, and I will turn at your bending)—that woman told me how it was: for when the new king was born, a black fairy with a smiling face came and sat within the doorway. She had a spindle, and would always spin. She wanted to teach them how to spin, but they did not like her, and they loved to do nothing at all. So they turned her out.

'But after her came a brown fairy, with a grave face, and she sat on the black fairy's stool and gave them much counsel. They liked that still less; so they got spindles and spun, for they said: "She will go now, and we shall have the black fairy again." When she did not go they turned her out also, and after her came a white fairy, and sat in the same seat. She did nothing at all, and she said nothing at all; but she had a sorrowful face, and she looked up. So they were displeased. They turned her out also; and she went and sat by the edge of the lake with her two sisters.

'And everything prospered over all the land; till, after shearing-time, the shepherds, because the king was a child, came to his uncle, and said: "Sir, what shall we do with the old wool, for the new fleeces are in the bales, and there is no storehouse to put them in?" So he said: 'Throw them into the lake."

'And while they threw them in, a great flock of finches flew to them, and said: "Give us some of the wool that you do not want; we should be glad of it to build our nests with."

'They answered: "Go and gather for yourselves; there is wool on every thorn."

'Then the black fairy said: "They shall be forgiven this time, because the birds should pick wool for themselves."

'So the finches flew away.

'Then the harvest was over, and the reapers came and said to the child king's uncle: "Sir, what shall we do with the new wheat, for the old is not half eaten yet, and there is no room in the granaries?"

'He said: "Throw that into the lake also."

'While they were throwing it in, there came a great flight of the wood fairies, fairies of passage from over the sea. They were in the form of pigeons, and they alighted and prayed them: "O cousins! we are faint with our long flight; give us some of that corn which you do not want, that we may peck it and be refreshed."

'But they said: "You may rest on our land, but our corn is our own. Rest awhile, and go and get food in your own fields."

'Then the brown fairy said: "They may be forgiven this once, but yet it is a great unkindness."

'And as they were going to pour in the last sackful, there passed a poor mortal beggar, who had strayed in from the men and women's world, and she said: "Pray give me some of that wheat, O fairy people! for I am hungry, I have lost my way, and there is no money to be earned here. Give me some of that wheat, that I may bake cakes, lest I and my baby should starve."

'And they said: "What is starve? We never heard that word before, and we cannot wait while you explain it to us."

'So they poured it all into the lake; and then the white fairy said: "This cannot be forgiven them"; and she covered her face with her hands and wept. Then the black fairy rose and drove them all before her—the prince, with his chief shepherd and his reapers, his courtiers and his knights; she drove them into the great bed of reeds, and no one had ever set eyes on them since. Then the brown fairy went into the palace where the king's aunt sat, with all her ladies and her maids about her, and with the child king on her knee.

'It was a very gloomy day.

'She stood in the middle of the hall, and said: "Oh, you cold-hearted and most unkind! my spell is upon you, and the first ray of sunshine shall bring it down. Lose your present forms, and be of a more gentle and innocent race, till a queen of alien birth shall come to reign over you against her will."

'As she spoke they crept into corners, and covered the dame's head with a veil. And all that day it was dark and gloomy, and nothing happened, and all the next day it rained and rained; and they thrust the dame into a dark closet, and kept her there for a whole month, and still not a ray of sunshine came to do them any damage; but the dame faded and faded in the dark, and at last they said: "She must come out, or she will die; and we do not believe the sun will ever shine in our country any more." So they let the poor dame come out; and lo! as she crept slowly forth under the dome, a piercing ray of sunlight darted down upon her head, and in an instant they were all changed into deer, and the child king too.

'They are gentle now, and kind; but where is the prince? Where are the fairy knights and fairy men?

'Wand! why do you turn?'

Now while Mopsa told her story the wand continued to bend, and Mopsa, following, was slowly approaching the foot of a great precipice, which rose sheer up for more than a hundred feet. The crowd that followed looked dismayed at this: they thought the wand must be wrong; or even if it was right, they could not climb a precipice.

But still Mopsa walked on blindfold, and the wand pointed at the rock till it touched it, and she said: 'Who is stopping me?'

They told her, and she called to some of her ladies to untie the handker-chief. Then Mopsa looked at the rock, and so did the two Jacks. There was nothing to be seen but a very tiny hole. The boy-king thought it led to a bees' nest, and Jack thought it was a keyhole, for he noticed in the rock a slight crack which took the shape of an arched door. Mopsa looked earnestly at the hole. 'It may be a keyhole,' she said, 'but there is no key.'

CHAPTER SIXTEEN

Failure

❊

We are much bound to them that do succeed;
   But, in a more pathetic sense, are bound
   To such as fail. They all our loss expound;
They comfort us for work that will not speed,
And life—itself a failure. Ay, his deed,
   Sweetest in story, who the dusk profound
   Of Hades flooded with entrancing sound,
Music's own tears, was failure. Doth it read
Therefore the worse? Ah, no! So much to dare,
   He fronts the regnant Darkness on its throne. —
So much to do; impetuous even there,
   He pours out love's disconsolate sweet moan—
He wins; but few for that his deed recall:
Its power is in the look which costs him all. [20]

At this moment Jack observed that a strange woman was standing among them, and that the train-bearing fairies fell back, as if they were afraid of her. As no one spoke, he did, and said: 'Good morning!'

'Good afternoon!' she answered, correcting him. 'I am the black fairy. Work is a fine thing. Most people in your country can work.'

'Yes,' said Jack.

---

20. **costs him all** Orpheus, the son of a Muse, managed to rescue his wife Eurydice through the power of his lyre, but lost her by looking back at Hades before they had reached the safety of the upper world.

'There are two spades,' continued the fairy woman; 'one for you, and one for your double.'

Jack took one of the spades—it was small, and was made of silver; but the other Jack said with scorn:

'I shall be a king when I am old enough, and must I dig like a clown?'

'As you please,' said the black fairy, and walked away.

Then they all observed that a brown woman was standing there; and she stepped up and whispered in the boy king's ear. As he listened his sullen face became good tempered, and at last he said, in a gentle tone: 'Jack, I'm quite ready to begin if you are.'

'But where are we to dig?' asked Jack.

'There,' said a white fairy, stepping up and setting her foot on the grass just under the little hole. 'Dig down as deep as you can.'

So Mopsa and the crowd stood back, and the two boys began to dig; and greatly they enjoyed it, for people can dig so fast in Fairyland.

Very soon the hole was so deep that they had to jump into it, because they could not reach the bottom with their spades. 'This is very jolly indeed,' said Jack, when they had dug so much deeper that they could only see out of the hole by standing on tiptoe.

'Go on,' said the white fairy; so they dug till they came to a flat stone, and then she said: 'Now you can stamp. Stamp on the stone, and don't be afraid.' So the two Jacks began to stamp, and in such a little time that she had only half turned her head round, the flat stone gave way, for there was a hollow underneath it, and down went the boys, and utterly disappeared.

Then, while Mopsa and the crowd silently looked on, the white fairy lightly pushed the clods of earth towards the hole with the side of her foot, and in a very few minutes the hole was filled in, and that so completely and so neatly that when she had spread the turf on it, and given it a pat with her foot, you could not have told where it had been. Mopsa said not a word, for no fairy ever interferes with a stronger fairy; but she looked on earnestly, and when the white stranger smiled she was satisfied.

Then the white stranger walked away, and Mopsa and the fairies sat down on a bank under some splendid cedar trees. The beautiful castle looked fairer than ever in the afternoon sunshine; a lovely waterfall tumbled with a tinkling noise near at hand, and the bank was covered with beautiful wild flowers.

They sat for a long while, and no one spoke: what they were thinking of is not known, but sweet Mopsa often sighed.

At last a noise—a very, very slight noise, as of footsteps of people running—was heard inside the rock, and then a little quivering was seen in the wand. It quivered more and more as the sound increased. At last that which had looked like a door began to shake as if someone was pushing it from within. Then a noise was distinctly heard as of a key turning in the hole, and out burst the two Jacks, shouting for joy, and a whole troop of knights and squires and serving-men came rushing wildly forth behind them.

Oh, the joy of that meeting! Who shall describe it? Fairies by dozens came up to kiss the boy king's hand, and Jack shook hands with everyone that could reach him. Then Mopsa proceeded to the castle between the two Jacks, and the king's aunt came out to meet them, and welcomed her husband with tears of joy; for these fairies could laugh and cry when they pleased, and they naturally considered this a great proof of superiority.

After this a splendid feast was served under the great dome. The other fairy feasts that Jack had seen were nothing to it. The prince and his dame sat at one board, but Mopsa sat at the head of the great table, with the two Jacks one on each side of her.

Mopsa was not happy, Jack was sure of that, for she often sighed; and he thought this strange. But he did not ask her any questions, and he, with the boy king, related their adventures to her: how, when the stone gave way, they tumbled in and rolled down a sloping bank till they found themselves at the entrance of a beautiful cave, which was all lighted up with torches, and glittering with stars and crystals of all the colours in the world. There was a table spread with what looked like a splendid luncheon in this great cave, and chairs were set round, but Jack and the boy-king felt no inclination to eat anything, though they were hungry, for a whole nation of ants were creeping up the honey-pots. There were snails walking about over the table-cloth, and toads peeping out of some of the dishes.

So they turned away and, looking for some other door to lead them farther in, they at last found a very small one—so small that only one of them could pass through at a time.

They did not tell Mopsa all that had occurred on this occasion. It was thus:

The boy-king said: 'I shall go in first, of course, because of my rank.'

'Very well,' said Jack, 'I don't mind. I shall say to myself that you've gone in first to find the way for me, because you're my double. Besides, now I think of it, our Queen always goes last in a procession; so it's grand to go last. Pass in, Jack.'

'No,' answered the other Jack; 'now you have said that, I will not. You may go first.'

So they began to quarrel and argue about this, and it is impossible to say how long they would have gone on if they had not begun to hear a terrible and mournful sort of moaning and groaning, which frightened them both and instantly made them friends. They took tight hold of one another's hand, and again there came a loud sighing, and a noise of all sorts of lamentation, and it seemed to reach them through the little door.

Each of the boys would now have been very glad to go back, but neither liked to speak. At last Jack thought anything would be less terrible than listening to those dismal moans, so he suddenly dashed through the door, and the other Jack followed.

There was nothing terrible to be seen. They found themselves in a place like an immensely long stable; but it was nearly dark, and when their eyes got used to the dimness they saw that it was strewn with quantities of fresh hay, from which curious things like sticks stuck up in all directions. What were they?

'They are dry branches of trees,' said the boy-king.

'They are table legs turned upside down,' said Jack; but then the other Jack suddenly perceived the real nature of the thing, and he shouted out: 'No; they are antlers!'

The moment he said this the moaning ceased, hundreds of beautiful antlered heads were lifted up and the two boys stood before a splendid herd of stags; but they had had hardly time to be sure of this when the beautiful multitude rose and fled away into the darkness, leaving the two boys to follow as well as they could.

They were sure they ought to run after the herd, and they ran, but they soon lost sight of it, though they heard far on in front what seemed at first like a pattering of deers' feet, but the sound changed from time to time. It became heavier and louder, and then the clattering ceased, and it was evidently the tramping of a great crowd of men. At last they heard words, very glad and thankful words; people were crying to one another to make haste, lest the spell should come upon them again. Then the two Jacks, still running, came into a grand hall, which was quite full of knights and all sorts of fairy men, and there was the boy king's uncle, but he looked very pale. 'Unlock the door!' they cried. 'We shall not be safe till we see our new Queen. Unlock the door; we see light coming through the keyhole.'

The two Jacks came on to the front, and felt and shook the door. At last the boy-king saw a little golden key glittering on the floor, just where the one narrow sunbeam fell that came through the keyhole; so he snatched it up. It fitted, and out they all came, as you have been told.

When they had done relating their adventures, the new Queen's health was drunk. And then they drank the health of the boy-king, who stood up to return thanks, and, as is the fashion there, he sang a song. Jack thought it the most ridiculous song he had ever heard; but as everybody else looked extremely grave, he tried to be grave too. It was about Cock Robin and Jenny Wren, how they made a wedding feast,[21] and how the wren said she should wear her brown gown, and the old dog brought a bone to the feast.

> ' "He had brought them," he said, "some meat on a bone:
> They were welcome to pick it or leave it alone." '

The fairies were very attentive to this song; they seemed, if one may judge by their looks, to think it was rather a serious one. Then they drank Jack's health, and afterwards looked at him as if they expected him to sing too; but as he did not begin, he presently heard them whispering, and one asking another: 'Do you think he knows manners?'

So he thought he had better try what he could do, and he stood up and sang a song that he had often heard his nurse sing in the nursery at home.

> 'One morning, oh! so early, my belovèd, my belovèd,
> All the birds were singing blithely, as if never they would cease;
> 'Twas a thrush sang in my garden, "Hear the story, hear the story!"
>   And the lark sang, "Give us glory!"
>   And the dove said, "Give us peace!"
>
> 'Then I listened, Oh! so early, my belovèd, my belovèd,
> To that murmur from the woodland of the dove, my dear, the dove;
> When the nightingale came after, "Give us fame to sweeten duty!"
>   When the wren sang, "Give us beauty!"
>   She made answer, "Give us love!"
>
> 'Sweet is spring, and sweet the morning, my belovèd, my belovèd;
> Now for us doth spring, doth morning, wait upon the year's increase,
> And my prayer goes up, "Oh, give us, crowned in youth with marriage glory,
>   Give for all our life's dear story,
>   Give us love, and give us peace!" '

'A very good song too,' said the dame, at the other end of the table; 'only you made a mistake in the first verse. What the dove really said was, no doubt, "Give us peas." All kinds of doves and pigeons are very fond of peas.'

'It isn't peas, though,' said Jack. However, the court historian was sent

---

21. **wedding feast** Jack fails to see that the "ridiculous" song is directed at himself; the nursery rhyme is intended to remind Jack of "Jenny," the name he is trying to repress, and to prepare him for his displacement.

for to write down the song, and he came with a quill pen, and wrote it down as the dame said it ought to be.

Now all this time Mopsa sat between the two Jacks, and she looked very mournful—she said hardly a word.

When the feast was over, and everything had vanished, the musicians came in, for there was to be dancing; but while they were striking up the white fairy stepped in, and, coming up, whispered something in Jack's ear; but he could not hear what she said, so she repeated it more slowly, and still he could neither hear nor understand it.

Mopsa did not seem to like the white fairy: she leaned her face on her hand and sighed; but when she found that Jack could not hear the message, she said: 'That is well. Cannot you let things alone for this one day?' The fairy then spoke to Mopsa, but she would not listen; she made a gesture of dislike and moved away. So then this strange fairy turned and went out again, but on the doorstep she looked round, and beckoned to Jack to come to her. So he did; and then, as they two stood together outside, she made him understand what she had said. It was this:

'Her name was Jenny, her name was Jenny.'

When Jack understood what she said he felt so sorrowful; he wondered why she had told him, and he longed to stay in that great place with Queen Mopsa—his own little Mopsa, whom he had carried in his pocket, and taken care of, and loved.

He walked up and down, up and down, outside, and his heart swelled and his eyes filled with tears. The bells had said he was to go home, and the fairy had told him how to go. Mopsa did not need him, she had so many people to take care of her now; and then there was that boy, so exactly like himself that she would not miss him. Oh, how sorrowful it all was! Had he really come up the fairy river, and seen those strange countries, and run away with Mopsa over those dangerous mountains, only to bring her to the very place she wished to fly from, and there to leave her, knowing that she wanted him no more, and that she was quite content?

No; Jack felt that he could not do that. 'I will stay,' he said; 'they cannot make me leave her. That would be too unkind.'

As he spoke he drew near to the great yawning door, and looked in. The fairy folk were singing inside; he could hear their pretty chirping voices, and see their beautiful faces, but he could not bear it, and he turned away.

The sun began to get low, and all the west was dyed with crimson. Jack dried his eyes, and, not liking to go in, took one turn more.

'I will go in,' he said; 'there is nothing to prevent me.' He set his foot on the step of the door, and while he hesitated Mopsa came out to meet him.

'Jack,' she said, in a sweet mournful tone of voice. But he could not make any answer; he only looked at her earnestly, because her lovely eyes were not looking at him, but far away towards the west.

'He lives there,' she said, as if speaking to herself. 'He will play there again, in his father's garden.'

Then she brought her eyes down slowly from the roseflush in the cloud, and looked at him and said: 'Jack.'

'Yes,' said Jack; 'I am here. What is it that you wish to say?'

She answered: 'I am come to give you back your kiss.'

So she stooped forward as she stood on the step, and kissed him, and her tears fell on his cheek.

'Farewell!' she said, and she turned and went up the steps and into the great hall; and while Jack gazed at her as she entered, and would fain have followed, but could not stir, the great doors closed together again, and he was left outside.

Then he knew, without having been told, that he should never enter them any more. He stood gazing at the castle; but it was still—no more fairy music sounded.

How beautiful it looked in the evening sunshine, and how Jack cried!

Suddenly he perceived that reeds were growing up between him and the great doors: the grass, which had all day grown about the steps, was getting taller; it had long spear-like leaves, it pushed up long pipes of green stem, and they whistled.

They were up to his ankles, they were presently up to his waist; soon they were as high as his head. He drew back that he might see over them; they sprang up faster as he retired, and again he went back. It seemed to him that the castle also receded; there was a long reach of these great reeds between it and him, and now they were growing behind also, and on all sides of him. He kept moving back and back: it was of no use, they sprang up and grew yet more tall, till very shortly the last glimpse of the fairy castle was hidden from his sorrowful eyes.

The sun was just touching the tops of the purple mountains when Jack lost sight of Mopsa's home; but he remembered how he had penetrated the bed of reeds in the morning, and he hoped to have the same good fortune again. So on and on he walked, pressing his way among them as well as he could, till the sun went down behind the mountains, and the rosy sky turned

The Queen's Farewell

gold colour, and the gold began to burn itself away, and then all on a sudden he came to the edge of the reed-bed, and walked out upon a rising ground.

Jack ran up it, looking for the castle. He could not see it, so he climbed a far higher hill; still he could not see it. At last, after a toilsome ascent to the very top of the green mountain, he saw the castle lying so far, so very far off, that its peaks and battlements were on the edge of the horizon, and the evening mist rose while he was gazing, so that all its outlines were lost, and very soon they seemed to mingle with the shapes of the hill and the forest, till they had utterly vanished away.

Then he threw himself down on the short grass. The words of the white fairy sounded in his ears: 'Her name was Jenny'; and he burst into tears again, and decided to go home.

He looked up into the rosy sky, and held out his arms, and called: 'Jenny! O Jenny! come.'

In a minute or two he saw a little black mark overhead, a small speck, and it grew larger, and larger, and larger still, as it fell headlong down like a stone. In another instant he saw a red light and a green light, then he heard the winnowing noise of the bird's great wings, and she alighted at his feet, and said: 'Here I am.'

'I wish to go home,' said Jack, hanging down his head and speaking in a low voice, for his heart was heavy because of his failure.

'That is well,' answered the bird. She took Jack on her back, and in three minutes they were floating among the clouds.

As Jack's feet were lifted up from Fairyland he felt a little consoled. He began to have a curious feeling, as if this had all happened a good while ago, and then half the sorrow he had felt faded into wonder, and the feeling still grew upon him that these things had passed some great while since, so that he repeated to himself: 'It was a long time ago.'

Then he fell asleep, and did not dream at all, nor know anything more till the bird woke him.

'Wake up now, Jack,' she said; 'we are at home.'

'So soon!' said Jack, rubbing his eyes. 'But it is evening; I thought it would be morning.'

'Fairy time is always six hours in advance of your time,' said the bird. 'I see glow-worms down in the hedge, and the moon is just rising.'

They were falling so fast that Jack dared not look; but he saw the church, and the wood, and his father's house, which seemed to be starting up to meet him. In two seconds more the bird alighted, and he stepped down from her back into the deep grass of his father's meadow.

'Goodbye!' she said. 'Make haste and run in, for the dews are falling'; and before he could ask her one question, or even thank her, she made a wide sweep over the grass, beat her magnificent wings, and soared away.

It was all very extraordinary, and Jack felt shy and ashamed; but he knew he must go home, so he opened the little gate that led into the garden, and stole through the shrubbery, hoping that his footsteps would not be heard.

Then he came out on the lawn, where the flower-beds were, and he observed that the drawing-room window was open, so he came softly towards it and peeped in.

His father and mother were sitting there. Jack was delighted to see them, but he did not say a word, and he wondered whether they would be surprised at his having stayed away so long. His mother sat with her back to the open window, but a candle was burning, and she was reading aloud. Jack listened as she read, and knew that this was not in the least like anything that he had seen in Fairyland, nor the reading like anything that he had heard, and he began to forget the boy-king, and the apple-woman, and even his little Mopsa, more and more.

At last his father noticed him. He did not look at all surprised, but just beckoned to him with his finger to come in. So Jack did, and got upon his father's knee, where he curled himself up comfortably, laid his head on his father's waistcoat and wondered what he would think if he should be told about the fairies in somebody else's waistcoat pocket. He thought, besides, what a great thing a man was; he had never seen anything so large in Fairyland, nor so important; so, on the whole, he was glad he had come back, and felt very comfortable. Then his mother, turning over the leaf, lifted up her eyes and looked at Jack, but not as if she was in the least surprised, or more glad to see him than usual; but she smoothed the leaf with her hand, and began again to read, and this time it was about the Shepherd Lady

I

'Who pipes upon the long green hill,
 Where meadow grass is deep?
The white lamb bleats but followeth on—
 Follow the clean white sheep.
The dear white lady in yon high tower,
 She hearkeneth in her sleep.

'All in long grass the piper stands,
 Goodly and grave is he;
Outside the tower, at dawn of day,
 The notes of his pipe ring free.
A thought from his heart doth reach to hers:
 "Come down, O lady! to me."

'She lifts her head, she dons her gown:
  Ah! the lady is fair;
She ties the girdle on her waist,
  And binds her flaxen hair,
And down she stealeth, down and down,
  Down the turret stair.

'Behold him! With the flock he wons
  Along yon grassy lea.
"My shepherd lord, my shepherd love,
  What wilt thou, then, with me?
My heart is gone out of my breast,
  And followeth on to thee."

II

' "The white lambs feed in tender grass:
  With them and thee to bide,
How good it were," she saith at noon;
  "Albeit the meads are wide.
Oh! well is me," she saith when day
  Draws on to eventide.

'Hark! hark! the shepherd's voice. Oh, sweet!
  Her tears drop down like rain.
"Take now this crook, my chosen, my fere,
  And tend the flock full fain:
Feed them, O lady, and lose not one,
  Till I shall come again."

'Right soft her speech: "My will is thine,
  And my reward thy grace!"
Gone are his footsteps over the hill,
  Withdrawn his goodly face;
The mournful dusk begins to gather,
  The daylight wanes apace.

III

'On sunny slopes, ah! long the lady
  Feedeth her flock at noon;
She leads them down to drink at eve
  Where the small rivulets croon.
All night her locks are wet with dew,
  Her eyes outwatch the moon.

'Over the hills her voice is heard,
  She sings when light doth wane:
"My longing heart is full of love.
  When shall my loss be gain?

> My shepherd lord, I see him not,
> But he will come again." '

When she had finished Jack lifted his face and said, 'Mamma!' Then she came to him and kissed him, and his father said: 'I think it must be time this man of ours was in bed.'

So he looked earnestly at them both, and as they still asked him no questions, he kissed and wished them goodnight; and his mother said there were some strawberries on the sideboard in the dining-room, and he might have them for his supper.

So he ran out into the hall, and was delighted to find all the house just as usual, and after he had looked about him he went into his own room, and said his prayers. Then he got into his little white bed, and comfortably fell asleep.

That's all.

Part Four

A TRIO OF ANTIFANTASIES
SPEAKING LIKENESSES

✳

Speaking Likenesses is probably the most brilliant, and is certainly the most unsettling, work in this collection. It is also our most unapologetically unhappy one. Like many of our authors, Christina Rossetti found in children's literature a perverse release from the cheerfulness demanded of good women. The sullen children in *Speaking Likenesses* are punished into happiness, but their punishments are fiendish enough to satisfy the balefulness they claim to exorcise. "I trust you will all be very good and happy together," says Flora's mother blandly at the beginning of a ghastly birthday party. To be good is to be happy, but to be happy is impossible.

The violence of *Speaking Likenesses* is familiar even in classic Victorian children's texts: Lewis Carroll's *Alice* books carry their heroine into a more pugnacious country than the well-mannered England she escapes, while Hans Christian Andersen's hopeful protagonists are mauled and mutilated for their expectations. Christina Rossetti, however, may be more deeply troubling than these sentimentally sadistic men, for *Speaking Likenesses* offers as rationale neither the nonsense of *Alice* nor the moralistic coherence of Andersen's tales. *Speaking Likenesses* appears to be sternly moral. It eschews the puns and nonsense verses of Wonderland, but its morality is as nonsensical as Carroll's language games. Unlike Andersen's grim logic, Rossetti's punishments fit no crimes. Perpetuated on unhappy children, they are detonations from an angry world.

Speaking Likenesses is told under suitably grim conditions. Most Victorian storytelling was associated with festivity and conviviality; even hallucinatory ghost stories such as Ewing's "Christmas Crackers" (reprinted in part 2) were part of Yuletide jollity. But *Speaking Likenesses,* which Rossetti dismissed as a "Christmas trifle" when her publishers brought out the book in December of 1873, relies on a narrator who goads her audience into ferocious charitable sewing. "No help no story," proclaims the narrating aunt to her five little nieces. "However, as I see thimbles coming out, I conclude you choose story and labour." Story and labor, charity and sewing: these disciplines are as necessary as punishments in combating a world whose cruelty is familiar and casual. Even Edith, the one relatively unscathed child in the tales, reflects on the retributions that would follow if she fails to boil a kettle of water: "Her relations, friends, and other natural enemies," she is convinced, "would be arriving, and would triumph over her" if she mismanaged this simplest of tasks. Story and labor, sewing and charity, do not make the world kinder, but they may steel girls and women against "natural enemies" who are everything and everybody.

By having the utilitarian aunt insist that her "dear little girls" busy themselves with their sewing and darning needles, Rossetti refers her reader back to her highly popular children's book, *Sing-Song: A Nursery Rhyme Book* (1872), whose title page featured Arthur Hughes's fine drawing of a little girl industriously hemming a pocket-handkerchief with needle and thread. But whereas Victorian reviewers praised the lyrics of *Sing-Song* for offering what one of them, John Colvin, called "a music suited to baby ears," the asperity of the aunt who delights in subverting the expectations of her listeners struck them as unpleasantly jarring. The defiant negativism of a book which Rossetti had originally called *Nowhere* seemed an ugly addition to the Victorian canon of childhood. Surveying the children's books that appeared for Christmas of 1873, John Ruskin pronounced the lavishly illustrated *Speaking Likenesses* the most distasteful of the lot. He held on to it, he claimed, simply "for the mere wonder of it: how could she or Arthur Hughes sink so low after their pretty nursery rhymes?" (*Works,* 37:155).

The book that offended Ruskin flaunts its antagonism to "pretty" conventions. The narrator herself seems designed as a parodic version of all those stern but kindly schoolmistresses and godmothers, governesses and maiden aunts so prevalent in more than a century of didactic children's books by English women writers, from Sarah Fielding's 1749 *The Governess* to Margaret Gatty's 1858 *The Fairy Godmother.* In their own youth, the Rossetti children had professed to despise moral fables such as *Sandford and Merton* or *The Fairchild Family.* Although *Speaking Likenesses* belongs to that genre, the revulsion seems to have lingered when Rossetti deformed her "mentoria" (in Mitzi Myers's apt name for such female educators) into a tyrannical bully. The despot who demands absolute silence as she tells her stories turns on her listeners with a sarcastic impatience that springs from perpetual annoyance. She dismisses their questions derisively: "How many children were there at supper?—Well, I have not the least idea, Laura, but they made quite a large party: suppose we say a hundred thousand."

Rossetti appears to derive a perverse pleasure in creating a storyteller hostile to the fantastic and the extraordinary. If, as noted in our introduction to the previous section, Jack, the protagonist of Ingelow's *Mopsa the Fairy*, eventually found unimaginativeness a blessing, the aunt who acts as pseudo-narrator of *Speaking Likenesses* positively exults in literal-mindedness. Paradoxically, she again and again denies her imaginative control over stories of her own invention. When the children plead that she build a second tale around a frog who had played a trivial role in the first story, she insists on her incompetence because, quite simply, she "was not there." In a final indignity that again undercuts the children's hope that their aunt might prove to be as "wonderful" a purveyor of magic as some of her rival storytellers, the frog in the second story remains as insignificant as ever. Even more than such rivals as Ingelow and Carroll, Rossetti knows that to carry children into exotic wonderlands may only expose the darker side of an adult imagination.

Rossetti's own imagination, therefore, delights in acts of suppression. Ingelow's dull "Captain Jack" had at least some claim to the role of hero, but the frog who assumes no prominence in a nonstory describing a nonaction is the creation of a writer whose subversive indirections go beyond Ingelow's. Wonder, Rossetti's narrator seems to have decided, is not good for children, and in this belief at least the narrator may well act as a "speaking likeness" of the author herself. In *Speaking Likenesses* the writer who had created in "Goblin Market" a poem every bit as fantastic and spellbinding as "The Ancient Mariner" went out of her way to fashion an antifantasy. In addressing girls on the verge of womanhood, she no longer pretended to create "music suited to baby ears."

Like many traditional fairy stories relying on triple wishes or featuring triple journeys successively undertaken by three siblings, *Speaking Likenesses* is composed mystically in threes. Not only are there three stories, but in the most powerful, the first and the last, the unhappy heroine endures three ordeals: Flora is forced to play three increasingly vicious games, and Maggie undergoes three temptations on her cold Christmas Eve journey to the doctor's house. The stories ascend as the Christian soul does, from Flora's birthday hell to Edith's purgatory—whose fire fortunately never quite gets lit—to the martyred Maggie's chilly heaven. If, in the first and most memorable story, Flora celebrates her eighth birthday in hell, her hell is surely, like a junior version of Sartre's, other children; moreover, it is not a prophecy warning the girl away from sin, but a dark mirror of the already-existing England into which Flora is going to have to grow up.

Like the Nick of Rossetti's cautionary parable (reprinted in part 2), Flora is guilty of a bad soul, not bad deeds. Unlike Nick, though, Flora wishes no harm. Her tense birthday party arouses nothing worse than understandable world-weariness: "is it really worth while to be eight years old and have a birthday, if this is what comes of it?" Most children's stories would teach Flora a chipper affirmative, but the dream-vision Rossetti inflicts on her is so grim an image of community that it can only reinforce her birthday despair.

No nonsense leavens the birthday party in the yew tree; Flora finds kindness only in the tables, chairs, and tea things that accommodate themselves to the malevolent children who use them. The obligingness of objects and the malice of people are nightmare refractions of the cozy consumerism of Rossetti's England, whose technology—displayed in rich profusion at the Great Exhibition of 1851—promised a paradise of domestic comfort to aggressive middle-class spectators who were far from domesticated themselves.

The children prepare for play by a dark inversion of the pantomime transformation scenes that were supposed to delight young audiences: they change into hybrid animals and instruments of pain, becoming the antagonism that rules them. The warlike games inflicted on Flora, and the solitary violence of the Queen whose birthday is celebrated so inhumanely, are closer to Victorian realities than Lewis Carroll's whimsical parodies. The "horrid game" of Hunt the Pincushion, whose sole object is to torture the smallest, weakest, fattest, most crippled, or otherwise ostracized child, exemplifies all the sadistic games England boasted of: the team sports that were the focus of public schools, socializing boys to their imperial destiny, and the equally savage marriage games that determined the destinies of respectable girls. Ostensibly, the Queen's birthday party will drive out the demons in Flora's angry heart, but actually it is an unstinting immersion in the society Flora already inhabits.

The second game, Self Help, that heroic nostrum of the aspiring middle class, is a still balder image of social reality than Hunt the Pincushion. In it, "the boys were players, the girls were played"—a pithy picture of Victorian gender relations—in a game whose sole purpose is assault. The final pastime replicates the claustrophobic Victorian family. Surveillance and starvation, those components of respectable family life, lead, in *Speaking Like-nesses,* to an apocalyptic final battle incited by the Queen. Arthur Hughes' powerful illustration of this battle makes explicit not only the interchange-ability of children and monsters, but the untamable aggression that com-poses Flora's dream of social reality.

When Flora is finally jarred out of her dream to chastened expectations—of birthday parties and of people in general—we experience no Carrollian regret at the loss of her dream country. For, as Rossetti makes clear, she has dreamt only the world she knows. Most dreams in children's literature offer some sort of escape from social constraints. In Burnett's "Behind the White Brick" (reprinted in part 2), for instance, Jem tried to erase her anger at her punitive aunt by dreaming of a dainty storybook child called Flora (in what seems a deliberate tribute to Rossetti's story). Jem's escapist dream is ineffectual as a sublimation of her anger, but Rossetti's Flora dreams ines-capability. Her dream vision is an uncompromising indoctrination.

The second tale, a purgatorial account of Edith trying vainly to boil water in a forest, is (like purgatory itself perhaps) notable for its flatness compared to the vivid violence of the first and last stories. Unlike the dreamer Flora, Edith must operate in a waking world. Her communion with the "wood abo-rigines" is shorn of the transfiguring potential girls like Snow White are al-lowed to experience with forest creatures. By simply and blandly reflecting Edith's domestic incompetence, these animals are the equivalent of the "speaking likenesses" Flora encountered in the previous story. Flora's birth-day party has prepared us for one conflagration at least; we are warned that Edith is ominously proud. Still, the chastening fire we anticipate never blazes. One after another, the lucifers Edith tries to light are wasted. It is just as well, for, as the frog had earlier noted (though no one heard him) the kettle that Edith tried to bring to a boiling point contained no water.

Read superficially, this middle story, which seems to endorse the bland moral that little girls should not play with matches, leaves us only with an uneasy sense of disastrous potential. But Edith's story is, of course, an elab-orate put-on in which Rossetti uses the aunt as her surrogate to mock the expectations of her own audience. We are teased by the multiple narrative possibilities only to find each of these squelched. The frog turns into no magical frog prince; a fox who appears out of a LaFontaine fable, only to look at some sour grapes and walk away, performs no function other than the useless task of brushing Edith's frock with his tail. Yet one seemingly trivial detail catches the attention of one of the aunt's listeners: the kettle hangs on a tripod. When asked, "Why a tripod, Aunt?" the narrator explains with seeming matter-of-factness: "Three sticks, Maude, are the fewest that can stand up firmly by themselves; two would tumble down and four are not wanted."

Rossetti here calls attention to the structure she has fashioned. Her own narrative tripod stands on the bare minimum of three stories; a fourth tale is not wanted, yet the two stronger legs of her structure, the first and third stories about monster children, need the support of the weak, middle non-story to prop up the whole. It is this shaky and shortest tale that holds together her triptych. Less fantastical than the others, it is the most destructive, for its mockery is aimed at Wordsworthian exaltations of the powerful child. When Edith and her animal friends fail to light the fire, the girl's old nurse comes with a new box of matches and some newspapers and kindling. The bonfire she starts bursts into flames as the crestfallen child hurries home.

The climax of *Speaking Likenesses* is an allegory of dying. Instead of fire at the end, we get cold. Like those classic nineteenth-century nightmares, *Frankenstein* and *Dracula*, *Speaking Likenesses* ends in a perishing arctic world. In most children's stories, Christmas Eve is a time of delicious magic, but for Maggie, the only underprivileged child we meet, delicious possibilities are forbidden dreams that culminate in visions of death.

Walking through the forest to the wealthy doctor's house with Christmas booty he has carelessly forgotten, Maggie heroically refrains from touching the accoutrements of jollity she carries. On her journey, this paragon of deprivation confronts and resists three temptations, all of them images of her own denied desires, overcoming in turn her loneliness, her hunger, and her longing for a rest that will freeze into death.

Through these self-conquests, her journey home is transfigured. Omens consecrate her resistance; her earlier temptations turn into animals she can rescue, and the northern lights blaze in celebration of her self-denial. Her path seems more magnificent than a mere return: it may lead to heaven. Maggie's joyful return to her grandmother's warmth is less a conventional happy ending than a celestial welcome.

✳

Salvation, in *Speaking Likenesses,* is the death of desire, and may be death itself. Flora dreamed the savagery of growing up; Edith mocked our narrative expectations by becoming the nonheroine of a nonstory; only Maggie achieves something like a happy ending by killing all her needs.

Today, the misery and violence of these three stories would certainly, in the judgment of Ruskinian experts, render them unfit for children, but in Victorian England, children's literature accommodated a more liberal emotional range than it does today. Had *Speaking Likenesses* been marketed as adult fiction, Victorian critics would certainly have denounced Rossetti's harsh view of both childhood and growth. In a century whose taboos differed from our own, children alone were licensed to share her despair.

Speaking Likenesses

Come sit round me, my dear little girls, and I will tell you a story. Each of you bring her sewing, and let Ella take pencils and colour-box, and try to finish some one drawing of the many she has begun. What Maude! pouting over that nice clean white stocking because it wants a darn? Put away your pout and pull out your needle, my dear; for pouts make a sad beginning to my story. And yet not an inappropriate beginning, as some of you may notice as I go on. Silence! Attention! All eyes on occupations, not on me lest I should feel shy! Now I start my knitting and my story together.

✳

Whoever saw Flora on her birthday morning, at half-past seven o'clock on that morning, saw a very pretty sight. Eight years old to a minute, and not awake yet. Her cheeks were plump and pink, her light hair was all tumbled, her little red lips were held together as if to kiss some one; her eyes also, if you could have seen them, were blue and merry, but for the moment they had gone fast asleep and out of sight under fat little eyelids. Wagga the dog was up and about, Muff the cat was up and about, chirping birds were up and about; or if they were mere nestlings and so could not go about (supposing, that is, that there were still a few nestlings so far on in summer), at least they sat together wide awake in the nest, with wide open eyes and most of them with wide open beaks, which was all they could do: only sleepy Flora slept on, and dreamed on, and never stirred.

Her mother stooping over the child's soft bed woke her with a kiss. "Good morning, my darling, I wish you many and many happy returns of the day," said the kind, dear mother: and Flora woke up to a sense of sunshine, and of pleasure full of hope. To be eight years old when last night one was

merely seven,[1] this is pleasure: to hope for birthday presents without any doubt of receiving some, this also is pleasure. And doubtless you now think so, my children, and it is quite right that so you should think: yet I tell you, from the sad knowledge of my older experience, that to every one of you a day will most likely come when sunshine, hope, presents and pleasure will be worth nothing to you in comparison with the unattainable gift of your mother's kiss.

On the breakfast table lay presents for Flora: a story-book full of pictures from her father, a writing-case from her mother, a gilt pincushion like a hedgehog from nurse, a box of sugarplums and a doll from Alfred her brother and Susan her sister; the most tempting of sugarplums, the most beautiful of curly-pated dolls, they appeared in her eyes.

A further treat was in store. "Flora," said her mother, when admiration was at last silent and breakfast over: "Flora, I have asked Richard, George, Anne and Emily to spend the day with you and with Susan and Alfred. You are to be queen of the feast, because it is your birthday; and I trust you will all be very good and happy together."

Flora loved her brother and sister, her friend Emily, and her cousins Richard, George and Anne: indeed I think that with all their faults these children did really love each other. They had often played together before; and now if ever, surely on this so special occasion they would play pleasantly together. Well, we shall see.

1. **merely seven** Carroll's Humpty-Dumpty tells the *Looking-Glass* Alice, who is seven years and six months old, that anything past seven (her age in *Wonderland)* is an "uncomfortable sort of age."

Anne with her brothers arrived first: and Emily having sent to ask permission, made her appearance soon after accompanied by a young friend, who was spending the holidays with her, and whom she introduced as Serena.

[What an odd name, Aunt!—Yes, Clara, it is not a common name, but I knew a Serena once; though she was not at all like this Serena, I am happy to say.]

Emily brought Flora a sweet-smelling nosegay; and Serena protested that Flora was the most charming girl she had ever met, except of course dearest Emily.

"Love me," said Serena, throwing her arms round her small hostess and giving her a clinging kiss: "I will love you so much if you will only let me love you."

The house was a most elegant house, the lawn was a perfect park, the elder brother and sister frightened her by their cleverness: so exclaimed Serena: and for the moment silly little Flora felt quite tall and superior, and allowed herself to be loved very graciously.

After the arrivals and the settling down, there remained half-an-hour before dinner, during which to cultivate acquaintance and exhibit presents. Flora displayed her doll and handed round her sugar-plum box. "You took more than I did and it isn't fair," grumbled George at Richard: but Richard retorted, "Why, I saw you picking out the big ones." "Oh," whined Anne, "I'm sure there were no big ones left when they came to me." And Emily put in with a smile of superiority: "Stuff, Anne: you got the box before Serena and I did, and *we* don't complain." "But there wasn't one," persisted Anne. "But there were dozens and dozens," mimicked George, "only you're such a greedy little baby." "Not one," whimpered Anne. Then Serena remarked soothingly: "The sugar-plums were most delicious, and now let us admire the lovely doll. Why, Flora, she must have cost pounds and pounds."

Flora, who had begun to look rueful, brightened up: "I don't know what she cost, but her name is Flora, and she has red boots with soles. Look at me opening and shutting her eyes, and I can make her say Mamma. Is she not a beauty?" "I never saw half such a beauty," replied smooth Serena. Then the party sat down to dinner.

Was it fact? Was it fancy? Each dish in turn was only fit to be found fault with. Meat underdone, potatoes overdone, beans splashy, jam tart not sweet enough, fruit all stone; covers clattering, glasses reeling, a fork or two dropping on the floor. Were these things really so? or would even finest strawberries and richest cream have been found fault with, thanks to the children's mood that day?

[Were the dishes all wrong, Aunt?—I fancy not, Ella; at least, not more so than things often are in this world without upsetting every one's patience. But hear what followed.]

Sad to say, what followed was a wrangle. An hour after dinner blindman's buff in the garden began well and promised well: why could it not go on well? Ah, why indeed? for surely before now in that game toes have been trodden on, hair pulled, and small children overthrown. Flora fell down and accused Alfred of tripping her up, Richard bawled out that George broke away when fairly caught, Anne when held tight muttered that Susan could see in spite of bandaged eyes. Susan let go, Alfred picked up his little sister, George volunteered to play blindman in Susan's stead: but still pouting and grumbling showed their ugly faces, and tossed the apple of discord to and fro as if it had been a pretty plaything.

[What apple, Aunt?—The Apple of Discord, Clara, which is a famous apple your brothers would know all about, and you may ask them some day. Now I go on.]

Would you like, any of you, a game at hide-and-seek in a garden, where there are plenty of capital hiding-places and all sorts of gay flowers to glance at while one goes seeking? I should have liked such a game, I assure you, forty years ago. But these children on this particular day could not find it in their hearts to like it. Oh dear no. Serena affected to be afraid of searching along the dusky yew alley unless Alfred went with her; and at the very same moment Flora was bent on having him lift her up to look down into a hollow tree in which it was quite obvious Susan could not possibly have hidden. "It's my birthday," cried Flora; "it's my birthday." George and Richard pushed each other roughly about till one slipped on the gravel walk and grazed his hands, when both turned cross and left off playing. At last in sheer despair Susan stepped out of her hiding-place behind the summer-house: but even then she did her best to please everybody, for she brought in her hand a basket full of ripe mulberries which she had picked up off the grass as she stood in hiding.

Then they all set to running races across the smooth sloping lawn: till Anne tumbled down and cried, though she was not a bit hurt; and Flora, who was winning the race against Anne, thought herself ill-used and so sat and sulked. Then Emily smiled, but not good-naturedly, George and Richard thrust each a finger into one eye and made faces at the two cross girls,

The Apple of Discord

Serena fanned herself, and Alfred looked at Susan, and Susan at Alfred, fairly at their wits' end.

An hour yet before tea-time: would another hour ever be over? Two little girls looking sullen, two boys looking provoking: the sight was not at all an encouraging one. At last Susan took pouting Flora and tearful Anne by the hand, and set off with them for a walk perforce about the grounds; whilst Alfred fairly dragged Richard and George after the girls, and Emily arm-in-arm with Serena strolled beside them.

The afternoon was sunny, shady, breezy, warm, all at once. Bees were humming and harvesting as any bee of sense must have done amongst so many blossoms: leafy boughs danced with their dancing shadows; bell flowers rang without clappers: —

[Could they, Aunt?—Well, not exactly, Maude: but you're coming to much more wonderful matters!]

Now and then a pigeon cooed its soft water-bottle note; and a long way off sheep stood bleating.

Susan let go the little hot hands she held, and began as she walked telling a story to which all her companions soon paid attention—all except Flora.

Poor little Flora: was this the end of her birthday? was she eight years old at last only for this? Her sugar-plums almost all gone and not cared for, her chosen tart not a nice one, herself so cross and miserable: is it really worth while to be eight years old and have a birthday, if this is what comes of it?

"—So the frog did not know how to boil the kettle; but he only replied: I can't bear hot water," went on Susan telling her story. But Flora had no heart to listen, or to care about the frog. She lagged and dropped behind not noticed by any one, but creeping along slowly and sadly by herself.

Down the yew alley she turned, and it looked dark and very gloomy as she passed out of the sunshine into the shadow. There were twenty yew trees on each side of the path, as she had counted over and over again a great many years ago when she was learning to count; but now at her right hand there stood twenty-one: and if the last tree was really a yew tree at all, it was at least a very odd one, for a lamp grew on its topmost branch. Never before either had the yew walk led to a door: but now at its further end stood a door with bell and knocker, and "Ring also" printed in black letters on a brass plate; all as plain as possible in the lamplight.

Flora stretched up her hand, and knocked and rang also.

She was surprised to feel the knocker shake hands with her, and to see the bell handle twist round and open the door. "Dear me," thought she,

The Knocker Shakes Hands with Flora

"why could not the door open itself instead of troubling the bell?" But she only said, "Thank you," and walked in.

The door opened into a large and lofty apartment, very handsomely furnished. All the chairs were stuffed arm-chairs, and moved their arms and shifted their shoulders to accommodate sitters. All the sofas arranged and rearranged their pillows as convenience dictated. Footstools glided about, and rose or sank to meet every length of leg. Tables were no less obliging, but ran on noiseless castors here or there when wanted. Tea-trays ready set out, saucers of strawberries, jugs of cream, and plates of cake, floated in, settled down, and floated out again empty, with considerable tact and good taste: they came and went through a square hole high up in one wall, beyond which I presume lay the kitchen. Two harmoniums, an accordion, a

pair of kettledrums and a peal of bells played concerted pieces behind a screen, but kept silence during conversation. Photographs and pictures made the tour of the apartment, standing still when glanced at and going on when done with. In case of need the furniture flattened itself against the wall, and cleared the floor for a game, or I dare say for a dance. Of these remarkable details some struck Flora in the first few minutes after her arrival, some came to light as time went on. The only uncomfortable point in the room, that is, as to furniture, was that both ceiling and walls were lined throughout with looking-glasses: but at first this did not strike Flora as any disadvantage; indeed she thought it quite delightful, and took a long look at her little self full length.

[Jane and Laura, don't *quite* forget the pocket-handkerchiefs you sat down to hem. See how hard Ella works at her fern leaves, and what pains she is taking to paint them nicely. Yes, Maude, that darn will do: now your task is ended, but if I were you I would help Clara with hers.]

The room was full of boys and girls, older and younger, big and little. They all sat drinking tea at a great number of different tables; here half a dozen children sitting together, here more or fewer; here one child would preside all alone at a table just the size for one comfortably. I should tell you that the tables were like telescope tables; only they expanded and contracted of themselves without extra pieces, and seemed to study everybody's convenience.

Every single boy and every single girl stared hard at Flora and went on staring: but not one of them offered her a chair, or a cup of tea, or anything else whatever. She grew very red and uncomfortable under so many staring pairs of eyes: when a chair did what it could to relieve her embarrassment by pressing gently against her till she sat down. It then bulged out its own back comfortably into hers, and drew in its arms to suit her small size. A footstool grew somewhat taller beneath her feet. A table ran up with tea for one; a cream-jug toppled over upon a saucerful of strawberries, and then righted itself again; the due quantity of sifted sugar sprinkled itself over the whole.

[How could it sprinkle itself?—Well, Jane, let us suppose it sprang up in its china basin like a fountain; and overflowed on one side only, but that of course the right side, whether it was right or left.]

Flora could not help thinking everyone very rude and ill-natured to go on staring without speaking, and she felt shy at having to eat with so many eyes upon her: still she was hot and thirsty, and the feast looked most tempting. She took up in a spoon one large, very large strawberry with plenty of cream; and was just putting it into her mouth when a voice called out crossly: "You shan't, they're mine." The spoon dropped from her startled hand, but without any clatter: and Flora looked round to see the speaker.

[Who was it? Was it a boy or a girl?—Listen, and you shall hear, Laura.]

The speaker was a girl enthroned in an extra high armchair; with a stool as high as an ottoman under her feet, and a table as high as a chest of drawers in front of her. I suppose as she had it so she liked it so, for I am sure all the furniture laid itself out to be obliging. Perched upon her hair she wore a coronet made of tinsel; her face was a red face with a scowl: sometimes perhaps she looked nice and pretty, this time she looked ugly. "You shan't, they're mine," she repeated in a cross grumbling voice: "it's my birthday, and everything is mine."

Flora was too honest a little girl to eat strawberries that were not given her: nor could she, after this, take even a cup of tea without leave. Not to tantalize her, I suppose, the table glided away with its delicious untasted load; whilst the armchair gave her a very gentle hug as if to console her.

If she could only have discovered the door Flora would have fled through it back into the gloomy yew-tree walk, and there have moped in solitude, rather than remain where she was not made welcome: but either the door was gone, or else it was shut to and lost amongst the multitude of mirrors. The birthday Queen, reflected over and over again in five hundred mirrors, looked frightful, I do assure you: and for one minute I am sorry to say that

Flora's fifty million-fold face appeared flushed and angry too; but she soon tried to smile good-humouredly and succeeded, though she could not manage to feel very merry.

[But, Aunt, how came she to have fifty million faces? I don't understand. —Because in such a number of mirrors there were not merely simple reflections, but reflections of reflections, and reflections of reflections of reflections, and so on and on and on, over and over again, Maude: don't you see?]

The meal was ended at last: most of the children had eaten and stuffed quite greedily; poor Flora alone had not tasted a morsel. Then with a word and I think a kick from the Queen, her high footstool scudded away into a corner: and all the furniture taking the hint arranged itself as flat as possible round the room, close up against the walls.

[And across the door?—Why, yes, I suppose it may have done so, Jane: such active and willing furniture could never be in the way anywhere.—And was there a chimney corner?—No, I think not: that afternoon was warm we know, and there may have been a different apartment for winter. At any rate, as this is all make-believe, I say No. Attention!]

All the children now clustered together in the middle of the empty floor; elbowing and jostling each other, and disputing about what game should first be played at. Flora, elbowed and jostled in their midst, noticed points of appearance that quite surprised her. Was it themselves, or was it their clothes? (only who indeed would wear such clothes, so long as there was another suit in the world to put on?) One boy bristled with prickly quills like a porcupine, and raised or depressed them at pleasure; but he usually kept them pointed outwards. Another instead of being rounded like most people was facetted at very sharp angles. A third caught in everything he came near, for he was hung round with hooks like fishhooks. One girl exuded a sticky fluid and came off on the fingers; another, rather smaller, was slimy and slipped through the hands. Such exceptional features could not but prove inconvenient, yet patience and forbearance might still have done something towards keeping matters smooth: but these unhappy children seemed not to know what forbearance was; and as to patience, they might have answered me nearly in the words of a celebrated man—"Madam, I never saw patience."

[Who was the celebrated man, Aunt?—Oh, Clara, you an English girl and not know Lord Nelson![2] But I go on.]

"Tell us some new game," growled Hooks threateningly, catching in Flora's hair and tugging to get loose.

Flora did not at all like being spoken to in such a tone, and the hook hurt her very much. Still, though she could not think of anything new, she tried to do her best, and in a timid voice suggested "Les Grâces."

"That's a girl's game," said Hooks contemptuously.

---

2. **not know Lord Nelson!** The mock protestation may satirize more than the incongruous mixing of fantasy and history lessons. If little Clara, an "English girl," does not know the name of the hero of Trafalgar, Horatio Nelson (1758–1805), she would hardly catch the patriotic ring of the middle name of one of Rossetti's more formidable rivals in the market of children's literature, Juliana *Horatia* Ewing.

"It's as good any day as a boy's game," retorted Sticky.

"I wouldn't give *that* for your girl's games," snarled Hooks, endeavouring to snap his fingers, but entangling two hooks and stamping.

"Poor dear fellow!" drawled Slime, affecting sympathy.

"It's quite as good," harped on Sticky: "It's as good or better."

Angles caught and would have shaken Slime, but she slipped through his fingers demurely.

"Think of something else, and let it be new," yawned Quills, with quills laid for a wonder.

"I really don't know anything new," answered Flora half crying: and she was going to add, "But I will play with you at any game you like, if you will teach me;" when they all burst forth into a yell of "Cry, baby, cry!—Cry, baby, cry!"—They shouted it, screamed it, sang it: they pointed fingers, made grimaces, nodded heads at her. The wonder was she did not cry outright.

At length the Queen interfered: "Let her alone;—who's she? It's *my* birthday, and we'll play at Hunt the Pincushion."

So Hunt the Pincushion it was. This game is simple and demands only a moderate amount of skill. Select the smallest and weakest player (if possible let her be fat: a hump is best of all), chase her round and round the room, overtaking her at short intervals, and sticking pins into her here or there as it happens: repeat, till you choose to catch and swing her; which concludes the game. Short cuts, yells, and sudden leaps give spirit to the hunt.

[Oh, Aunt, what a horrid game! surely there cannot be such a game?—Certainly not, Ella: yet I have seen before now very rough cruel play, if it can be termed play.—And did they get a poor little girl with a hump?—No, Laura, not this time: for]

The Pincushion was poor little Flora. How she strained and ducked and swerved to this side or that, in the vain effort to escape her tormentors! Quills with every quill erect tilted against her, and needed not a pin: but Angles whose corners almost cut her, Hooks who caught and slit her frock, Slime who slid against and passed her, Sticky who rubbed off on her neck and plump bare arms, the scowling Queen, and the whole laughing scolding pushing troop, all wielded longest sharpest pins, and all by turns overtook her. Finally the Queen caught her, swung her violently round, let go suddenly,—and Flora losing her balance dropped upon the floor. But at least that game was over.

Do you fancy the fall jarred her? Not at all: for the carpet grew to such a depth of velvet pile below her, that she fell quite lightly.

Flora and the Children in the Enchanted Room

Indeed I am inclined to believe that even in that dreadful sport of Hunt the Pincushion, Flora was still better off than her stickers: who in the thick of the throng exasperated each other and fairly maddened themselves by a free use of cutting corners, pricking quills, catching hooks, glue, slime, and I know not what else. Slime, perhaps, would seem not so much amiss for its owner: but then if a slimy person cannot be held, neither can she hold fast. As to Hooks and Sticky they often in wrenching themselves loose got worse damage than they inflicted: Angles many times cut his own fingers with his edges: and I don't envy the individual whose sharp quills are flexible enough to be bent point inwards in a crush or a scuffle. The Queen must perhaps be reckoned exempt from particular personal pangs: but then, you see, it was her birthday! And she must still have suffered a good deal from the eccentricities of her subjects.

The next game called for was Self Help. In this no adventitious aids were tolerated, but each boy depended exclusively on his own resources. Thus pins were forbidden: but every natural advantage, as a quill or fishhook, might be utilized to the utmost.

[Don't look shocked, dear Ella, at my choice of words; but remember that my birthday party is being held in the Land of Nowhere. Yet who knows whether something not altogether unlike it has not ere now taken place in the Land of Somewhere? Look at home, children.]

The boys were players, the girls were played (if I may be allowed such a phrase): all except the Queen who, being Queen, looked on, and merely administered a slap or box on the ear now and then to some one coming handy. Hooks, as a Heavy Porter, shone in this sport; and dragged about with him a load of attached captives, all vainly struggling to unhook themselves. Angles, as an Ironer, goffered or fluted several children by sustained pressure. Quills, an Engraver, could do little more than prick and scratch with some permanence of result. Flora falling to the share of Angles had her torn frock pressed and plaited after quite a novel fashion: but this was at any rate preferable to her experience as Pincushion, and she bore it like a philosopher.

Yet not to speak of the girls, even the boys did not as a body extract unmixed pleasure from Self Help; but much wrangling and some blows allayed their exuberant enjoyment. The Queen as befitted her lofty lot did, perhaps, taste of mirth unalloyed; but if so, she stood alone in satisfaction as in dignity. In any case, pleasure palls in the long run.

The Queen yawned a very wide loud yawn: and as everyone yawned in sympathy the game died out.

A supper table now advanced from the wall to the middle of the floor, and armchairs enough gathered round it to seat the whole party. Through the square hole,—not, alas! through the door of poor Flora's recollection,—floated in the requisite number of plates, glasses, knives, forks, and spoons; and so many dishes and decanters filled with nice things as I certainly never saw in all my lifetime, and I don't imagine any of you ever did.

[How many children were there at supper?—Well, I have not the least idea, Laura, but they made quite a large party: suppose we say a hundred thousand.]

This time Flora would not take so much as a fork without leave: wherefore as the Queen paid not the slightest attention to her, she was reduced to look hungrily on while the rest of the company feasted, and while successive dainties placed themselves before her and retired untasted. Cold turkey, lobster salad, stewed mushrooms, raspberry tart, cream cheese, a bumper of champagne, a méringue, a strawberry ice, sugared pine apple, some greengages: it may have been quite as well for her that she did not feel at liberty to eat such a mixture: yet it was none the less tantalizing to watch so many good things come and go without taking even one taste, and to see all her companions stuffing without limit. Several of the boys seemed to think nothing of a whole turkey at a time: and the Queen consumed with her own mouth and of sweets alone one quart of strawberry ice, three pine apples, two melons, a score of méringues, and about four dozen sticks of angelica, as Flora counted.

After supper there was no need for the furniture to withdraw: for the whole birthday party trooped out through a door (but still not through Flora's door) into a spacious playground. What they may usually have played at I cannot tell you; but on this occasion a great number of bricks happened to be lying about on all sides mixed up with many neat piles of stones, so the children began building houses: only instead of building from without as most bricklayers do, they built from within, taking care to have at hand plenty of bricks as well as good heaps of stones, and inclosing both themselves and the heaps as they built; one child with one heap of stones inside each house.

[Had they window panes at hand as well?—No, Jane, and you will soon see why none were wanted.]

I called the building material bricks: but strictly speaking there were no bricks at all in the playground, only brick-shaped pieces of glass instead. Each of these had the sides brilliantly polished; whilst the edges, which were meant to touch and join, were ground, and thus appeared to acquire a certain tenacity. There were bricks (so to call them) of all colours and many different shapes and sizes. Some were fancy bricks wrought in open work, some were engraved in running patterns, others were cut into facets or blown into bubbles. A single house might have its blocks all uniform, or of twenty different fashions.

Yet, despite this amount of variety, every house built bore a marked resemblance to its neighbour: colours varied, architecture agreed. Four walls, no roof, no upper floor; such was each house: and it needed neither window nor staircase.

All this building occupied a long long time, and by little and little a very gay effect indeed was produced. Not merely were the glass blocks of beautiful tints; so that whilst some houses glowed like masses of ruby, and others shone like enormous chrysolites or sapphires, others again showed the milkiness and fiery spark of a hundred opals, or glimmered like moonstone: but the playground was lighted up, high, low, and on all sides, with coloured lamps. Picture to yourselves golden twinkling lamps like stars high overhead, bluish twinkling lamps like glowworms down almost on the ground; lamps like illuminated peaches, apples, apricots, plums, hung about with the profusion of a most fruitful orchard. Should we not all have liked to be there with Flora, even if supper was the forfeit?

Ah no, not with Flora: for to her utter dismay she found that she was being built in with the Queen. She was not called upon to build: but gradually the walls rose and rose around her, till they towered clear above her head; and being all slippery with smoothness, left no hope of her ever being able to clamber over them back into the road home, if indeed there was any longer such a road anywhere outside. Her heart sank within her, and she could scarcely hold up her head. To crown all, a glass house which contained no vestige even of a cupboard did clearly not contain a larder: and Flora began to feel sick with hunger and thirst, and to look forward in despair to no breakfast to-morrow.

Acoustics must have been most accurately studied, —

[But, Aunt, what are acoustics?—The science of sounds, Maude: pray now exercise your acoustical faculty.]

As I say, they must have been most accurately studied, and to practical purpose, in the laying out of this particular playground; if, that is, to hear distinctly everywhere whatever might be uttered anywhere within its limits, was the object aimed at. At any rate, such was the result.

Their residences at length erected, and their toils over, the youthful architects found leisure to gaze around them and bandy compliments.

First: "Look," cried Angles, pointing exultantly: "just look at Quills, as red as fire. Red doesn't become Quills. Quills's house would look a deal better without Quills."

"Talk of becomingness," laughed Quills, angrily, "you're just the colour of a sour gooseberry, Angles, and a greater fright than we've seen you yet. Look at him, Sticky, look whilst you have the chance:" for Angles was turning his green back on the speaker.

But Sticky—no wonder, the blocks *she* had fingered stuck together!—Sticky was far too busy to glance around; she was engrossed in making faces at Slime, whilst Slime returned grimace for grimace. Sticky's house was blue, and turned her livid: Slime's house—a very shaky one, ready to fall to pieces at any moment, and without one moment's warning:—Slime's house, I say, was amber-hued, and gave her the jaundice. These advantages were not lost on the belligerents, who stood working each other up into a state of frenzy, and having got long past variety, now did nothing but screech over and over again: Slime: "You're a sweet beauty,"—and Sticky (incautious Sticky!): "You're another!"

Quarrels raged throughout the playground. The only silent tongue was Flora's.

Suddenly, Hooks, who had built an engraved house opposite the Queen's bubbled palace (both edifices were pale amethyst coloured, and trying to the complexion), caught sight of his fair neighbour, and, clapping his hands, burst out into an insulting laugh.

"You're another!" shrieked the Queen (the girls all alike seemed well-nigh destitute of invention).

Her words were weak, but as she spoke she stooped: and clutched—shook—hurled—the first stone.

"Oh don't, don't, don't," sobbed Flora, clinging in a paroxysm of terror, and with all her weight, to the royal arm.

That first stone was, as it were, the first hailstone of the storm: and soon stones flew in every direction and at every elevation. The very atmosphere seemed petrified. Stones clattered, glass shivered, moans and groans resounded on every side. It was as a battle of giants: who would excel each emulous peer, and be champion among giants?

The Queen. All that had hitherto whistled through mid-air were mere pebbles and chips compared with one massive slab which she now heaved up—poised—prepared to launch—

"Oh don't, don't, don't," cried out Flora again, almost choking with sobs. But it was useless. The ponderous stone spun on, widening an outlet through the palace wall on its way to crush Hooks. Half mad with fear, Flora flung herself after it through the breach—

And in one moment the scene was changed. Silence from human voices and a pleasant coolness of approaching twilight surrounded her. High overhead a fleet of rosy grey clouds went sailing away from the west, and outstripping these, rooks on flapping black wings flew home to their nests in the lofty elm trees, and cawed as they flew. A few heat-drops pattered down on a laurel hedge hard by, and a sudden gust of wind ran rustling through the laurel leaves. Such dear familiar sights and sounds told Flora that she was sitting safe within the home precincts: yes, in the very yew-tree alley, with its forty trees in all, not one more, and with no mysterious door leading out of it into a hall of misery.

She hastened indoors. Her parents, with Alfred, Susan, and the five visitors, were just sitting down round the tea-table, and nurse was leaving the drawing-room in some apparent perturbation.

Wagga wagged his tail, Muff came forward purring, and a laugh greeted Flora. "Do you know," cried George, "that you have been fast asleep ever so long in the yew walk, for I found you there? And now nurse was on her way to fetch you in, if you hadn't turned up."

Flora said not a word in answer, but sat down just as she was, with tumbled frock and hair, and a conscious look in her little face that made it very sweet and winning. Before tea was over, she had nestled close up to Anne, and whispered how sorry she was to have been so cross.

And I think if she lives to be nine years old and give another birthday party, she is likely on that occasion to be even less like the birthday Queen of her troubled dream than was the Flora of eight years old: who, with dear friends and playmates and pretty presents, yet scarcely knew how to bear a few trifling disappointments, or how to be obliging and good-humoured under slight annoyances.

※

"Aunt, Aunt!"

"What, girls?"

"Aunt, do tell us the story of the frog who couldn't boil the kettle."

"But I was not there to hear Susan tell the story."

"Oh, but you know it, Aunt."

"No, indeed I do not. I can imagine reasons why a frog would not and should not boil a kettle, but I never heard any such stated."

"Oh, but try. You know, Aunt, you are always telling *us* to try."

"Fairly put, Jane, and I will try, on condition that you all help me with my sewing."

"But we got through our work yesterday."

"Very well, Maude, as you like: only no help no story. I have too many poor friends ever to get through *my* work. However, as I see thimbles coming out, I conclude you choose story and labour. Look, these breadths must be run together, three and three. Ella, if you like to go to your music, don't stay listening out of ceremony: still, if you do stay, here are plenty of buttonholes to overcast. Now are we all seated and settled? Then listen. The frog and his peers will have to talk, of course; but that seems a marvel scarcely worth mentioning after Flora's experience."

※

Edith and a teakettle were spending one warm afternoon together in a wood. Before proceeding with my story, let me introduce each personage to you more particularly.

The wood should perhaps be called a grove rather than a wood, but in Edith's eyes it looked no less than a forest. About a hundred fine old beech-trees stood together, with here and there an elegant silver birch drooping in their midst. Besides these there was one vine which, by some freak, had been planted near the centre of the group, and which, year after year, trailing its long graceful branches over at least a dozen neighbours, dangled bunches of pale purple grapes among its leaves and twisted tendrils. The kettle was of brilliant copper, fitted up with a yellow glass handle: it was also on occasion a pleasing singer. Edith was a little girl who thought herself by no means such a very little girl, and at any rate as wise as her elder brother, sister, and nurse. I should be afraid to assert that she did not reckon herself as wise as her parents: but we must hope not, for her own sake.

The loving mother had planned a treat for her family that afternoon. A party of friends and relations were to assemble in the beech-wood, and partake of a gipsy tea: some catch-singing might be managed, cold supper should be laid indoors, and if the evening proved very delightful, the open-air entertainment might be prolonged till full-moonrise.

Preparations were intrusted to nurse's care, others of the household working under her, and she promising to go down to the beeches at least half an hour before the time fixed for the party, to see that all was ready. An early dinner throughout the house and no lessons in the schoolroom set the afternoon free for the gipsy feast.

After dinner Edith dressed her doll in its best clothes, tied on its broad-brimmed hat and veil, and hooked a miniature parasol into its waistband. Her sister was busy arranging flowers for the supper-table, her brother was out taking a walk, nurse was deep in jams, sandwiches, and delicacies in general; for nurse, though going by her old name, and still doing all sorts of things for her old baby, was now in fact housekeeper.

None of these could bestow much attention on Edith, who, doll in arm, strolled along into the kitchen, and there paused to watch cook rolling puff paste at her utmost speed. Six dozen patty-pans stood in waiting, and yawned as they waited.

Edith set down her doll on the window-seat and began to talk, whilst cook, with a goodnatured red face, made her an occasional random answer, right or wrong as it happened.

"What are we to have besides sandwiches and tarts?"

"Cold fowls, and a syllabub,[3] and champagne, and tea and coffee, and potato-rolls, and lunns, and tongue, and I can't say what besides."

"Where are the fowls, cook?"

"In the larder, where they ought to be, Miss Edith, not lying about in a hot kitchen."

"Do you like making tarts?"

"I like tarts, but not often."

"Cook, you're not attending to what I say."

"No, the attendance is just what I should not have liked."

Edith looked about till a bright copper kettle on a shelf caught her eye. "Is that the kettle for tea?"

"Yes, miss."

The doll gazing out of window was forgotten, while, mounting on a stool, Edith reached down the kettle.

"I will carry the kettle out ready."

"The fire will have to be lighted first," answered cook, as she hurried her tarts into the oven, and ran out to fetch curled parsley from the kitchen-garden.

"I can light the fire," called out Edith after her, though not very anxious to make herself heard: and thus it happened that cook heard nothing beyond the child's voice saying something or other of no consequence.

So Edith found a box of lucifers,[4] and sallied forth kettle in hand. Striking on the burnished copper, the sun's rays transformed that also into a re-

3. **syllabub** a frothy dessert made of milk and spices
4. **lucifers** safety matches, so called because of their sulphurous smell

splendent portable sun of dazzling aspect. The beautiful sunshine bathed garden, orchard, field, lane and wood; bathed flower, bush and tree; bathed bird, beast and butterfly. Frisk, the Newfoundland dog, and Cosy, the Persian cat, meeting their young mistress, turned round, to give her their company. Crest, the cockatoo, taking a constitutional on the lawn, fluttered up to her shoulder and perched there. The four went on together, Frisk carrying the kettle in his mouth, and Crest pecking at the match-box. Several lucifers dropped out, and not more than six reached their destination.

Edith knew that the gipsy party was to be held just where the vine grew, and thither she directed her steps. A pool, the only pool in the wood,

gleamed close at hand, and mirrored in its still depths the lights, shadows, and many greens of beech-tree, birch-tree, and vine. How she longed for a cluster of those purple grapes which, hanging high above her head, swung to and fro with every breath of wind; now straining a tendril, now displacing a leaf, now dipping towards her but never within reach. Still, as Edith was such a very wise girl, we must not suppose she would stand long agape after unattainable grapes: nor did she. Her business just then was to boil a kettle, and to this she bent her mind.

Three sticks and a hook dependent therefrom suggested a tripod erected for the kettle: and so it was.

[Why a tripod, Aunt?—I have been wondering at the no remarks, but here comes one at last. Three sticks, Maude, are the fewest that can stand up firmly by themselves; two would tumble down, and four are not wanted. The reel? here it is: and then pass it to Clara.]

Within the legs of the tripod lay a fagot, supported on some loose bricks. The fagot had been untied, but otherwise very little disturbed.

By standing on the fagot, Edith made herself more than tall enough to hang the kettle on its hook: then jumping down she struck her first match. A flash followed; and in one instant the match went out, as might have been expected in the open air and with no shelter for the flame. She struck a second lucifer, with the like result: a third, a fourth, with no better success. After this it was high time to ponder well before sacrificing a fifth match; for two only remained in the broken box.

Edith sat down to reflect, and stayed quiet so long, with her cheek leaning on her hand and her eyes fixed on a lucifer, that the aborigines of the wood grew bold and gathered round her.

[Who were the aborigines, Aunt?—The natives of the wood, Laura; the creatures born and bred there generation after generation.]

A squirrel scampered down three boughs lower on the loftiest beech-tree, and cracked his beech-mast audibly. A pair of wood pigeons advanced making polite bows. A mole popped a fleshy nose and a little human hand out of his burrow—popped them in, and popped them out again. A toad gazed deliberately round him with his eye like a jewel. Two hedgehogs came along and seated themselves near the toad. A frog—

[*The* frog, Aunt?—Yes, Laura,]

—*the* frog hopped at a leisurely pace up the pond bank, and squatted among the long grasses at its edge.

The wonder is that Frisk, Cosy, and Crest, let this small fry come and go at pleasure and unmolested; but, whatever their motive may have been, they did so. They sat with great gravity right and left of their mistress, and kept themselves to themselves.

Edith's situation had now become, as it seems to me, neither pleasant nor dignified. She had volunteered to boil a kettle, and could not succeed even in lighting a fire. Her relations, friends, and other natural enemies would be arriving, and would triumph over her: for if her fire would not light, her kettle would certainly never boil. She took up the fifth lucifer and prepared to strike—paused—laid it back in the box: for it was her last but one. She sat on thinking what to do, yet could think of nothing to the purpose: of nothing better, that is, than of striking the match and running the risk. What should she do?

She had not even so much as half an eye to spare for the creatures around

Edith Thinking How She Shall Light Her Fire and Boil Her Kettle

her, whilst they on their side concentrated their utmost attention on her. The pigeons left off bowing: the squirrel did not fetch a second beechmast.

"Oh dear!" exclaimed Edith at last; "what shall I do?"

Two voices, like two gurgling bottles, answered, "Couldn't you fly away, dear?" and the two pigeons bowed like one pigeon.

Edith was so thoroughly preoccupied by her troubles as to have very little room left in her mind for surprise: still, she did just glance at the pigeons before answering, "I wish you'd advise something sensible, instead of telling me to fly without wings."

"If you can only get so much as one twig to light," called out the squirrel hopefully, "I'll fan the flame with my tail."

"Ah," retorted Edith, "but that's just it: how am I to light the first twig with lucifers that do nothing but go out?"

A pause. "What should you say," suggested the mole, rubbing his hands together, "to my rearranging the sticks?"

"Very well," answered Edith, "do what you please." But she looked as if she did not expect much good to result from the mole's co-operation.

However, the mole clambered up one of the bricks, and then by pushing and pulling with his handy little hands, really did arrange the sticks in a loose heap full of hollows and tunnels for admitting currents of air; and so far matters looked promising.

The two hedgehogs sat silent and staring; why they came and why they stayed never appeared from first to last; but the frog hopped past them, and enquired, with a sudden appearance of interest, "Does not the kettle want filling?" No one noticed what he said, so he added under his breath, "Perhaps it is full already."

[Was it full, Aunt?—No, Maude, there was not a drop in it: so after all it was fortunate that it hung above black sticks instead of over a blazing fire, or it would soon have been spoilt. Remember, girls, never put an empty kettle on the fire, or you and it will rue the consequence.]

The toad peered with his bright eye in among the sticks. "I should vote," said he mildly, "that the next lucifer be held and struck inside the heap, to protect the spark from draughts."

[How came the toad to be so much cleverer than his neighbours, Aunt?— Well, Jane, I suppose such a bright thought may have occurred to him rather than to the rest, because toads so often live inside stones: at least, so people have said. And suppose his father, grandfather and great-grandfather all inhabited stones, the idea of doing everything inside something may well have come naturally to him.]

The toad's suggestion roused Edith from despondency to action. She knelt down by the tripod, although just there the ground was sprinkled with brickdust and sawdust; thrust both hands in amongst the wood, struck a match, saw it flash,—and die out. "Try again," whispered the toad; and as she could devise no better plan she tried again.

This sixth and last venture was crowned with success. One twig caught fire, as a slight crackling followed by a puff of smoke attested. The squirrel took his seat on a brick and whisked his tail to and fro. The hedgehogs turning their backs on the smoke, sniffed in the opposite direction; waiting as I suppose for the event, though they showed not the least vestige of interest in it.

"Now," cried the frog hopping up and down in his excitement and curiosity, "Now to boil the kettle."

But that first spark of success was followed by a dim, smoky, fitful smouldering which gave merely the vaguest promise of a coming blaze. A pair of bellows would have answered far better than the squirrel's tail: and though, with a wish to oblige, the two wood-pigeons fluttered round and round the tripod, they did not the slightest good.

Just then a fox bustled up, and glanced askance at Frisk: but receiving a reassuring and friendly nod, joined the party under the shady vine-branches. This fox was a tidy person, and like most foxes always carried about a brush with him: so without more ado he went straight up to Edith, and gave her dusty frock a thorough brushing all round. Next he wrapped his fore paws about the vine, and shook it with all his force; but as no grapes fell,[5] though several bunches bobbed up and down and seemed ready to drop into his mouth, he gave one leap upwards off all four feet at once towards the lowest cluster he could spy; this also failing he shook his head, turned up his nose, shrugged his shoulders, muttered, "They must be sour" (and this once I suspect the fox was right), trotted away, and was soon lost to view among the beech-trees.

"Now," cried the frog once more, "now for the kettle."

"Boil it yourself," retorted Edith.

So the frog did not know how to boil the kettle, but he only replied, "I can't bear hot water." This you may remark was a startling change of tone in the frog: but I suppose he was anxious to save his credit. Now if he had only taken time to look at what was under his very eyes, he might have saved his credit without belying his principles: for

5. **no grapes fell** an allusion to the fable by LaFontaine

The fire had gone out!
And here my story finishes: except that I will just add how
As Edith in despair sat down to cry,
As the pigeons withdrew bowing and silent,
As the squirrel scudded up his beech-tree again,
As the mole vanished underground,
As the toad hid himself behind a toadstool,
As the two hedgehogs yawned and went away yawning,
As the frog dived,
As Frisk wagged, Cosy purred, and Crest murmured, "Pretty Cockatoo," to console their weeping mistress,
Nurse arrived on the ground with a box of lucifers in one hand, two fire-wheels in the other, and half-a-dozen newspapers under her arm, and exclaimed, "Oh, my dear child, run indoors as fast as you can: for your mother, father, brother and sister are hunting up and down all over the house looking for you; and cook is half out of her wits because she cannot find the kettle."

※

"My dear children, what is all this mysterious whispering about?"
"It's Jane, Aunt."
"Oh, Maude, I'm sure it's you quite as much."
"Well then, Jane and Maude, what is it?"
"We were only saying that both your stories are summer stories, and we want you to tell us a winter story some day. That's all, Aunty dear."
"Very well, Maudy dear; but don't say 'only,' as if I were finding fault with you. If Jane and you wish for a winter story, my next shall freeze hard. What! now? You really do allow me very little time for invention!"
"And please, Aunt, be wonderful."
"Well, Laura, I will try to be wonderful; but I cannot promise first-rate wonders on such extremely short notice. Ella, you sitting down too? Here is my work for you all, the same as yesterday, and here comes my story."

※

Old Dame Margaret kept the village fancy shop. Her window was always filled with novelties and attractions, but about Christmastide, it put forth extra splendours, and as it were blossomed gorgeously. Flora's doll, her sugar-plum box and hedgehog pincushion, came I should say from this very window; and though her hoops and sticks for *les grâces* can scarcely have looked smart enough for a place of honour, they emerged probably from somewhere behind the counter.

[Did Edith's doll come out of the window too?—Yes, Clara, if Flora's did I have no doubt Edith's did; for as they say in the Arabian Nights, "each was more beautiful than the other."]

In spite of her gay shop, Dame Margaret was no fine lady, but a nice simple old woman who wore plain clothes, and made them last a long time: and thus it was that over and over again she found money to give or lend among her needy neighbours. If a widow's cow died, or a labourer's cottage was burnt down, or if half-a-dozen poor children were left orphans, Dame Margaret's purse would be the first to open, and the last to shut; though she was very cautious as to helping idlers who refused to help themselves, or drunkards who would only do more harm with more money.

I dare say her plain clothes and her plain table (for she kept a plain table too) were what enabled her, amongst other good deeds, to take home little Maggie, her orphan granddaughter, when the child was left almost without kith or kin to care for her. These two were quite alone in the world: each was the other's only living relation, and they loved each other very dearly.

Hour after hour on Christmas Eve, business raged in Dame Margaret's shop. I shrink from picturing to myself the run on burnt almonds, chocolate, and "sweeties" of every flavour, all done up in elegant fancy boxes; the run on wax dolls, wooden dolls, speaking dolls, squeaking dolls; the run on woolly lambs and canaries with removable heads; the run on everything in general. Dame Margaret and Maggie at her elbow had a busy time behind their counter, I do assure you.

[Did Maggie serve too?—Yes, Jane; and it was her delight to run up steps and reach down goods from high shelves.]

About three o'clock, the shop happened for a moment to be empty of customers, and Dame Margaret was glancing complacently round upon her diminished stock, when her eye lighted on some parcels which had been laid on a chair and forgotten. "Oh dear, Maggie," exclaimed she, "the doctor's young ladies have left behind them all the tapers for their Christmas tree, and I don't know what besides." Now that doctor resided with his family in a large house some distance out of the village, and the road to it lay through the outskirts of an oak forest.

"Let me take them, Granny," cried Maggie eagerly: "and perhaps I may get a glimpse of the Christmas tree."

"But it will soon be dark."

"Oh, Granny, I will make haste: do, please, let me go."

So kind Dame Margaret answered, "Yes; only be sure to make great haste:" and then she packed up the forgotten parcels very carefully in a basket. Not merely the red tapers, but a pound of vanilla chocolate, a beautiful bouncing ball, and two dozen crackers, had all been left behind.

Basket on arm, Maggie started for the doctor's house: and as she stepped out into the cold open air it nipped her fingers and ears, and little pug-nose. Cold? indeed it was cold, for the thermometer marked *half-a-dozen* degrees of frost; every pond and puddle far and near was coated with thick sheet ice, or turned to block ice from top to bottom; every branch of every bare oak shivered in a keen east wind. How the poor little birds kept warm, or whether in fact any did keep warm on the leafless boughs, I cannot tell: I only know that many a thrush and sparrow died of cold that winter, whilst robin redbreast begged crumbs at cottage windows. His snug scarlet waistcoat could scarcely keep hungry robin's heart warm; and I am afraid to think about his poor little pretty head with its bright eye.

Maggie set off on her journey with a jump and a run, and very soon got a fall: for without any suspicion of what awaited her she set her foot on a loose lump of ice, and down she went, giving the back of her head a sounding thump. She was up again directly, and ran on as if nothing had happened; but whether her brain got damaged by the blow, or how else it may have been, I know not; I only know that the thwack seemed in one moment to fill the atmosphere around her with sparks, flames and flashes of lightning; and that from this identical point of time commenced her marvellous adventures.

Were the clouds at play? they went racing across the sky so rapidly! Were the oaks at play? they tossed their boughs up and down in such rattling confusion! Maggie on her travels began to think that she too should dearly like a game of play, when an opening in the forest disclosed to her a green glade, in which a party of children were sporting together in the very freest and easiest manner possible.

Such a game! Such children! If they had not been children they must inevitably have been grasshoppers. They leaped over oaks, wrestled in mid-air, bounded past a dozen trees at once; two and two they spun round like whirlwinds; they darted straight up like balloons; they tossed each other about like balls. A score of dogs barking and gambolling in their midst were evidently quite unable to keep up with them.

[Didn't they all get very hot, Aunt?—Very hot indeed, Maude, I should think.]

The children's cheeks were flushed, their hair streamed right out like

Maggie Meets the Fairies in the Wood

comets' tails; you might have heard and seen their hearts beat, and yet no one appeared in the least out of breath. Positively they had plenty of breath amongst them to time their game by singing.

"One, two, three," they sang, —

"One, two, three," they sang, —

"One, two, three," they sang, "and away,"—as they all came clustering like a swarm of wasps round astonished Maggie.

How she longed for a game with them! She had never in her life seen anything half so funny, or so sociable, or so warming on a cold day. And we must bear in mind that Maggie had no playfellows at home, and that cold winter was just then at its very coldest. "Yes," she answered eagerly; "yes, yes; what shall we play at?"

A glutinous-looking girl in pink cotton velvet proposed: "Hunt the pincushion."

"No, Self Help," bawled a boy clothed in something like porcupine skin.

[Oh, Aunt, are these those monstrous children over again?—Yes, Ella, you really can't expect me not to utilize such a brilliant idea twice.]

"No, running races," cried a second girl, wriggling forward through the press like an eel.

"No, this,"—"No, that,"—"No, the other," shouted every one in general, bounding here, spinning there, jumping up, clapping hands, kicking heels, in a tempest of excitement.

"Anything you please," panted Maggie, twirling and leaping in emulation, and ready to challenge the whole field to a race; when suddenly her promise to make haste crossed her mind—her fatal promise, as it seemed to her; though you and I, who have as it were peeped behind the scenes, may well believe that it kept her out of no very delightful treat.

She ceased jumping, she steadied her swinging basket on her arm, and spoke resolutely though sadly: "Thank you all, but I mustn't stop to play with you, because I promised Granny to make haste. Good-bye;"—and off she started, not venturing to risk her decision by pausing or looking back; but feeling the bouncing ball bounce in her basket as if it too longed for a game, and hearing with tingling ears a shout of mocking laughter which followed her retreat.

The longest peal of laughter comes to an end. Very likely, as soon as Maggie vanished from view among the oak-trees the boisterous troop ceased laughing at her discomfiture; at any rate, they did not pursue her; and she soon got beyond the sound of their mirth, whilst one by one the last echoes left off laughing and hooting at her. Half glad that she had persisted

in keeping her word, yet half sorry to have missed so rare a chance, Maggie
trudged on solitary and sober. A pair of woodpigeons alighting almost at her
feet pecked about in the frozen path, but could not find even one mouthful
for their little empty beaks: then, hopeless and silent, they fluttered up and
perched on a twig above her head. The sight of these hungry creatures
made Maggie hungry from sympathy; yet it was rather for their sakes than
for her own that she lifted the cover of her basket and peered underneath
it, to see whether by any chance kind Granny had popped in a hunch or so
of cake, —alas! not a crumb. Only there lay the chocolate, sweet and tempting, looking most delicious through a hole in its gilt paper.

Would birds eat chocolate, wondered Maggie, —

[Would they, Aunt?—Really, I hardly know myself, Laura: but I should
suppose some might, if it came in their way.]

—and she was almost ready to break off the least little corner and try,
when a sound of rapid footsteps coming along startled her; and hastily shutting her basket, she turned to see who was approaching.

A boy: and close at his heels marched a fat tabby cat, carrying in her
mouth a tabby kitten. Or was it a real boy? He had indeed arms, legs, a
head, like ordinary people: but his face exhibited only one feature, and that
was a wide mouth.[6] He had no eyes; so how he came to know that Maggie

6. **wide mouth** The Mouth Boy, who plays Wolf to Maggie's Little Red Riding Hood,
clearly is a "speaking likeness" of the hunger she represses as successfully as Lizzie does in
Rossetti's *Goblin Market.*

and a basket were standing in his way I cannot say: but he did seem some-how aware of the fact; for the mouth, which could doubtless eat as well as speak, grinned, whined, and accosted her: "Give a morsel to a poor starving beggar."

"I am very sorry," replied Maggie, civilly; and she tried not to stare, because she knew it would be rude to do so, though none the less amazed was she at his aspect; "I am very sorry, but I have nothing I can give you."

"*Nothing,* with all that chocolate!"

"The chocolate is not mine, and I cannot give it you," answered Maggie bravely: yet she felt frightened; for the two stood all alone together in the forest, and the wide mouth was full of teeth and tusks, and began to grind them.

"Give it me, I say. I tell you I'm starving:" and he snatched at the basket.

"I don't believe you are starving," cried Maggie, indignantly, for he looked a great deal stouter and sleeker than she herself did; and she started aside, hugging her basket close as the beggar darted out a lumpish-looking hand to seize it. "I'm hungry enough myself, but I wouldn't be a thief!" she shouted back to her tormentor, whilst at full speed she fled away from him, wondering secretly why he did not give chase, for he looked big enough and strong enough to run her down in a minute: but after all, when she spoke so resolutely and seemed altogether so determined, it was he that hung his head, shut his mouth, and turned to go away again faster and faster, till he fairly scudded out of sight among the lengthening shadows.

Had this forest road always been so long? Never before certainly had it appeared so extremely long to Maggie. Hungry and tired, she lost all spirit, and plodded laggingly forward, longing for her journey's end, but without energy enough to walk fast. The sky had turned leaden, the wind blew bleaker than ever, the bare boughs creaked and rattled drearily. Poor des-olate Maggie! drowsiness was creeping over her, and she began to wish above all things that she might just sit down where she stood and go fast asleep: never mind food, or fire, or bed; only let her sleep.

[Do you know, children, what would most likely have happened to Maggie if she had yielded to drowsiness and slept out there in the cold?—What, Aunt?—Most likely she would never have woke again. And then there would have been an abrupt end to my story.]

Yet she recollected her promise to make haste, and went toiling on and on and on, step after tired step. At length she had so nearly passed through the forest that five minutes more would bring her out into the by-road which led straight to the doctor's door, when she came suddenly upon a party of

Maggie and the Sleepers in the Wood

some dozen persons sitting toasting themselves around a glowing gipsy fire, and all yawning in nightcaps or dropping asleep.

They opened their eyes half-way, looked at her, and shut them again. They all nodded. They all snored. Whoever woke up yawned; whoever slept snored. Merely to see them and hear them was enough to send one to sleep.

A score or so of birds grew bold, hopped towards the kindly fire, and perched on neighbouring shoulder, hand, or nose. No one was disturbed, no one took any notice.

If Maggie felt drowsy before, she felt ready to drop now: but remembering her promise, and rousing herself by one last desperate effort, she shot past the tempting group. Not a finger stirred to detain her, not a voice proffered a word, not a foot moved, not an eye winked.

At length the cold long walk was ended, and Maggie stood ringing the doctor's door-bell, wide awake and on tiptoe with enchanting expectation: for surely now there was a good prospect of her being asked indoors, warmed by a fire, regaled with something nice, and indulged with a glimpse of the Christmas tree bending under its crop of wonderful fruit.

Alas, no! The door opened, the parcel was taken in with a brief "Thank you," and Maggie remained shut out on the sanded doorstep.

Chilled to the bone, famished, cross, and almost fit to cry with disappointment, Maggie set off to retrace her weary steps. Evening had closed in, the wind had lulled, a few snowflakes floated about in the still air and seemed too light to settle down. If it looked dim on the open road, it looked dimmer still in the forest: dim, and solitary, and comfortless.

Were all the sleepers gone clean away since Maggie passed scarcely a quarter of an hour before? Surely, yes: and moreover not a trace of their glowing fire remained, not one spark, not one ember. Only something whitish lay on the ground where they had been sitting: could it be a nightcap? Maggie stooped to look and picked up, not a nightcap, but a wood-pigeon with ruffled feathers and closed eyes, which lay motionless and half frozen in her hand. She snuggled it tenderly to her, and kissed its poor little beak and drooping head before she laid it to get warm within the bosom of her frock. Lying there, it seemed to draw anger and discontent out of her heart: and soon she left off grumbling to herself, and stepped forward with renewed energy, because the sooner the pigeon could be taken safe indoors out of the cold, the better.

Mew, mew, mew: such a feeble pitiful squeak of a mew! Just about where the Mouth had met her a mew struck upon Maggie's ear, and wide she opened both ears and eyes to spy after the mewer. Huddled close up against the gnarled root of an oak, crouched a small tabby kitten all alone, which mewed and mewed and seemed to beg for aid. Maggie caught up the helpless creature, popped it into her empty basket, and hurried forward.

But not far, before she paused afresh: for suddenly, just in that green glade where the grasshopper children in general and one glutinous girl in particular had stood hooting her that very afternoon, her foot struck against some soft lump, which lay right in her path and made no effort to move out of harm's way. What could it be? She stooped, felt it, turned it over, and it was a shorthaired smooth puppy, which put one paw confidingly into her hand, and took the tip of her little finger between its teeth with the utmost

friendliness. Who could leave such a puppy all abroad on such a night? Not Maggie, for one. She added the puppy to her basketful, —and a basketful it was then!—and ran along singing quite merrily under her burden.

And when, the forest shades left behind her, she went tripping along through the pale clear moonlight, in one moment the sky before her flashed with glittering gold, and flushed from horizon to zenith with a rosy glow; for the northern lights came out, and lit up each cloud as if it held lightning, and each hill as if it smouldered ready to burst into a volcano. Every oak-tree seemed turned to coral, and the road itself to a pavement of dusky carnelian.

Then at last she once more mounted a door-step and rang a door-bell, but this time they were the familiar step and bell of home. So now when the door opened she was received, not with mere "Thank you," but with a loving welcoming hug; and not only what she carried, but she herself also found plenty of light and warmth awaiting all arrivals, in a curtained parlour set out for tea. And whilst Maggie thawed, and drank tea, and ate buttered toast in Granny's company, the pigeon thawed too, and cooed and pecked up crumbs until it perched on the rail of a chair, turned its head contentedly under its wing, and dropped fast asleep; and the kitten thawed too; and lapped away at a saucerful of milk, till it fell asleep on the rug; and the puppy—well, I cannot say the puppy thawed too, because he was warm and cordial when Maggie met him; but he wagged his stumpy tail, stood bolt upright and begged, munched tit-bits, barked, rolled over, and at last settled down under the table to sleep: after all which, Dame Margaret and Maggie followed the good example set them, and went to bed and to sleep.

THE END.

Biographical Sketches

Frances Hodgson Burnett (1849–1924)

The acute deprivation Frances Eliza Hodgson experienced in her early life and her subsequent move, as a teenager, from England to America eventually fueled her enormous success as a writer. Her profitable literary career allowed Burnett to recover a family fortune lost when her father, a merchant who had provided Manchester industrialists with opulent home furnishings, suddenly died in 1853. Left with five young children, her mother tried to take over the furnishing business, but after losing her house and status, she decided in 1865 to move to Tennessee, where the family's vicissitudes only worsened. Frances soon began to make money by putting to use the literary training she had received as a voracious reader of fiction. Placing stories in ladies' magazines, she soon graduated to more ambitious fictional constructs and achieved recognition with her first full-length book, *That Lass o' Lowries* (1877), in which she exploited the fascination which a British class system held for American readers insisting on their own ideology of classlessness. This same formula would be given a new twist when, after at least a dozen more adult books, the publication of *Little Lord Fauntleroy* (1886) made Burnett the best-selling author of children's books on both sides of the Atlantic. By then the mother of two boys, Burnett quickly transformed *Fauntleroy* into an equally well-received play (1889) on the London and New York stage. Though *Fauntleroy* continued to offer roles for young actresses and actors who played the curly-headed boy in films, its reputation was soon displaced by the acclaim of the two children's books deservedly regarded as Burnett's best, *A Little Princess* (1905) and *The Secret Garden* (1911). In these later works the Cinderella motif of loss and recovery is invested with emotional powers that stem from an identification with the resilience shown by Sara Crewe and Mary Lennox. That identification may have been eased by the self-scrutiny the novelist conducted in an autobiography, *The One I Knew Best Of All* (1893). Like her son Vivian's *The Romantick Lady* (1927), Burnett's memoir provides rich biographical details ably processed by more discriminating biographers and critics, notably Ann Thwaite and Phyllis Bixler (see Further Readings).

Juliana Horatia Ewing (1841–1885)

Juliana Horatia Gatty, who married Major Alexander Ewing in 1867, came from a family with military, clerical, and literary affiliations. She owed her middle name "Horatia" to the personal devotion to Lord Horatio Nelson's memory shown by her maternal grandfather, the naval chaplain in whose arms the admiral had died. From her mother, Margaret Scott Gatty, who had married a genial but impoverished Yorkshire clergyman, she learned that female authorship and middle-class gentility were not incompatible. Aware that her interest in natural history could be marketed for child readers, Mrs. Gatty supplemented her husband's meager income by publishing, between 1855 and 1871, five volumes of her *Parables From Nature,* which proved far more successful than her mixture of moralism and fantasy in *The Fairy Godmothers* (1851). Mrs. Gatty soon recognized that the creative imagination of her second daughter, to whom she entrusted the care of eight younger siblings, greatly surpassed her own. She thus used Julie as the model for the fictional character of a teenage storyteller, "Aunt Judy," whom she credited with the tales retold in *Aunt Judy's Tales* (1859) and *Aunt Judy's Letters* (1862). By 1866, when her publishers encouraged Margaret Gatty to found the girl's monthly she called *Aunt Judy's Magazine,* Juliana Horatia had already made a name of her own, and soon became the prime contributor to her mother's magazine. Even a two-year stint in Canada, to which her husband had been sent, failed to interrupt her steady production of superior children's fiction. Her novel, *From Six to Sixteen* (1875), the reminiscences of an Anglo-Indian orphan girl transplanted to Yorkshire, was credited by Kipling as inspiring his own, later work. (Frances Hodgson Burnett, too, seems to borrow from it in *The Secret Garden.*) Army settings are employed in *Jackanapes* (1879) and *The Story of a Short Life* (1885), works that also reveal a fascination with early death that may have reflected Ewing's last years of painful and crippling illness before her death at the age of forty-four.

Jean Ingelow (1820–1897)

Born in Northern England like Frances Hodgson and Juliana Horatia Gatty, Jean Ingelow led a more sequestered life than her two contemporaries. Although eventually she too would have to leave the North, she clung to the remembered Lincolnshire landscapes of her childhood in both her poetry and prose. The eldest of nine children in a family suffering financial losses almost as severe as those which had crippled the Hodgsons, Jean never quite experienced deprivations as acute as those undergone by the fatherless Frances. Brought up very strictly by a Calvinist mother who frowned on writing as a form of self-indulgence, she was eventually allowed to exercise her literary talents. A book of poems, *A Rhyming Chronical of Incidents and Feelings* (1850), was quickly followed by an earnest religious novel *Allerton and Dreux; or, the War of Opinion* (1851). Although Ingelow would produce superior works of adult fiction in books such as *Off the Skelligs* (1872), with its lyrically activated childhood memories, she became best known as a poet whose various collections of verse sold over 200,000 copies in the United States alone. Her "High Tide on the Coast of Lincolnshire," still reprinted in twentieth-century anthologies, was so popular at the time that her admirers proposed that she succeed Tennyson as England's Poet Laureate. Although Ingelow had published stories for children before the appearance of *Mopsa the Fairy* (1869), these had been in the didactic mode. Her return to fantasy in some of the stories she eventually gathered in *Wonder-Box Tales* (1887) seems far more guarded. Neither the anonymous *Some Recollections of Jean Ingelow* (1891) nor a 1972 biography by Maureen Peters offer the kind of detailed information we possess about Burnett, Ewing, or Nesbit. As reclusive as an adult woman as she had been as a child, Jean Ingelow was determined to lead the uneventful external life she defiantly celebrated in one of her stories, "The Life of Mr. John Smith."

Mary Louisa Stewart Molesworth (1839–1921)

Though born in Holland, Mary Louisa Stewart grew up in Manchester, where her father had become a senior partner in a firm of merchants and shippers. Her education was more extensive than that of most girls of her generation. She was sent to a Swiss boarding school and also was privately tutored by Elizabeth Cleghorn Gaskell, the novelist, and her husband William, neighbors and friends of the Stewarts. More important to her later career, however, were her annual visits between 1841 and 1848 to her maternal grandmother in Scotland. In an 1894 article, "How I Write My Children's Stories," Molesworth credited this "delicate and dainty" old lady for stimulating her early imagination: "She seemed to me very old—more like a *great* grandmother; . . . I can see her now, sitting in a favourite window, looking out on the lawn of a very old country house in Scotland, with my brothers and myself, and later on a little sister, round her in a group, while she told us 'The Fair One With Golden Locks,' or 'The Brown Bull of Norrowa,' and sometimes stories of herself or of her own children when they were young." After the grandmother's death, Mary Louisa repeated to her younger siblings the precious stories she had hoarded. Her storytelling skills would resurface soon after her marriage, at the age of twenty-two, to Captain Richard Molesworth, a dashing Crimean veteran. Just as Elizabeth Gaskell began to write novels after the death of a beloved child, so did Mary Louisa turn to fiction after losing the oldest of her four daughters as well as an infant son (two more sons were born later). Her first children's book, *Tell Me A Story* (1875), was dedicated to this seven-year old daughter, whose death is also recounted, from a child's point of view, in one of the volume's tales. Yet before becoming a prolific writer of children's books, Molesworth tried her hand at adult novels, which she published under the pseudonym of a childhood friend, Ennis Graham, who had disappeared in Central Africa with her father. The breakdown of her marriage led her to build on the success of *Tell Me A Story*. Separated in 1879 from her husband, no longer able to count on parental aid after her father's death, Molesworth wrote story after story to support her surviving five children. Her last published work *Fairies Afield* (1911), reputedly was her hundredth book. Given this daunting output, the high quality of most of her writings seems all the more remarkable. Equally at home in works of realism such as *The Carved Lions* (1895) and in fantasies such as *Four Winds Farm* (1887), Molesworth is at her best in the subtle interpenetration of the two, as in *The Cuckoo Clock* (1876) and *The Tapestry Room* (1877), her best known works. Lance Salway reprints "On the Art of Writing Fiction for Children," one of four articles she wrote on the subject, while Roger Lancelyn Green and Marghanita Laski have written sensitive appreciations of her work. (See Further Readings.)

Edith Nesbit (1858–1924)

Unlike Burnett, Ewing, or Molesworth, Edith Nesbit never assumed the name of her husband, Hubert Bland, whom she married in 1880, when she was seven months pregnant. Her unconventionality was evident in other ways. She was a cofounder of the Fabian Society, together with George Bernard Shaw, H. G. Wells, and Bland, and wrote some of the group's early socialist manifestos. She also dispensed with late-Victorian fashion by cutting her hair short, wearing practical clothing, and smoking in public. Her sexual politics were equally liberal. She not only condoned her husband's infidelities (and at least contemplated several extramarital affairs of her own) but also adopted two illegitimate children Bland had fathered upon seducing their household companion, Alice Hoatson. In other respects, however, the circumstances that led to Nesbit's becoming a major author of children's books seem amply familiar. Hers, too, was a story of indigence overcome by a marketable inventiveness. Her father, a scientist who ran an agricultural college near London, died when she, the youngest of his four children, was only three. Her mother (who also had a daughter from a previous marriage) tried to run the college herself before deciding to move to France for the health of Edith's oldest sister. The uprooting, which left Edith and her two brothers planted in various boarding schools, left its mark on the girl's psyche. A series of twelve articles, "My Schooldays," which ran in *The Girl's Own* in 1896–97, dwells on traumas resolved only when all family members were reunited in a Kent country house. When her mother's savings were finally dissipated, London replaced the short-lived pastoral setting to which Nesbit returned in her best children's stories. After meeting Christina Rossetti, she vowed to become "a great poet" and began to submit her verses to sundry magazines. Her economic situation worsened when her husband's business partner absconded with all their funds while Bland was recovering from a smallpox infection. As sole breadwinner, Edith fell back on her genteel education, producing hand-painted greeting cards inscribed with her own verses and giving recitations in working men's clubs. Still persisting in her self-image as poet, she produced verse narratives and birthday books. Not until the stories of the Bastable children, first published in magazines and then collected as *The Story of the Treasure Seekers* (1899), did Nesbit at last find her true métier. The second Bastable book, *The Wouldbegoods* (1901) was followed by the Psammead stories of *Five Children and It* (1902), *The Phoenix and the Carpet* (1904), and *The Story of the Amulet* (1906), in which Nesbit not only mixes realism and magic, as Molesworth had done, but also introduces a rich vein of humor. A slightly patronizing tone towards both her child heroes and child readers may be attributable to Nesbit's reluctant assumption of a role at odds with her earlier literary aspirations. Yet this friction also yields wonderful results whenever she mocks the very conventions she uses, in *Nine Unlikely Tales* (1901), for example, a book which unfortunately remains out of print, unlike some of her other titles. Her sequence of childhood recollections has been recently reprinted under the title *Long Ago When I Was Young,* illustrated by Edward Ardizzone; there are two excellent biographies by Doris Langley Moore and Julia Briggs (see Further Readings).

Christina Rossetti (1830–1894)

Christina Rossetti was the youngest of four children born in successive years to Gabriele Rossetti, a political exile from Italy who taught at King's College, and Frances Polidori, whose English mother had married an Italian immigrant, Gaetano Polidori. Well-educated, and loyal to the memory of her disgraced brother John Polidori—Lord Byron's physician and traveling companion, author of *The Vampyre,* opium addict, and eventual suicide—Mrs. Rossetti exerted a strong influence on Christina, who dedicated each of her books to the woman she called "My Beloved Example, Friend." Above all, she seems to have bequeathed to her youngest child a compelling need to reconcile an unconventional "passion for intellect" with an almost ascetic religious pietism. Christina's older siblings resolved this clash by taking more one-sided positions: whereas her sister Maria became an Anglican nun known for a fine commentary on *The Divine Comedy,* her brothers Dante Gabriel and William Michael embraced, respectively, the Bohemian freedom and the agnosticism allowed to male Victorian artists and intellectuals. Christina's efforts at blending contrary outlooks are evident in a 1850 manuscript, *Maude: Prose and Verse,* which her brother William finally published in 1897, three years after her death, as a presumed "Tale for Girls." This tripartite novel reveals the self-divisions of the nineteen-year-old whose poetry had already been favorably received (her grandfather published a volume of her juvenile verses in 1847 and her brothers printed seven later poems in *The Germ,* the Pre-Raphaelite journal they had helped to found). Parceling herself out among four young women, Christina has Maude, her morbid heroine, ask Agnes, a friend, who she would become "if you could not be yourself": "would you change with Sister Magdalen [who has become a nun], with Mary [who has married], or with me?" Agnes replies that she wants none of these options: "at present I fear you must even put up with me as I am. Will that do?" Yet Maude, racked by doubts, gives in to a death-wish, and Agnes is left to preserve specimens of her poetry together with a lock of her hair. Split identities also operate in what remains Christina Rossetti's best-known poem, "Goblin Market," a work as haunting and rich as Coleridge's "The Ancient Mariner." There, however, the sororal selves of Lizzie and Laura do not remain at odds, like Maude and Agnes, but manage to blend and fuse. The 1862 volume of *Goblin Market and Other Poems* and her 1866 *The Prince's Progress and Other Poems,* both of which were extremely well-received, led to the perception of Rossetti as a potential children's poet, since goblins and princes were presumably the staple of fairy tales and since she had offered two prose tales, "Nick" and "Hero: A Metamorphosis" in *Common Place and Other Short Stories* (1870). Yet when Rossetti finally published *Sing-Song: A Nursery Rhyme Book* (1872), which she did not inscribe to her mother but rather "dedicated without permission to the Baby who suggested them," she eschewed narrative altogether. Though her verses and Arthur Hughes's illustrations were highly praised, she made little money from the book. What is more, its publication coincided with the onslaught of Graves disease, a form of hyperthyroidism that still baffled Victorian medicine. She remained a pain-racked invalid for the last twenty years of her life. The angry aunt in *Speaking Likenesses* (1874), so adept at describing physical and mental discomforts, may have much to do with the poet who could write, "I am sick of self, and there is nothing new; / Oh weary impatient patience of my lot!— / Thus with myself: how fares it, Friends, with you?" Undaunted, Christina Rossetti continued to publish major works of devotional poetry and prose. Two years before her death from cancer, she still managed to produce a commentary on the Apocalypse, *The Face of the Deep* (1892). It, too, was dedicated to "My Mother," but with the added lines, "For the First Time to her Beloved, Revered, Cherished Memory." Among the Rossetti biographies, those by Georgina Battiscombe and Lona Mosk Packer are the best. (See Further Readings.)

Anne Isabella Thackeray Ritchie (1837–1919)

Anne Thackeray and her sister Minny became their father's charges when, shortly after Minny's birth in 1840, their mother's postpartum depression turned into an incurable insanity that necessitated her lifelong confinement to a French asylum, where mental patients were treated with greater care than in England. William Makepeace Thackeray had originally married Isabella Shawe in Paris, but found London a better locale for marketing his writings and drawings. Unable to offer the children a home until he could improve his financial situation, he entrusted them to his mother and stepfather, who had joined a community of Anglo-Indian retirees in Paris. The six years Anne spent with her grandparents before the girls rejoined their father in London in 1846 contributed to her intellectual precocity. The success of Thackeray's *Vanity Fair* brought him and his daughters in contact with many notable figures Anne later memorialized: Carlyle, Tennyson, and Charlotte Brontë, whom she found "somewhat grave and stern, specially to forward little girls who wish to chatter." Thackeray took his daughters with him whenever he went abroad: his own children's book *The Rose and the Ring* (1854) was begun as an entertainment for Anne and Minny and an American girl, Edith Story, whom they met in Rome. In Italy, they also became acquainted with the Brownings, to whom Ritchie would later devote a third of her *Records of Tennyson, Ruskin, and Browning* (1892). Thackeray encouraged Anne's interest in writing and increasingly treated her as an intellectual equal. When he became editor of the new *Cornhill Magazine* in 1860 he proudly published one of her first essays, "Little Scholars," an account of her visits to various working class schools. Thackeray's death occurred the same year that Anne published her first novel, *The Story of Elizabeth* (1863), which George Eliot found "charmingly written." The emotional support Anne had received from her father was now generously extended by other Victorian intellectuals; it was in the circle of the Tennysons and Julia Cameron, the photographer, that the Thackeray sisters met members of a younger generation such as Ellen Terry, C. L. Dodgson (not yet Lewis Carroll), and Leslie Stephen, whom Minny married in 1867. The Stephen household, which Anne joined, produced further contacts with younger writers such as Henry James and Thomas Hardy. The early 1870s saw Anne's career accelerating, with the publication of *Old Kensington* (1873), *Bluebeard's Keys and Other Stories* (1874), and *Toilers and Spinners, and Other Essays* (1874), following in rapid succession. Yet when her sister suddenly died in 1875 and Leslie Stephen asked her to take charge of his household to care for her niece, who inherited Isabella Shawe's insanity, it seemed that Anne's cherished independence was about to be sacrificed. Only Stephen's involvement with Julia Duckworth, whom he eventually married and who would bear him four more children, including Virginia Woolf and Vanessa Bell, offered some promise of relief. But the writer hitherto known as "Miss Thackeray" became "Mrs. Richmond Ritchie" in 1877, when at the age of thirty-nine, she decided to accept, against Leslie Stephen's protestations, the marriage proposal of a cousin who was only twenty-three. After the birth of a healthy daughter, Hester, in 1878, and of a son she named William Makepeace after her father, in 1880, she resumed her literary career. She wrote on earlier women writers she found especially congenial in *Madame de Sevigné* (1881), *A Book of Sybils: Mrs. Barbauld, Mrs. Opie, Miss Edgeworth, Miss Austen*

(1882), and in *Blackstick Papers* (1908), as well as in her introductions to novels by Elizabeth Gaskell, Maria Edgeworth, and Mary Russell Mitford; but she clearly regarded her 1911 introductions to the Centenary Edition of her father's novels as a crowning labor of love uniting her with the Victorian past. Virginia Woolf's 1919 obituary catches "the paradoxes and fascinations" of Ritchie's art with an empathy that resembles Ritchie's own. It is reproduced in Winifred Gérin's appreciative biography (see Further Readings).

Further Readings

A Selection of Primary Texts in Print

Browne, Frances. *Granny's Wonderful Chair.* Harmondsworth: Puffin/Penguin, 1986.

Burnett, Frances Hodgson. *The One I Knew The Best Of All: A Memory of the Mind of a Child.* New York: Arno, 1980.

———. *The Racketty Packetty House.* New York: Harper, 1975.

Carter, Angela. *The Bloody Chamber and Other Adult Tales.* New York: Harper, 1981.

———. ed. *Sleeping Beauty and Other Favourite Fairy Tales.* Illustrated by Michael Foreman. London: Victor Gollancz, 1982.

Clifford, Lucy. *Anyhow Stories Moral and Otherwise* (1882), reprinted with a preface by Alison Lurie. New York: Garland Publishing, 1977.

Cott, Jonathan, ed. *Beyond the Looking Glass: Extraordinary Works of Fairy Tale and Fantasy.* New York: R. R. Bowker, 1973.

David, Alfred and Mary Elizabeth Meek, eds. *The Twelve Dancing Princesses and Other Fairy Tales.* Bloomington: Indiana University Press, 1974.

Demers, Patricia, ed. *A Garland from the Golden Age: An Anthology of Children's Literature from 1850 to 1900.* Toronto: Oxford University Press, 1983.

De Morgan, Mary. *On a Pincushion and Other Fairy Tales* (1877) and *The Necklace of Princess Fiorimonde and Other Stories* (1880), reprinted with a preface by Charity Chang. New York and London: Garland Publishing, 1977.

Dundes, Alan, ed. *Cinderella: A Casebook.* New York: Wildman, 1983.

Ewing, Juliana Horatia. "In Memoriam, Margaret Gatty." In Lance Salway, *A Peculiar Gift.* Harmondsworth: Kestrel/Penguin, 1976.

Grimms' Fairy Tales [1823, 1826]. Illustrated by George Cruikshank and translated by Edward Taylor. Harmondsworth: Puffin/Penguin, 1971.

Hearn, Michael Patrick. *The Victorian Fairy Tale Book.* New York: Pantheon, 1988.

Ingelow, Jean. *Off the Skelligs,* reprinted from the 1872 edition. New York: AMS Press, 1988.

Lang, Andrew. *Blue Fairy Book,* ed. Brian Alderson. Harmondsworth: Puffin/Penguin, 1987.

Le Prince de Beaumont, Madame. *Beauty and the Beast.* Translated and illustrated by Diane Goode. New York: Bradbury Press, 1978.

Mieder, Wolfgang. *Disenchantments: An Anthology of Modern Fairy Tale Poetry.* Hanover: University of Vermont Press, 1985.

Molesworth, Maria Louisa. *The Cuckoo Clock.* New York: Dell, 1987.

———. "Hans Christian Andersen"; "Juliana Horatia Ewing"; and "On the Art of Writing Fiction for Children." In Lance Salway, *A Peculiar Gift.* Harmondsworth: Kestrel/Penguin, 1976.

Nesbit, E[dith]. *Beauty and the Beast.* New York: Viking Penguin, 1988.

———. *The Last of the Dragons and Some Others.* Harmondsworth: Puffin/Penguin, 1982.

———. *Long Ago When I Was Young.* Introduced by Noel Streatfield and illustrated by George Buchanan and Edward Ardizzone. New York: Dial Books, 1987.

———. *The Magic World.* Harmondsworth: Puffin/Penguin, 1988.

Opie, Iona and Peter, eds. *The Classic Fairy Tales.* London: Oxford University Press, 1974.

Philip, Neil. *The Cinderella Story: The Origins and Variations of the Story Known as "Cinderella."* London: Penguin, 1989.

Ritchie, Anne I. *The Works of Miss Thackeray.* New York: AMS Press, 1988.

Rossetti, Christina. *Maude: Prose and Verse.* Edited and with an introduction by R. W. Crump. Hamden, Conn.: Archon Books, 1976.

———. *Goblin Market.* New York: Dover, 1982.

———. *Sing-Song: A Nursery Rhyme Book.* New York: Dover, 1969.

Salway, Lance. *A Peculiar Gift: Nineteenth Century Writings on Books for Children.* Harmondsworth: Kestrel/Penguin, 1976.

Sawyer, Ruth. "Wee Meg Barnilegs and the Fairies." In *The Way of the Storyteller.* Harmondsworth: Penguin, 1986.

Stephen, Julia Duckworth. *Stories for Children, Essays for Adults,* ed. Diana Gillespie and Elizabeth Steele. Syracuse: Syracuse University Press, 1987.

Woolf, Virginia. *Nurse Lugton's Curtain.* Illustrated by Julie Vivas. London: Bodley Head, 1991.

———. *The Widow and the Parrot.* Illustrated by Julian Bell and with an afterword by Quentin Bell. San Diego: Harcourt Brace Jovanovich, 1982.

Zipes, Jack. *Don't Bet on the Prince: Contemporary Feminist Fairy Tales in North America and England.* New York: Routledge, 1989.

———. *Victorian Fairy Tales: The Revolt of the Fairies and Elves.* New York: Methuen, 1987.

Selected Secondary Readings

Auerbach, Nina. "Alice and Wonderland: A Curious Child," and "Falling Alice, Fallen Women, and Victorian Dream Children." Pp. 130–48 and 149–68 in *Romantic Imprisonment: Women and Other Glorified Outcasts.* New York: Columbia University Press, 1980.

———. "Little Women." Pp. 55–73 in *Communities of Women: An Idea in Fiction.* Cambridge, Mass.: Harvard University Press, 1978.

Avery, Gillian. *Childhood's Pattern: A Study of the Heroes and Heroines of Children's Fiction, 1770–1950.* London: Hodder and Stroughton, 1975.

Avery, Gillian, and Julia Briggs, eds. *Children and Their Books: A Celebration of the Work of Iona and Peter Opie.* Oxford: Clarendon Press, 1989.

Battiscombe, Georgina. *Christina Rossetti: A Divided Life.* New York: Holt, Rinehart, and Winston, 1981.

Bettelheim, Bruno. *The Uses of Enchantment: The Meaning and Importance of Fairy Tales.* New York: Knopf, 1976.

Bixler, Phyllis. *Frances Hodgson Burnett.* Boston: Twayne, 1984.

Blom, Margaret Howard and Thomas E. Blom, eds. *Canada Home: Juliana Horatia Ewing's Fredericton Letters, 1867–1869.* Vancouver: University of British Columbia Press, 1983.

Bottigheimer, Ruth B. *Grimms' Bad Girls and Bold Boys.* New Haven: Yale University Press, 1987.

———., ed. *Fairy Tales and Society: Illusion, Allusion, and Paradigm.* Philadelphia: University of Pennsylvania Press, 1986.

Briggs, Julia. *A Woman of Passion: The Life of E. Nesbit, 1858–1924.* New York: New Amsterdam Books, 1987.

Cadogan, Mary, and Patricia Craig. *You're A Brick, Angela! A New Look at Girls' Fiction from 1839–1975.* London: Victor Gollancz, 1976.

Carpenter, Humphrey. *Secret Gardens: The Golden Age of Children's Literature.* Boston: Houghton Mifflin, 1985.

Clark, Beverly Lyon. "A Portrait of the Artist as a Little Woman." *Children's Literature* 17 (1989), 81–97.

Darnton, Robert. "Peasant Tell Tales: The Meaning of Mother Goose." In *The Great Cat Massacre.* New York: Basic Books, 1984.

Dusinberre, Juliet. *Alice to the Lighthouse: Children's Books and Radical Experiments in Art.* New York: St. Martin's Press, 1987.

Dyhouse, Carol. *Girls Growing Up in Late Victorian and Edwardian England.* London: Routledge and Kegan Paul, 1981.

Estes, Angela M. and Kathleen Margaret Lant. "Dismembering the Text: The Horrors of Louisa May Alcott's *Little Women.*" *Children's Literature* 17 (1989), 98–123.

Fester, Richard, Marie E. P. Konig, Doris F. Jonas, and A. David Jonas. *Weib und Macht: Fünf Millionen Urgeschichte der Frau.* Frankfurt: S. Fischer, 1979.

Fromm, Gloria G. "E. Nesbit and the Happy Moralist." *Journal of Modern Literature* 11 (March 1984), 45–65.

Gérin, Winifred. *Anne Thackeray Ritchie: A Biography.* Oxford and New York: Oxford University Press, 1983.

Gilead, Sarah. "Magic Abjured: Closure in Children's Fantasy Fiction." *PMLA* 106 (March 1991): 276–93.

Green, Roger Lancelyn. *Mrs. Molesworth.* New York: Henry Z. Walck, 1964.

———. *Tellers of Tales: Children's Books and Their Authors from 1800 to 1964.* London: Edmund Ward, 1965.

Grylls, David. *Guardians and Angels: Parents and Children in Nineteenth-Century Literature.* London and Boston: Faber and Faber, 1978.

Hearne, Betsy. *Beauty and the Beast: Visions and Revisions of an Old Tale.* With an Essay by Larry DeVries. Chicago: University of Chicago Press, 1989.

Honig, Edith Lazaros. *Breaking the Angelic Image: Woman Power in Victorian Children's Fantasy.* New York: Greenwood Press, 1988.

Kast, Verena. *Mann und Frau im Märchen: Eine Psychologische Deutung.* Olten: Walter-Verlag, 1983.

———. *Wege Aus Angst und Symbiose: Märchen Psychologisch Gedeutet.* Olten: Walter-Verlag, 1982.

Keyser, Elizabeth Lennox. "'Quite Contrary': Frances Hodgson Burnett's *The Secret Garden.*" *Children's Literature* 11 (1983): 1–13.

Knoepflmacher, U. C. "Avenging Alice: Christina Rossetti and Lewis Carroll." *Nineteenth-Century Literature* 41 (1986), 299–328.

———. "The Balancing of Child and Adult: An Approach to Victorian Fantasies for Children." *Nineteenth-Century Fiction* 37 (1983): 497–530.

———. "Little Girls Without Their Curls: Female Aggression in Victorian Children's Literature." *Children's Literature* 11 (1983): 14–31.

———. "Of Babylands and Babylons: E. Nesbit and the Reclamation of the Fairy Tale." *Tulsa Studies in Women's Literature* 6 (1987): 299–325.

Laski, Marghanita. *Mrs. Ewing, Mrs. Molesworth, Mrs. Hodgson Burnett.* London: Arthur Barker, 1950.

Luethi, Max. *Once Upon A Time: On the Nature of Fairy Tales.* Bloomington: Indiana University Press, 1976.

Lurie, Alison. *Don't Tell the Grown-ups: Subversive Children's Literature.* Boston: Little Brown and Company, 1990.

Maxwell, Christabel. *Mrs. Gatty and Mrs. Ewing.* London: Constable, 1949.

Moers, Ellen. "Educating Heroinism." In *Literary Women,* 211–42. Garden City, N.Y.: Doubleday, 1976.

Moore, Doris Langley. *E. Nesbit: A Biography.* Philadelphia: Chilton Books, 1966.

Myers, Mitzi. "Impeccable Governesses, Rational Dames, and Moral Mothers: Mary Wollstonecraft and the Female Tradition in Georgian Children's Books." *Children's Literature* 14 (198?): 31–59.

Packer, Lona Mosk. *Christina Rossetti.* Berkeley: University of California Press, 1963.

Peters, Maureen. *Jean Ingelow: Victorian Poetess.* Ipswich: Boydell Press, 1972.

Prickett, Stephen. *Victorian Fantasy.* Bloomington: Indiana University Press, 1979.

Rose, Jacqueline. *The Case of Peter Pan, or, The Impossibility of Children's Fiction.* London: Macmillan, 1984.

Rose, Karen. "'Fairy-born and human-bred': Jane Eyre's Education in Romance." Pp. 69–89 in *The Voyage In: Fictions of Female Development,* ed. Elizabeth Abel, Marianne Hirsch, and Elizabeth Langland. Hanover: University Press of New England, 1983.

Sale, Roger. *Fairy Tales and After: From Snow White to E. B. White.* Cambridge, Mass.: Harvard University Press, 1978.

Sircar, Sanja. "The Victorian Auntly Narrative Voice and Mrs. Molesworth's *Cuckoo Clock.*" *Children's Literature* 17 (1989): 1–24.

Stone, Harry. *Dickens and the Invisible World: Fairy Tales, Fantasy, and Novel-Making.* Bloomington: Indiana University Press, 1979.

Streatfeild, Noel. *Magic and the Magician: E. Nesbit and Her Children's Books.* London: Ernest Benn, 1958.

Tatar, Maria. *The Hard Facts of the Grimms' Fairy Tales.* Princeton: Princeton University Press, 1987.

Thwaite, Ann. *Waiting For The Party: The Life of Frances Hodgson Burnett, 1849–1924.* New York: Scribner's, 1974.

von Franz, Marie-Louise. *The Feminine in Fairy Tales*. Dallas: Spring, 1972.

Watson, Jeanie. "'Men Sell Not Such in Any Town': Christina Rossetti's Goblin Fruit of Fairy Tale." *Children's Literature* 12 (1984): 61–77.

Zipes, Jack. *Breaking the Magic Spell: Radical Theories of Folk and Fairy Tale*. Austin: University of Texas Press, 1979.